AMERICAN KILL SWITCH

END OF DAYS
BOOK 3

JOHN BIRMINGHAM

1

THE FALLEN REALM OF MEN

Full moon lay over the streets of Bachman, a small town on the edge of the badlands, and nature reclaimed her dominion there with surprising swiftness. Three coyotes emerged from the shadows of Cottonwood Park and trotted up the middle of Wilbur Avenue in the silver moonlight, possessed of such confidence that to see them, you might imagine the kingdom of men had never risen in the first place, let alone fallen so recently. The carnivore pack froze at the rear of a squat, brown cinderblock bunker where a tattered flag promising COFFEE lay in the parking lot, the faded plastic swatch feebly slapping the concrete in a cool breeze. It posed no threat to them, and they resumed their passage along the gravel road, their claws clicking on the hardscrabble, small puffs of fine, red dust rising a few inches from the paw prints they left in their wake.

The long drought had been hard on Bachman, but harder yet were the days that followed.

The coyotes paused again at the corner of Evans and Wilbur, their heads turning with one mind to the tiny blur of dirty orange and white fur that flashed through the intersection.

A cat.

Specifically, Tugger, once upon a time, the much loved and

ruinously overfed companion of Mrs Joan Swithen, widow of John, and owner of the town's *Corner Store*, which was not located on the corner of Evans and Wilbur streets but two doors down. Tugger did not look quite so portly these days. With matted pelt and sunken eyes that burned with feral mania, he darted from one pool of shadow to the next, wary of the predators that had reclaimed the nights, the days, and all the spaces in between.

It had been two and a half months since Mrs Joan Swithen had spooned out the last tin of Tugger's favourite *Chicken & Turkey in Tasty Gravy*. Less time since Joan had laid down on her bed, dizzy and nauseous with the most awful headache, the first symptoms of the catastrophic blood sugar episode that would soon lay her down for good.

There being no more insulin for Joan, you see.

And no more tins of *Chicken & Turkey in Tasty Gravy* for Tugger.

Not that Tugger went hungry for too long. Old Joan didn't lay herself down in a bath of tasty gravy, but she was an invaluable source of protein when things got tight.

In sublime concert, the three coyotes turned away from the wretched and scrawny feline. Its turn would come. For now, though, they lifted their snouts to the sky where a dark and savoury feast of much greater allure hung just out of reach. The leader of the pack, an alpha male, bared his fangs. A low and spiteful growl turned into a howling lamentation as all three carnivores protested the perverse injustice of finding such a repast, swaying just out of reach. Three nights, they had stolen into the fallen realm of men, drawn by the heady scent of meat, and for three nights they had gone hungry, unable to leap high enough to drag the carcass down from where it hanged.

They tried.

Leaping and twirling in the air, snapping at the lowermost limbs, desperate to sink fang into flesh and tear the promised meal from its strange eyrie.

Crows had picked at the carcass, first taking the softest, sweetest meats. The eyes. The lips. The cheeks. The pack leader's sense of smell told him that the black-winged mutilators had rained down a small storm of fleshy scraps, but other bottom-feeding scavengers had left not so much as a tiny shred for the pack.

It was an outrage, and they howled long into the night at the travesty and displeasure of it.

Until a gunshot cracked and a single bullet sparked off the tarmac.

The pack fled in all directions.

They would surely come back together in the darkness, on the old familiar trails, or perhaps in the lair they had newly made, inside the single-bedroom apartment annexe out the back of the *Corner Store*, just down from the corner of Evans and Wilbur.

But not for hours.

Not until the danger had passed.

For it seemed that men had returned.

"You missed," Rick said, teasing.

James O'Donnell lowered the rifle and shook his head.

"No," he said evenly. "I put that shot exactly where I wanted."

Rick Boreham smiled and nodded but said nothing. He knew a good deal about James O'Donnell, having survived the trek across North America with him, and two things he would swear to: James was a great shot with that Ruger, but he would not lightly take a life with it. Not even to put down a wild dog pack set on tearing a human body to pieces.

Not since the body was long dead.

Rick brought the binoculars up to his eyes again. They were nothing like the fancy night vision specs he'd used in the Rangers. Just a plain old pair of Nikon 7s, salvaged from a camera shop back in Glenwood, Iowa. Walmart, Best Buy, gun shops, it was pointless even looking in them. They'd all been stripped, or they were occupied by random militia who shot first and kept shooting. But not many folks had thought to loot a camera shop.

That had been another idea of James's.

For a man who was down on himself as being useless for anything but desk work, the former investment guy was always coming up with hacks and tricks for getting them through just one more day. He'd been the one who'd known because he just knew that stuff, that some big bank or investment house in Omaha, Nebraska, had a storehouse of emergency supplies just outside the city. A lot of it was useless. N95 masks and NBC suits. Crazy stuff like that. But there were also freeze-dried rations, medicine, and fuel, and although somebody had raided the cache—they'd used a forklift to break through the doors—there was still enough good scrounging to get them halfway to Wyoming.

"Those coyotes coming back?" James asked.

Rick scanned the dead town again. Nothing.

"Don't reckon so," he conceded.

"There you go then. Should we check it out?"

"Not yet," Rick Boreham murmured, slowly sweeping the town from one end to the other.

His eyes were still good, and with a full moon high overhead and a bright wash of starlight behind that, he had no trouble scoping out the streets of Bachman from their vantage point on a small hill half a mile to the east of town.

The 7th Cavalry had fought some skirmish here during the Sioux Wars, and a white stone cairn marked the graves of four troopers from the 7th who would forever stand sentinel over a small pergola and barbecue area. An oddball convoy of dusty, road-worn vehicles idled in the parking lot of the memorial—three SUVs, two motor homes and Tammy Kolchar's big ass Oldsmobile. Sentries armed with an even more oddball collection of firearms and melee weapons had taken up observation posts, giving them good cover from all approaches. Andrew Nesbitt, a schoolteacher from Kalamazoo, Michigan, was carrying the heaviest artillery. He'd moonlighted after school hours with some website development and cryptocurrency trading and insisted he'd picked up on the Chinese attack well before the NSA.

"You could've dropped a fucking dime, buddy," Michelle Nguyen smacked back whenever he brought it up.

Another sweep with the Nikons.

Just to be sure.

Nothing moved in the town save for the body swaying from a lamp post with a hand-scrawled sign pinned to a tattered tee shirt.

Looter.

That was the one the coyote pack had been after.

Three more swung gently in the night breeze in the second, smaller park at the far end of the main street, but there wasn't much left of them. The park was, or had been, more of a kids' playground to judge by the swing sets and seesaws. But the swings had been pressed into service as makeshift gallows, and the bodies hanging there had swung low, leaving them vulnerable to ground scavengers. The extra distance made it impossible to decipher whatever signs hung around their necks, but Rick was pretty sure they didn't say '*Looter*'.

He lowered the binoculars after another minute of quiet surveillance.

"Good to go," he said. "I'll take Nez and Pete."

James nodded.

They turned and walked back to the group.

Everyone had climbed out of the vehicles to stretch their legs, but not everybody had the luxury of simply strolling around the recreation area or kicking back in the pergola for a thermos of coffee and a quick bite of deer jerky. Necessity had taught them the need for vigilance, and Rick had trained everybody, including the kids, to play their part.

The children, ten of them now, all sat in the pergola, where the eldest, the Bloomfield kid, entertained the others by reading from a Batman comic, turning it around and showing off each panel as he read the dialogue. He was quiet. They were all quiet.

They'd learned. Each of them was, in their way, just about the luckiest kid in the world at that point – although Tammy Kolchar's Bobby and Wynona and her friend Roxarne's little Jakey and Liana were probably the most fortunate, having been saved by Rick from the cooking pot of pervert cannibals. When Rick told those little ones they had chores to do, there was no grumbling or feet draggin'. There were just chores done well and done quickly.

Michelle was waiting by James's vehicle, her face a map of anxiety. She chewed on her lower lip and poured over a map on the hood of the Sierra.

"Looks like your basic pissant little burg," she said as they approached. "I'd guess a population of four or five hundred before the attack. Fits the profile of a food desert. Not a lot of fresh arugula, but plenty of firearms, mostly for range work—"

Rick cut her off.

"Town's dead," he said.

Michelle looked up, a deep line between her eyebrows as she frowned.

"Oh. So, no barricades or guards or anything?"

"Nothing," James said.

"Four bodies hanging in plain sight. One of them tagged as a looter. Can't say as to the others, but I'd guess they were outsiders."

"Any insiders left?"

Both men shook their heads.

"Doesn't look like it," James said. "There's plenty of animals in the open. Game and prey."

Michelle started to fold up the map. A Rand McNally they'd picked up from a ransacked Tesla supercharging station back in Iowa.

"Anything to salvage?" she asked.

"Not much in the way of food, I'd guess," James replied. "But there is a Texaco. Might be worth checking the pumps."

"Okay," she said, taking in a breath as though readying herself to lift a heavy weight. "Whose turn is it?"

Rick held up his hand.

She breathed out—a ragged sigh.

"Good."

"Hey!" Rick said, but without rancour.

"I just hate it when James goes," Michelle said. "He's no good at this shit."

"Hey," James protested, with a little more feeling than Rick.

Michelle fixed him with her fiercest don't-even-try-me glare.

James backed down.

"Fair enough," he conceded. "You are better at this than me," he added, lightly punching Rick.

The former Ranger shrugged.

"Misspent youth."

He waved to a couple of the men standing guard around the perimeter of the memorial park, Andrew Nesbitt and Peter Tapsell, gesturing for them to come over.

They hurried across the dead brown grass at a trot.

"S'up, guvnor?" Tapsell asked.

"Get some extra ammo and grab your magic goggles, Nez," Rick said. "We're going to town."

2

ALL THOSE POINTS OF LIGHT

Jodi Sarjanen cried when Ellie gave her the camera, but her tears were clean and unspoiled by bitterness. The camera wasn't great. Just one of those disposable cardboard things that people put out at weddings and birthday parties so everyone could snap away, and out of three or four hundred exposures, you might get lucky with maybe a dozen usable shots. But it was the thought that went into it, the effort of finding such a thing, and the danger her girlfriend must have risked to secure it.

"Baby, you shouldn't have done this," Jodi protested, even though she was so glad to have it.

"For you, anything," Ellie said, kissing her by the campfire light.

"Sparklers!" Damo cried out and lit two of them like a magic trick. The children cheered and clapped, and God only knew where he'd found them. Maybe the same place Ellie got the camera.

"And cake!" young Pascal added happily.

"And cake," Eliza Jabbarah confirmed.

"But how?" Jodi gasped as Pascal's younger sister Beatrice appeared from the lengthening shadows behind the battered, dust-coated Land Rover with a small chocolate cake. Damo hurried over to plant the sparklers into the icing and led them all in a chorus of 'Happy Birthday.'

She'd known her birthday was coming up, but she honestly wasn't sure when. Her phone wasn't working. Nothing like that had worked in ages.

When the last singing fell away, Jodi heard Karl's voice from somewhere in the darkness.

"Happy birthday, Miss Jodi."

"Thank you, Karl," she called back.

And sighed, wiping the tears from her eyes.

"This is the best birthday ever, you guys."

Turning back to Ellie, she said, "Seriously, how did you even make a cake? We don't have a stove."

Ellie smiled and shrugged.

"If you got a good pot, you got a stove, baby," she said. "I've been saving the ingredients since we got off the boat."

Damo's boat, she meant. The *Lasseter's Reef*. That boat had never had such a good run on the water before. Until Damo and the others had fled from San Francisco in the yacht, it'd mainly served as a floating bar, rarely leaving its berth at the marina.

They'd left the *Reef* somewhere on the Sacramento River about a thousand miles back many weeks ago. Maybe even two or three months now. It was hard to keep track of the days when you were outside all the time, constantly moving, but slowly, carefully, to avoid the troubles that so often followed encounters with other people. They'd been doing that, avoiding other people, since Northern California. There were all sorts of crazy militias like the stupid Freedom Legion and biker gangs like the Hells Angels running wild back there. Nazis and cannibals, too, they'd heard. But out here, in the real west, it was just them, often for days or weeks.

The sparklers died away, the last bright shooting fragments of light dying out in the dark, leaving their faces illuminated by the orange glow of the campfire coals.

Oh yeah, Jodi thought. *Cake.*

She'd seen the black cast iron camp pot sitting in the coals earlier that afternoon; the lid clamped on firmly. Ellie had shooed her away when she'd asked what was cooking. Something Karl had trapped or shot, she figured. That was mostly what they ate now, along with field greens and mushrooms picked by the children and sorted into edibles and everything else by Ellie. She must have been baking the cake then.

Jodi had taken the kids, her little boy Maxi and Pascal and Beatrice, the two Canadians they were trying to get home, and done some reading and writing with them. It was her turn. All the grown-ups took the children for some form of schooling for at least an hour every day. Damo for math and science. Karl for history because he'd been a real History Channel buff back when there was a History channel, and he got it bundled for free with his cable.

Back when there was cable.

Jodi did art and English, and Ellie filled in the gaps. Usually with cooking lessons.

Between them, they kept all three children occupied and learning something most days as they inched north and east towards Damo's farm up near Canada. She had a new appreciation for how hard teachers worked. Teaching kids all day was exhausting.

"I should get a picture of the cake," Jodi said, climbing to her feet and quickly ratcheting the scroll wheel around on the little cardboard Kodak. It clicked into place for the first exposure.

"But won't it be too dark?" Ellie said. She looked beautiful in the firelight, Jodi thought.

"Take my picture, Mom," Maxi demanded. "Take mine."

"And me," Beatrice added. "I want to be in the cake picture too."

Pascal, at twelve, going on thirteen, was too old and way too cool to get worked up like that, but Jodi could tell he didn't want to be left out, so she told him to move his butt in with the others. He rolled his eyes but hurried to be included.

"I can make it work with the firelight," she said. "You just have to lay on your tummies, feet away from the campfire, all your faces pointing in at the cake. Be quick, so the icing doesn't melt."

They arranged themselves for the photo, and Jodi wondered how

Ellie had made icing all the way out here. They were camped in a field in the bow of a small river somewhere in the northern reaches of Wyoming. It was cold but not lethally so. Not yet. Everybody dressed warmly, under multiple layers, but the air was beautifully clean and crisp. Almost startling in its clarity. And the weather remained warmer than it should have been, even as all the pollution disappeared. For once, that wasn't a bad thing. Damo said a real winter up here could kill you if you weren't ready for it, and they weren't. Not really. They had to get to his farm.

Jodi could hear the river gurgling away off in the distance. The first stars were beginning to wink into life across the huge expanse of sky. Only one thing was big enough to interrupt that vast, dark vessel of the heavens. Just one lonely mountain a couple of miles away. A striking, singular peak that Damo called the Devils Tower. He said it had been in movies and everything. Karl called it the Close Encounters mountain and promised to find a copy of the film for the kids to watch.

"Now they've seen the real thing."

It did look very familiar to Jodi, and if she hadn't lost her camera bag to that douchewad mugger back in San Francisco at the start of all this, she would have spent hours framing and shooting the Tower.

It was spectacular. A grand stone pillar punched a mile into the sky, blotting out a thick wedge of stars when full night fell. She and Ellie had snuck away to make love under the stars last night. Afterwards, lying in her lover's arms, wrapped in a thick blanket, she shivered deliciously and stared in awe as a shooting star disappeared into the negative space carved out of the densely packed star field. Perhaps they could sneak away again tonight once the children were asleep. Although it wasn't really sneaking because both Damo and Karl knew where they were and for damn sure what they were doing.

Ellie was a loud and spirited fuck wherever they did it.

The boys were kind enough to pretend they couldn't hear.

She took the photo.

The clunky mechanical noise of the camera's cheap plastic shutter was strangely satisfying. It was her first photograph since they'd escaped the city. And it was strangely thrilling, not knowing whether it had worked out. It was like a small secret locked inside the flimsy cardboard box. She might never even see it. What were the chances of getting the roll developed?

Pretty small, if she was being honest.

But Jodi had never been so pleased with an image.

Ellie stepped in to rescue the cake, to carve it up, putting one slice aside for Karl for when he returned from patrolling out in the dark.

"Is there ice cream?" Maxi asked, and Ellie snorted before Jodi could tell him off for being so inconsiderate.

"You see any cold-looking cows out here, Maxi?"

"No," he said.

"Then that's a hard no on the ice cream, kid," Ellie said. "But there's extra chocolate in the cake."

All three kids were happy with that. Damo too.

The big Australian mining engineer inhaled his piece in two bites, loudly sucking the chocolate icing off his fingers.

"Nice one, mate," he said. "Right up there with your posh chocolate soufflé back at the shop, I reckon."

By the shop, he meant *Fourth Edition*. The restaurant he'd owned, where Ellie had been the head chef.

"Not even close, Damo", she snorted, "But you gotta work with what you got. I reckon we'll be good to move on in the morning. That deer meat will have dried out by then. The jerky will keep for a year. We'll need to keep up our greens and a bit of fruit, but we won't have to worry about protein again. Not if we can get to your place before winter bites."

Damien Maloney sucked air in through his teeth.

"Yeah, that's a bloody big if, mate. We're gonna need fuel for the Land Rover, and I don't like that clanking sound she makes when she gets up near sixty or so."

"Damo," Jodi scolded him gently, frowning and nodding at the three children. They had agreed not to discuss their problems in front of the kids. The younger two had nightmares.

Sorry, Damo mouthed, putting up his hands in mock surrender.

"Good to hear the jerky's done," he said aloud.

Ellie looked over at the drying racks Karl had made from sticks and twine. She couldn't see much in the dark, but she could smell the smoke Ellie had used to finish the preserving process. Karl had shot a big buck, and Ellie broke down the carcass. They buried the offal and skin to avoid drawing in predators and scavengers. The meat sat packed in salt for three days—swimming pool salt they'd bartered for back in California when they'd left the boat and traded it for the old 4x4 they'd been in ever since.

It was Ellie who'd suggested they'd need salt for drying out meat since they could no longer just walk into the freezer on Damo's yacht. Jodi's heart swelled as she looked through the low flames into her love's eyes. She was so proud of Ellie. She was brave and fierce and would kill anyone who threatened Jodi or Max.

Or any of their strange, extended family.

Because Damo felt like family. He had, even before everything went sideways. And Karl was like a long-lost brother, or uncle, come home from his travels. Except their home was the road now, and specifically, the smaller, quieter back roads where they weren't as likely to encounter anyone. And you could not look after children, as they had looked after Pascal and Beatrice, without feeling like those children were part of you somehow.

Jodi got teary again and hurried to eat half of her slice before dividing the rest of the cake between the kids. One messy bite each. It took her mind off things. About everything they had lost. It was easier out here in the countryside. When they'd still been close to San Francisco, she'd found it incredibly sad, all the shops and businesses that were closed. All the streets empty. People hiding away, frightened of each other. Sometimes, she would play a song on Ellie's iPod, and the words would make her cry just because they reminded her of how much had changed and how it would never change back.

Jodi Sarjanen was pretty sure of that.

The world they had known was not going to reappear magically. Not Damo and Ellie's restaurant. Not her camera bag or her job shooting photographs of big-name bands and singers, which hadn't paid much, but which was still amazingly cool and seemed even cooler and more amazing the further she got from it. None of that was coming back. She and Ellie would never have cocktails at their favourite bar in Temescal again. Maxi would never see his friends. Pascal and Beatrice might get back to their dad in Canada. Damo was pretty determined to make that happen. And their dad was a Mountie or something, so he'd be looking for them.

But it wasn't like they could drop them at an airport and wave goodbye.

There was no flying around anymore.

No visiting friends or family, far away, or even just across the street.

It had all gone, and nothing good had replaced it.

She shuddered and flinched away from the memories of everything they'd seen back on the coast. The sort of people they'd driven further and further east to avoid. Terrible people doing terrible things.

But, of course, they'd done some hard things themselves.

Ellie had killed men now. Karl and Damo, too. Only Jodi had not had to do that, and Ellie promised she would never.

You let me take care of that shit, babe.

Jodi stood up and moved around the campfire to sit next to Ellie.

"Happy birthday, lover," Ellie said, and Jodi said thank you, but she was thankful for having a warm hug to hide inside.

The Devil's Tower grew darker in the west, blotting out all those points of light. Maybe a thousand. Maybe more.

3

THE SKY CARES NOTHING FOR MEN

Jonas Murdoch wished he had a horse. This would be so much cooler if he could ride into town at sunset to accept the surrender on some badass giant hell-horse with armour and shit. Still, the Legion's war wagons were fucking badass, and the mayor of Three Forks, Montana, was one loud 'boo' away from filling his pants. Also, he'd yielded the town, so...

You know. Mercy.

A cold wind blew down from the mountains, where the snow-frosted peaks turned pink and bronze in the sunset, the northerly gusts arriving in waves that you could see coming for miles across the open grasslands and river valleys. A few thin clouds streamed high overhead at day's end, up where jetliners once left contrails tracing their path across the wilds of the northwest. Collapsing distance, compressing time. Now, the sky was a vast, darkening blue silence, empty and open and utterly indifferent to any challenge that the remnants of humanity might throw at it.

A curse for a thunderhead. A fist raised against a tornado.

The sky cared nothing for man and never had.

Difference was, Jonas thought, now there was fuck all a man could do about it.

Best he could hope for was to tend to his own affairs. And right now, at this time and place, the affairs of men were entirely concerned with the surrender of Three Forks to the forces of the Legion.

His Legion. The greatest thing he'd ever done. Like, way more fucking metal than his stupid podcast, as undeniably fucking metal as that'd been too.

Jonas stared out the window over the fields of crops and shit and gazed off toward the mountains where shadows reached through valleys and gorges in the failing light.

He wondered if Joe Rogan was alive somewhere.

Because how weird but awesome was it that five internet minutes ago, Rogan was the biggest podcaster on the planet, and then he went to Spotify for like a hundred million bucks? Then the fucking Chinese stomped the world, and now it was Jonas, pimp rolling through the ruins in a six-wheeled Merc?

Answer, it was really fucking weird and rock-out-with-your-cock-out awesome.

Sure, some grandad big-band shit was playing on the stereo, but Tommy Podesta loved that stuff, and he was driving. That was the rule. You drove; you got your choice of tunes. This rig they rode in was a fucking monster. A Mercedes Benz G63, the civilian derivative of the long-range patrol vehicles used by the SAS in Afghanistan and Iraq. His four-man personal guard sat on cushioned benches in the rear tray, with two bright red Ford Rangers rolling fore and aft as an escort. More heavily armed men rode in the escort vehicles, but the declarative statement of the Legion's superior firepower, hammerskin mojo and hardcore motherfucking Vader cred stood proud in the back of the Rangers. Two pairs of twin-mounted 50 cal. machine guns on swivel mounts.

Jonas had been shocked at what you could do with those things.

Not many places were built to take that sort of damage. In a nice little town like Three Forks, emphasis on little, his guys could have stood off with the 50s and demolished it block by block over a couple of hours.

Two or three hours. Max. Depending on how often they had to swap out the barrels. The mayor and the good folk of Three Forks, not being completely fucking retarded, had opted to bend the knee.

Jonas leaned forward to get a better look at the town as they approached up a long, straight run of blacktop from the south. Fields green with winter crops and fringed with cottonwood trees stretched away on both sides in the watery, amber light. The land was flat here, but the valley was a watershed for both the Missouri and Mississippi rivers. He knew that Three Forks was surrounded by a lush riverine delta of fresh, clean-running watercourses that fed the headwaters of the Missouri and separated the fertile plains from the pine forests and rocky heights of the Bridger Mountain range to the north. The town was compact, maybe a mile from end to end. The tallest structures were white-painted silos at the rail yard, looking almost golden in the setting sun.

It was a good get for the Legion of Freedom. A long way from grubbing in the community gardens at Silverton.

"You want something, boss?" Chad Moffat asked from the passenger seat up front.

"Just a look-see at our latest acquisition," Jonas said.

He was always careful to speak collectively.

Their conquests.

The Legion's triumphs.

Never his. Always theirs.

A mouth-breather like Chad wouldn't notice, but others would. His driver, for instance, Tommy 'The Tripod' Podesta, he was a fucking guy you kept close and watched closer. A made guy, perhaps. Mobbed up, for sure. Back in Miami, working for that shitbird Hondo, Jonas had stood up in court for a couple of guys like the Tripod.

How could he not be at least a minor fucking Soprano with a handle like that?

They'd added him to their merry band about two weeks after Silverton. Dude was leaned over the engine of a fucking Lincoln town car on State Route 2, the sleeves of his silk shirt rolled up to the elbow, his stripy fucking tie—an honest to goddamn necktie—thrown back over his shoulder to protect it from the engine grease. That was your classic Tripod right there. Even in the middle of an apocalyptic train wreck, this stylish goombah was taking care to keep it sharp.

Jonas knew in both his gut and his head that a man like Podesta could be a sword and a shield, or he could be the angry motherfucker plunging a dagger into your back because he felt himself disrespected or disregarded or even short-changed a buck-fifty on what he thought he was owed. A man like Podesta, if you wanted his loyalty, you had to make him believe he had yours. So let the motherfucker have his big band show tunes.

"Looks like the sorta shithole you end up in Wit Sec," the Tripod said, taking one hand from the wheel of the Merc and pointing up ahead at the line of silos. Except, instead of human hands, Jonas would swear under oath that this gorilla had a couple of gigantic, hairy pork hocks.

The convoy approached the edge of town at a stately thirty miles an hour.

They could have put pedal to the metal and rolled in like fucking Vikings with a fash-metal symphony blaring out of massive speakers on a flatbed truck.

Would have been almost as cool as riding in like Caesar on a big black warhorse.

But Jonas had learned to take his time, all the better to ramp up some tension in the crowd that had gathered, on his order, in the baseball field on the southern outskirts of the settlement. It would be chilly there as the light and warmth leaked out of the day. The ball ground lay between a small but very useful airfield and a railway siding. Jonas could see what looked like a thousand people standing together on the infield, under the guns of his Legion and half a dozen war wagons.

But he was much more interested in the rail siding. Eight refrigerated boxcars painted bright red stood out against the uniform white of silos and warehouses. His intelligence gimps told him they were full of beef which had been bound for the port of Seattle. More than enough to feed the Legion for the winter... If they didn't have to feed the good burghers of Three Forks, too.

Or Cardwell or Harrison or any of the other thirty-four towns and villages and bee's dick little places he'd put under his protection. The sort of protection Tommy, 'the Tripod' Podesta, had undoubtedly offered as a service once upon a time.

"What's the mayor's name," he asked.

"Jennings," the Tripod answered. "Fuckin' country club Republican."

"Do they have a country club?" Chad asked, sitting up straighter. No doubt dreaming of gym facilities.

"Golf club, if that counts," Podesta grunted.

Chad slumped. It didn't.

"All righty then. Let's go meet Mayor Jennings," Jonas said, cutting off any conversation before it could start.

THE ARMOURED CONVOY pulled into a parking lot that would have played host to tailgate parties on Friday nights just like this, Little League families on Saturday mornings, and maybe even a farmers' market a couple of times a month. Now, it was occupied by two flatbed trucks converted into heavy gun platforms —the Legion's war wagons—and the two troop carriers delivering the Cohort to Three Forks.

The troop carriers were just a pair of salvaged Greyhounds. Still, the Cohort was a hundred of the hardest motherfuckers specially selected from the three thousand-strong Legion to serve as Jonas's personal guard. They got the best rations, the first pick of any plunder and pussy, and unlike the rest of his army, they had no other duties. Some were ex-military. A couple were even former cops, which hadn't sat well with the Tripod at first, but they'd proved themselves solid hires in the sack of Wenatchee, all the way back in Washington state.

The Commander of the Cohort, Luke Bolger, a former guard from a private prison outside of Wenatchee, stood to attention and saluted as Jonas climbed down from the rear cabin of the big Merc. He never allowed anybody to open the door for him, but he readily returned Bolger's salute, a closed fist over the heart. Then they shook hands as Chad jumped down from the passenger side to land with a crunching thud. The one-time PT was a massive unit. Even bigger than when Jonas met him in Silverton. These days, thanks to the Legion, he got a lot more food and time for weight training. It was almost as though the giant six-wheeled utility had birthed a human version of itself. The shotgun cradled in his hands looked like a child's toy, a trick of perspective. It was a Mossberg Shockwave with a fifteen-inch barrel and an extended clip. Chad also wore a splitting maul slung across his back, a weird sort of half-sledgehammer, half axe, and it did not look like a toy. The handle was as thick as Jonas Murdoch's forearm, and the steelhead looked heavy enough to smash through a bank vault door if you swung it hard enough.

Chad, a tectonic slab of slow-twitch muscle fibre raised to sentience, took up his position a little behind and to the side of Jonas. He wasn't strictly needed as a bodyguard. It was more like security theatre, but it was still great theatre having a 'roid ape with a fucking warhammer back there – even though anybody who raised a hand against Jonas would die in a bullet storm from the half-dozen of Luke Bolger's men assigned to close personal protection of the Centurion.

Yes, okay, so what if Jonas was back on his bullshit? It's not like these fuckers knew he was even referencing his dope podcast with his self-proclaimed title. Who was going to question him on it?

Half a mile of bodies were swinging from telephone poles outside Wenatchee because the mayor and council back there hadn't shown the requisite respect for the Legion in its earliest incarnation. Jonas had offered to safeguard the town against the depredations of all the inmates who'd escaped from that private gaol just outside of town. Or maybe the Chinese had released them, but what did it fucking matter anyway? Some of those guys were his guys now, and Wenatchee was where the Legion of Freedom came into the world.

It was fascinating to Jonas, as an amateur student of history, just how quickly things had rolled back to earlier states of being as soon as the Chinks had swept the legs out from under modern America.

When you took away the scaffolding of norms and law and conventions and shit, you were left with the raw stuff of life. The full Hobbesian buffet. Not just domination and violence, but the most primitive ways of channelling and containing that shit. Personal codes of honour. The syntax of respect. The sort of things he'd learned in Florida, amazingly enough, from cartel and mafia clients like Podesta. Even as low-level and chickenshit as they'd been. When the state can no longer stand as a guarantor of civilised norms and behaviour, smart motherfuckers took matters into their own hands.

This was, in essence, the message Bolger had delivered to Ross Jennings, mayor of Three Forks, not five minutes earlier, as Jonas's convoy made its ever-so-dignified approach along Bench Road.

"Sorry? What do I call him?" Jennings asked.

"Centurion."

"What?"

"Centurion. Or sir. But man, he really digs Centurion."

"MISTER MAYOR," Jonas beamed, striding across the baseball diamond, his hand out to shake with Ross Jennings as though they were meeting at the golf club to iron out the last few details of a real estate deal before celebrating with beers and cigars out on the veranda.

The assembled townsfolk, easily more than a thousand, remained silent and wary. There was the slightest murmur of conversation from the very back of the crowd, but everyone around him seemed to be holding their breath. The sports field did have lights but not enough power to run them, so Leo Vaulk had organised a truck full of Tiki torches, which now burned in an ever-brighter circle around the periphery of the gathering.

"Mister Murdoch... I mean... Cent..er... sir," Mayor Jennings said.

Jonas smiled and took the man's proffered hand in both of his, pumping it once, twice, three times.

"Please. Mister Mayor," he said. "Call me Jonas. And you're Ross, right?"

Jennings' eyes darted to Luke Bolger, who stared back at him coldly.

"Ross, yes," he said. "Ross Jennings. Mayor of Three Forks. And I... I run the GM dealership."

"Oh, that's great, man," Jonas said, slapping him on the shoulder just a little too hard. "American made. Good for you."

He didn't feel sorry for Jennings. That'd be stupid. But he could sort of empathise with the poor bastard.

Jonas had been nervous the first time he'd negotiated the surrender of a whole town. It was such a weird trip. Such a totally fucking out-of-context problem for a Twenty-First century American mind to grapple with that it did put the zap on your head.

And he'd been the guy accepting the surrender, not having to offer it.

That was back in September, about three days after Wenatchee. Some bumpkin village called Entiat an hour up the Columbia River. One thousand souls who'd kept themselves whole by fishing and working the market gardens sprawled over both riverbanks. The place was perfectly well situated to feed itself but basically indefensible. They'd heard about Wenatchee because Jonas made sure they did.

So, he knew it was perfectly natural for old Roscoe here to be a little ropey with stage fright. After all, it looked like almost every one of his constituents had turned out for the ceremony.

As ordered.

Jonas did not need to humiliate him. That wasn't what this was about. But he did need these people to understand that things had changed. Everything had changed. Again.

"Do you mind?" he said to Jennings, smiling as Bolger took the man's elbow and pulled him aside. Gently and discretely but forcefully.

Jonas smiled even wider and stepped up onto the pitcher's mound. It gave him just enough elevation to see over the heads of the crowd. They were primarily white, of course. That was why he'd come to this part of the country. Well, that, and it was close to where he'd started, and there was plenty of food, and not too many mouths needed feeding with it. But it was good that they were white. They were his people, even if they didn't understand that yet.

He took a deep breath. Steadied the butterflies in his stomach. Not many, but there were a couple. He summoned his old courtroom voice, letting it roll out across the field of anxious, staring faces.

"Good day to you," he shouted, although it was more theatrical projection than a carnival barker's yell. "My name is Jonas Murdoch. I lead a community organisation called the Legion of Freedom, and we are here to help."

He let the last words roll away on the cool morning breeze. The faces in front of him weren't openly hostile because these people weren't stupid. They were unarmed. Or disarmed, to be honest. That was a lesson learned from another flyspeck town called Gypsum. That was before Wenatchee and Entiat, back when they weren't even the Legion, just his guys, Brad, Leo and Dale, a couple of Joe Wolfenden's militia crew, and some of Darren O'Shannassy's boys. Anyone who escaped Silverton when the fucking bikers nuked it from orbit. Just over a dozen of them all up, and they'd gone to Gypsum on rumours of a warehouse full of potatoes.

Not a rumour, it turned out.

A true fact, as Leo Vaulk liked to say.

There wasn't much security for those 'taters either. A couple of old coots with hunting rifles who agreed to let Jonas and company stay on in town if they helped bring in the next harvest of spuds.

Long story short, picking potatoes was fucking ass-breaking work, and only Dale Juntii seemed happy to do it. After two days in town, Jonas and Leo turned their guns on the Gypsum Emergency Committee and sent them out into the fields to pick the fucking things. Would have been fine, too, except one of the old pricks had buried a casket full of guns out there, and next thing you know, they've picked off both of Wolfenden's leftovers and shot one of O'Shannassy's guys in the dick.

That was an unholy fucking mess, but not as big a mess as they made of those spud-fuckers when they were done with them.

And so now it was policy. Only the Legion could be armed on its turf.

"These are hard days for our country," Jonas continued, confident in the hundred guns of the Cohort to keep him safe from any crazy fuckers in this audience. "Hard days for you."

A few heads nodded, perhaps cautiously, but only in the crowd.

His men, and the few women who'd proven themselves worthy of promotion to the Cohort, swivelled their heads like gun turrets, sweeping the assembled multitude, looking for any sign of disruption or danger. There was none. They had learned well these last months how to break any spirit of resistance long before it got going.

"You have endured here in your homes with no support from the government. State or Federal."

More nodding.

"You have withstood privation, borne this burden, taken it all on your shoulders."

They agreed with that.

Jonas Murdoch spoke the truth.

"But it gets harder every day. Medicines run low. Supplies dwindle. Some of them vital, like fresh fruit and vegetables...."

He'd been a bit surprised how quickly scurvy had become an issue when a ready source of vitamin C could not be found. The heads, which had started nodding in agreement, were doing so with more conviction now. There weren't a lot of orange groves in this part of the country.

"... And of course, some supplies are vital... but a little embarrassing."

He grinned at the confusion he could see on their faces. He smiled with a lopsided grin and winked.

"Who'd a thunk toilet paper would ever be worth its weight in gold, hey?"

He got a laugh with that. A genuine laugh. And he felt that organic connection. It was suddenly just there.

The toilet paper line was something he'd worked on across a dozen of these ceremonies. Initially, when he'd accepted the surrender of Colton, a small farming town of about four hundred frightened souls hunkered down between the Snake River and the border with Idaho, he'd made a joke about toilet paper being worth its weight in Benjamins and the only one who'd laughed was fucking Tomi Yates. And he was pretty sure she was laughing at him, not with him.

But he'd eventually put that treacherous bitch in the ground, and he'd worked on his material, and by the time he'd moved through Idaho and into western Montana, he was getting pretty good at working a crowd. Even when that crowd was scared, resentful, and deeply disturbed at how the whole world had taken a sudden, violent turn for the worse.

So, the citizens of Three Forks, the newest subjects of the Legion, duly laughed with good-natured relief at his joke. Maybe if he was joking about toilet paper, this wouldn't end so badly, even after all those things his 'envoys' had said to the city council before the surrender. They used soft words but promised terrible consequences if those words went unheeded.

But that was then.

And who the hell was Jonas to disabuse them of their delusions now?

"So that's the first thing we're gonna take care of," he said, his voice booming as another vehicle pulled up at the edge of the baseball field. A small commercial truck, its arrival timed perfectly.

"I said we've come to help, and help is in that truck," Jonas said.

Now, all heads did turn in the direction he was pointing.

"We have medical supplies. Food. And simple goods and products which are suddenly not so simple to lay on hands on these days. Batteries..." A small cheer went up somewhere in the crowd. "Toilet paper." A bigger cheer. "And two pallets of whiskey and cigarettes."

An enormous cheer this time.

A few hats flew up, tossed high into the sky by jubilant owners. Jonas waited for the commotion to die down before speaking again.

"We will have need of some discussions with your town leadership about how you can help us to help other towns and villages and maybe even a few cities get back on their feet. But for now, you folks need to know that the worst is over. You have come through the other side."

A cheer roared out. And clapping started. It was members of the Cohort at first but quickly picked up by the crowd.

Jonas stepped down off the pitcher's mound, followed by the cheering. The protection detail formed around him, but he kept his smile in place as they moved him back toward the Merc. He saw Tommy Podesta giving Mayor Jennings the good news that he was needed at an urgent meeting. Immediately. Meanwhile, Brad Rausch pulled up the roller door on the back of the truck, and the Legion's Civilian Aid crew dropped to the tarmac to begin unloading the relief supplies.

"I just got word from Leo," Bolger whispered. "Manhattan ain't for folding."

Jonas kept smiling and waving.

"Okay," he said out the side of his mouth. "Looks like Mayor Jennings is gonna get to prove his loyalty right up front."

4

GOTTA GET YOUR MACROS

Jonas was not so arrogant as to take Jennings' chair.

Okay, fine.

He was that arrogant. But he wasn't stupid with it. The Legion had a chokehold on Three Forks, but you could get out of a chokehold if you knew how. Especially if you moved before it cranked on. And he could not afford to crank it on here. Not yet.

Truth was, he couldn't crank the motherfucker on anywhere yet.

He was consolidating his rule.

He'd been 'consolidating' since getting his ass out of Silverton in one piece.

So, Jonas let the mayor keep his cheap swivel chair and at least some of his dignity. But he made sure that Bolger delayed the guy just long enough for Tommy Podesta to drive the half-dozen blocks up Main Street to what passed for City Hall. They pulled into the angle parking slot directly out front. Three Forks' seat of government was underwhelming for such a prosperous-looking town. An ugly brick bunker that reminded Jonas of a bail bond office or a payday loan joint. It sat between a quilting supply store and The Plaza, a wood-panelled bar and casino that looked like the sort of place that served breakfast margaritas to degenerate gamblers like Podesta. The Tripod was already licking his lips as he pulled on the parking brake.

"Tommy, I don't think the slots'll be rolling today. Not even for you, man," Jonas said.

It wasn't just that most of the town had been forced to turn out at his arrival ceremony. Money itself had ceased to have any value. The collapse of the banks back on the first day of the Chinese attack had wiped away trillions of dollars in real wealth, but with it went something even more valuable.

Trust.

Nobody *trusted* the value of money as a medium of exchange anymore.

And without trust, that shared belief in the mythology of dollars and cents likewise had no value. That's partly why Jonas was here.

Three Forks *was* wealthy. It had in abundance those things which had become the currency of survival. Food, water, and defensible shelter. Of course, they hadn't defended it very well, which was how come Jonas was here to redistribute their wealth.

He told his security detail to wait on him outside but gestured for Chad and the Tripod to come along. Chad went first, toting his shotgun in one hand like an old duelling pistol. He had the warhammer casually laid over his other shoulder.

Podesta, who'd probably kicked down a few doors for the Mob in his time, hung back, waiting for the massive bullet sponge to go first. He and Jonas exchanged a look. Jonas tried not to smirk. He succeeded. The Tripod shrugged.

Podesta was armed, but unlike Chad or the Cohort, he was discreet about it, tucking a plain old forty-five into a shoulder holster under his jacket.

Just like the day Jonas and crew met him, Tommy 'The Tripod' Podesta was the only man in all the Legion who still wore a suit and tie.

"*Standards,*" he said when anyone asked him. "*I got standards, you fuckin' mope.*"

Tommy entered the building, reaching into his jacket as if for his wallet. Or perhaps to give one of his manboobs a squeeze. They were a considerable pair of hairy fucking knockers, even after three months without a decent bowl of pasta, but when nothing and nobody came at them, the Tripod let his hand fall away. Jonas followed him in.

A woman stood nervously behind a reception counter. Chad loomed over her with his giant maul like she was a carnival strength tester he was thinking of giving one good whack. Just to see if he could ring the little bell.

She tried to speak, but her voice failed her.

Jonas smiled.

"Good afternoon. We have a meeting with Mayor Jennings," he said.

Again, her lips moved, but nothing came out.

"Hey, beautiful," Tommy said. "What's your name?"

"M-Marion Bates," she said, as if unsure.

"Well, Marion, be cool. It's gonna be okay. You're gonna be all right. Why don't you fetch us a cup of joe? I bet the mayor still got old Joe Coffee on tap, right?"

Marion nodded quickly, jerkily, as if relieved to be able to help.

"Yes," she squeaked in a tiny voice.

"I'll take mine black and short," Tommy smiled, pinching his thumb and forefinger together. "The boss here, he don't drink coffee. He's one a them health nuts. And this vanilla gorilla..." he jerked a thumb at Chad, "... he's even worse. All he drinks are fuckin' raw eggs and wheat grass juice if you can believe it. And you could believe it if you ever smelled his farts, let me tell ya. Just look at this mook, would ya? He looks big, but it's mostly egg farts that can't get out, making him bloat like that."

He gave Chad an old-fashioned noogie, right on the flattop.

Chad laughed and shrugged.

"Gotta get your macros right," he said.

Jonas watched, impressed, as Podesta's pantomime routine chilled out this skittish old biddy. He was playing a caricature of himself, but one she would recognise and maybe even appreciate. Like a piece of the old world, come back to life.

"Mayor Jennings likes his Folgers," Marion said, her voice shaking but louder. Just a little more confident. "I'll see if I can rustle one up."

"Ooh, rustling's a serious crime, Marion," Podesta purred. "But I won't tell if you won't, darlin'."

He winked at her, and she blushed.

Jonas gaped. This fucking guy was hitting on Jennings' secretary.

He shook his head as she hurried into a little kitchen to set an electric jug to boil.

"Come on, Disco Stu, boogaloo this way."

Podesta grinned and followed Jonas behind the counter and into the mayor's office. Marion started to protest that they couldn't go in there, but Jonas smiled his winningest smile.

"We'll be good."

And he left Mayor Jennings his chair.

IF ROSS JENNINGS was disconcerted to find three barbarians inside his gates, he did an excellent job of hiding it. He thanked Marion for his coffee and sent her home before settling himself behind his desk.

Jonas sat in one of two cheap plastic chairs in front of the desk.

"You got your parade, Mister Murdoch," Jennings said. "Is there something else I can do for you?"

Chad, who was standing just behind Jonas, moved closer to Jennings. He didn't unsling the warhammer. He didn't have to. Podesta stood in a corner, sipping his coffee, looking bored. Jonas smiled.

"It's more about what we can do for you, Mister Mayor," he said.

Jennings sighed. "Can we not pretend?"

"Sorry?" Jonas said, raising an eyebrow.

"Can we stop pretending that you're here to help us? I know what you're here for. I know what you're doing. I've been hearing about you and your... *Legion*... for weeks now. Been taking in refugees from the towns you took over. And the ones you didn't."

Chad did start to unsling the hammer then, but Jonas laid a restraining hand on him.

"And what is it you think I've been doing, Mister Mayor? What do those refugees tell you?"

Podesta slurped loudly on his coffee. They all looked at him.

"Sorry," he said. "But this tastes like shit." He dropped the cup and saucer on top of a filing cabinet, where it landed with the crash of breaking China.

"Because we didn't come here to drink your shitty fucking coffee," Jonas said.

Jennings jabbed a finger at him.

"You're trying to build some little kingdom to replace the government."

Jonas shrugged.

"But we do need to replace the government. They went away."

"You don't know that," Jennings said.

"I do," Jonas said. "I saw it happen. You might think they're coming back. That's why you let us in without a fight. You're thinking that someday soon the state troopers, or the National Guard, or the 101st fucking Airborne are gonna open the country up again and make everything the way it was."

He could tell he'd hit a nerve. The color rose in Jennings' face, and the muscles in his jawline jumped with the effort of biting down on whatever it was he'd been about to say. Probably some promise of dire consequences for thugs and grifters like Jonas when the current crisis passed, and things got back to normal. Jonas leaned in to press the advantage.

"You've been hanging on for that, haven't you, Mister Mayor? Jonesing for some sweet normality. But I got sour news for you, Ross. This is the new normal. Unknowable numbers of dead. The survivors hunkered down. And us. We're the new normal."

Jonas leaned back in his cheap plastic chair and spread his arms expansively. He was enjoying his monologue, which he'd been polishing since Colton. But he also knew he'd reached a tipping point with Jennings, and the man could fall either way. Podesta knew it, too. You could feel it in his wariness across the room.

Chad?

He was probably thinking sexy thoughts about deadlifts.

Jennings' shoulders slumped just enough to notice.

"What is it you want?" he asked. "Food, I suppose. The meat in the refrigerated cars down the siding. That's what brought you here, isn't it?"

"Protein is important," Jonas grinned. "Macros, Chad, am I right?"

"Fuck yeah, macros."

"But no, Mister Mayor. We're not here to rape and pillage. We only do that to places where they don't let us in. I'm sure those refugees told you that."

Jennings said nothing, but Jonas could see all the wheels turning inside his head. Fact was, the Legion did not punish those towns that submitted without resistance. Only those who offered defiance. And unlike those asshole bikers who'd all but destroyed themselves taking Silverton, the Legion never raided a town they had not first reduced from afar.

But Jennings knew that. Jonas was right; Jennings had heard a lot from those refugees. Some of them were genuine escapees. And some had been sent by Jonas to spread the good word.

"We're not gonna clean you out," Jonas promised.

Jennings looked up warily.

"We will redistribute some of that food supply because there are towns under my protection where people will starve if we don't. And I will not allow people, or my people, to starve. But I meant what I said down at the baseball field. I know you have shortages here because everyone has shortages everywhere." He leaned in and lowered his voice, for emphasis, an old trick he'd learned for working a jury. "In the big cities on the coast, people aren't just killing each other over food; they're killing each other *for* food."

Jennings blanched and looked to Podesta and Chad for confirmation.

Podesta nodded grimly.

Chad smiled. "Protein," he said.

"So, you need to give me a list of all the shit that's short around here," Jonas continued. "I can guess, but if you're any good at your job, you'll know. You get me that list, and I'll try my best to make good on it. But things are short everywhere, Jennings and it's time to lift your sights a little. Look beyond the last street in Three Forks."

Mayor Jennings rubbed at his eyes.

"I'll have Marion send you the latest stocktake," he said, sounding tired. "We've run out of many medications. Lost some good folk because of it, and there are machine parts we need for power and water we just can't get. The grid failed early, and we've done what we can with solar and wind, but we've been pumping water from the rivers. Purification's becoming an issue and—"

Jonas held up his hands.

"Okay, okay. I got it. I'm not the mayor here. You are, Ross. These problems? You're gonna solve them — with our help. But it's still your show. I'll need some rooms in town for about two dozen of my people right away. Admin people, not fighters. They'll see to your needs and what you can spare. You got a hotel, a motel, something like that?"

Jennings thought about it.

"There's the Lewis and Clark Motel, I guess, a few blocks up Main. It's mostly been empty since this whole thing. We had some refugees in there. Montana folk. But we try to billet them and—"

Again, Jonas held up his hands.

"Details, Ross. Details. I know you've been as kind-hearted as you can be to outsiders without being soft about it. That's how we get through this. Kind-hearted when we can be," Jonas said. He stared directly into Ross Jennings' eyes. "Hard when we have to."

The Mayor of Three Forks moved his head in a way that could have been a nod.

"On which topic," Jonas resumed, "I have a favour to ask."

"Oh?" Jennings said, sounding worried.

"Yeah. Your neighbours over in little Manhattan. Is that right? Manhattan? Like the city?"

"Yes," Jennings said, his stomach already turning at the thought of what this lot might try to do to the small Montana town.

"Yeah, they're not as kind-hearted as they could be," Jonas said. "Not as welcoming. They don't like to share. And I don't want to go hard on them. But I will, Ross. Unless you can help me convince them to come on board for the big win."

5

THE BREATH OF AN EMPTY WORLD

They approached Bachman on foot. It was harder to pick out three men and a dog creeping through whispering fields of dead grass and scattered clumps of trees than it would be to lay the sights of a weapon on one of the vehicles. They were quieter, too.

Andrew Nesbitt led the way. Nez was the only one of them with night vision gear. Rick Boreham and Peter Tapsell walked in behind him. A good ten or twelve yards behind spread out to either side, making them a trickier target to cut down with one lucky burst. Rick's dog Nomi was impossible to spot with her midnight black coat. She kept her head down, scanning from side to side, sniffing the soft desert air for unfamiliar-man scent.

She wouldn't bark or even growl if she caught a whiff of somebody she did not know from the convoy. She would simply drop to the ground, alerting Rick to the presence of the Unknown.

It was a hell of a thing, he thought, coming up on a small town in America like some jihadi stronghold in Afghanistan, but you could never be too careful. In most places still occupied and halfway functional, you couldn't get within five hundred yards. They'd thrown up stockades and firing platforms and turned themselves into strategic hamlets, stabilised villages, or whatever the current term of art might be. At the start of their journey, the radio in James' SUV occasionally flared up with news of government plans, strategies, programs, and policies to push out from the stronghold cities and reclaim the heartland towns. You still heard about the strongholds a bit.

But never *from* them, Rick thought, as he carefully stepped around an abandoned truck tire in the middle of a stony field. The strongholds were silent.

The smaller rural townships, anywhere under about fifteen hundred souls with access to water and nutrition, seemed to pull through. But they shook out into all sorts. Some of them, the sentries would start firing on you as soon as you came within range. Some you could roll right up to the gates, or whatever passed for gates, and haggle for trade goods. Some places just felt bad as soon as you laid eyes on them. Rick usually made that call, but Michelle Nguyen was pretty good at reading them, too, which made sense. Her being a professional threat assessment geek and all.

But of course, that was a long time ago, in a galaxy far, far away.

Michelle's fancy satellite phone hadn't successfully jacked into any national command networks for more than two months now.

All she got was hissing silence or the occasional burst of static.

In the here and now, they advanced on Bachman.

Population unknown, but probably four to five hundred before the Chinese attack.

Possibly none, three months after it.

Rick moved forward slowly, trusting Nez to warn them of booby traps or snares and Nomi to pick up human threats at longer range.

He wasn't expecting trouble. Not specifically. And not out here in the fields around a ghost town. But you could never be too careful.

Where once he would have stepped lightly, his eyes darting left and right looking for a strangely shaped mound of garbage or a discarded box that just wasn't sitting right because of the IED hidden inside, Rick Boreham moved across the field to the east of Bachman, listening for human voices, or the sound of furtive movement, waiting on a sudden flicker of torchlight, or the wavering red dot of a targeting laser stabbing out from a low roofline, or a hunter's blind.

The night was cold, and the air so clean he felt he could reach up and sweep handfuls of stars from the sky. They shone with an almost sensual diamond brilliance.

Mel, his woman, she loved nights like this. There was no absolute privacy in the caravan they had assembled by chance and misadventure, but once or twice on the long road, they had managed to steal away for a few hours, leaving Nomi with the others.

Rick stepped. And stopped.

The toe of his boot had touched something hard and unnatural. Metallic. Years of condensed trauma tried to explode into the world through his nerve endings, but it was not a landmine. Even as the panic sweat tingled on his skin, he could see by the light of the moon and stars that he'd stepped on a discarded Coke can. Probably tossed here by a farm hand years ago.

He waved Pete Tapsell to go on.

The rangy old Brit resumed his careful, creeping advance.

Rick breathed out raggedly. Taking a moment.

He kept his weapon raised and his preconscious mind open to the world. Any threat would come from out there, and he let the world flood through his senses. But a small part of him still tried to slip away to the night they'd camped at that lake in South Dakota. A reservoir made by damming the Missouri River and flooding miles of deep, crenellated valleys. He'd been exhausted, his nerves shot by what they had seen and all they had done to get through the megadeath zones south of the Great Lakes. Mel had insisted they rest. Everybody was spent, and they were only halfway done with the journey to Montana.

That was a wonderful night.

Rick shook his head, quietly cursing himself and dragging his focus back into the now.

There would be no more wonderful nights with Mel if he fucked this up and they walked into an ambush.

Thirty yards ahead, on the outskirts of town, Nez held up a hand and lowered himself to one knee. Rick and Pete followed him down to the hard-baked earth. Nomi sat a few feet ahead of her owner. Utterly silent. Rick watched the outline of the point man.

They'd found Andrew Nesbitt near El Paso.

El Paso, Illinois, in case you were wondering.

That was about as far south as they got.

Again, it was James who suggested they add Nez to their growing caravan because they had a bunch of kids to look after now, and he was the first schoolteacher they'd encountered.

Nez maintained they'd taken him into their tribe because he was a badass road warrior with a pick-up full of guns and ammo. But the country was overrun by asshole preppers and Mad Max superfans. So no, Nez was with them because he ran a badass road school out of Ramona Tilley and Sparty Williams' RV. Nesbitt did have a spanking pair of Armasight NVGs, but in conditions like this, Rick was more than happy with his Nikons.

He raised the binoculars and slowly swept the town, east to west.

Two main roads ran parallel to each other, forming the town's backbone. Four smaller streets crossed them irregularly to make up a small grid. The squared-off angles and straight lines fell to straggling disorder at the edge of settlement, where a few of the crosstown streets faded to nothing in the hardscrabble and drifting dust. Rick couldn't see most of it, of course, but he had a good picture in his head from the road maps back at the convoy. Up ahead of them, a municipal park occupied the equivalent of two blocks and the chain-link fence where Nez had taken a knee marked the south-eastern limit of the town's built environment. The trees were dead, and what-ever grass had covered the grounds of the park had long ago died with them. The topmost branches of the tallest trees moved in the chill desert wind, and their moonlit shadows called forth deep, race memories of claws and talons.

Rick ignored the crawling sensation that ran up his back and neck.

Shadows were harmless.

The things that hid inside shadows were not.

He scanned the empty streets and listened to the breath of an empty world. He heard the creaking sign suspended outside Jim's Barber Shop. The flapping of a flag, or maybe some advertising banner. The whisper of wind and dust.

A predator howled briefly but far away. A wolf or coyote. A feral dog.

"Good girl," he said in a low voice to Nomi, who ignored thousands of years of evolutionary biology to shut the hell up.

Her tail thumped once on the ground in acknowledgment, raising puffs of fine grey dust, but otherwise, she remained utterly silent.

She was a very good girl, and she did like to be told so.

Nez got to his feet, and a second later, Rick and Pete did the same.

They stepped off again.

Rick ignored the old familiar pull towards shelter and cover. A hundred thousand years of human evolution urged him to accelerate. To cover the last hundred yards towards what looked like safety as fast as he could run.

He ghosted forward, one slow step at a time, sweeping his tactical arc with the AR-15 he'd taken from a dead man all those thousands of miles ago. Nez and Pete moved just as slowly.

He'd taught them that. He'd taught everyone in the convoy how to move.

Well, everyone except Mel. She already knew.

They stepped over the drooping length of chain-link, which marked the edge of the larger of Bachman's two parks. A few hardy buckthorn trees had retained their foliage in the drought and the dry weeks of autumn, but most of the park's cover of flowering crab apples and black walnut had died a while back. Honeysuckle and sand cherry shrubs looked to have run wild. Water gurgled from the ground by a cluster of cement tables and coin-op barbecues—a broken water pipe.

Rick could imagine the life that would have been lived here. The steady flow of road traffic headed east and west on the interstate. The slow but powerful heartbeat of ranching and farming that continued all year round. The exodus of the town's young people to college, business, and war. The slower but just as inevitable return of the prodigal sons and daughters later in their lives. Independence Day parades would have trundled up one of the main streets and back down the other, ending in a celebration here in the park. The seasons would come and go in their turns, and the routine triumphs and challenges with them. So it had been for a hundred and fifty years. Maybe more. But no longer for Bachman, Montana.

They crossed the arid dustbowl of the park and came together in the shelter of a small pergola that matched almost exactly the one at the Cavalry Memorial.

"Scout," Rick said quietly to Nomi.

She padded away into the dark.

Nomi would not venture far into the streets of the empty town, but she was the closest thing they had to long-range recon. No artificial lamplight burned through the darkness anywhere, and even under the silver-blue chill of moon and stars, she quickly became one with pooling shadows.

"Feels a bit odd this one, I reckon," Peter Tapsell said in a low voice.

Rick had taught them not to whisper, too.

"That's why we're checking it out, man," Nez replied.

"Quiet, fellas," Rick said softly. "Let's just wait a while and see."

And so they did.

The only things that moved in the next ten minutes were the lone body hanging from that lamppost two blocks north and Nomi when she came trotting back from her brief exploration of the town. She dropped her butt at Rick's feet and waited for her reward. He fetched a small piece of jerky from a shirt pocket and rewarded her for a well-done job.

Had she encountered anything untoward, she would not have sat and grinned at him, expecting a treat. Nor would she have capered about, insisting they come to investigate. Instead, she would have stood pointing her snout in whichever direction she wanted them to move.

"Nomi's good," Rick said.

"More than good, she's a bloody wonder dog," Pete said quietly. "Aren't you, girl?"

Nomi agreed that indeed she was, her tail wagging vigorously and stirring up a small dust storm.

"What do you think, Pete?" Rick asked.

Tapsell was an optimist but with a dark sense of humour. He'd explored for gold and diamonds in most places they could be found and probably had more time in the boonies than Rick because of it. He professed to love being in the desert, any desert and walking over ground not often trodden or, even better, never mapped or traversed before he got there. He laid claim to some weird experiences in even weirder places.

"The sort that makes you wonder, guv."

But Rick trusted the man and his judgment. Tapsell was quiet and almost reverent when he spoke of such things, and he knew more than enough of the gritty and unglamorous realities of places that Rick had been, places like Rwanda, Iran, and the Hindu Kush, that Rick did not doubt even his tallest tales. Including a claim to have *almost been* a professional cricketer, a path he did not follow because he'd also been "a *very* professional drinker."

"Looks like it just dried up and blew away," Tapsell said. "It's a long way from anywhere. Would've started running out of supplies on the first day."

Rick pointed at the body hanging from the lamppost in the moonlight.

"Wouldn't have done that on the first day. Probably not even the first week or two," he countered.

"No," Tapsell agreed. "But a month in? Not a problem. He was probably an outsider, anyway."

"Like us," Nez said.

"They got no walls, no gates," Rick said. "No defences to speak of."

"Yeah, mate, that's why they're all dead, eh?" Tapsell said.

Rick grunted noncommittally.

"No warnings on the State Route coming in, either. That bridge back on the Big Powder River that would've been the spot to choke off any traffic from the south. Two men with hunting rifles could hold that bridge."

"Yeah, and they didn't," Pete shrugged. "Not everywhere's the same, Rick. Some places pulled through. These poor buggers didn't."

"No," he conceded. "They did not. Best we go find out why before the others come through. Advance to cover. Take it in turns. I'll go first. Nez, you got your magic goggles. You keep a lookout and come up last."

The other two men agreed to the movement plan, and Rick clicked his tongue for Nomi to follow.

He moved out from behind the pergola and into the town proper.

The three-man team advanced slowly, methodically, leapfrogging each other up the main street. Nomi stayed with Rick, padding along at his heel.

He knew James would be still watching over them from the memorial hill, his eye to the scope of the Ruger. Sparty Williams was there with him, surveying the town with the giant, tripod-mounted telescope he'd been hauling around Wyoming when things fell apart. Sparty, a freelance travel writer once upon a time, took pictures of the moon and the night sky. A hobby that had become a job had saved his life when Zero Day found him hundreds of miles from anywhere.

They had good cover. Steady overwatch. And Nomi.

But it still felt off.

Even Nomi felt it. The deeper they got into town, the more she fretted.

Perhaps it was the spectre of that corpse, swaying ever so gently in the night breeze. Maybe the scent of the cat or the coyotes they had seen.

Rick ignored the rhythmic creaking of the hangman's rope as best he could while they advanced up the wide-open street. A few cars and pick-ups remained parked where their owners had left them. As they settled onto the rims, their tires began to bulge below. Rick noted that none appeared to have been siphoned for gas. The caps of their fuel tanks remained closed.

It would be worth checking them for gas in the morning.

But again, it felt off.

Surely other parties had come through here before?

Half the stores had broken windows.

The door of a hair and beauty salon creaked back and forth in the wind, and a few sad scraps of litter flapped and rolled almost wearily up the main stem, carried on the cool breeze. But the town had not been looted. Nothing had burned. Nomi whimpered but did nothing to alert Rick to any specific threat. He reached down and gave her a reassuring pat. She nuzzled his hand.

Nez moved past him, taking them closer to the dead man, dangling from a rope in the darkness. He stopped momentarily to pick something up from the road's surface before carrying on to shelter under the awning of Jim's Barber Shop.

As Rick passed by him on his next move forward, Nez held up something small between thumb and forefinger, the thing he'd bent down to pick up from the road. Rick took the offering and recognised it immediately. A shell casing.

5.56mm.

Just one?

His next lay-up point put him just short of the body. He could read the sign hung from the neck.

LOOTER.

He paid closer attention to the building facades, and once he started to look for the evidence, he found it. Bullet holes and ballistic scarring. Chewed up masonry and woodwork.

He was sure that come daylight if they cared to explore those shopfronts with shattered glass, they would find plenty of spent rounds.

It should have made him happy, in a way.

This was normal.

But it was still... sort of... wrong.

Pete Tapsell was the first to reach the gallows, where the other three bodies swayed. He surveyed the street and the roofline before turning his attention to the dead.

"Nasty," he said.

It was. Crows had been at their faces.

"Let's keep moving," Rick said. "If this is a trap, these guys are the bait. Come on."

They left the dead to their own company.

SISTER NADINE TENSED her shoulders and tightened the grip on her scythe, but the Rector laid a hand on her shoulder, and she relaxed as the calming spirit of the Lord flowed into her.

Rector Adam did not need to speak to his flock. They were disciplined fishers of men, and all of this had been before. All of this would be again. The Rector peered through the small gap between the slats on the salon's second floor. He knew not to venture near the window. They all did.

He narrowed his eyes.

The heathen scouts had ignored the dark fruit he had displayed for them.

They proceeded instead through the streets of New Jerusalem with the same, revealing precaution. These were no innocent pilgrims. The Rector was confident that the tall one with the chase-hound was their leader. He presented colder than the hinges of Hell, and his canis daemon was well trained to the employments of the Tempter.

Rector Adam smiled without mirth, the expression of a man who had prepared well to do the Lord's work.

The hound had been a complication, but what was this earthly plane if not one difficulty after another on the way to perdition or glory? Alerted by his seekers at the bridge, he had prepared for chase-hounds.

And for heathen scouts coming armed to New Jerusalem.

"Be still before the Lord and wait patiently for him," the Rector mouthed in silent prayer. "Do not fret when people succeed in their ways or carry out their wicked schemes. For those who are evil will be destroyed, but those who hope in the Lord will inherit the land."

He would not fret, nor would his flock.

They would wait patiently, and those who were evil would be destroyed.

6

ANOTHER ONE-OH-ONE

While Rick Boreham led Andrew Nesbitt and Peter Tapsell through the deserted streets of Bachman, three hundred miles to the west, Jonas Murdoch ate a hard-boiled egg, a rye cracker, and a nice piece of cheese in the back of his Mercedes. Chad organised lunch on the run, and Jonas supposed he should be grateful it wasn't another endless buffet of Chicken Sriracha protein bars. Moffat had found a stash of them a week or so back, and he'd been living on the damned things ever since – which meant Jonas, too, as Headquarters toured the Legion's ever-expanding realm.

The eggs were good and fresh, with rich golden yolks. Free range, obviously. The only eggs you got these days came from small farms or backyard chicken coops. The massive factories full of battery hens that had filled the shelves at Walmart and Krogers were all gone, just like Walmart and Krogers, and everything that had once operated at industrial scale.

"Hey, Chad. Where'd you get the cackleberries, man?" Jonas asked as they motored down I-90 toward the tiny hamlet of Manhattan. Tommy had some terrible fucking Frank Sinatra album playing on the stereo, but the rule was the rule. Driver's choice.

"You want more, boss? I got a dozen sweegs boiled up back in

Three Forks while you was talking to the mayor. They got a little chicken ranch there; one of the guys told me about it."

Jonas snorted at the idea of a chicken ranch, but he took another egg, squeezing the still-warm ovoid in his fist until it cracked. It was a strangely pleasing sensation. He peeled the shell into a cup holder. Somebody would clean that out later.

"I'm gonna take one-a-them too," Tommy Podesta said from behind the wheel. "But you gotta peel it for me, Chad. And get all the shell off of it this time. And gimme some a that cheese too. It ain't so fuckin' bad that shit."

The Tripod was right.

Everything except the rye crackers was fresh and dense with flavour.

The good folks of Three Forks, Montana, had their shit together if they were still eating like this three months after the fuckin' slants dropped the hammer. They would make an excellent addition to the Legion if they learned the habit of obedience.

Jonas ate the egg in two bites and the hunk of semi-hard yellow cheese in one. It wasn't much of a feast for a conquering hero, but these days he did most of his conquering with his ass comfortably planted in the back of the Merc or across a desk from some hapless cuck like Mayor Jennings. He tried to keep his CrossFit up, but who'd a thunk it? Turns out, building an empire, even a little one like his, was all about meetings and planning and administrivia, and it wasn't unusual for him to work late into the night.

He flashed back to the management gimps running the Amazon warehouse in Seattle for a moment. Soft cocks, all of them reeking of cologne, perfume, and microwave meals. Not a drop of honest sweat among them. Not like Jonas and the workers down on the floor.

In the front seat, Chad farted.

The Tripod cursed and rolled down the windows, letting the air roar, which had the virtue of drowning out all the grandad crooning from Sinatra.

"Jesus, you fucking animal," Podesta said. "How much of that spicy chicken shit you been eating?"

Chad Moffat just laughed.

Jonas ignored them. They were good guys. Useful. But neither man was what you would call a strategic thinker. He had precious few of them.

Luke Bolger, the boss of his Cohort? Yeah, Luke could see the big picture, for sure.

And Mathias Runeberg, his numbers guy. He had that rare ability to see around corners.

But if Jonas was being honest, most of the Legion were just dumb fucking grunts. Patriots, sure. And loyal to a fucking fault. But none of them was likely to catch the attention of the judges at the Nobel Committee.

He rolled down the back window and stared at the passing landscape. They were cruising the valley at around sixty miles per hour, close enough to warp speed these days, even out on the open highway.

This stretch of the interstate was only passable because his engineers had already cleared it of dead Teslas, truck rollovers and one big pile-up at the turn-off to some place called Logan. It was smaller than Manhattan and Three Forks, and it'd died months ago. The highway ran through irrigated farmland, and from his elevated position, Jonas could see dozens of vast, dark green fields. Far away to the north, a line of blue, haze-shrouded hills blocked out the horizon. He had a briefing paper from Mathias Runeberg listing all the assets and resources that would accrue to the Legion in this area once they brought it under control. But then, that's why he had Mathias. To turn his big throbbing galaxy brain to the minute details of stuff like that.

What Jonas knew was this...

The country around here was rich enough to feed his three-thousand-strong army and the sixty-thousand-plus citizens of the Legion he had already brought under his protection.

But all the subjects he'd just added by way of Three Forks and its surrounding territory also had to be resourced and catered for now. Some of Luke Bolger's smarter lieutenants would sift through the rolls of the town's fighting-age population and conscript a levee to add another company to their available combat strength. And naturally, they'd be dispatched to the far corners of the Legion's territory. You couldn't expect them to turn on their neighbours if those neighbours resisted his ambassadors' entreaties – as they just had in Manhattan.

But every conquest brought with it the need to add more territories and new recruits to support and supply the population already under his yoke, as well as those who had just been added.

It never fucking ends, Jonas thought.

A week before taking Three Forks, he'd asked Runeberg in frustration when they could turn to consolidation rather than conquest, and the operations chief had just smiled.

"When winter finally piles the snow up high enough to stop us."

And now that Three Forks was gained, he was on the road again.

So much winning that he was getting sick of it.

It would be nice, Jonas thought as they sped past the burned-out, rusted ruins of another significant pile-up to kick back and enjoy his conquests one day. When you thought about it, the only time he'd had a chance to chill the fuck out was back in Silverton, and he'd enjoyed that for just a couple of weeks. Strange how fondly he remembered that place now because when he was there, most of the normies and losers had shat him to frustrated tears.

Even boning Tomi Yates got boring after a while. Until she threatened to rat him out at the end. That'd spiced things up. It'd been the end of sexy little Tomi, too.

But thinking back on her tight, treacherous little ass, he stirred.

It'd been a week since he got his pipes cleaned by that sexy fucking black bitch back at Deer Lodge, and the pressure was building. He was gonna have to wrap up this Manhattan thing quickly and get his ass back to Three Forks, see what the recruiters had turned up. In a place that big, there was always some honey looking to lie down next to the big dog.

It was good, but Jonas sometimes wondered whether it might have been better if none of this shit had gone down. Things had been breaking for him at the ass end of the summer. But of course, he never did get to enjoy his podcast, *The Centurion*, breaking out just before everything fell apart. The more he thought on it, the darker his mood grew. It was almost as though fate was mocking him. Always showing him what he could have and ripping it away before he could enjoy it.

"We're about five minutes out," Podesta announced as they swept past a sign alerting them that the thriving little burg of Manhattan, Montana, was four miles distant.

It broke the downward spiral of his thoughts.

"How d'you reckon the real Manhattan is doing right now?" he said.

Chad turned around to answer him.

"Dude, it'd be fucking gnarly with cannibals and shit, for sure."

Chad was always up for a bull session about cannibals and shit. He was confident most of the country was overrun with them by now. Mostly, it amused him until he remembered his little boy was out there somewhere.

Then, they had to deal with Sad Chad.

"Gimme another one of those eggs, man," Jonas said, looking to distract him.

The convoy of SUVs and gunned-up Ford Rangers slowed a minute further down the freeway. Jonas leaned forward for a better view as he finished off the chicken bullet. Beyond the lead vehicle, one of the big, red gun wagons, he saw a collection of trucks, flatbeds, and a couple of minibusses doing duty as troop carriers. They were all stationary, parked on the interstate in a temporary vehicle fort a couple of hundred yards short of the off-ramp. Two former lifeguard towers, liberated from an *Oceans of Fun* water park, rose over the armed encampment, providing an elevated view across the open fields between the highway and the outskirts of the small town.

"How come they set up this far out?" Jonas asked.

Podesta kept his eyes on the road. "Bolger says, the way the town's built if they got any closer, they'd get caught in a crossfire."

Jonas hadn't studied any tactical maps, but he trusted the Cohort chief to make the right call. The Tripod slowed down and steered them off the road into a breakdown lane. It put the mass of all those other vehicles between Jonas and any snipers who might be scoping for him from an attic or a rooftop somewhere across that field.

Tommy cut the engine, and all three men climbed out, with Chad taking up his usual position just behind the boss.

Luke Bolger was waiting for Jonas, flanked by two of his officers, all of them dressed in matching forest camouflage.

It was a serious business, laying down a siege.

"Hey, Luke," Jonas said. "What's happening?"

Bolger did not salute. That was a protocol he had insisted upon. Salutes could draw sniper fire. Jonas thought that was a bit over-wrought, but these guys would literally take a bullet for him, so what the fuck. He could indulge them.

"It's another one-oh-one," Bolger said.

He meant a fortified town.

In the administration's last days, the President had issued Executive Order 14101, authorising local government authorities to secure America's towns and cities against any threats 'by whatever means possible.' The adult population of the United States was deemed to be drafted into the military and seconded to local militia units under the command of the senior elected official in their local government area.

It meant precisely nothing in the cities, which had already fallen, but in thousands of smaller towns, it had created a legal permission structure to raise fortified walls against the outside world.

Jonas sighed.

"Okay. Do we got a line to the mayor or the sheriff or whatever fuckin' big man is left over there?" he asked.

Bolger shook his head.

"Not so much, no. We sent a party over to negotiate. They shot them down halfway there."

"Whoa! Hardcore."

"Yeah," Bolger growled. "This looks like a tougher nut to me, boss. I don't want to waste more of my guys on it."

Jonas raised an eyebrow.

"Your guys?"

Bolger grinned sardonically.

"Sorry. Our guys."

"Okay, good call. But we have one more card to play before we fumigate the place."

He looked around for Tommy Podesta. The Tripod wasn't hard to find in his fucking blue business suit. He was standing over near the chow wagon, nursing a steaming cup of joe.

It would be a nice coffee, too. Jonas insisted that the frontline grunts always got the best rations. Better even than he did. It wasn't that big a deal, though. He was trying to keep his carbs and sugar budget in balance. Still, it was a good look for a leader, he reckoned, and he was all about the optics.

"Hey, Tommy," he called out. "I think it's time for Mister Mayor to earn his pay."

Ross Jennings did not much like the look of this. He sat in the back seat of the converted Ford Ranger, guarded by a couple of Murdoch's gun thugs. They stood outside smoking and talking but always watching. He wasn't restrained in any way. No handcuffs or zip ties. And they'd been courteous about telling him not to move.

They called him Mister Mayor and said it wasn't safe to get out of the vehicle and wander around.

Jennings was no fool. He knew the immediate danger did not come from the two hundred or more heavily armed men in the lee of the eccentric armoured convoy. If he tried to get out and get away, his guards would probably break his legs.

Sitting in the back of the converted pick-up, waiting to play whatever role had been chosen for him, Jennings tried to remember when he had first learned of these gangsters. Because that's all they were, in the end, notwithstanding their love of military cast-offs and absurd

Roman references. They were just a bunch of ruffians. That's what'd made it so hard to untangle the first rumours of organised banditry from the chaos and violence of everything coming apart. It had almost been worse when the TV news had still been on. At least when the news networks went dark, he'd no longer had to contend with half the town losing their minds at Hannity or that Maddow woman every night.

To be honest, it had been a blessing.

The things they'd seen in places like LA.

Jennings shivered, and not with the cold.

It was probably seven or eight weeks after they stopped hearing from the Governor's office in Helena or anyone in Washington when he first got wind of something happening beyond the Divide. Not just rumours of biker gangs or crazy stuff like Mexicans from California taking over everything, but whispers about some militia forces or a unit of the Oregon National Guard finally rolling out of their barracks to restore a semblance of order. The Legion was none of those.

Ross Jennings closed his eyes and frowned, trying to get it straightened out in his memory.

The city council had voted quickly to take a series of prudent, practical steps to secure Three Forks under the auspices of the President's Executive Order. Still, they had not raised a stockade wall or dug trenches and strung razor wire like in some places.

Not like Paul Davis and Tony Neilson over in Manhattan, for instance.

But he remembered the day they voted to impound the refrigerated goods train stuck at the siding down on Talc Road.

"Boy, howdy, wasn't that a show," he said to himself.

Jennings was given to talking out loud when he was on his own and needed to think something through. He found it helped organise his thoughts.

"And that was, let's see, that was the same Thursday night that Doc Siewert said we would start losing folks if we didn't get their medicines in. And he was right about that, as it turned out."

The furrows in his brow grew deeper as he dredged his memory of those crazy days.

"Let's see; we locked everyone down the first week of September. Put the curfew on and took stock of all the food in town."

That was when they were still getting CNN, Fox, and all the others because he remembered the little TV in the council offices showing the hunger riots in the cities back east.

"And we voted to close the town the following Tuesday, didn't we? Yes, that's right. Because I remember talking to Paul about it just before the phones went out."

So, the first real indication that something was up—you know, besides the end of the world—was probably a little after that, when a rider came down the I-90 from Cardwell, warning that a bunch of outlaw motorcycle gangs were tearing up little places like Cardwell and Three Forks over in Washington state.

Ross Jennings was lost in deep concentration now. He looked like a man in prayer, his head bowed forward, his hands clasped together between his knees. He stared at the cuffs of his pants without really seeing them.

"And we got those refugees from Seattle in the valley a week after that."

That had been the hardest thing he'd ever had to do. Not just as mayor but as a man, and a man of strong faith at that.

The Bible did not mince words on the matter. Way back in Leviticus, the good Lord insisted that if your brother became poor and could not maintain himself, "you shall support him as though he were a stranger and a sojourner, and he shall live with you."

But when strangers and sojourners had appeared on the horizon west of Three Forks, the town itself was already desperately poor in the way of foodstuffs and medicines, and they couldn't maintain both their own and all who came to them.

Thoughts and prayers were all they had to offer.

The rail yard full of frozen beef notwithstanding.

Mayor Jennings rubbed his hands together so tightly that he squeezed the blood from his fingers.

He was far enough lost in his thoughts that he didn't notice the big, well-dressed man approaching along the breakdown lane.

He jumped in surprise when Tommy Podesta pulled open the door and grabbed him by the arm to pull him out.

"Mister Mayor," the Tripod said cheerily. "It is your time to shine."

7

THE FIDEL CASTRO OF GRIFTERS

For as long as he lived, Ross Jennings would never forget that smile. Jonas Murdoch had the smile of a hammerhead shark. A wide and hungry maw, full of teeth. However, unlike a shark's black, soulless eyes, Murdoch's seemed to dance with a delighted sparkle.

"Your honour!" he called out as Jennings emerged from the back of the improvised gun truck, spreading his arms as if to sweep Jennings into a brotherly embrace. The warlord was standing in the shelter of some sort of armoured car. Two of them had rolled up in the last hour and a half. They looked like the sort of thing you used to see paramilitaries riding around in places like the Middle East or South America. At least when there had been TV news and websites to carry that sort of footage, once upon a time. The vehicles were big, six-wheeled brutes with the thick, sloping armour of their troop cabins broken only by dark and tiny slit windows and firing loops. They were painted in desert tan, and Jennings assumed that Murdoch, more likely some of his goons, had hijacked them from a military base.

He was more than a little surprised to see the words PORTLAND CITY SCHOOL DEPARTMENT stencilled onto the armour of the nearest vehicle.

Murdoch and a couple of his henchmen stood around a small fold-up card table, eating bread rolls and drinking coffee. Jennings could smell hot corned beef and melted butter. The coffee steamed in the crisp late morning air, and he felt his stomach rumbling and mouth-watering. Jennings did his best to keep a neutral expression on his face. He didn't want to give Murdoch even the slightest impression that the man had any leverage over him – which was laughable when he thought about it. Ross Jennings was now surrounded by nearly two hundred heavily armed men and women. Mostly men. And what looked like a small regiment of armoured vehicles and the makeshift heavy gun platforms the terrorists in Africa called 'technicals'.

"Come and get some vittles, Roscoe," Murdoch said as Jennings approached. "Do you say vittles out here in cow country? I've always been a city boy, and I'm just trying to fit in."

"We just call it food," Jennings said, more sourly than he'd intended.

For some reason, Murdoch and his cronies found that hilarious, and the next few moments were filled with their braying laughter. The show ended only when Jonas Murdoch stopped laughing.

"Seriously, man," Murdoch said, putting one arm around Jennings' shoulder and leading him away from the small buffet, "you should have gone into stand-up. You have a way with words."

Jennings shrugged off the man's arm.

"I assume you have something you want me to do," he said.

Murdoch smiled and nodded.

"People say you should never assume anything, don't they?" he smiled. "And then they do that tired joke about making an ass of you and me, but honestly, Ross, yes. I do have something for you to do, and I'm glad you're thinking ahead. That's what I'm all about, man. I try to think ahead."

They came to a small gap between the two armoured cars. Jennings saw that the second one had been scavenged from the police department in Kennewick. It was covered in a cage arrangement, and he realised with a start that it was a defence against rocket attacks.

He wondered if the police officers of Kennewick had suffered many rocket attacks of late.

Murdoch steered Jennings into a spot where he had a clear line of sight across an open field to the edge of Manhattan. He could see Ed Cormack's auto repair shop about a mile away. Ed specialised in European vehicles, and Jennings had put his eldest daughter's old Renault in there several times. He wished she would just get something reliable, like a Toyota, but Chrissy had bought that car with her own money before going to the Academy, and she loved it with an irrational passion. Murdoch was still talking, mostly about himself, and Jennings wanted to tune it all out, but the man would not shut up.

"I was thinking ahead when I got out of Seattle on the first day," he said. "I was thinking ahead when I laid up in a friendly little town called Silverton. Have you ever heard of Silverton, Ross? No? That's a pity. It was a nice place until a bunch of asshole bikers rolled on it and fucked everything up. But that's okay!" He boomed, full of life and self-regard. "I planned for that too, which is how I got out. I plan for everything, Ross because it's a sixth sense, don't you think? Planning is just seeing into the future and getting ready for it."

God Almighty, Jennings thought. This guy is like the Fidel Castro of grifters. It's not enough that he has to shake you down, but he has to deliver a seven-hour speech while doing it.

"You see, I knew what was going to happen, Ross," Murdoch went on. "Not exactly, you understand. I didn't know exactly what the Chinese would do or even that it would be the Chinese. But just between you and me, Ross, one leader to another. I could tell all that shit we were into; it could not keep going. Sending good American jobs out to a bunch of shithole countries. One law for the rich, another for everyone else. Forcing all that diversity and empowerment crap down a man's throat until he had no choice but to gag on it. Yeah, I knew when that whole rotten system took a hit, a real hit, it was going to come apart."

Murdoch turned Jennings to look at him directly. Man to man.

"That's why I'm standing here in charge of a Legion, and what you're about to do is walk out across that potato field, or whatever the hell it is, and make my Legion, our Legion, a little bit bigger. Because I see the future, Ross. And your neighbours over there, they have no future outside the Legion. Inside, they'll be kickin' it—hookers and blow for everyone. Or, you know, adequate nutrition, shelter, and security. Outside, winter is coming. And wolves. And, like, fuckin' bikers of the apocalypse and shit."

Murdoch waved his hands around.

"I know, Ross, I know. I do get carried away with my cultural references. That's why I'm sending you out there to talk to them, Ross. You're a level-headed guy. A good man. A trusted neighbour. Probably a registered Republican, am I right?"

He grinned. It reminded Jennings of that terrible Batman movie about the Joker. The one that didn't even have Batman in it. Why would people do that?

"You know I was, Murdoch. Your spies knew all about us before you ever came through the gap."

Murdoch nodded as if satisfied.

"Yes. Yes, I did. Which is why I know you are going to knock this out of the park, Ross. I need you to get yourself over there and convince those guys to come on board for the big win. You can do it. You know I speak the truth. Seriously, winter is coming, and we need to hunker down and help each other out. Nobody else is coming. Your friends over there? I know they have more than enough for themselves. If they are not inclined to be community-minded and lean more toward selfishness and short-sightedness, they do not have a future. You need to convince them of that, Mr Mayor."

Murdoch grinned at him again. A tingle started at the base of Jennings's spine and quickly ran up his back and into his shoulders and neck. His balls crawled up inside his body.

"And what if I can't convince them?" He said, struggling to get the words out past a dry throat.

The smile disappeared from Murdoch's face.

"I'm afraid, Ross, that the Legion cannot tolerate threats within its territory. We won't *take* this town if it doesn't yield. We will reduce it. You tell them that."

The giant bodyguard with the sledgehammer and the shotgun reappeared at a signal from Murdoch. Jennings looked around the temporary encampment. Most everyone was staring at him.

"Best you get a move on," Jonas Murdoch said. He tapped two fingers on the expensive-looking wristwatch he wore. It was almost certainly stolen or looted.

"Tick-tock," he said.

The bodyguard pointed out across the field with his oversized hammer.

"That way, dude."

"Oh! I almost forgot," Murdoch said. He grinned and pointed two fingers at the side of his head, imitating a gun. His thumb fell like a hammer, and he made a shooting noise, crossing his eyes. "Here, take this with you, and make sure you keep it on the whole time."

Jennings was more than surprised when Murdoch handed him a phone. He didn't know what sort it was, just that it wasn't an iPhone. His family were all iPhone users.

Murdoch read the expression on his face.

"Nah, man, it doesn't work. Not like that anyway. The cell networks are still down. But it can take a memo. So, I want you to turn it on, keep the volume jacked up, and record everything happening while you're over there. I want a record of whatever you say to them, not just your recollection."

Jennings started to object but gave up. What was the point? They would just shoot him and send someone else if he didn't do it.

He put the phone in his pocket and started walking.

It took him a moment or two to get control over his feet and his legs. They felt like balloons, and he stumbled a little as he threaded his way between the massive armoured vehicles. Somebody started clapping, and he stopped and turned. It was Murdoch, smiling and politely applauding him as though he was stepping up at some garden party to make a speech. All the legionnaires, or whatever they call themselves, followed his example, and Ross Jennings stumbled down the embankment of the interstate, followed by the sound of warm applause.

Good Lord, he thought. This can't be happening.

But it was. He was walking across the onion field – he could see now that a new crop was sprouting through the rich brown earth – he was walking across the onion field outside Manhattan, and two or maybe even three hundred armed bandits were clapping him as he went.

Jennings was still dressed for his office. He wore the brown suede boots his daughter Amy had bought him for Father's Day last year. A pair of khaki drill pants. A blue cotton shirt and a light sports jacket. He had left his hat back in the converted pickup.

The sun was high overhead, but it was not especially hot at this time of year. A breeze whispered in from the east, carrying the smell of hops and malt. There were two craft breweries in Manhattan, and he was surprised to realise they were still working. Perhaps that's why Murdoch and his horde were so keen to capture the town. Maybe they were after the beer.

No. That wasn't the story. At least not the whole story, Jennings knew. They wanted Manhattan for the same reason they wanted Three Forks. The oldest reason of all. Blood and soil. Warm bodies for their militia. Food and shelter. The new currency.

He did not like the chances of this turning out well.

Paul Davis, the mayor of Manhattan, was not the sort of man who would blink at a threat. And Tony Nielsen, his sheriff, was even less likely to back down. Davis had been courteous and helpful in the first weeks of the crisis, but when the president signed that executive order authorising incorporated municipalities to see to their defences by whatever means they deemed necessary, he had turned his town into a fortified hamlet. Unlike Three Forks, Manhattan was surrounded by razor wire and man traps. There were heavily armed patrols, both regular and irregular, walking the streets. Mayor Davis had warned him to keep his residents a reasonable distance from the town and the river to the north. He had snipers scattered at random high points, with orders to shoot down outsiders.

Jennings' scalp started prickling again when he imagined that some of them must have him in their sights by now. He wondered who. There was no shortage of hunters and veterans in Manhattan or Three Forks. He might have as many as half a dozen sets of crosshairs laid on him as he picked his way through the soft soil of the onion field. He could only hope they would recognise him and relax their trigger fingers. Three figures lay in the dirt up ahead. Two looked as if they had melted into the earth. The third lay in the unnatural attitude of one suddenly ripped from the living world. His back was arched, and two arms raked at the sky behind his head.

Jennings could imagine him flying backwards, his hands thrown up in shock at the impact of the bullet that killed him.

Without thinking, he started to veer ever so slightly away from them.

A bullet cracked past him five hundred yards from the edge of town. His bowels turned to water, but he forced himself to keep walking. He raised his hands to show he was not armed and resolutely turned his face towards his destination. He also quietly intoned the Lord's prayer and the 23rd Psalm to steady his nerves and, honestly, to give him something to think about other than what it might feel like to have a bullet pass through his forehead and emerge from the back of his skull.

"Yea, though I walk through the valley of the shadow of death, I will fear no evil: for thou art with me—"

Another bullet kicked up dirt about twelve feet to his left.

Strangely, that made him feel better. That was such a wide miss for a good rifleman with a long arm and a scope that he was sure it was just a warning. A shot across his bow. He kept walking.

His arms ached with the effort of holding them high, and once or twice, he nearly tripped and fell on his face. Two more warning shots bracketed his left and right, but he pressed on. He relaxed when he was close enough to make out the man shooting at him from a small attic window at the town's western limit.

It was Sheriff Nielsen.

He was pretty sure Tony Nielsen wouldn't gun him down.

When no more bullets chewed up the earth around his feet or whistled and cracked past his head, Ross Jennings thought about lowering his hands. His shoulders ached fiercely—the arthritis playing up. But from an abundance of caution, he kept them high and kept walking.

Approaching the town from the southwest, he was a little taken aback by the work Davis and Nielson had done to build out Manhattan's defences. The town presented as a compact pentagon, and each of the five sides had been reinforced with earthworks. Barbed wire was not unusual in cattle country, but it was surprising to see it wrapped tightly around a familiar town. Also unexpected were the firing pits and guard towers they had built here.

"That'll be far enough, Ross," a voice called out. "You can put your hands down if you want."

That was a merciful release—the familiar voice, Paul Davis, and dropping his hands. Jennings could not recall the last time he'd felt such relief.

He peered into the entrenchments, looking for the town's mayor. He didn't see Davis, but a young man in army camouflage gear appeared behind a John Deere tractor and waved him in.

A trench line zigzagged in front of him, and he thought he might have to do some climbing to get across it, but a couple more young men appeared from within the deep ditch with a plank length to carry him from one side to the other. He recognised one of them, Buddy LaMothe, who'd gone to Montana State in Bozeman on a scholarship to play point guard for the Hawks.

"Hey, Buddy," Jennings said. "Good to see you got home. I caught that game you played against Billings back when... well... Before all this."

It was a helluva thing, but a bright, genuine smile cracked open the grim lines of the young man's face.

"Thank you, sir. I had a good game, but, you know, they still played better than us on the night."

"Basketball was the winner, buddy," Jennings smiled.

LaMothe grinned, nodded and pointed to a gap between a couple of boarded-up houses.

"Mr Davis and the sheriff will see you through there, sir."

"It's good to see you, son," Jennings said.

"You too, sir."

The plank across the trench line was at least two feet wide, but he put his arms out for balance as he walked across. It wasn't the most stable platform. Stepping down on firm ground on the other side, Ross Jennings felt himself in a familiar and utterly foreign place.

They had turned Manhattan into a fortress. Trench lines ran everywhere, studded with foxholes. Everybody was armed. It was nothing like Three Forks. Jennings and the city council had moved heaven and earth to keep things as normal as possible in their town. It had not been easy. The Jennings family line ran back to the founding of Three Forks in 1908, when his great-great-grandfather, a cattleman from the Red River plains of Texas, came north with 2000 head of German Angus. The Jennings clan had served the town of Three Forks ever since. Three mayors, ten councilmen, a schoolmaster, generations of cavalrymen, and one Air Force woman, his own eldest daughter, Chrissy. That was a lot of institutional memory—a long bloodline with deep remembrance of hard times past. And Jennings had drawn heavily on it to pull the town through the current difficulties.

He wondered, looking around at the fortifications Paul Davis had built here, whether he had done nearly as well as he thought. When the long-haul trucks stopped arriving at the loading docks of The Three Forks Market and the Cash Dollar grocery store, he hadn't supposed to start digging trenches and run barbed wire. His thoughts had turned immediately to how long the crisis might go on and how he could keep everyone fed if it were longer than the governor's office was saying.

Perhaps he should have attended to the matter of guns before shoring up their butter reserves.

"It's always nice to have visitors, Ross," a familiar voice called out. "But I can't say I care much for the company you brought with you."

Paul Davis appeared from around the corner of a small engineering workshop. He was carrying a rifle in one hand and wore a pistol on his hip. Davis swapped the gun to his left hand before he and Jennings shook. Jennings then put a finger to his lips, carefully removed the phone from his pocket and showed Davis that they were being recorded.

The other man nodded.

Jennings put the phone back in his top jacket pocket.

"So, I guess these fellas will be this Legion we've been hearing about," Davis said.

"I'm afraid so," Jennings confirmed. "They sent me as a messenger."

Davis nodded.

"Yeah, makes sense. We killed the other three they sent. So, I suppose you better give me the message, Ross. Although I can probably work it out for myself. Something about an unconditional surrender?"

Jennings nodded.

"Something like that. You want to talk it over in your office?"

He heard footsteps approaching, and a few moments later, Sheriff Nielson appeared wearing a bulletproof vest. He tipped the brim of his straw hat in Jennings's direction.

"Ross," Nielsen said.

"Tony," Jennings replied. "My thanks for not shooting me before."

The sheriff sketched him a brief, passing grin.

"Least I could do. You still owe me twenty bucks from our poker game."

"My word, you are correct, and I had forgotten. My apologies, Sheriff. I have been busy."

"We all have," Mayor Davis said. "And I fear we are only going to get busier still. You let these clowns into Three Forks, Ross?"

Ross Jennings sighed and nodded.

"We took a vote. Not just the council, Paul. The whole town. Heard from both sides, those who wanted to fight and those who didn't. Heard from some people who had fought Murdoch and his gang. Heard from some others who just ran."

Davis and Nielsen listened in silence, their faces unreadable.

"I'll give them this," Jennings said. "They don't mess around with weasel words or doublespeak. They told us if we joined their legion, they would come in peacefully, take stock of our resources, redistribute what we didn't need, and provide for what we don't have. If we refused to join, they would reduce the town."

Sheriff Nielsen frowned.

"What do you mean reduce?"

Ross Jennings shifted awkwardly.

"I don't think they mean by ten per cent, Tony. I've seen the sort of firepower they'd be using. It looks like they got a lot of it from army bases, the National Guard, or something. Big machine guns. Rocket launchers. That sort of thing. They're not messing around. When we took the vote, we heard from a couple of people we let in as refugees, back when we could still do that. They came to us from a place called Wallace, back up the I-90. Except Wallace isn't there anymore. Murdoch and his Legion reduced it. To ashes. I'm sorry, fellas. There'll be no talking him out of it. For whatever reason, he wants this town. Probably because he wants the valley for the winter crops."

The two men digested what he had said. They were silent for a long time. Paul Davis spoke first.

"How did you vote, Ross?"

The phone in his jacket felt very heavy.

"I voted to fight them," he said.

There didn't seem to be much point in lying. Now that the Legion had moved into Three Forks, it wasn't like he could hide his vote from Murdoch.

Both Nielsen and Davis nodded as if they approved.

"But the town voted no?" Davis said.

"That's how it went," Jennings answered. "And I have to respect the vote."

"Of course," Davis said as if the question should not even be asked.

They fell quiet again. This time, it was Jennings who broke the silence.

"So, what's your answer, Paul? What are you going to do?"

Davis nodded slowly.

"We took our vote, too. You tell Mr Murdoch he can go to Hell. Manhattan will fight."

8

EVERY PROBLEM A NAIL

The voices on the recording were muffled and occasionally obscured by static, probably from the phone mic rubbing against Ross Jennings' pocket fabric. But Jonas didn't need a crime lab to clean up the audio.

"We took our vote, too," Mayor Davis said. *"You tell Mr Murdoch he can go to Hell. Manhattan will fight."*

That was enough.

Jonas had everything he needed to know. He tapped the on-screen button to end playback.

"You know, it's good to be the one on this end of the wire, for a change," Tommy Podesta said.

Jonas grunted.

They sat in his Merc with the doors closed and the heater running. Fuel wasn't an issue yet. He had plenty of salvage teams out siphoning gas from abandoned vehicles.

Outside, the last of the day's warmth had disappeared as the sun dipped under the high line of old, eroded mountains to the west. Twilight was closing in on the Legion, and with it, darkness, rushing up the valley in long, pooling shadows. The Samsung's home screen lit up Jonas's face from below, and he could see his reflection in the car window.

Without streetlights, heating or any of the comforts and amenities of civilisation, night fell upon the valley like a swift black sword, cleaving the observable world from those things that happened in the dark. Luke Bolger maintained good light discipline among the Cohort and the other ranks of the wider Legion.

There were four hundred troops on site now, but not all of them with the main detachment on the interstate. Small blocking forces had taken up positions around Manhattan to bottle up any escapees. Jonas could not see much beyond the windows of his car. Bolger did not allow campfires, cigarettes, or any source of light that might attract fire from the besieged town. He did not think it likely that Manhattan's defenders possessed heavy weapons. They'd have used them by now. But Luke Bolger was a cautious man by nature. It was why Jonas trusted him, for now, with command of his personal guard and operational responsibilities for the Legion as a whole. That was a lot of power in the hands of one subordinate, but Jonas calculated that it was not in the man's nature to take advantage of it.

That would require a boldness of spirit that Luke Bolger did not possess.

What he did possess, however, was a flinty-eyed facility for reckoning the odds and shortening risk. He had already recommended that they address the tactical problem of Manhattan with what he called 'action from a distance.'

Bolger proposed to 'fumigate' the place in the jargon of the Legion's frontline fighters. He wanted to demolish the town with vehicle-mounted 50-calibre machine guns. That was Luke Bolger's idea of nimble tactics. Standoff and solve a problem with overwhelming firepower. Machiavelli, he was not.

Marshal Zhukov? Yeah, that was a fair compare, Jonas thought.

"You good boss?" The Tripod asked.

Jonas had gone quiet in the back.

"Yeah, I'm good, man. I never like doing this. Seems kinda wasteful, is all."

Tommy Podesta turned around in the driver's seat.

"It is, boss. It's a terrible waste and a real shame. But that's no reason not to do a thing. Not if it's gonna save you the trouble of an even bigger waste down the road. These assholes, we seen their type before. We know what happens if you leave them be. They don't respect you. It ain't a mercy to them. It's a provocation. You walk on past guys like this. I guarantee they'll kick you in the ass the first chance they get. They're fuckin' rats."

In Tommy Podesta's moral universe, there was no creature lower or more deserving of extermination than a rat.

"You speak a hard truth, brother," Jonas said. "Come on, let's get it done."

He tossed the Samsung and climbed out of the back of the Mercedes. The bitter chill of nightfall knifed through his leather jacket. Podesta, now wearing a scarf and a heavy overcoat against the rapidly advancing frigid gloom of the evening, followed him out, tapping an old-fashioned hat down into place for good measure. Chad was waiting just outside for them. The spicy chicken sriracha farts had become insufferable, leading to his banishment. He was talking with Bolger and a couple of the Cohort guys about why prioritising strength training over cardio was more important when you had to choose.

"And when you don't have to make a choice, you still gotta go with the heavyweights," he said. "It's just science."

They saw Jonas emerging from the car and came to a form of attention. Nobody saluted, of course. Nobody's posture changed. Nothing like that. They just stopped talking and waited on him to decide what next.

This is how it had been since Silverton.

Jonas had lit out from that shit show with just a handful of true believers. There was Chad, of course, and Brad Rausch and Leo Vaulk. And one genuine badass, Dale Juntii. Brad and Leo were still with him. As it turned out, Rausch was a damned good mechanic, and he'd been employee of the fucking month when they'd had to rely entirely on salvaged motors and siphoned gas to get their asses out of Dodge. He was still useful to have around, keeping an eye on the Legion's growing transport division - but his naturally anti-social mojo meant that he mostly kept to himself. And Leo, who hadn't been worth a pinch of shit in the fight with the bikers, did bring two virtues to everything they'd done since. He knew how to run a business and was loyal as a broken dog, which meant Jonas could trust him to keep an eye on both Mathias and Luke.

Dale? That was another sad story.

But he'd played his role.

And now it was time for Jonas to get into character and play his.

"Gentlemen," he said, raising his voice in theatrically loud good humour. "It appears we have a bug problem in town. I suggest we call for the exterminators."

"All right!" Chad Moffat cried out. "I fuckin' love fireworks."

"Consider it done," Luke Bolger said. Satisfied, as always, with the simple solution.

Luke was a hammer, and every problem a nail.

He nodded to Jonas, about the closest he ever came to a salute in the field and turned away to begin preparations. Jonas waved Tommy Podesta over and told him to drive Mayor Jennings back to Three Forks in the Merc.

"It's better that he doesn't watch this," Jonas said. "But I'm gonna stay here with the boys. Drop Jennings back home. Tell Leo to keep an eye on him and make sure he doesn't do anything about the regrets he's gonna be feeling. You can come back and get me later. This'll probably take an hour or so."

Podesta nodded sombrely. "You gonna stay for the after party, boss?"

"Not here, no," Jonas said.

Somewhere nearby, Luke Bolger shouted orders to his officers, and they, in turn, relayed his instructions down the chain of command. He heard engines turning over and boots pounding on the tarmac of the interstate. A few war whoops and rebel yells drifted back to him through the darkness. "But I do feel like a party," Jonas said. "If Leo has opened the O Club back in town, make sure we got cold drinks and hot bitches to go."

"You got it, boss," the Tripod said, nodding in approval.

Bolger had already worked out the firing lines and positioned the Legion's gun wagons accordingly. There were four converted pickups in the gun line, a mix of Fords and Toyotas. It galled Jonas to admit it, but the Toyotas had proved more reliable in all the months of campaigning. Eventually, they were going to have to swap out the American vehicles. For now, though, he could still enjoy the show. He walked behind one of the heavily armoured troop carriers they'd salvaged from some police station a couple of states ago, took the soft plugs he always carried in his pocket for this occasion and worked them deep into his ears. The small waxy blobs didn't completely block out all noise, but they deadened the sound of battle prep.

He heard muted voices, muffled engines and the softened shouts of Luke Bolger yelling orders to the troops.

Jonas didn't need to say anything; for that matter, neither did Bolger.

This would be the fifth... No, the sixth town they had reduced for open defiance. Jonas did not enjoy the necessity. He wasn't a psychopath. But he was a student of history. He'd once listened to a couple of chapters of an audiobook about Genghis Khan in preparation for a podcast, and he knew that one of the Maximum Mongol's most innovative, most effective policies was extending mercy to those who bent the knee and performative annihilation to all who did not.

Shooting the shit out of one bunch of uppity assholes had a measurable effect on the willingness of the next ones in line to consider the advantages of signing on with the Legion of Freedom. There was a mathematical certainty to it. If you destroyed one town, you could be almost 100% certain that the next five or six would roll over and give it up without a fight.

A couple of minutes after he had given the order to reduce Manhattan, Luke Bolger ambled over. No need to hurry. They had all done this before. They knew how it played out. Jonas removed one of the earplugs. It occurred to him that he should get some noise-cancelling headphones.

"We're good to go," Bolger said.

"Okay then. Light 'em up."

Bolger shouted the order down the line, and the gun wagons opened fire.

Brad Rausch and his travelling machine shop didn't have blue-prints to work from when designing the Legion's mobile artillery. With the Internet nothing more than a fond memory, they couldn't even call up an image of the 'technicals' favoured by warlords and militia fighters in places like Somalia. But American ingenuity long predated the Internet. It had taken Brad less than two days to convert the first F-150 to a mobile gun platform, and he had been refining the design ever since.

Each rig loaded out with a twin-barrelled system capable of sending up to 1200 rounds down range every minute. Of course, if you just prayed and sprayed like that, you'd melt the barrels, so the effective rate of fire was much lower.

Didn't matter.

Hundreds of rounds of 50 Cal tracer and armour-piercing could chew through the defences of a podunk little burgh like a child's play-fort constructed of marshmallow and balsa wood.

Even with his earplugs in place, Jonas placed his hands over his ears to protect his hearing from the deafening roar of the heavy guns. He waited a few seconds after the eruption of fire before stepping out from behind cover to watch the show.

It was awesome.

Eight sinuous rivers of hellfire. Orange and yellow and red. The yellow stream emanated from a command vehicle firing 'bright' tracer, which ignited as soon as it left the muzzle, arcing across the length of the open field and marking the targets for the other wagons to service.

"It's better than fucking Star Wars, man!" Chad Moffat yelled over the uproar.

The other platforms fired 'subdued' rounds, which did not light up until they were halfway across the field, creating a weirdly magical effect where deadly torrents of bright red fire emerged from the middle of nowhere.

The effect on the small town's wooden framed houses and lightly built sheds and barns was devastating. It was always devastating.

By the time Jonas had stepped out of cover to observe the destruction, a couple of streets had already been demolished, the ruins burning freely.

Here and there, single points of light flared in defiance as lone riflemen attempted to fight back. He supposed he was at some risk from the odd, angry shot coming back at them from the dark, but it was a calculated risk. It was good to let his fighters see him taking the same chances as them.

And the terrible arc of bright yellow tracers adjusted quickly to find those lone positions, drawing multiple streams of red and orange thunderbolts down on top of them.

Jonas flinched and ducked as a massive explosion lit up the north-western quarter of the town. A roiling blue-green inferno.

"Propane tanks," Bolger shouted over the uproar.

Jonas unclenched his teeth and nodded.

He checked his watch. They had been firing for less than two minutes.

Manhattan was already aflame. Reduced to ashes and blood.

9

THE INNOCENCE OF STRANGERS

James had the watch when Rick and the others returned from scouting the town. They hadn't entirely circled the wagons at the Cavalry Memorial, but the half-dozen strong convoy had laagered up as well as they could manage. The two motor homes afforded the lookouts perched on their roofs' sweeping moonlit views downslope, across the river to the darkened town and back east towards the black ribbon of the interstate. Sparty William's Winnebago and Bruce Goldie's Jayco stood at twelve and six o'clock, respectively, with Sparty's Minnie Winnie giving them the long view down to Bachman.

The Bloomfield kid was up there at the moment. He was young but had sharp eyes and could stay awake all night on a couple of Cokes and chocolate bars. Goldie stood at the watch atop his camper van on the far side of the rough, broken circle of motor vehicles. He had a fold-up chair with him, but only to hold the many packets of Twinkies and the giant Thermos of Irish coffee he needed to get through to dawn.

The rear fender of Goldie's van backed onto one corner of the small, covered pergola where picnickers could seek shade on a hot day. The front of Tammy Kolchar's *Oldsmobile* all but kissed the far corner. The three SUVs, including James's *Sierra*, described a ragged half circle back around to the front grill of Bruce Goldie's Jayco, and within that improvised barricade, they had pitched their tents. It was a makeshift arrangement that served them well across all of their campsites on the road. More than once, it had saved them from scavenger raids.

Stepping carefully, James skirted the outer row of tents but stayed within the steel ring of vehicles. He could hear a couple of adults snoring and one child whimpering. He shivered inside the lamb's wool lining of his bomber jacket. At least the cold was good for keeping him awake, although James knew that as winter came on and the mercury dropped below freezing, that would change. Eventually, it got so cold that your body heat leached away into the night, and the phantom, killing warmth of hypothermia crept up on you, tempting you to stop, rest, and close your eyes forever.

James shrugged the rifle off one shoulder, swapping it over to the other as he slipped past the small tent he shared with Michelle. He stopped and listened carefully. She often started snoring about an hour before dawn. He wasn't sure why because she slept quietly for the rest of the night. But, standing just outside of their tent, straining his ears, he heard nothing. She was so quiet that he started to worry. He was just about to pull back the tent flap and check in on her when he heard the distinctive three-tone whistle that Laurence Bloomfield used to alert the other sentries to any change in their situation.

James checked his watch, a Seiko he'd picked up from the ruins of a looted pawn shop back in North Dakota. Unlike his Apple Watch, it didn't need constant recharging. The luminous dial was easy to read.

4.53 AM.

Laurence whistled again. The same three notes. It was a bird call or something he'd learned at summer camp, but repeating the same notes meant there was no immediate danger, just something for James to come and check out.

He breathed out, watching his breath steam, relieved. Michelle, the threat specialist, said he worried too much.

End of the goddamned world, and she thought he worried too much.

But she was right. James did, especially about her. It had been a long time since they'd heard any real news about the wider world, but the last radio reports they'd picked up—from some BBC guy in Hong Kong—man, they'd been grim. So many dead in China that the government had stopped counting, and then the government had just stopped. Everything was gone over there.

James stepped away from their tent, careful not to trip on the tie-downs. Reversing his course, he moved as quickly as he could back around to the larger of the convoy's two RVs. Laurence Bloomfield was waiting at the top of the small step ladder, providing roof access.

"Rick's coming back," he said quietly. "And the others."

"Thanks," James said. "I'll come up."

He climbed the ladder, careful not to make too much noise or to rock the Winnebago on its axles. There were usually six or seven kids asleep inside, as well as Sparty and Ramona. Climbing onto the roof of the big RV, he cautiously stepped onto the fibreglass surface. Laurence knew to back away, spreading out the weight. A few of them had discussed bolting a platform up there, something like the rudimentary observation deck Bruce Goldie had rigged up on top of his Jayco, but they'd never really had the time or resources to do it. Probably wouldn't either, until they got to the ranch, and then they wouldn't need it.

Blinking the sandman from his tired eyes, James peered into the darkness, trying to spot the returning scouts. The moon was high and bright, and only a few thin clouds obscured the great stellar band of the Milky Way, but his distance vision had been getting worse since college, and the world beyond the circle of the campsite was a nocturnal blur.

"Over there, see?" Laurence said, pointing downhill toward the town.

James squinted in the direction the boy had picked out, but it was hopeless. He could see nothing. That's why Laurence was up here, and James was down on the ground, walking the perimeter.

"You sure it's them?" James asked.

"Yeah. I can see Nomi. And I recognise Mister Tapsell's funny walk, from when he hurt his back playing cricket, and the way Mr Boreham sort of floats from place to place."

James smiled.

"Close enough," he said, reassured more by Nomi's presence than anything else and even more impressed by Laurence's ability to pick her out of the dark. "But keep an eye on them, Laurence. Let me know if you change your mind. And don't be quiet about it. Wake everyone up."

"Will do, sir," the kid said.

James patted his shoulder and climbed down to put some water on to boil. The scouts would probably have cocoa, or tea in Peter Tapsell's case, rather than coffee. They would want to rest for a while before leading a salvage team back into the town, assuming it was clear. And while James might not be much of a lookout or even a guard, he could boil the hell out of a pail of water on one of those coin-operated barbecues. By the time Laurence challenged the scouts for the night's password—it was 'felafel'—James had a pot bubbling in the dark and the fixings for whatever hot drink they needed.

Rick, Pete and Nez climbed over the low, improvised barrier of spare tires, closing the space between the Winnebago and James's Sierra. At the same time, Laurence and Bruce Goldie kept an even sharper watch on the approaches to the cavalry memorial to make sure nobody was using the distraction of their return as cover for a stealthy approach. The three men and Nomi padded around to join James at the propane-fired barbecue by the pergola.

"That barbie's nice and warm," Tapsell said. "Saw some very unhappy-looking brass monkeys out there tonight."

"Anything else?" James asked as he poured steaming water into three mugs. Black tea for Pete. Cocoa for Rick and Nez.

"We checked out the grocer, the gas station, a couple of other places," Rick said, taking his drink with thanks. He rewarded Nomi with a scratch behind the ear and some jerky. She curled up near the warmth of the barbecue and chewed on the dried meat. "Place was empty. But weird," he said.

"Creepy as hell, you mean," Nez muttered. "It's like the goddamn Marie Celeste down there. Or that Left Behind show."

"Except there was nobody left behind," Tapsell said.

James looked at Rick. They knew each other well enough by now that they could have whole conversations without words. As though the long road here had compressed a lifelong friendship into three months.

Rick just shook his head.

"Can't say what happened," he said. "There've been some firefights, for sure, but no way of telling whether that was before or after the place emptied out—coulda been outsiders fighting over supplies. Coulda been townsfolk fighting off outsiders who tried to take their supplies. No way to tell in the dark."

"Does it look like we can resupply?" James asked.

Rick nodded but slowly.

"Reckon so. The grocery still had stuff on the shelves and more in a storeroom out back."

"Really?" James said. That was a surprise. Most obvious places had been stripped bare by now. You had to work the ruins to turn up a decent stash.

Rick Boreham sipped at his cocoa and breathed in the steam. His eyes were far away, as though he was seeing the town for the first time, scoping out every shadow.

"I did say it was weird. But I dunno; it's pretty isolated out here, too. Not like south of Chicago or Minneapolis."

"What about the bodies?" James said. "The ones they hanged."

"First one was a looter, according to the sign around his neck," Peter Tapsell said.

James had seen that for himself through the scope of his Ruger.

"The others were reporters," Rick added. "Or one reporter, a woman and two crew. Camera guy and a sound guy, I guess. Whoever hanged 'em also hung a sign on 'em. Said 'Fake News'. You couldn't see it from here, but their van was around the corner, a block or so up the main street. KBZK."

"Huh," James went. "I know that station. CBS affiliate out of Bozeman, near my folks' place. They're a long way from home."

"Maybe they got caught on the road," Nez suggested.

"Maybe. How long?" James asked Rick.

He meant how long Rick thought it had been since they died, but he didn't need to spell it out.

Rick shrugged, "Call it two or three weeks?"

He looked to Nez, who nodded.

"Guess so," the teacher said. "From the state of the bodies. But that's just a guess. We didn't do a lot of human autopsies in high school science."

James frowned.

"But the networks stopped broadcasting months ago."

Nez waved off the point with his free hand.

"Like I said. Maybe they just got caught on the road. Couldn't get back to Bozeman."

"Or maybe they were running away, and they ran out of road," Tapsell suggested.

While they had been talking, the horizon to the east had slowly come into view, an ever-so-slight divide between the lightening sky and the still-dark land. James realised he could see Bruce Goldie's rotund outline on the roof of the Jayco van.

"So, what do you think?" he asked Rick.

The former ranger made a face.

"We need to resupply, and it's all hard road between here and the Gallatin. If we keep the kids, the older folk and a couple of shooters hunkered down in camp and take the rest back with Nez's trailer, I reckon we should be able to load out by lunchtime. Get moving again."

"Guess we better check with the boss ladies," James said.

MICHELLE NGUYEN WOKE a few minutes before James came to get her. She lay curled up in the extra-large sleeping bag, listening to the murmur of voices. She could not make out the words, but recognising James's slow, familiar drawl – yet oddly meticulous pronunciation of every syllable – amid the dense thread of male voices, she relaxed and almost drifted back to sleep. The others must be back, she thought, before her thoughts slipped sideways, away from the campsite, far from Montana, and back to the day they had met, back in Washington at the start of all this.

She missed Washington.

No, that wasn't true.

She missed living in a city. Any city. She had lived in nearly a dozen during her twenty-six years. She missed meeting her cousins at Pike Place Markets in Seattle, shopping for crabs to flash fry with chilli and garlic. She missed walking to her favourite bar in the Marais district of Paris, gasping for a glass of red wine and a cigarette at *Cafe Barav*. She missed the subway in New York, hopping on at a station, any station, and heading out somewhere, anywhere, for a day's gallery hopping or clothes shopping. She missed people; she missed crowds.

She missed being able to trust millions of strangers.

God, how she missed trusting herself to the innocence of strangers. A hell of an indulgence for someone with her history.

In her drowsy half-waking state, Michelle shied away from memories of how that trust had been taken from her, moment by moment, since the start of the war. Or was it a war? As best she knew, there'd hardly been a shot fired, except for that first Chinese thrust. After that, hostilities had turned into an exchange of viral packets.

She just wanted to sleep and to forget. She wanted everything to go back to how it had been. Before she'd met James. It had all gone wrong from that day on.

And yet, she loved him.

James O'Donnell was her world now.

To wish the Hell of this world gone was to wish herself into loneliness.

Fuck.

She was awake.

"Baby? You awake in there?"

It was James, somewhere just outside the tent.

"Michelle?"

"Coming," she croaked. Like, literally fucking croaked. She fumbled in the darkness for her water bottle but couldn't find it.

She couldn't find her flashlight either.

She yawned hugely and pushed herself up on her elbows. Her elbows dug into the camp mat, which lay on the hard-baked earth of eastern Montana, and she could feel every rock, every crack in the crust of the planet beneath her.

"We need to bounce a few things off you?" James said. "When you're good."

Michelle blinked in the dark, but it did not help.

When she was good?

So, never, then?

As full awareness crept over her, so did the memory, realisation, and weight of all she had done, what she'd been part of, even if it was just a tiny part. Off to the side.

With it came the nausea.

A billion dead.

Maybe more.

No. Definitely more.

The Plan Jericho models she had gamed out projected two or even three billion dead.

She shook her head. Hard. As if to cast out by force the profane thoughts inside of her skull.

"No," she said through gritted teeth. "Not this shit again."

Nothing for it. Michelle snaked out of the bag, wearing her jeans and a fleecy long-sleeved tee. Pulled on her Docs. Found the ski jacket she'd picked up when the first real cold snap had caught up with them back in Iowa.

They needed her here.

It didn't matter what she'd done in a past life, as an analyst and before that as an operator. In this one, she was loved and needed.

Michelle Nguyen climbed out of the darkness and over the

corpses of two or even three billion dead. Same as she had yesterday. Same as she would tomorrow.

JAMES HEAPED two teaspoons of instant coffee into a chipped steel mug for Michelle. She would have coffee. He was sure of that. For Melissa Baker, he made tea. Or rather, he asked Peter Tapsell to. A Brit like Mel, Pete insisted he and his people were genetically favoured with inherently superior tea-making skills.

Pete dangled a teabag into a mug and poured hot water over it.

Michelle appeared, swimming inside the puffer jacket they'd liberated from a truck rollover back in Iowa at least two months ago. They had no creamer or sugar for anyone, but they were all used to that now.

"Thanks," Michelle said, her voice small and cracked as she took the drink from him.

Nobody said anything to her. Nobody would be fool enough to ask anything of Michelle Nguyen before she'd had that first hit of caffeine. They all knew better.

James watched her discretely, looking for signs she had not slept.

Michelle often had nightmares, but she would never tell him what they were about.

She didn't have to. Michelle also talked in her sleep. Weird, grammatically correct, but utterly bizarre conversations with ghosts about other numberless ghosts. In her sleep, she was chased by an army of nameless dead people.

"Morning all!"

Mel Baker appeared from the tent she shared with Rick. Unlike Michelle, she had no trouble waking up and throwing herself into the day. However, she did have trouble keeping her morning voice down, and James cringed to think of how many people she'd just woken up.

About the same as every morning.

Half the damn camp.

He heard voices and rustling sleeping bags as the former London policewoman took her black, unsweetened tea from Pete Tapsell.

"Thanks, guv'," she said, no quieter than before. "Don't suppose I could have a bacon buttie to go?"

"Fraid not, Luv. Just sold the last one to my best customer," Tapsell said.

He nudged Nomi with the toe of his boot. She panted and rolled over for a tummy rub.

"Oh, her again," Mel said. "Just my luck. So, what's up, lads?"

"Spooky town," Rick said.

"You wot mate?" Mel grinned as though that was the best news she'd heard all morning. She blew steam from her mug of hot tea. "You found a spooky ghost town? No way."

Michelle had finished her coffee in a couple of long pulls.

"Spooky, how?" she asked, her eyes red-rimmed and watery.

Rick briefed them both on the recon mission, with Nez and Pete adding occasional details for color. When they finished, the two women exchanged a look. Like Rick and James, they had become close friends well before the convoy grew from just the four of them into the much larger caravan they now led.

"Doesn't pass the sniff test," Michelle said. "Smells like ass to me."

"I couldn't make a call without seeing it myself," Mel said.

"What about checking it out in daylight?" James said.

Rick shook his head.

"Reason we go in at night is the cover. I don't like the feel of this place, but we need those supplies. We'll run out of gas for the RVs and Tammy's car before we get to the next town. If we go back, we can go heavy. Recon in force, get what we need, and get out. Keep the camp locked down, sentries up."

Rick mainly spoke to Michelle, who seemed to be the main holdout.

They all looked at her.

After a moment, she said, "Why do I have to be the bad guy?"

Mel smiled.

"It's those wicked tattoos, darlin'."

10

THE CREATION OF AN IMAGE

"Never thought I'd miss airports and planes and all that shit," Damien Maloney said as they packed up the campsite. "But if I walked into a functioning fucking airport right now, I reckon I'd get a fat so fucking hard you could crack fleas on it."

Ellie snorted, then checked that none of the kids was around.

They'd started to pick up some of Damo's more colorful verbal habits, despite the best efforts of the grown-ups and even Damo himself to teach them otherwise.

"I'm allowed to swear cos I'm Australian, and we don't know any better," Damo would tell them every time they did it, "but you're not, and you do, so shut the fu.... Oh no, there I go again. Everyone drop and give me twenty!"

And all three kids would squeal with laughter and drop into a set of push-ups. Damo, too. They'd been doing this with star jumps, knee-high running bursts, and a dozen other flavours of high-intensity cardio and strength intervals since leaving the boat behind. Damo's once considerable paunch wasn't entirely gone, but it had shrunk. His arms and shoulders had lost their soft outlines, and he no longer had to stop to find his breath during physical labour.

He broke down the tents and stacked away the folding chairs and camp grill while Ellie packed the deer jerky into airtight plastic containers.

She located the children a short distance away, in a field of wild-flowers that sloped down to the river. Letting the children burn off some energy before the long hours of driving made for a much easier trip, and Karl kicked a ball for them to chase through the dormant patches of starwort and snowberry. It was late in the year, and only a few hardy petals still blazed under the morning sun. Ellie could imagine it would be spectacular here in high summer.

Jodi stood on the roof of the Land Rover, arranging their gear while watching the ball game and occasionally scanning the distance with a pair of binoculars. She looked like a model for a J. Crew photo shoot. Karl, too, would scope out the approaches as the children charged away after one of his long kicks.

"You think we'll make it to Montana today?" Ellie asked as Damo kicked dirt over the coals of last night's fire.

"Fuckin' hope so, mate," he said. "I'm getting a bit antsy about having our arses hanging out in the breeze when winter comes. I'd like to get off the road before then."

"We don't have fuel to make it all the way there," she reminded him.

Damo was one of those men whose focus on the ends could blind him to the fact that he didn't have the means to get there. Ellie, on the other hand, was all about detail. It had worked well for them as a partnership at the restaurant, but the stakes were much higher now.

He poured water over the mound of dirt he'd kicked onto the coals. Steam and smoke hissed quietly from a couple of places.

"Yeah, I know. We'll need to siphon as we go. But it'd be good to refill properly and score a couple of spare cans if poss'. A full tank would see us home, for sure. Let's get Karl and have a gander at the map, eh?"

Ellie shaded her eyes and smiled up at Jodi.

"Hey baby, can you swap with Karl? We're gonna plan the route."

Jodi had been sweeping the horizon with the binoculars they'd taken from Damo's boat.

"Sure," she said, letting them hang from the lanyard. Before climbing down, she pulled out her birthday present, the disposable camera Ellie had found for her, and took a photo of them with the Devil's Tower in the background.

"No, don't pose," Jodi said. "Just act natural."

"That's impossible," Damo protested. "Nobody can *act* natural. It's a contradiction in—"

Jodi snapped a shot of him jutting his chin at her, hands on hips, while Ellie smirked off to one side.

"Perfect," she said, slipping the camera away again and using the small, three-step ladder built into the rear cabin of the Land Rover to climb down.

"When this is all over, you'll thank me," she said. "Nobody's keeping a journal or a diary or anything. We should be recording this. For the children, at least."

"Mate, when this over, I'm gonna drink so much fucking rum-n-Coke, I'm not gonna remember a fucking thing about it," Damo said.

"Then it's even more important that somebody else does," Jodi pushed back.

Her eyes sparkled in the morning light, and even tired, dirty and ragged from three months on the road—or three months on the run —Jodi Sarjanen was a vision of impossible fortune and beauty to Ellie. There were days, even now, when she wondered why this woman had chosen her. It seemed so improbable, so wrong, that in her darker moments, she could imagine all this shit that'd happened was just the world trying to right itself because someone like Ellie Jabbarah wasn't meant to be with a woman like Jodi Sarjanen.

"Hey, Karl, swap you," Jodi called out, turning and dancing away through the field of sleeping wildflowers.

Damo and Ellie finished packing the last few things into the back of the Land Rover, making sure to leave space for the kids to sit while Karl climbed the hill back toward them. He arrived sweating but smiling.

"Never gets old," he said. "Unlike me."

"Testify, brother," Damo said.

They unfolded the road map on the vehicle's hood and scoped out their options. In matters of road transport, they took their lead from Karl Valentine, the same way everyone deferred to Ellie about how to feed themselves. Karl had driven trucks for the Army in Iraq and even more trucks for long-haul freight companies when he got back. He studied the big Rand McNally tourist map, tracing a stubby forefinger over the thin grey lines, charting all their possible routes through northern Wyoming.

"We got enough gas to get us this far," he said, using the same finger to describe an arc that would put them halfway to the Canadian border.

"Fucking awesome," Damo said.

"Yeah, but that's without detours or backtracking if we get jammed up someplace they don't like us and won't let us through," Karl added, with his customary note of caution. He was always the one calling the long odds. "And you can bet that's gonna happen. It always does. There's a good chance the further north we get that we might even brush up against those Legionnaire fellas again. They were headed east, as I recall."

They had long ago settled on a principle for negotiating all such encounters.

They always backed down wholly and immediately. Nobody wanted another fight like the one they'd had on the lake back at the Three River Reach. It was a wonder they'd all survived, a miracle that nobody had been badly hurt.

"Soooo..." Karl went on. "I think these are the options if we're still avoiding settlements bigger than a thousand people."

"And we are," Damo confirmed.

"And we're not headed back west any time soon," Ellie added. "Not with those Legion assholes swinging their dicks around."

"Didn't think so," Karl nodded. He outlined three routes north, all of which avoided major arteries or crossroads. The big state roads and federal highways were impassable in too many places. Sometimes, massive pile-ups blocked them. Sometimes, a single truck had crashed or jack-knifed. The interstate crossovers were always a mess, and minor crossroads were just as often dangerous for other reasons. Choke points, Karl said and refused to even think about driving through.

"Better a day late in this life than years early in the next," he would say.

Worrying over the map on the hood of their battered off-roader, however, he was less concerned with avoiding the massive snarls and random ambushes they'd learned to anticipate back in the coastal states, where the population density was so much greater. Or where it had been, at least. In the sweeping rangelands, deserts and occasional mountain wilds of the central west, he tried to plot them a course that offered a chance of replenishing their meagre supplies without unduly exposing them to hazard or disaster.

The tip of his finger moved up a long, meandering track; the nails chewed short, the whorls of his fingerprints dirty with grime, ash and the grit of a life now lived almost entirely out of doors.

"I think this might be the best of our prospects," he said. "There's a couple of small places along the way, and I reckon we'd finish up somewhere around here."

He circled a spot in southeast Montana.

"Place called Bachman."

"Batman?" Damo said.

"Bachman," Ellie corrected him. "But I've never heard of it either."

"No reason you would," Karl said. "Ain't much there—maybe three or four hundred folks. Friendly enough, when I drove the 212 a couple of times. Hauling timber east and cheese to the south."

"Cheese?" Ellie smiled, suddenly interested.

Karl nodded, "Fancy cheese from Canada, Miss Ellie. Anyways, I know there's a couple of small airfields and a golf course nearby. Not likely occupied now, but probably got a few drops of fuel lying around... If we can't barter for some or siphon enough along the way."

Damo looked at Ellie, and she shrugged.

"Sounds like a plan," she said.

Damo folded up the map and whistled for Jodi and the kids to hurry back.

"Batman it is, then," he said.

THE KIDS WERE CHARGING back through the grass, trampling it underfoot, when Jodi heard Damo's traffic-stopping whistle. Pascal had the ball, which he tossed to Maxi like a rugby player, who caught it effortlessly before passing it carefully to Beatrice. She tucked the ball under one arm and raced on with her head down and one hand out to fend off any defensive tackles—another example of Damo's influence. Jodi's third eye, which framed the world in portrait or landscape, saw a perfect moment rushing towards her. She whipped out her birthday present and snapped off one exposure without even bothering to put the viewfinder to her eye. It would work, or it would not.

Somehow, being stripped of her technology made things so much easier. She did not need to fuss around with multiple lens choices, camera bodies, or lighting. Digital ISO meant nothing to her now. Creating an image had once involved hours of thought and decision chains that could wind through hundreds of choices, any one of them a point of failure. And that was before she loaded the raw files to image processing and started to edit. For Jodi, photography had always been a complex process that demanded planning, judgment, and disciplined execution.

Now, she just raised the little cardboard Kodak and squeezed off the shot.

And just as quickly, the moment she had seen coming was gone. Maxi and his new best friends, his only friends, swept around her, the two boys yelling 'Charge' as they ran up-slope back to the others.

Had she caught that brief half-second when everything lined up perfectly?

She looked down at the cheap little camera and smiled.

She had no idea. Again.

But she could imagine that inside the little yellow box, the past magically lived on, and no matter what happened out here in the world of real things, it would always live on. Somewhere, there were people, and there would come a place and they would matter and mean that there was always love in the world.

Jodi started shaking just a little bit and was surprised to discover when she examined her feelings that it was with relief. Standing in that field with a clean, cool breeze slipping over her skin, listening to the laughter of the children, watching her friends bent to the mission of seeing them all safely to the refuge of Damo's farm, Jodi Sarjanen felt for the first time, in a very long, long time, that everything would turn out okay.

She started walking back to the others.

Maxi had already made it to the Land Rover and talked with Damo and Karl.

He jumped up and down, flapping his arms as though he might take wing.

Instead, he turned and sprinted back to Jodi, crying out as he ran, "Mom! Mom!"

He was almost breathless with excitement when he reached her.

"What is it, Maxi? What's going on?" she laughed, almost as giddy as him, but simply because of his happiness.

Maxi leapt the last few feet to land in front of her like a superhero, dropping to one knee and pretend-punching the ground.

He looked up, his eyes wide. He lowered his voice to be as deep and gravelly as he could manage.

"We're going to Batman," he said.

11

THE JAGGED RELICS OF HIS SOUL

Even with a trailer hanging off the ass-end of Pete Tapsell's pickup, they covered the ground back to town much quicker than walking in. Last night's three-man crew, the salvage team bolstered by Mel, Tammy, Lew Gibb and Sparty Williams, left the Cavalry Memorial just as the sun inched over the lip of the world. Anybody watching them from Bachman would do so, squinting into the sunrise. Of course, Rick knew, they could wear sunglasses or shade their eyes with one hand or a baseball cap, but you had to give yourself every chance; it wouldn't be easy for somebody staring through the sights of a hunting rifle to aim at the approaching vehicle. Not for a precision shot, anyway.

Nobody said much of anything as they left the camp. It wasn't the first time they had done this, and the seven people in the salvage team had all proven themselves more adept or inclined to this work than those they'd left behind. After the previous night's scouting mission, Nez and Pete were freshly caffeinated and good to go. Tapsell drove, and Nez sat in the rear of the cabin, catching a few minutes' shuteye. Rick rode upfront, letting his gaze sweep back and forth across the outskirts of the town. From a mile out, it looked unremarkable. Benign. They could've been driving up on any small town in America in the last fifty years.

Mel sat directly behind him, occasionally leaning forward into the space between the front seats, staring at Bachman with almost hostile intent and sizing it up like a perp.

Sparty Williams sat between Mel and Nez, listening to an old podcast, oblivious to the hazards of the morning.

In the rear tray of the pickup, Tammy Kolchar and Lew Gibb, the long-retired gym coach from San Jose, carried on the only conversation, a willing exchange about the relative merits of store-bought versus handmade barbecue sauce. Tammy was a passionate evangelist for Sweet Baby Ray's smoky divinity.

"Four bucks worth of smoky, squeezable heaven, Lew."

"Four whole dollars to light a chemical fire in my mouth? I don't think so, young lady."

Two minutes after they set out, true dawn came on them, and it came quick, with a diamond cutting edge that sheered across the world with clarifying cruelty. This would be hellish country in the summer, Rick thought. Even now, with the mild weeks of autumn succumbing to the first real cold snaps and hoar frosts of the fast-approaching winter, the morning light revealed the low, scrubby steppe lands of eastern Montana in a hard and unforgiving mood.

No birdsong gentled the condition of this new day. Perhaps if he rolled down the window, he might hear the distant howl of those coyotes they'd scared off last night or the bitter call of a crow, hungry to rake at those corpses, swinging from the hangman's rope. The palette of the landscape here was all granite grey and parched yellow ochres. A few patches of dark green stood out from the small oases of parkland at the edge of Bachman, but they accentuated the severity and desolation of everything else.

Tapsell, with years of experience driving off-road in Africa, took them in across some farmer's field that lay fallow for the season and all the seasons to come. It offered the most direct approach to the small Texaco they had scouted out last night. Mel started to ask questions a minute or two out from their destination.

"So, did you boys see any sign of life last night? Anything electrical like? Even one of those bug zappers? You know, for barbecues and stuff."

"Nothing like that, no," Rick said.

"There was that sewage leak in the park," Tapsell said. "Might mean something, you reckon?"

"Yeah. Don't play in the park," Rick said.

"What about them bodies?" Mel asked. "How badly was they picked over?"

They'd had this conversation back at the camp, but Mel wasn't one to leave anything to chance, and Rick did not mind. Better to circle a thing five or six times than just blow past it and miss the one detail that will get you killed.

"They weren't fresh," Rick said as the pick-up bounced over a small irrigation ditch at the edge of the field, crashing through a line of knee-high shrubs and settling back into a smooth passage on the sealed road leading up to the gas station.

Tammy's voice came to them from the rear bed, a little muffled but still strident.

"Hey! Fireball! Easy on the ass hammer, man."

"Sorry," Tapsell called back out the window. "Not sorry," he said in a lower voice to himself.

They were close now. The town looked very different by day. More desolate, if that was possible. And haunted by something worse than whatever Rick had sensed or imagined in the dark, at the edge of perception. Goddamned coyotes or dogs gone feral. Probably. He shifted in his seat, trying to take in a wide angle while he still could. Once they pulled up and got to work, it would be harder to withdraw.

They drove into the Texaco and stopped in the middle of the tarmac, away from the pumps. No way they'd be working. Nobody moved or said anything for a second.

Finally, Tammy Kolchar spoke up from the back.

"A shitty job don't get no less shitty for letting it stew," she said before adding. "Not even in your fancy handmade sauce, Lew."

"Redneck Barbie is right," Rick said, climbing out of the vehicle.

"Let's get it done. Lew, Tammy, keep an eye out and don't be shy if you get a bad feeling about anything."

"I get that creepy itch tells me something is not right; I intend to scratch it with a couple of buckshot rounds," Tammy said, hopping down from the rear tray.

"I'll see about the fuel situation," Tapsell said, opening his door and stepping out carefully.

They all dismounted.

Everybody carried long arms, and most wore handguns as a backup. To Rick, they looked a motley bunch, but he knew the appearance was deceptive. This was an evolution they had practised dozens of times coming out west. Ignore the random collection of weapons and the complete absence of any chain of command, and you'd see a pretty tight crew spread out to do their jobs with the sort of quiet efficiency honed by prolonged exposure to risk and challenge.

Andrew Nesbitt stood guard over Peter Tapsell while the British man searched for and quickly found an access point to the gas station's underground storage tanks. Lew Gibbs and Tammy Kolchar took up overwatch at different corners of the tarmac, both seeking good cover. Rick and Mel headed straight for the small convenience store. It wasn't the best prospect they had for resupplying the caravan with food, but it was worth checking out.

One of the big plate glass windows was broken, with a spider web of cracks radiating from a single impact. But Rick could already tell it wasn't from a bullet. Whatever had struck the glass had not passed through.

The view inside was not severely compromised, and he could see that although the shelves weren't full, neither had they been denuded by the panic buying that characterised the early days after the attack or the looting and scavenging that came later.

"I see what you mean by spooky," Mel said. "It's a bit weird, innit, Luv?"

"Weird and then some, baby," Rick said. "Stay sharp, move quick, let's go."

They entered the shop as their former professions had taught them and as they'd learned working together over the past couple of months. Rick went first. He always went first.

He broke left. Mel went right.

They swept the interior of the Texaco's convenience store. It was a pretty basic setup. No fast food court. Only two freezers, one of them given over to soda. A half-empty bottle of vanilla Coke stood alone on a shelf. The second cold unit looked like it might have once held foodstuffs, but there was nothing in there now.

The shelves in the retail section were similarly bare of food. No road food like corn chips, chocolates or cookies. But they were not entirely empty. Plenty of automotive supplies remained. Wiper fluid, engine oil, that sort of thing. And all the usual crap you found in these places was still there. Ancient CDs, cheap sunglasses, insect repellent, sun-faded magazines. Mel grabbed a couple of pump packs of Natrapel bug spray.

"Let's check out the storeroom," Rick said

They took as much care as they would have breaking into a Taliban stronghold, approaching the open doorway behind the counter with guns up. Mel dropped hers fractionally to let Rick pass in front of her and breach the room. If they'd had stun grenades, he would've tossed one in for good measure. Instead, they made do with what they had: experience and reaction time.

There was no threat back there.

The storeroom was gloomy but not so dark that he couldn't see all four corners. It was surprisingly neat. Cardboard boxes lined the walls on sets of steel shelving. No hiding places. No ambush points. Rick lowered his weapon. He tried the light switch by the door but got nothing. That was reassuring in its way.

"Hello-ello-ello, what 'ave we got here then?" Mel said, inspecting one of the shelves up close.

"What've you found?" Rick said.

"The good stuff," Mel answered. "Chef Boyardee's *Beefaroni* and Chilli Mac. Not in the same can, but. In case you were getting excited."

"I wasn't," Rick said. "But I wondered why the shelves out front got cleared, but these didn't. It doesn't make sense."

"No, it doesn't," Mel agreed. "So I reckon we should bag what we can and scarper. Maybe send Nez and Lew back here to help carry some of this stuff."

Rick took one sealed cardboard box of Chef B's Cheesy Burger Macaroni under one arm, keeping his other free. Mel took a box and followed him out.

Peter Tapsell was working the hand pump to pull gas out of the storage tanks when they emerged into the morning light. Nez stood nearby, watching the street. Lew and Tammy maintained their overwatch from opposite ends of the tarmac. A cool breeze blew in from the north and set the tired, plastic bunting hanging over the pumps to flapping quietly. A Dairy Queen sign hanging from the roof outside the store swung a few inches back and forth in the breeze, creaking on a rusty chain. The loudest noise was Pete, grunting away at the hand pump. He had laid out four large plastic containers. One of them was already filled, sealed and set aside. Two stood empty and waiting. Bright green gasoline squirted into the third.

"Lew, Nez," Rick said, not needing to raise his voice. "If it's clear out here, there's some cans of food we could load up from the storeroom out back. Standard rules."

They wouldn't take everything. They never did. Others might be along after them and in more need of the forage.

"On it," Andrew Nesbitt replied. "Unless you want a rest, Pete."

"Nah, mate, I'm good. Got me rhythm going here. You go do the shopping."

Lew Gibb, who had been kneeling behind a small shed that Rick now saw was some sort of dog wash, stood up and started back across the tarmac.

The arrow that struck him in the hip would probably have hit him in the chest or the head if he hadn't moved.

It still struck him, however, with a thick, wet crunch, and he went down screaming.

A shotgun roared out.

Tammy was firing from the other end of the gas station, swearing loudly but not loudly enough to be heard over the boom of her sawn-off pump action.

Rick had already let go of the box of the Cheeseburger Macaroni, but only a fraction of a second earlier. As the heavy, awkward weight started to fall from his grip, an arrow thudded into it. It would have plunged into his chest, somewhere between his ribs, had he not been protected by the pallet of Mac. Everything slowed down. The way it always slowed down.

He was not in the Korangal Valley or Sadr City anymore. He'd been walking out of a Texaco in a small town in Montana. But the part of him that lived forever in those other places, where men had tried to kill him, and he had taken their lives instead, that part of him which slept fitfully and lightly under cover of everyday life, it woke up.

And that part of Rick Boreham was not entirely human.

It was something alien and extra, forged from the jagged relics of his soul and the injured pieces of his body in the war that never ended.

Not for him.

Eighty-seven days they had been on the road, and eighty-six of them, Michelle Nguyen had commenced with the same ritual. Two cups of coffee and fifteen minutes of fruitlessly trying to report to her chain of command at the National Security Council.

Once a week, Michelle recharged her satellite phone by plugging it into the cigarette lighter in James's Sierra. She did this whether it needed recharging or not. Which it never did. Because she was never able to make contact. By the end of the first week, when they had been camped in the National Park back in the Canaan Valley, Rick had carefully suggested she was wasting her time.

"The satellites are gone," he said.

She sighed, admitted he was almost certainly correct and went on trying to plug herself back into the national security grid. Most mornings, at least to begin with, she also scanned the FM and AM radio bands, looking for news networks or local stations, picking through the frequencies for tiny fragments of information. Like a chicken scratching at the bare ground.

As the salvage team drove away, James and Bruce closed up the wagon circle to secure their campsite again. James got to work brewing Michelle's second cup of coffee, delivering it to her at the picnic table where she sat alone noodling away on the satellite phone. Just as everybody had learned not to speak to her before she had that first cup of coffee, they all knew she would not be interrupted when playing with that phone. Even the kids had learned to give her the space.

The children, eleven of them, were all in the pergola, eating their breakfast, which today consisted of Bruce Goldie's rock-hard 'road cookies' soaked in a warm pot of long-life milk. The road cookies were some sort of oatmeal and dried fruit slab, which Bruce baked up whenever the opportunity and ingredients presented themselves. Ramona Tilley, a librarian from West Fargo, had the kids mostly under control, partly thanks to Laurence Bloomfield. He occupied a unique ecological niche between the youngest of the grown-ups – Tammy and Roxarne – and the oldest of the little kids, Bobby Kolchar. Tammy's boy.

They'd found Laurence walking the I-94 in what looked like filthy grey painters' overalls but which had started life as a pristine white karate uniform. He had been travelling with his dojo to a tri-state karate championship in Grand Forks, North Dakota, when Unit 61398 had launched its digital blitzkrieg on North America. Laurence had made it to the dormitory at NDU but left two days after the power went down, and the food ran out. He intended to walk home, a trip of many thousands of miles. Laurence wore his karate uniform over three layers of clothes because he didn't want to leave it behind. It provided a little extra warmth, and being twelve years old, he thought the sight of his blue belt might deter any attackers encountered on the open road.

Instead, it caught Melinda Baker's eye on a long stretch of highway about a hundred miles west of Grand Forks. Laurence was not the only hiker they encountered, of course. They'd picked up most of the children in the caravan early, from the remnants of one unlucky primary school excursion, trying to walk out of the Canaan Valley after their teacher disappeared, having 'gone for help'. They'd driven past many thousands of people south of the Great Lakes, all fleeing the cities to the north.

But Laurence was the only one dressed for a karate lesson in the middle of an apocalypse.

And luckily for him, Mel was driving that day. The ex-copper was even more recently an ex-judo instructor whose radar locked onto Laurence's *gi*, his training uniform, where Rick or James might have ignored it in the weird, random dreamscape of a civilisation accelerating toward total collapse. After all, they hardly needed to add a small, itinerant house painter to their crew.

"That Bloomfield kid was a good hire, wasn't he?" James said, carefully setting down the battered steel mug of black coffee where Michelle couldn't spill it on the sat-phone. He shrugged the rifle off his shoulder and leaned it against the table.

"Huh?" she said, looking up from the handset. Her brow creased in concentration.

"Laurence. He's pretty mature for a kid. I mean, he *is* just a kid, really," James said.

Michelle glanced at the small group of children gathered under the shelter of the pergola. Laurence, who'd been up since midnight to stand his watch, was now reading from a book while Ramona Tilley served bowls of warm, long-life milk and only slightly softened road cookies. Nomi sat patiently awaiting her road cookie, having been excused from a return trip to Bachman. Laurence had challenged the smaller kids to sit as still as Rick's dog, and they had settled into the challenge.

"Yeah, I guess so," Michelle said. "Better him than me. Kids are just, ugh. You know."

James didn't mind kids when they were well-behaved, which

these mostly were. But he did know that if Michelle Nguyen had ever had a biological clock, she'd unplugged it and thrown it out years ago.

Michelle sighed and pushed the satellite phone away.

"No luck?" James asked.

After eighty-seven days, it was a legitimately stupid question, but he wasn't expecting an answer. He just was inviting her to vent.

To his surprise, she didn't. Instead, Michelle sighed again.

"I just want everything to be like it was, James."

She looked at him and pushed a handful of long, uncut hair out of her eyes. The purple and blue highlights that had so wholly undone him back in Washington had all faded away. She so needed a cut and color.

Her eyes were red. She'd been crying or trying not to.

"Sometimes when we're driving, listening to music, and we haven't seen a dead town for a while," she said. "Or had to go around some massive pile up, or hayseed fortress, sometimes it almost feels normal, you know? Like nothing weird even happened. And then I remember it did, and we're in this thing, we're actually *in it,* and there's no rewind. We can't get back to before. We can only go forward, but what's in front of us feels even worse than what we've already been through."

She stared at him.

"Anyway, that's my bleak existential monologue for this morning. How's your day going?"

Before he could answer, she reached out and took his hand, pulling him closer.

"I think I want to go back to bed. With you."

A quiet, suspended moment ballooned up to surround them. Just the two of them. James felt himself stirring at the thought.

A single rifle shot cracked out, splitting the day into everything that came before that shot and all that happened after.

James spun away from Michelle, automatically reaching for his rifle.

She was already up and running, bent double, pistol out, yelling at the children to get down and stay down. Nomi was barking, running in a tight circle around the children as though herding them like sheep.

Crack!

Another gunshot, then another and another.

They seemed to be coming from all around.

Return fire was heading out, too. The Bloomfield kid and Bruce Goldie had been quicker to react than James.

He ran for the coin-op barbecue, a big, three-plate unit constructed of heavy concrete blocks. It was gas-powered, but the bottles were safely stored inside a small recess. It was the best cover they had. A high-velocity round could pass right through a motorhome.

Everything moved quickly, too fast for James to make real sense of it. More gunshots banged out but hit nobody. He couldn't even tell what the shooters were aiming at.

Children screamed and cried out in panic. Ramona and Roxarne tried to wrangle them all under the heavy wooden tables screwed down to the concrete floor of the pergola. It wouldn't afford them much protection, James thought.

He ran crouched to the small redoubt between the Oldsmobile and the Winnebago. Constructed of spare tires, it offered a view downslope towards the town. A bullet crashed into the driver-side window of the Olds just as James slid into cover. He had not managed to get his head up for a quick look over the thick rubber rampart before Michelle and Roxarne thumped down beside him, Michelle still armed with her little handgun, Roxarne carrying a cut-down shotgun.

She and Tammy were very fond of shotguns.

Roxarne flipped the weapon over the rim of their hideout and squeezed off a round at nothing and nobody that James could see.

"Who's out there?" he shouted at her.

"The fuck do I know?" Roxarne shouted back. She racked another round and blasted it out, not bothering to raise her head out of cover to aim.

James didn't need to ask whether anybody was on top of the motorhomes. He knew they weren't. The Bloomfield kid had taken himself off to the far side of the wagon circle and sat with his rifle, hunched into a tight ball behind the front wheel of the Sierra. He was small enough that the tires should protect him unless the gunfire came from the other direction, back towards the interstate.

"Bruce!" James yelled out. "Can you cover the back door?"

The barrel-chested South African gave him a thumbs up.

They had swept Bruce Goldie into their group back in Iowa. He'd been travelling home 'the long way' from some Rugby tournament in Hong Kong, seeing America as it was meant to be seen. *'From a giant fucking six-wheeled McMansion with Netflix and a hot tub.'*

Bruce shouted something back in Afrikaans, which he never used with anyone but Tapsell. James had no idea what he said, but the meaning was clear. Anybody trying to get in that way was going to die.

"They ain't even shooting at us," Roxarne shouted.

"What?" Michelle yelled back over the uproar.

"They ain't shooting at us," Roxy said. "I don't reckon so anyways. Not unless they're aiming to miss."

"What the fuck are you talking about?" Michelle said as she fired through a small gap between two tires. Michelle did not have a bottomless well of patience for dealing with Tammy and Roxarne. Mostly, she kept her distance from them and they from her.

"I mean, they had the drop on us, but nobody's been hit. Not even grazed. But rounds keep chopping up the leaves and stuff. See?"

She pointed at the branches of the trees, which provided shade over the picnic area. As James looked up, a couple of rounds shot through the foliage, cutting down a shower of twigs and bark. Michelle's gaze followed his, and her eyes narrowed in suspicion.

"Hmm," she went.

"What are you doing?" James asked as she moved a few inches away from him.

Before he could stop her, she stood up in a practised shooter's stance, raised her baby Glock, and cranked out three rounds. The small, black subcompact cycled quickly through the salvo with a flat, choppy report that sounded more like multiple whip cracks than a firearm. Michelle dropped back into cover before James could pull her down.

"The fuck are you doing?" he shouted. "Are you crazy?"

"No. I'm working the odds," she said with surprising detachment. Not for the first time, James wondered if she had done more than draft research papers for the government. "Roxarne is right. They're not trying to kill us. They just want us pinned down."

"Jesus Christ, Michelle! And what if they were trying to kill us?"

"Some of us would already be dead," she said as if it was self-evident.

The volume of fire had not decreased, but neither had it found any targets within the ring of the modern wagon corral. Occasionally, a single round crashed into metal or glass on one of the vehicles, but mostly, the fire was directed above them into the trees.

"What the hell are you talking about?" James asked.

"What'd you see?" Roxarne said.

"That's the better question," Michelle said as a bullet blew out a tire somewhere with a loud bang. Roxarne swore vividly, but Michelle ignored her.

"I made at least four shooters in the open," she said. "Basic fire and movement drill, except they were shooting into the trees to keep our heads down. I'd say there's plenty more than four of them out there. No idea who they are before you ask. But I do know what they want."

"What?" James said.

"Us," Michelle answered.

"Or them," Roxarne nodded towards the cowering, screaming children as if she had suspected all along.

"Goddamn it," James hissed. He chambered a round, popped up just far enough to peer anxiously over the stack of tires, and fired in the direction of the only human shape he could see moving on the hillside. He missed and was back under cover before a volley of return fire came in, aimed directly at their hiding place. They all hunkered down tight behind the rampart as maybe a dozen rounds chewed into the rubber wall.

Roxarne laughed.

"Ha. Any year your tires save you is a good year," she snorted before raising her shotgun to fire blindly over the top again.

"I don't understand," James protested. And he didn't. None of this made any sense. Why shoot at people you didn't want to hurt?

"I think they want to get close enough to rush us," Michelle explained. "To pick you and Bruce out for sure. Maybe Ramona too. They don't want the cars or the supplies. They want warm bodies."

"What? James said. "Seriously. Cannibals again?"

Michelle Nguyen shook her head. "No. Not cannibals. Slavers."

12

AN AUSPICIOUS PLACE TO FALL

The Rector was displeased. Some venial wretch had erred grievously in loosing the first stone without permission, and Rector Adam was confident he knew which of his errant children it was, too. The bright orange arrow sticking out of the sinner's thigh was a material confession.

Brother Orin had yet again succumbed to the Tempter's compulsions.

He would be made to atone unless the good and merciful Lord took him to his bosom during the tempest of this day. A possibility, indeed. The heathen fighters had thus far acquitted themselves with inconvenient competence even as the terrible swift sword of Jerusalem's redemption cut at them.

The Rector urged his host into battle from his vantage point raised high above the martyrs' field—previously, the attic storeroom of the Western Chic' Ladies Boutique. These times were sent to try the righteous and the unrighteous alike, and now that it was done and could not be undone, it should not matter that Brother Orin, curse him for a fool, had marred the Rector's elegant design by intemperate action. The action was writ, and the Lord saved only those who saved themselves.

"Cry havoc, sister," he shouted to Nadine, his fastest runner, "Cry havoc and pour on as the Flood."

The young woman was clad today in leggings, affirmation of her role as his voice, and so God's voice, on the field of contention. She signed herself, tracing the lines of the holy rood tree he had carved into her visage as a token of his favour. Nadine bowed her head and promised urgently, "Thy will and His will to be done."

Goodsister Nadine spun away and hurried down the stairs to pass his order throughout the host.

Rector Adam had faith in Nadine. An accomplished fisher of men, she had never failed him, not in the field nor the pillow chamber. She would see to his fulfilment. Turning back to the window but taking care to conceal his presence from capricious fate, he peered down upon the battle, struggling to put aside his annoyance with Brother Orin.

Lo, but it was difficult.

The archers were supposed to loose their shafts *in concert*, cutting down the heathen foe in one fell stroke. Brightly colored arrows stuck out from the body of the automobile and the wheeled wagon they had brought into Jerusalem, intent on plunder and conversion. More lay in great profusion around the tiny storefront, bent and broken, spent without reward. Meanwhile, the heathen band had retreated inside the structure and seemed willing to receive any final charge within.

Oh, but this was vexing.

He had sent most of his long guns out to lay siege against the caravan encircled upon the hill outside the walls of New Jerusalem. There, the real prize was to be had. Not just the supplies these unrepentant sinners stole in their trek across the fallen lands but fresh lambs for his flock. New believers for Jerusalem. And what use were long guns here, anyway? Outsiders were always-always-*always* drawn to the pumps of the abandoned gas station, like Philistines to a wine shop. The Texaco always had been an auspicious place to fall upon outsiders.

And yet the spark of just one bullet might raise a conflagration to consume them all.

This! This was why the Rector held it such a grave necessity that all must follow his design in the execution of the ambush. Cut down the enemy's scouts and soldiers with silent swiftness and ferocity, but have a care to the cauldron in which they fought and light no fires there.

Was that so hard to understand?

Apparently so, if you were Brother Orin.

Below him, the flock, reformed as a wolf pack for the hunt, wavered at the jump. A score of them did little work but hesitation, unsure of what must come next until Nadine arrived within their midst to urge them forward on to glory.

Rector Adam roused himself in excitation at vision of the Goodsister, praying under his breath.

"Exercitus sine duce corpus est sine spiritus."

An army without a leader is a body without a spirit.

And he had imbued this his army with a righteous spirit through his vessel Nadine. Snatching the bow out of Brother Orin's hands, she used it as both a marshal's baton and an overseer's whip, lashing and leading the penitent forward to redeem their failures.

The Rector smiled at last.

This day would yet belong to him, and he would reward Goodsister Nadine with his undivided tribute in the pillow chamber come evensong.

"No, don't fire," Mel Baker yelled as they retreated to the storeroom.

"You ain't the boss of me," Tammy Kolchar shouted back, punching home the point with two blasts from her radically shortened shotgun. She fired directly into the human crush of crazy fucking desert druids at the outer doors of the little shop. Glass shattered, and voices screamed in pain and shock. The first blast killed some psychotic hippie chick swinging around a bloody great hunting bow. The second chewed a big hole in the crowd of Manson family outcasts that Bow Girl had led in a charge across the tarmac, nearly ploughing them under in one rush.

"The storeroom, get in the storeroom," Rick shouted over the squall of screaming and confusion, not all of it from their attackers.

Poor Lew Gibb had two arrows in him now, one poking out of his chest, and he was moaning pitiably in the back while Peter Tapsell tried to push the shaft through and out the other side. Tapsell's face was a bloody mask from a long, lipless machete wound to his scalp. Sparty Williams was vomiting and clutching at the arrow through his knee and had gone a sickly shade of grey with blood loss and pain.

Nobody knew where Nez had buggered off to, and Mel was terrified that he was trapped outside with this mob of Old Testament lunatics. They were dressed like extras from some bloody Holy Grail fan club, and they'd carved up their faces like complete fuckin' nutters. Wasn't no creepy little crosses between their eyebrows neither, but massive bloody biblical runes slashed from ear-to-ear and forehead to chin, like some bizarre, bloody mutilation cult.

It was a right proper fucking freak out seeing those maniacs coming at you, and she'd forced herself to imagine the florid scars as being nothing more than convenient aiming points. Just so she wouldn't lose her bottle thinking too much about the horrible things.

Worked a bloody treat, too, until she remembered they were in a bloody petrol station, and ol' Pete'd been cranking away at his do-it-yourself hand pump less than a minute ago, splashing fumes and petrol droplets everywhere.

"You'll blow us up," Mel yelled at Tammy, who was racking another shell into that sawn-off shottie of hers. A right fucking blagger's gun it was, spreading pellets everywhere in a ridiculous ballistic spray of hot lead and metal sparks.

Tammy fired again before Mel could stop her, and she cringed in anticipation of the explosion that was surely coming when their luck ran out.

But for now, it held, and the only damage done was to the angry mass of murder-lemmings all piled up and falling over themselves at the broken doors, some trying to get in, some trying to get out, all of them yelling and screaming up a blue storm.

"Fuck yeah!" Tammy hollered in triumph. At least four of the crazies went down with that last shot. Not dead, not all of them that Mel could see, but none of them likely to offer much in the way of trouble.

"Tammy!" Rick shouted. "Mel's right. You'll set off the pumps or the cans that Pete left out there. Ceasefire. Now."

"And do what?" Tammy demanded, pretty reasonably if Mel had to admit it.

How could they save themselves without their guns?

"Fall back. Into the storeroom, both of you," Rick barked.

It was an order. Not an answer.

Mel started to back away from the counter. Tammy tried to load another shell, but Rick pushed her back.

"Go!"

Mel got an arm around Tammy's neck, pulled her off her feet and dragged her through the narrow opening, fighting all the way. She was worse than a drunken East End scrubber on welfare night.

"Rick! Come on," Mel shouted, suddenly frightened that he would try it on with some stupid gesture, barring the door with his body or something. And for one terrible second, it seemed he might do that. Rick used his shoulder to shove Mel and Tammy into the smaller, more defensible space of the storeroom, then turned back to face the mob, who were spilling inside over the bodies of their fallen.

"No! Rick, don't," Mel cried out.

But he didn't charge into the melee. Instead, he reached low to pull something from beneath the shop counter.

A pair of tyre irons.

He threw one to Mel, who had to let go of Tammy to catch it. He tossed his rifle back, too, and Mel passed it on to Sparty Williams, who'd propped himself up against a large box of Chef Boyardee's microwaveable lasagne. He'd snapped off the arrow shaft jutting out of his leg and wiped some of the sick from his face. He looked ready to die, defending his slab of oven-ready carbs and cheese sauce.

The mob came on. They were armed with improvised clubs and edged weapons. Garden tools. Hammers. And axe handles.

They roared as one, but in concert now—some sort of battle cry.

"Cor-pus Christi! Cor-pus Christi!"

Rick and Mel stood shoulder to shoulder in the doorway, each holding a tire lever and a handgun.

"There's not that many of them," Rick Boreham snarled. "Maybe thirty or so. We can do this, Mel. Just hack them down."

"Cor-pus Christi! Cor-pus Christi!"

The leading edge of the tight-packed horde broke over the counter and around the ends. Mel could not even conceive of them as individual attackers now. They were just one seething mass of arms and legs. Eyes rolled back to whites, and spittle flying from bared teeth.

And those scars.

Those raw and hideous disfigurements seemed so fearsome until Rick began to literally deface them with fresh wounds of his own making.

A thin, demented berserker landed directly in front of them, swinging a length of bicycle chain. Rick drove a kick into his groin and smashed the tire iron down on the side of his head. Blood and hair and gobbets of torn scalp hit Melissa Baker in the face, but she did not notice. By then, Mel was flailing away with her heavy steel rod. She was distantly aware of Tammy Kolchar levering her way into the tight space between them, jabbing into the crowd with a length of wood – an old mop or a broom handle, perhaps? – snapped at one end and weaponised into a crude stabbing spear that Tammy thrust deep into the horde.

"Cor-pus chris-ti! Cor-pus chris-ti!" howled the feral mob.

"Here-we-go, here-we-go, here-we-go!" Mel bellowed into the face of the chanting savages as she hacked away at them.

Recognising the cadence of *The Stars and Stripes Forever*, Tammy and Rick joined Mel in her war cry straight from the terraces of

England's football stadiums. The stupid, repetitive chant gave them something to channel against the animal fury of their would-be killers. From behind her, Mel could hear Peter Tapsell pick up the never-changing chorus, adding his voluble baritone to the mix.

"'Ere-we-go-'ere-we-go-'ere-we-go...'"

And all the while, she thrashed and bludgeoned down anything in front of her. Her arms grew heavy, and her lungs burned. Her vision swam. Beside her, Rick Boreham carved and sliced into meat and bone like a human threshing machine. Behind her, Tammy Kolchar stabbed and prayed and roared defiance.

And none of it, Mel knew, would make any difference.

There were too many of them.

They were going to lose, and they were going to die.

13

THE WAGON CIRCLE

They did not have enough guns to hold the small circular fort of SUVs and motor homes. James knew that before the first attacker breached their defences. Ramona stayed with the children, keeping them huddled under the picnic tables in the rotunda while Nomi growled and stalked around them, all the fur along her spine raised in thick, bristling defiance. That left five adults and one very young teenager to receive the enemy, who looked at least forty or fifty strong. It was hard to tell. The volume of fire coming up the hill had not slacked off despite Michelle and Roxarne claiming kills. James thought he might have winged one guy, but the terror of battle, of other human beings trying to *kill* them, seemed to have shattered everything into jagged mirror shards of disordered continuity. He had become unmoored from time itself. Had they been under fire for hours or minutes? He couldn't say. Was there some line of inference between the trigger he had just pulled, the bark of the rifle, and the oddly graceful, twirling pirouette described by some nameless man in unremarkable working clothes just thirty yards away? Who could tell?

Unlike Rick and possibly Michelle, James O'Donnell had no experience with this sort of thing. The raiders and bandits they'd chased off previously had not been so organised or numerous as this. They were just desperate, starving people. Refugees fleeing the cities and not well suited to a life of brigandage. This was a form of Hell. The uproar was constant: guns firing, people yelling, children screaming, and Nomi barking. He couldn't think, and James was a thinker. It was really all he'd done since leaving his parents' farm, and he had been good at it. People had paid him to do it for them.

But now, beside him, crouched low behind their barricade of car tyres, Michelle and Roxarne, each in their way, seemed better suited to the urgencies of battle. Roxy swore and snarled and unloaded shot after shot, channelling all her rage at the threat to her children down through the barrel of that shotgun. Where Roxarne was all furious wrath and maternal passion, Michelle Nguyen was rational and calculating.

She analysed the threats and worked the odds.

The lines of Michelle's face were all drawn deeper and longer than James had ever seen, but they were the natural cracks in the frozen surface of a winter lake. What lay beneath them was cold and dangerous.

James poked the barrel of his Ruger out through a slot between the tyres and pulled the trigger on a sprinting figure he realised afterwards was probably a woman.

She had a woman's shape, and her scream, as she crumpled, was undeniably feminine.

He froze.

"I just shot a woman. Who the hell are these people?"

Roxarne bobbed up and loosed a blast in the same direction.

"Only winged her, Jimbo. But I finished that bitch off."

Michelle nodded grimly. She reached over and grabbed a handful of James's shirt, pulling him in closer.

"There's a couple of different groups out there," she said. "Or units or whatever. Not all of them have guns. Some aren't even armed. The ones with guns might be driving the others ahead of them. I dunno. But if you get a chance to pick off a shooter, concentrate on them."

"Got it," Roxarne said.

James patted his pockets with shaking hands, looking for more ammo.

Nothing.

"I'm out," he said at last.

"We've got more ammo in the tent," Michelle said. "We'll cover you. Bring the spare clips for me, too. In my day pack. Go!"

And with that, both women sent a volley of fire downslope. Michelle didn't need to say anything to Roxarne. They acted in concert like birds suddenly turning and swooping in flight.

There was no question of second-guessing her. The sudden heavy metal chorus of their combined fire was a kick in the pants that got James moving.

He stayed low.

Rick had taught them that.

He desperately wanted to take just one brief moment to look and see who was attacking them, to understand what sort of people might do that, but he kept moving instead. Rick had taught him that, too.

His legs felt heavy and numb. They hadn't fallen asleep. They were more like phantom limbs, somehow not his own, and he tripped and stumbled a couple of times over his own feet. He hurried past the huddled children, waving at Nomi to stay where she was. Rick's dog started barking as soon as she saw him. She was dancing and leaping in tight, frantic circles. The children cried out to her.

Nomi, no.

Stay with us.

Ramona had crawled under the table with the children and sheltered them with her body as best she could, but there were too many for her to cover. The gunfire continued, wild and almost indiscriminate. It still seemed mostly aimed to pin them down, if it was aimed at all. A steady shower of leaf matter and small, shattered branches rained down from the tree cover.

Nomi blurred away, a midnight black streak flashing across the campsite, between the tents, barking and heading for Laurence Bloomfield.

James stopped and stared after her.

The boy—and he was just a boy—was fighting a grown man who had broken into the camp. A husky, balding fireplug of a man in faded blue bib coveralls and heavy working boots. He was easily two-and-a-half times the size of the Bloomfield kid, and he'd come through the improvised wagon circle in the gap between one of the SUVs and the rear fender of Bruce Goldie's Jayco.

Bruce was hobbling towards them at his best speed, but he was seventy-one years old, and his glory days as a rugby player were far behind him. Laurence had lost his rifle, and the intruder was armed only with a club hammer, not a gun. But one swing of that thing would smash the boy's head like a rotten cantaloupe.

The man, his face a purple mask of gross, distended fury, skinned back white lips from yellow teeth and swung again. Laurence skipped back, a nervy little rabbit jump, and the heavy steelhead of the mallet whistled past his jaw, the momentum dragging the man a quarter turn away and opening a short line of attack for the teenager. Laurence reversed his twitchy retreat and moved in quickly, scything a low roundhouse kick into the man's knee. James heard the joint crack and pop even in the shocking turmoil of the broader battle, with bullets zipping overhead and the constant storm of shredded leaves and twigs falling from the canopy above. The man cried out in pain and rage, but he did not go down, not even when Laurence snapped a second kick into the same limb.

The boy's aim was slightly off this time, landing a few inches north of the injured knee joint, smacking into the man's thickly muscled thigh. The club hammer started its return swing, and James cringed as he ran on. This hammer blow would surely smash the poor kid in the face or neck.

Instead, Bruce Goldie slammed into the attacker, his aging but heavy, barrel-chested bulk crashing home with full force. And then Nomi was there too, spearing into the thrashing tangle of arms and legs and sinking her teeth deep into the attacker's throat.

Even amid battle, it was a moment of horrifying and insensate savagery.

And it was over very quickly.

A strangled scream died in a wet susurrus of retching and gasping. Laurence's would-be murderer spent his last sucking breaths clawing at the raw and bloody pit Nomi had torn open in his throat. His heavy boots drummed a frantic beat into the stony ground, his back arched, and he fell still.

Nomi chewed and crunched at the meat in her jaws. Once. Twice. And on the third bite, she swallowed the lot, her tail quivering.

James felt a cold shudder run through his entire body, but it did not last. The hot blast of yet more murder to be done warmed his crawling flesh and carried him on. He came down next to Laurence as though sliding into first base.

"You okay, man?"

"I'm good, Mister O'Donnell," the boy said, his voice breathy and shaken.

He always called James 'Mister O'Donnell', which made James feel about eight hundred years old.

"Solid fucking bliksem, boss," Bruce Goldie groaned as he picked himself up off the ground.

To James, it sounded like 'Salad feckon bliksem bass', and he had no idea what any of it meant, but Goldie punched Laurence lightly on the shoulder and suggested they get back to it.

Or, *"Beck to et."*

He was covered in scratches and welts, and his leathery old hide would probably be a carnival of lurid bruising if they survived the day.

James turned back toward his tent, meaning to grab the ammunition. And at that moment, he understood that they would not survive.

The walls were breached.

His heart seemed to fall into a black hole when he saw that Michelle and Roxy were gone and the small fortress of car tires overturned. Cruel and brutish-looking strangers poured in through the breach, and he started to raise his rifle to fire directly into them before remembering he was out of bullets.

A pistol roared a few feet away.

Bruce Goldie stood in a weirdly formal shooter's stance. Not in a two-handed grip, feet wide apart like a cop or maybe a soldier. But side on, like an old-fashioned duellist or one of the athletes you sometimes saw at the Olympics when nothing else was happening— a medallist in some super obscure elite air pistol showdown or something.

Nothing obscure or elite about the handgun Bruce had pulled out, however.

It looked like a museum piece, an old cavalry pistol, the sort of antique hand cannon you might dig up from under the Memorial right here.

As James watched, transfixed, Bruce pulled back the hammer, sighted carefully along his thick, sunburned arm, and squeezed off one, carefully aimed round.

Fire and smoke leapt from the ancient pistol with a roar that sounded nothing like the precise and manufactured report of Michelle's little Glock.

Michelle!

His wandering mind, disoriented and unravelling in the chaos of their final minutes, accelerated back into motion.

Where was Michelle? And Roxarne?

"Fok diss donkey konts," Bruce Goldie growled as the old cavalry pistol clicked on an empty chamber.

He snatched up the heavy club hammer fallen from the dead man's hand and limped towards the crush of men and women, trying to squeeze through the collapsed wall of car tires.

James shook his head in astonishment.

Partly at Goldie, who was insane.

But mainly at the spectacle of those women fighting to break into the camp.

Women!

Who were these maniacs?

An eerie bubble seemed to have inflated around him. This could not be happening, so it wasn't for part of his mind. James O'Donnell wasn't standing in a picnic area, watching dozens of starving, feral humans claw and rake at each other to get at him and his friends.

That was insane.

These people were just people.

Not so long ago, they had been getting through their days, tending to their work, looking after families, probably watching too much TV and not getting enough fibre or fresh fruit and vegetables.

Not so long ago, surely?

And then he heard the familiar crack of Michelle's subcompact and the twinned roar of a sawn-off shotgun, and some of the blood-thirsty hordes fell to be trampled down by their own kind. James saw Roxarne and Michelle crouched over by the barbecue, shooting across the camping ground, firing into the attackers' flanks struggling through the breach.

I just want everything to be like it was, James, Michelle's voice whispered to him from across the unfathomable void between then and now. *Like nothing weird even happened.*

But more and then still, more of these unknowable creatures appeared at the edges of the camp, struggling to break through the crush. So many of them piled up outside the little wagon circle that Sparty Williams' motorhome was rocking back and forth on its axles as the press of human bodies surged and ebbed.

James didn't know what to do. He faltered between charging after Goldie, staying with Laurence, or going to Michelle.

"We're actually in it and there's no rewind," Michelle's voice, or the memory of it, said to him from some preternaturally quiet place within the widening maelstrom.

The bubble popped, and reality flooded back in through all of his senses.

He saw in all those bestial faces how close they were to being killed. He heard the cries of the terrified children, the strangely distant blast of Roxarne's shotgun, and the crackle and pop of firearms from outside the camp. The fear in his throat tasted of burning iron and salt.

"Come on, kid," James said, taking Laurence by the arm. "Stay with me."

They moved towards the pergola and the barbecue, where they would make their last stand.

The children were all there, hiding beneath the tables, and if this murderous rabble could be said to have a focus, it was moving in their direction.

James held onto Laurence with one hand and his empty rifle with the other.

Perhaps Michelle had grabbed the ammunition? Perhaps not.

He would swing it like a club if he had to.

The mob pressed in, closer to the barbecue. Their cries were thunderous.

The animal squall changed in tenor to something ghastly and shrieking as Bruce Goldie hammered at the leading edge of the mob with the heavy steel head of the dead man's club hammer.

Nomi raced into the fray, barking and biting, her black fur a sticky mess of blood and hackles.

Then, the tide seemed to turn.

Bruce went down.

Nomi yelped in fright or pain, and James changed direction again, leaving the kids cowering beneath the tables and running towards the heaving mob and his fallen comrade.

He was vaguely aware of Michelle's voice calling out to him from a thousand miles away.

He kicked a man who had thrown himself onto Rick's dog and tried to bite Nomi on the back of the neck. James's boot connected hard, and the shock ran up his leg. He lost balance and toppled over, knowing he would not get up again as he fell.

He saw Nomi free herself and dart away, and that was enough. Rick would say James O'Donnell had done enough.

The crowd closed around and then over him. A tsunami of thrashing arms and legs. A huge and monstrous centipede of stomping feet and roaring incoherent violence.

Pain flared in his head as someone kicked him. His neck and back. A hundred explosions of hurting all over his body.

He curled into a tight ball as best he could, wanting it to be over.

And then it was.

Almost as though another wave had crashed into the one that took him under.

He heard screams, cries, and gunshots, and it was confusing because he could tell them apart from each other again. The world was no longer one colossal storm of noise and pain. The dark flailing maul of attackers broke apart and disintegrated, the constituent bodies flying away or running away or dropping and dying.

James blinked mud and blood from his eyes.

He saw Bruce Goldie staring at him just two feet away as if they had woken from a nap under the soft winter sun of eastern Montana.

But Bruce, he thought, would never wake again.

James heard his name called over and over.

Fearfully. Angrily.

It was Michelle.

But it was not Michelle who reached down for him.

That was another stranger.

A newcomer, though, not an intruder.

James blinked again, wiping away tears and filth with numb, shaking fingers.

He did not recognise the man who pulled him out of the bloodied slurry, but he did recognise kindness and fellow feeling in the man's eyes. That simple shared humanity was a glass of cool water in Hell.

When the man spoke, his voice was unusual, foreign—like Bruce Goldie's had been.

"G'day mate," he said. "I think your missus might be looking for you. She seems a bit pissed off."

14

IN THE BADLANDS NOW

"What d'you reckon, mate?" Damien Maloney said, passing the big-arse Skymaster binoculars to Karl. They'd taken the oversized glasses with them when they traded his boat for the banged-up Land Rover.

Karl Valentine took the astronomical binoculars and studied the distant campsite for a minute or so. It sat on one of the low hills that rose above the gently undulating plains like a wave peak on a vast and fathomless ocean. Damo thought there might be seven or eight vehicles parked in a rough circle around some kind of shelter and a surprisingly large number of children for the handful of adults minding them. Karl's brow furrowed over the padded eyepieces.

"That's a war memorial," he said. "For the Seventh Cavalry, as best I can recall. General Custer's boys. You might have heard of them, even all the way Down Under."

Damo snorted.

"Bit of a wanker was what I heard, mate. Charged in where he wasn't wanted and got everybody killed."

"Not everyone," Karl said. "It was a good day for the Lakota, Arapaho and their friends."

He lowered the glasses and nodded into the distance.

"But that ain't for Lieutenant Colonel Custer. Little Big Horn was a-ways from here. That's a memorial for a couple of troopers who got themselves good and scalped all on their own. It's the main tourist attraction around these parts. The only one, truth be told, since we left the Devil's Tower in Wyoming."

The two men stood under the shade of a small thicket of honey-suckle trees and native birch. The Land Rover, running on fumes after they'd been forced to detour three times and zig-zag nearly two hundred miles off course, waited out of sight beneath what Karl called the 'military crest'.

To Damo, it was simply parked around the arse end of the hill where nobody could see it.

The two ladies and the little ones waited with the vehicle while the men scouted the approach to Bachman.

"What d'you reckon they're doing?" Damo asked, staring at the far away campsite.

"Having breakfast," Karl ventured. "See the smoke? As I recall, there was a nice little barbecue built for the memorial. Had myself a real good breakfast sandwich from a place in town there once, on my way back east. Lovely spot to sit and take in the air."

"And what about them?" Damo said. "You reckon they'd be up for company, or maybe some barter? All those bloody utes and caravans, they might have some spare gas they'd trade for Ellie's jerky or that salt fish we got left."

Karl raised the glasses again.

"Maybe. That's a lot of little kids to feed they got over there. But a lot of gas tanks to fill up too. Could be they're as empty as we are."

Jodi's voice surprised them.

"What do you mean, little kids?"

Jodi and Ellie had come up to see what they were talking about. The three children were sitting in the back seat of the Land Rover, playing with a Nintendo or something, to judge by all of the electronic beeps and bloops that Damo could hear.

Karl handed the binoculars over.

"Hard to tell, Miss Jodi," he said. "But from here, it looks like a school trip got caught on the road. Maybe a dozen kids in that party."

Jodi all but levitated when she took in the scene.

"Omigod," she said, quickly handing the glasses to Ellie. "They are kids! Just like ours. We have to go meet them, Damo. We have to," she insisted.

Damo threw up his hands, "Whoa, mate, I'm not saying no. I was just talking to Karl about whether they might be keen on a swap. But, Jodes, we don't know if they—"

"Er, Damo? Karl?"

It was Ellie.

She had walked a few steps away and was peering intently through the powerful Skymasters. Frowning.

"This doesn't look like a happy development."

She passed the binoculars to Karl. His face remained expressionless as he surveyed the distant tableau, but he swore softly and handed the glasses to Damo.

"What? What's happening," Jodi asked, dancing from one foot to the other.

"Just hang on, baby," Ellie said. Her tone was dark.

Damo swept the far-off camp with the big twin lenses. He immediately saw what Ellie Jabbarah meant. A small group advanced by stealth on the circle of cars and caravans. There was no question that they were sneaking up on their quarry, just as there was no doubt they intended them harm. The weapons they carried testified to that.

"Bugger," said Damo.

"What's going on?" Jodi demanded to know. "I hate it when you guys do this."

Damo gave her the binoculars.

"Looks like fuckin' bandits, mate. Up to all sorts of mischief."

Jodi Sarjanen did not long speculate about what she was seeing.

"We have to warn them. Now! We have to help," she said.

She didn't like what she saw in their faces when she dropped the glasses from her eyes.

"No!" Jodi said, "We can't just leave them to it. All those children. They're just little kids."

Damo looked at Karl and Ellie.

His one-time chef looked grim-faced and even nauseous. Karl, as was his nature, seemed to be awaiting orders. If Damo told him to drive away, he would, no matter what he thought of it.

"Pleeeeease," Jodi cried, reaching for her girlfriend's hand. "Baby, please, they're just little kids."

"So are Maxi and the others, babe," Ellie said. "We can't take them into that. Into what's about to happen over there. Or what I think is gonna happen."

"We don't have to," Jodi protested. "Just... just leave them here. But go now, we have to go now."

"Mate," Damo said, "we can't just leave the kids here on their own. There could be more of these fuckwits about."

Jodi threw her arms out theatrically and spun in a half circle.

"Where, Damo? Where? Seriously. Look around. There's nothing for miles. We just drove through miles of nothing. Everyone is over there."

She jabbed a finger toward Bachman and the little hilltop picnic ground.

Damo sighed.

Ellie folded her arms and stared at her own feet.

Karl shrugged.

"Fact is, we can't get much farther anyway," he said.

They all stared at him.

"What?" Ellie said, her tone sharp and interrogative.

Karl lifted his shoulders and showed them his open palms. Nothin' to hide.

"We ain't got much more'n a couple of miles worth of gas. And I mean that for real—maybe two or three. If we're in the Badlands now, we're in trouble. Could be the only help is over there. And their only help is over here, with us. I guess we should probably go. You and me at least, big fella," he said to Damo.

"Yes! Please!" Jodi said, almost crying. "We'll be alright. I can stay with the kids. Or I can go if you want me to go—"

"No fucking way!" Ellie said. "I'll go with Damo and Karl. You stay right here, and if we don't get back inside an hour or send someone to get you, you start walking back along the road we came in."

"Where?" Jodi asked.

"Anywhere but here," Ellie shot back. "That's the deal. You good with that?"

She was fierce, almost frightening. Damo had never seen Ellie speak to Jodes like that before, but he'd seen it plenty of times in the restaurant. She'd made up her mind that she was going, too.

THEY HEARD the first gunshots as they quickly unloaded the camping gear and the kids.

The children all wanted to know what was happening, and there was no bullshitting them. They'd been through enough to know what trouble sounded like.

"Baddies," Jodi said, kneeling in front of Maxi. "But Damo and the others are going to deal with it. We'll just wait here."

"But I want to go too," Maxi protested.

"You can't," Damo said sternly. He leaned down and lowered his voice. "If there's more baddies around, I need you and Pascal to look after Beatrice and your mum."

"Check your outdated gender norms this morning, Damo?" Ellie Jabbarah said as she brushed past, carrying a shotgun.

"Yeah, mate. They were fuckin' tops. Let's go."

Jodi wrangled the children into a huddle over by the luggage as the sound of distant gunfire intensified. It didn't grow louder, but it did get a lot heavier. She took a pistol from Ellie without saying anything. They hugged and separated.

"Damn," Karl muttered as he climbed in behind the wheel. "I hate this stuff. I always hated this stuff."

"Let's just get it done," Ellie said through clenched teeth, hurrying back to the vehicle.

Damo took the passenger seat up front. He clipped Karl's shotgun into the rack on the dashboard and checked the loads on his own weapons, a mismatched pair of handguns.

"All right then. Let's go," he said as Karl turned over the engine and gave it a little gas. The tank was so low he let the Land Rover roll down the far side of the hill until they hit level ground. The ride was rough, and despite Damo's hard-won fitness gains, his ageing body felt every jolt and bump. He was glad when they pulled onto a dirt track and were able to pick up speed on the smoother surface.

Ellie leaned forward, peering out ahead.

She was a good twenty years younger than either man, and her eyesight was sharper.

"This is a fuckin' shitshow," she said after scowling at the still distant tableau. "I don't understand this at all."

Karl concentrated on the road, such as it was. Damo tried squinting to bring the scene into focus, but it was still blurry and indistinct. He'd been ignoring his deteriorating eyesight for years.

"What's happening?" he asked. "What's it look like?"

"It's weird," Ellie said. "Looks like half of those clowns charging at the campsite are being chased up there by some other goons who are shooting at them. To get them moving or something. I dunno."

"Well, who's who in the fucking zoo, mate?" Damo said as they sped towards the gunfire and chaos. He wound down the window, and the sounds of the small battle grew louder, even over the roaring wind of their passage. "Who am I supposed to be shooting at?" he shouted.

"Anybody outside that wagon circle," Karl replied. "Reckon I seen this before."

Now that they were committed, Damo was surprised at just how quickly they would be in the thick of it. The unsealed road curved gently across the open ground between the cavalry memorial and their little hilltop hiding spot, and Karl was not sparing the horses to cover the gap quickly.

"The Hajis used to do that sometimes," he said. "Send people forward in front of their own, like bullet sponges or human shields. Hardly mattered which. Look-see over there?"

Damo followed where Karl briefly pointed and saw two men with rifles herding a group of maybe a dozen forward up the rising ground towards the circle of motor homes and SUVs on top of the hill. The larger group were armed with what looked like farm tools. Long-handled shovels and pitchforks. Axes and sledgehammers. Simple lengths of wood.

The gunmen mostly fired over their heads and sometimes into the ground at their heels.

"Bugger me," Damo said. "That's a bit rough."

Karl jerked the wheel slightly and laid a heavy foot onto the accelerator.

The mob saw them coming at speed, and for one mad second, a few started running toward the Land Rover.

Damo leaned out the passenger side window and fired at them, aiming over their heads. It broke up the charge, if it could be called a charge, and everyone scattered.

Everyone but the two gunmen, at least.

They hesitated until Damo loosed a few shots at them, and Karl leaned into the gas to speed up, heading directly for them.

One man fired, high and wide. The other broke and ran.

The boom of Ellie's shotgun from the rear window added to the crack of Damo's handguns. The rifleman who'd shot at them tumbled over. He struggled back to his feet and limped away.

"God, I hate this," Karl muttered, turning the wheel back towards the close-packed crowd which had piled up at the outer rim of the improvised fort. He said something else, but Damo couldn't hear it over the noise of their passage, the rattle of gunfire and the growing uproar of the heaving crowd.

Ellie's shotgun boomed and boomed again.

Damo targeted a couple of gunmen at the back of the crowd, unloading the rest of his magazine at them. One went down. The other turned and ran.

Most of the crowd broke then, and Karl did pump the brakes, but they still ploughed into the mob at sickening speed.

The crunching thud of hard steel hitting soft bodies was terrible, but not as bad as the screaming and mayhem which followed.

Karl leaned into the horn and backed up.

Damo fired over the heads of the crowd. Up close, they looked authentically mad but with hunger and fear.

Ellie shot one man in the chest.

He dropped the gun he was carrying and fell backwards into the dust.

It was enough to break the collective will. They panicked, and any lingering coherence disintegrated. Most had fled back down the hill and into the surrounding fields within a few seconds.

Some dropped to the ground, begging for help, for mercy.

Some lay where they fell, unable to move.

Damo threw open the door and jumped out, carrying just one pistol now. Not entirely sure of how many rounds it still had. He was aware of Ellie and Karl following him, but the carnage and chaotic aftermath of battle, or riot, or whatever the hell this was, over-whelmed his ability to understand what he was seeing. The stench of it was nauseating.

Most of the attackers looked like ordinary people who'd been living rough for months. They were pale and thin, all but emaciated. Their clothes hung from them in rags, but the shooters were differ-ent. They looked like—

His rational mind refused to process the image of the one nearest him. The man Ellie had shot in the chest.

He looked like a monk in robes. Or maybe a weird fucking Hare Krishna or something. But with a hideous-looking half-healed scar resembling a bloody crucifix carved into his face.

Unable to figure out what the fuck had happened out here, Damien Maloney turned his attention to what was happening inside the camp they'd come to; what? Rescue? Liberate?

He had no fucking idea.

For half a second, he faltered in his certainty that they had done the right thing.

They knew nothing, really. And because of that, they might have just stepped into something truly fucked up and heinous.

"James! James!"

Damo heard a woman's voice.

He found her quickly. A small Asian-American woman with wild tattoos and a desperate fearfulness in her eyes. She saw him and snapped up a handgun with practised speed and precision.

Damo threw up his own hands in theatrical surrender.

"Whoa. Steady on, love. We came to help."

Ellie and Karl appeared at his side, bearing arms, but neither threatened anybody inside the makeshift compound. It was a hell of a mess in there. Screaming kids. Dead bodies. Tents trampled down, and a small fire burning freely near the barbecue area. Ellie shouldered her shotgun and hurried into the campsite through a breach in their defences.

She gathered a small boy who had broken away from the others and hugged him until his howling subsided. Karl checked the pile of bodies that had jammed up the space between a couple of the vehicles.

"Where's James?" the woman shouted. "Is he out there with you?"

She was frantic. Close to unhinged.

Another woman, white, much older, was trying to round up about a dozen hysterical children and shepherd them into one of the motorhomes. A dog barked incessantly.

The last of the starving horde who could get away had done so. Only the wounded and the catatonic remained.

Ellie carried the small boy over to the dangerous-looking Vietnamese woman. She handed the kid to her as if returning a lost child at a playground.

"Hey Damo," Karl said, "I reckon this young fella might be who she's looking for. Is your name James, son?"

He stood over a man covered in mud and blood but not so obviously starved and destitute as the rabble which had attacked them. The woman inside the compound had decided to ignore Ellie and even the small boy she was trying to return.

"James! James!" she cried out.

The bloke on the ground seemed to respond to her voice.

Damo reached down to help him up.

"G'day mate," he said. "I reckon your missus might be looking for you."

15

THE SWORD THROUGH THESE YOUR LANDS

Rick Boreham had seen some hard fighting in his thirty-two years. One or two firefights, he still didn't know how he'd come through. But that was a matter of working the odds and wondering why he was still drawing breath on the other side.

This.

This was just weird.

The unholy maniacal bloodswarm of disfigured cultists melted away in three or four heartbeats.

In one moment, he was fully engaged in a frenzy of wild medieval combat, made all the more freakish by its setting in the pillaged remains of a Texaco on the edge of a modern ghost town. And before he had time to process any change in their circumstances, those circumstances were utterly transformed.

The savage, squalling mass of zealots did not so much collapse in front of him as they fell into a sudden, motionless stupor. A waking coma, of sorts.

The mob turned, nearly as one, issued a collective moan and fell to their knees.

Beside him, Tammy and Mel kept thrashing away, unable or unwilling to stop, until Rick pushed Tammy back into the storeroom and laid a heavy hand on Mel's shoulder.

"Look," he said.

She merely grunted. Slowing. Stopping at last.

Mel stared at him. Breathing hard. Her expression slack. Uncomprehending.

Her eyes were empty of any human feeling.

"Look," Rick said again, his breath short, his mouth dry. "It's Nez."

"Huh?" she went, but this time she did turn to look.

All their would-be killers had fallen to their knees, and their hands were empty of edged weapons and crude clubs. Instead, they prayed, quietly imploring Andrew Nesbitt to have mercy.

"Have mercy..."

"Please, mercy..."

"Have mercy on his soul..."

Nez, who had disappeared in the first moments of the attack, reappeared with a single prisoner under his control.

Another cultist, like the maniacs they'd been fighting,... but not like them.

Where they were dressed in plain brown sackcloth and disfigured by grotesque facial scars, this man was clad in black robes, and his face was untouched, save for a bright red cross daubed onto the skin rather than carved into it. With shaking hands, he gestured urgently at his followers to remain on their knees.

"Solid choice, padre," Rick muttered. Nez had jammed the muzzle of his rifle deep into the man's neck, just below the jawline. He had a thick handful of the dude's hair and had pulled his head back over the base of his spine, unbalancing him.

"And I will give you peace in the land," the man trilled nervously. "And you shall lay down your arms. Do it now, do it, and none shall make you afraid, for I will rid you of these beasts in good time, and neither shall the sword go through these your lands."

"The fuck is he talking about?" Tammy Kolchar asked. She had squeezed herself out of hiding to stand between Rick and Mel again.

"I think he's telling them to stand down," Rick said, and whether it was the man's words or the threat of the gun jammed into his throat, in just a few seconds, the entire host of escaped Dark Ages lunatics had prostrated themselves before him.

Rick and Mel moved quickly, exiting the chokepoint they had made of the storeroom door, establishing tactical dominance over the suddenly quiescent enemy. Tammy followed despite his waving her back.

"The hell I will," she said.

It was the weirdest ending to a battle Rick had ever experienced, but he wasn't about to waste the reprieve or the advantage.

"Nez, don't come in any further. Keep your distance from them," he called out.

"All right," Nesbitt called back. "I found this asshole across the street, directing traffic. Pretty sure he's the boss."

Rick put aside all his many questions about how Nez had escaped the initial assault and laid hands on ... whoever this asshole might be. Strange things happened in combat. Sometimes, you never figured out why.

"Pete, Tammy, gonna need you on the trigger out here," he called out. "Sparty, can you look after Lew?"

"Lew's gone," Sparty said from behind him in the storeroom.

Rick resisted the urge to turn around. He could not take his eyes off these homicidal nut jobs.

"Okay," he said. "I'm sorry. I didn't know. You good for now, man?"

Sparty's voice was tight with pain when he replied.

"I'll live," he said.

Rick Boreham took him at his word.

The four who could still walk cautiously emerged from the shelter of the storeroom and fanned out, picking their way through the wounded and the dead, avoiding the creepy, kneeling survivors as far as possible.

Rick detailed Mel and the others to positions where they could put fire down on any trouble that flared up. He took a minute to replace the seals on the Texaco's underground tanks and relocate the gas canisters Nez and Tapsell had already siphoned off.

He was still flying on the neurochemistry of combat and unexpected survival, but he knew that would pass, and he would crash. They would all come down in their own ways. He needed to wrap this quickly.

He needed to get—

The camp!

He hadn't thought of what might happen back at the campsite since this had kicked off.

Rick spun around, looking directly into the morning sun.

He winced, squeezing his eyes out and shading them with his free hand.

He could see that something was happening up there. Or had happened.

Smoke poured into the endless blue skies of Montana, and dozens of figures ran, walked and hobbled away in all directions from the small hill that was the final resting place and memorial to four troopers of the 7th Cav.

Rick's heart lurched, and he felt the last reserves of adrenaline sluicing through his nervous system in one final synaptic dump. Caution be damned, he hastened over to Nez and his prisoner on legs suddenly gone shaky and numb.

"The fuck did you do? Huh! The fuck did you do up there, asshole?"

The man started babbling some Old Testament shit, and a couple of the whackjobs nearest him began getting to their feet.

Nez spoke up in a warning voice.

"Rick. Look."

He thought Nez was warning him to have a care about the other prisoners, and he was ready to shoot them all down if the situation demanded it. But before the ungovernable impulse to mass murder could overrun him, Mel called out, "It's James. Look."

And Rick Boreham deliberately turned away from the dark temptations of wrath and vengeance to see a single vehicle racing across the open fields he had crossed in stealth the previous evening. It was James O'Donnell's Sierra, throwing up a trailing cloud of dust. They were travelling so fast that Rick worried they might hit a damned gopher hole and flip the vehicle.

"Keep an eye on them," he said. "If they move or try anything, kill the leader first and light the rest of them up."

He didn't wait for anyone to acknowledge his order; instead, he hurried back the way they had come in so recently. Rick stood on tippy toes, trying to get a better look, waiting on the arrival of the Sierra.

His heart was tripping along faster than it had during the fight. He thought he could see James behind the wheel. Maybe. But it was hard, looking into the morning sun.

It had better be James who got out of that vehicle, he promised himself. James or one of their people. Because anybody else was getting a bullet.

———

DAMO CLUNG to the grab bar of the SUV as they cannonballed through the fine red soil of the unploughed field to the east of Bachman. Karl hunched over the steering wheel, glowering fiercely at the terrain ahead, looking for any obstacles or ground features that might bring them undone. In the back seat, the young man they'd been introduced to as James O'Donnell, braced himself and urged them on.

"That's them, up there. For sure," he said, pointing at a servo on the edge of town.

It didn't promise to be a happy reunion. As they got closer, Damo could see some guy who looked like he'd crawled through an abattoir, apparently waiting to receive them with an assault rifle. Some other bloke had taken a priest or maybe a judge captive with a fucking shottie, and there were bodies everywhere.

"That's Rick. Thank god, that's Rick," the O'Donnell kid said from the back seat, pointing to the lone gunman, standing slightly apart from the others.

They bounced in their seats as Karl accelerated over a small ditch at the edge of the field and mounted the tarmac on the other side. Damo cursed as he hit his head on the roof. Karl pumped the brakes and slowed the SUV to a stop as the rifleman O'Donnell had pointed out raised his weapon to aim at them.

"For fucks sake," Damo said. "Doesn't anybody around here know how to say thank you?"

He started to open the door, but Karl's hand shot across the centre console and gripped his forearm.

"Better let Deadeye Dick over there see his pal first, I reckon. Mister O'Donnell, you good to get out and make the introductions?"

James looked almost dopey with confusion.

Probably in shock, Damo thought.

But the young man nodded, "Yeah, sure, good idea," and opened the back door.

"Rick, it's me," he said, climbing out. "It's good, man. These guys are friends."

The one called Rick lowered his weapon, and Damo felt his arsehole unpucker.

"Now you can get out," Karl grinned ruefully.

"Thanks, mate," Damo said. "Bloody long way to come just to get shot by accident."

"It's a long way to come to get shot at all," Karl replied.

They climbed out of the big SUV and into the cool Montana morning.

Damo didn't know what to make of the bizarre scene that greeted them. Dozens of monks kneeled face down on the tarmac of the gas station, which had been as badly messed up as the campsite back at the Cavalry memorial. He saw the red cross painted on the black-robed priest's face.

The gunman Ellie had shot was marked the same way.

"Bugger me," Damo said. "Fucking face painting fetishists. What sort of a town is this place, Karl?"

Karl shrugged, "Perfectly normal, last time I was here, man. I dunno. Maybe Stephen King moved in since then?"

O'Donnell and his friend Rick embraced fiercely and exchanged a few words that Damo couldn't catch, but the big fella seemed to relax a little.

Just a little.

Rick walked over to where Damo and Karl waited by the vehicle, looking a little ashamed of himself.

"Sorry about that before," he said. "We've had a morning."

"No problem," Karl Valentine said.

"Mate, any morning I don't get shot is a good morning, I reckon," Damo said. "My name's Maloney. Damien Maloney. But you can call me Damo, and this is my mate, Karl."

They shook hands.

"Rick Boreham," the other man said. "And thank you. James tells me you turned up in the nick of time."

"Like the cavalry," Karl nodded. He almost seemed to be enjoying himself now.

"Just like," Rick Boreham agreed. "We owe you guys. Seriously, thank you."

More handshakes and more thanks followed before Boreham's face turned dark again.

"But we're not done here," he said. "I don't know what's going on in this place, but we can't just let these people go."

He waved a hand at his prisoners.

Damo noticed that they seemed to be praying under their voices.

"And we can't leave the others too long," James O'Donnell added. "The attack sort of broke up when Damo and Karl here arrived with... what was your friend's name?"

"Ellie. She's my sous chef," Damo explained.

Boreham and O'Donnell stared at him blankly.

"She's a real good cook," Karl said as if that explained everything.

O'Donnell nodded. "Okay. Good to know. But anyway, we had maybe a hundred of those guys trying to get at us when Damo and Karl came along. They've scattered everywhere now, but they could come back."

"They're already back," Rick Boreham said, his voice low and dour. "Look."

He had the assault rifle slung over his shoulder. He unslung and raised the weapon in one fluid motion that told Damo he wasn't new to the game of soldiers.

Boreham walked over to the edge of the field, pointing the weapon at six or seven people running toward them.

They looked like the scarecrow figures Damo had seen earlier. Thin, pale, desperate. They cried out in small, indistinct voices. They raised their hands high in the air when Rick aimed at them. But they kept coming, staggering across the field as quickly as possible. One fell and face-planted into the dirt. Two others helped him and came on just as determined as before.

"Mate, I don't think they're attacking anyone," Damo said. "I reckon they're surrendering or coming for help or something."

"Why?" Rick Boreham said.

"No face paint."

16

GIRLFRIENDS, LIKE FOR REALS

Jodi Sarjanen did not do as she was told. She had promised Ellie that she would leave with the children if nobody came back for her within the hour. But nearly two hours after Ellie and the others had left, and the big fight at the other camping ground was over, Jodi and the kids were still sitting around under the honeysuckle trees, waiting. "Mom, can we recharge the batteries for the Switch?" Maxi asked.

"We'll see, baby," she said, only half listening to him. "I think the charger's in the car."

Maxi was unimpressed with that all-too-obvious parental deflection.

"Oh, but *we'll see* always means *nooooo*," he complained.

"Maxi, be quiet, please," Jodi said, frowning through the binoculars. "I'm trying to see what's going on."

"Is Damo coming back soon?" Pascal asked.

"And Ellie? Ellie too?" Beatrice added.

Jodi lowered the Skymasters. She had a headache from the stress of it all. They'd left her on her own with these children, and as far as she could tell, nobody had made a move to get to them.

It had been terrifying at first when she could see the fighting through Damo's binoculars.

Then, it had been anxious while she waited to see if Ellie or the others had been hurt. Or worse.

And now, after two hours, it was getting dull and kind of annoying.

Scary, too, at times. Twice, just after the fight, she'd had to chase off wild-looking men who approached them, begging for food and water. The second time, she'd even had to fire her gun in their direction. That had sent them running, but the idea that there could be more of them around was very worrying.

The kids seemed way better at handling this stuff than her. They'd watched the battle, excited and scared but mostly excited. They'd dutifully kept a lookout for strangers afterwards; indeed, Pascal had been the first to spot the scary men moving in on them.

And now, like all children left without distraction or stimulation, they were bored and growing fractious.

"Where's Ellieeeee?" Beatrice cried.

Indeed, Jodi thought.

Where. Was. Ellie.

She scanned the distant campsite again. Damo's binoculars were heavy but powerful. Easily as good as her best telephoto lens, wherever that might be now. Probably still stashed away in some evidence locker at the police station back in the city.

Jodi deliberately turned her thoughts away from San Francisco.

She could see Ellie moving around over there, doing God knows what. Sometimes, Ellie appeared to be talking to other people. Sometimes, she was carrying a child, not always the same one. A couple of times, Ellie even stopped whatever she was doing to climb on top of a big RV and wave to Jodi and the kids. A young man, possibly very young, sat on the roof of the camper van, watching Jodi and the kids through his binoculars.

He had a rifle, which made her nervous until she worked out he was watching over them.

That became obvious when he fired the rifle at some people she couldn't see until they started running away. After that, she told the children to recheck all the fields around them. That had kept them occupied for a while, but the two youngest, Maxi and Beatrice, eventually circled back to bugging her about charging the dead battery in their Nintendo.

The morning was cool, with a slight breeze adding to the chill of late autumn.

It wasn't going to get much warmer, and Jodi was starting to worry about what little warmth they did enjoy at the moment, leaking out of the day later in the afternoon.

At least they had food.

She had decided to feed the children their lunch when Pascal called out.

"A car. Look, an old car."

Jodi saw the vehicle, a genuine 70s antique or something, slowly approaching along the same unsealed country road on which Karl had driven away.

"That's a cool car. Can we have a ride, Mom?" Maxi asked.

"Maybe," she said, mainly to herself.

She used Damo's binoculars again to scope out the driver. Her hopes fell a little when she did not recognise the woman but soared when she realised Ellie was in the passenger seat.

"I don't think that car can get up here," Pascal said.

And he was right.

It was a hell of a ride, but it wasn't built for cross-country driving, and Jodi could see they'd have to meet it at the bottom of the hill.

"Okay, kids," she said. "We're gonna have to hike down to the road and carry all our stuff with us."

She expected them to complain, but they all cheered.

They wanted to get away as much as she did.

IT TOOK two trips to move everything down off the little knoll where they'd laid up, and on the second leg, they were helped by a young boy called Bobby Junior, which Maxi thought to be hilarious.

"Just like on TV," he said without further explanation.

The car, a dusty, battered Oldsmobile, pulled over at the side of the dirt track, and Ellie jumped out. Jodi ran down to her, and they hugged fiercely.

"Where were you? What happened? I was so worried," she babbled, her thoughts spilling together in a messy word salad.

"Oh baby, you do not want to know," Ellie said, pushing back out of their embrace for a second. "And you do *not* want to take the kids up there, believe me," she went on, throwing a glance back over her shoulder towards the campsite she had just left.

Jodi gathered her lover back into her arms again, squeezing hard, burying her face in the warm, familiar curves of Ellie's neck.

"Whatever you say, baby. I'm just so glad you're okay. What about Damo and Karl? Are they..."

"They're good," Ellie assured her. "They went into town to help out."

"Hey there," a woman said. "My name's Roxarne. But y'all can call me Roxy."

The driver was out of the car and leaning up against it, arms folded on the roof.

"Ellie tells me y'all are girlfriends, like for reals," she said.

"Yeah," Jodi said, unsure of what might be coming next. It'd been a long time since she'd had one of *those* conversations. Not since the mothers' group back in Oceanview, and those bitches were all dead. Probably.

"That's cool," the woman grinned. "I knew me some Ellen Degenerates back in Dillonvale."

Jodi flared at the term, but the woman was smiling harmlessly. There seemed to be no ill intent about her, no matter how ugly her language might be.

"Don't worry, she's cool," Ellie assured her in a whisper. She kissed Jodi on the ear.

"My friend Tammy and I are just normal friends. In case you might be wondering. I'm cool with you ladies banging clams, though, just so's we're clear. Tammy will be too. She's awesome. She's Bobby Junior and Wynona's mom, but Jakey and Liana are mine. And all we care about is getting these kids safe somewhere, so maybe we should all get the fuck gone now."

She climbed back into the Oldsmobile while Pascal and Bobby Junior loaded the last of the luggage into the trunk.

"Banging clams?" Jodi said.

Ellie rolled her eyes.

"A ride is a ride, baby. And this one is ours. Come on. We're gonna catch up with Damo and Karl."

The dirt road looped around the base of the hill where Roxarne and her friends had been camped.

"We're all moving into the town," the woman explained. "It ain't safe out here with all a-them freaks and goddamned weirdos about."

Jodi, who had squeezed into the back with the children, save for the little girl who rode up front between Ellie and Roxarne, bent down a little to look up-slope toward the camping ground. She could see that one of the big RVs had pulled out, and a couple of the other, smaller vehicles were following.

Roxarne's children were all very quiet, which seemed to dampen the spirits of Maxi and his friends as well, but they all perked up when Maxi showed them the Nintendo.

"Mom, we got batteries. Can we have the batteries?" the younger boy, Jakey, started up. His pestering tone was eerily similar to Maxi's.

Unlike Jodi, however, Roxarne did not even try to fend him off.

"Hell, yes!" She said. "Ellie, can you fetch that glove box open? There's a whole heap of batteries and Mophie chargers and stuff in there. We grab 'em up whenever we find 'em. Charge the Mophie's on the go."

"Don't you need them for important stuff? Like, I dunno, flashlights and radios?" Ellie said.

Roxarne laughed.

"Ain't nothing more important than keeping a car full of little ones entertained while you're trying to outrun the end of the damn world, girl. Fetch that recharger out and give 'em some juice. But don't you kids run it flat. I wanna play some too. What you got on that thing, Maxi? You got any Zelda?"

"I got Mario," Maxi answered.

The children cheered, all of them, and Jodi marvelled at how quickly Roxarne had flipped the mood in the car from tense and sombre to something much lighter.

"How long have you guys been on the road?" Jodi asked, knowing that it was a stupid question. They'd been running as long as everyone else. Since Zero Day. "Have you had much trouble getting here?" she added. Another dumb question, but what wouldn't be?

Roxarne was one of those drivers who hunched over the wheel as though she needed to watch the road roll under their front wheels.

"Oh man, you got no idea," she said as they left the shallow folds of the valley and hit a stretch of road running directly into town. It looked like the fields on either side had once been tilled for crops, but they had run to seed in the last few months and were knee-high with dry grass. A light breeze rolled over the pasture in waves.

"We got chased out of one place by about ten thousand zombies, it seemed. Not for real Walking Dead ones, of course, but it felt like it, didn't it, kids?"

"Fuck yeah," Bobby Junior concurred.

"Bobby!" Roxarne scolded. "Your momma gonna open a can of whup-ass on you, she hears you talking to company like that. And a second can on me for letting you get away with it. You fucking take it back right now."

"Hells yeah, I meant. Sorry, ma'am," Bobby Junior apologised, but he wasn't really paying attention to the grown-ups. Maxi had the Nintendo plugged into a power pack, and the children stared at the bright electric colors of the screen as if a portal to some magical realm had opened up in the back seat of the Oldsmobile.

"Share with the others, Maxi," Jodi warned, but he didn't need telling. He enjoyed his newfound status as the Switch Master, handing the device around like a powerful talisman.

Roxarne told them of their adventures, good and bad. She started with the escape from their hometown of Dillonvale back east and how they'd first hooked up with some travellers in a National Park in West Virginia before gathering more members of a pretty sizeable caravan headed to a farm in Montana. It belonged to someone in their party called James. She lowered her voice and spoke only in the vaguest terms about how they'd come to meet James and his friends Rick and Mel and Michelle in that park.

Jodi understood that the children had been in real danger but not what the nature of that danger might have been.

She and Ellie tag-teamed a recap of their escape from San Francisco with Ellie's boss Damo and with Karl, who'd rescued Jodi from a mugging and later from a potential murder, all on the first day of this thing.

"Y'all sailed away in a millionaire yacht?" Roxarne laughed, amazed. "You shoulda kept sailing."

It was not a long drive into Bachman, ten minutes or so at most, but Roxarne was a talker, and Jodi felt like she already knew many of the people in Roxy's little community before they reached town. There was Rick, a former soldier and their ass-kicker-in-chief. His girlfriend, Mel, who was a 'police lady' in London once but had moved to America with some other guy, not Rick, and it didn't work out. She was like their 'own personal PT now', Roxarne said. There was James, who was either a farm boy or a merchant banker; it was hard to tell which. His girlfriend Michelle, who Roxy thought was probably a spy. Some karate kid. A librarian. A schoolteacher. 'Poor Bruce', who was from South Africa but dead now, was "kil't by those crazies this morning". A whole bunch of school kids who had nothing to do with the schoolteacher. Some English guy. The roll call went on and on.

"It's like you've got a small town," Jodi said.

"Feels like a mad house on wheels most days," Roxarne said. "We're glad of it, though. Don't reckon we'd a made it this far without 'em."

As they neared the edge of town, they saw others on foot slowly trudging through the fields in groups of two or three. They looked ragged and starved. Hollow-eyed, sunken-faced, many of them wounded and bleeding.

"Who are they?" Jodi asked, worried that something was about to start up again. "Are they the ones who attacked you guys?"

Roxarne concentrated on the road, sparing only a glance out the riverside window.

"Yep," she said. "But t'weren't their fault, turns out. They was being forced to by this asshole called himself the Rector or the Reverend or something. Some kind of big religious cult guy. And these guys..." she jerked a thumb at two half-starved looking scarecrows carrying another between them "...they got themselves baptised into his stupid church whether they chose to or not."

Jodi craned her head as they drove past three of the closest figures.

It was hard to believe they were even Americans.

They looked like something you used to see on the news about wars and famines in other places.

As the Oldsmobile slipped past, they stopped and raised their bone-thin arms to wave. Two of them were crying, but Jodi Sarjanen had the unsettling sense that their tears were joyful.

17

NO CHOICE BUT TO RIDE

Bachman was a hell of a mess. Not the town so much as what had happened there. But Rick Boreham was less interested in that grim tale than he was in getting clear of the place. While James and the big-mouth Australian guy talked with one of the locals, Rick took charge of securing the prisoners.

That was one thing he knew how to do for sure.

The maximum asshole calling himself the Rector and all his true believers would have to be held as prisoners, and dangerous ones at that, while everything else got sorted.

"First thing we gotta do is break them up," Rick said.

"For sure," Mel agreed.

They still stood on the tarmac of the gas station on the edge of town. It was coming on for midday, with the autumn sun high over-head and warm when the breeze wasn't sweeping in from the Badlands. All of the captives in their weird sackcloth robes and their leader in his much tonier black satin vestments lay facedown on the concrete. Mel had supervised the job of tying their wrists together behind their backs. With no zip ties or handcuffs, they'd had to use whatever they could find nearby and had fettered the prisoners with an eclectic mix of restraints, from duct tape to pantyhose.

Now and then, one of them would complain, but Andrew Nesbitt would threaten to shoot their dear leader, and that usually shut them up. Or the Rector himself would, with a bit of encouragement from Nesbitt's boot and gun muzzle.

Rick wanted to put the lot of them on ice somewhere. As more of the townsfolk limped back into town, keeping them away from their former captors was getting hard.

As best he could tell, that was the deal here.

The cult had captured the town, and now the town was looking for payback.

"There's a lock-up a couple of streets over, according to them," Mel said, jerking a thumb in the direction of a couple of skeletal, half-crazed survivors watching avidly from the Texaco's compressed air station. "We could stack some of 'em in there. Lock a few more in the storeroom here. If we pushed that big coke machine behind the counter, I reckon it'd block the door nicely. And, I dunno, find somewhere secure for the rest. Padlock them into a barn or something. Gotta be a good barn around a cow town like this."

"Gotta be," Rick smiled at her obvious distaste for the environs of Bachman, Montana. It was the first time his face had lost any of its forbidding menace all morning.

Mel saw him smiling at her, and her face lit up in response.

"There he is, my pretty boy. It's like the sweetest little flower in a bloody great granite mountain your smile is, darlin'."

She leaned in and kissed him.

"You should give that pretty smile a little more sunlight."

Rick couldn't help it. He smiled some more.

JAMES O'DONNELL HAD BEEN in some pretty strange places and seen some weird and disturbing shit since this all started back in high summer. Standing under the late autumnal sun of his home state, watching a ghost town come back to life as the hungering, shrivelled spectres of its former inhabitants staggered into view was the damnedest thing so far.

"Fuck me, sideways," murmured the big Australian who'd saved his life less than an hour ago.

"I wouldn't know where to begin," James said absently. He was elsewhere. His mind wandering.

"Somewhere round the side, mate," Maloney lobbed back. "Usually."

And he fell silent again as they watched another group of stragglers appear from around a corner a little further up the road from the Texaco.

Their conversation was of a piece with the unfolding scene: absurd, disengaged, unplugged from anything real.

But what the hell is real here? James wondered.

These were the people he'd been trying to kill not so long ago—the same people trying to get into the camp to kill him. And Michelle and Roxy, and Laurence and Bruce.

Hell. They *had* killed Bruce.

He was still trying to process that. Bruce was gone.

But they weren't in the least way hostile. Not anymore.

Matter of fact, they were eerily submissive and even respectful.

"Mister O'Donnell?"

"Huh?"

"Mister O'Donnell? Are you okay?"

James blinked.

And seemed to fall back into himself as if from some great, unknowable height.

A different voice spoke in that thick accent. "Jimbo? You good, mate?"

James shook his head.

"I think I'm in shock," he said.

"Mister O'Donnell?"

He wasn't talking to Maloney, the Australian.

It was another man.

"Ray? Right?" he said.

The man nodded.

"Ray Clark, sir. I was... I was the letter carrier for Bachman. US Postal Service, sir. Twenty-three years. I delivered the mail here and Broadus and Powderville. I am... I guess I'm—"

"You're what's left of the local notables, are you, mate?" Damien Maloney said as the man seemed to lose the thread of his own words. "No mayor in town, then? No sheriff or anything?"

Ray Clark shook his head.

"Those people over there, they hung Sheriff Bannerman," he said, raising one skinny arm and pointing at the bizarre, almost medieval collection of women and men lying face down under the guns of Rick and the salvage crew. "Mayor Walters was already gone when they got here," Clark went on. "His medicines ran out, you see. I used to deliver them, too. Some of them, anyway. From Canada. It was cheaper, you see."

James nodded.

Once upon a time, he'd written a whole newsletter about Canada's thriving online trade in prescription medicines. Once upon a time, having a newsletter about stuff like that was a thing. That was how he came to meet Michelle. That must have been, what, two or three... hundred years ago.

"Mister Clark," he said as he struggled to regain some control over his wandering thoughts. "I'm sorry about, you know, what happened back up there—"

James gestured vaguely in the direction of the Cavalry Memorial.

Clark lifted his shoulders, sighed and let them slump.

"Hell of a thing that was, and not your fault, Mister O'Donnell, sir."

"Still..." James started to say.

But Ray Clark shook his head as firmly as he could in his infirm state.

"No, sir. This town owes you folks. You have set us free, Mister O'Donnell. And you, Mister...er?"

"Maloney," the Australian said when Clark obviously couldn't remember his name.

Had they been introduced, James wondered, but he caught himself before his mind could flitter away chasing that question.

He needed to dial in on this right now.

It seemed that Ray Clark was what passed for surviving authority in Bachman, and soon enough, it looked like any surviving townsfolk would be back in numbers. James, and now Maloney and his people, all had concerns they must see to.

"Mister Clark," he started, "We lost some people; you lost more. Some of them we killed—others we've done real harm to. I hope you can find it within yourselves to forgive us, sir, because we are in need of your forgiveness. And your help."

A small crowd was gathering a short distance from the Texaco.

Mel Baker had walked over to keep them in check. She looked just like the cop she had once been. James wondered how many townsfolk of Bachman, Montana would ever have seen a black police officer, let alone a black female 'Bobby' from old London town.

She was friendly but firm with them. Smiling but holding them back from the prisoners.

Two men and a woman who had come into town with Ray Clark, all of them looking as though they had slept rough and eaten bitter weeds and ground vermin for three months, stood a few yards away, shuffling back and forth, drawn toward the growing crowd at the gas station, but not wanting to break away from Clark.

They would flinch away whenever James looked over at them. Their presence was so powerfully woeful that he couldn't help but sneak the occasional peek at them. They drew his eye the way a wound sometimes itched for a finger to probe it.

"Any help we can render, we will do so gladly, sir," Ray Clark said.

"Petrol, mate. I mean, gas, sorry," Damien Maloney said.

He didn't mean to shout, but he was one of those men whose voice had a natural, booming quality, and Clark flinched a little under the aural assault.

But he nodded.

"There's still plenty of gas in the tanks here," he said. "And more out at the airfield. Not just Avgas, either. Old man Snell kept a pump out there for traffic coming east from the ranges."

"Sweet," Maloney said.

"And food," James added. "We need to trade for some food if that's possible. Not much. We haven't got much further to travel."

Ray Clark chewed at his lower lip.

"That might be more difficult," he said. "The Rector there had us on half rations. It was one of the ways they kept everyone in line. And how he made conversions, too. His... congregation ate better than we did."

Clark scowled at the man in the flowing black gown. Andrew Nesbitt was still standing over him, pointing a gun at the back of his head.

"Sounds like they'll have supplies then," Maloney said.

"I guess," Clark confirmed. "But part of the reason they set to waylaying travellers was to scavenge their food and supplies. And to collect..."

Clark stopped and chewed something over. It looked as if he was gnawing on a hard and bitter root. Finally, he found the words he needed.

"They collected breed stock. And culled the rest."

James and Maloney exchanged a look.

"Bugger me," the Australian said. "That bloke's a bit of an unshaved ball bag, isn't he."

"Indeed," Ray Clark agreed. Darkness filled his eyes as he glared at the captives under guard. It passed quickly, however, and he turned a grateful, almost kindly expression on the two outsiders.

"Mister O'Donnell, Mister Maloney, I can speak for the town because that's what I been doing these past..."

He trailed off.

"I don't know how long it's been. But we are done with this fellow now. Thanks to you. Fill your tanks. If you can find sustenance hereabouts, take what you need. We'll make do."

Clark's expression turned dark again as he pondered the bound and subdued prisoners.

"Once we've had a reckoning with these folks."

———————

THEY DID NOT LINGER in Bachman.

They drew the gas they needed and shared a meal with the newest members of their convoy.

Rick had been wary of Damien Maloney. On first impressions, he recalled all of the swaggering rich men Rick had once cleaned up after back at the Bretton Woods resort. But when he'd finally handed control of the prisoners over to Ray Clark and a posse of townsfolk and met the rest of Maloney's party under less difficult circumstances, he did warm to them. Part way, at least.

Also, Mel told him to take the pole out of his ass.

Except she said 'arse'.

"Bloody Aussies are all like that. It's just the convict strain coming through," she said, and Rick couldn't tell if she was joking.

But she spoke with Michelle, and both Michelle and James said that the crazies would have overrun the camp if not for the intervention of Maloney and his friends.

Nomi, who was always a better judge of people than Rick, approved of them, although that may have been due to all the deer jerky Maloney kept feeding her under the table.

The two parties came together for a meal in the larger of Bachman's public parks, where all the children could run a little wild, and the chef who was travelling with Maloney's crew turned out a surprisingly hearty meal on the park's propane barbecue plates.

Finding out about her was probably when Rick took his first real set against the Australian.

"Who the hell travels around the end of the world with their own damn chef?" he whispered to Mel, even as they tucked into the spicy fish tacos she had made for everyone. "Rich assholes, that's who," he muttered.

Mel rolled her eyes.

"She's a good cook, Luv. That's all. And she worked for him in his caf' back in the city. So, eat your fuckin' taco and behave."

Eventually, he behaved.

They had a chef *and* a driver travelling with them. But the 'driver' had been an E-4 with 7th Trans. He professed himself grateful and even humbled to have been invited along for the ride by Maloney and his two lady friends.

Mel rolled her eyes at that, too.

"They're not lady friends, Rick. They're lovers. Lush fucking girly finger friends. It's nice but, innit."

Rick made a discreet tactical withdrawal. Everyone else had filled up on tacos, smoked meat, and a salad that the cook, Ellie, scrounged up from the garden beds of the park. Rick was working on his fourth taco, sitting by himself on a bench, taking in the rays. The tacos were pretty damned good and fresh as hell. He wondered where she'd got the fixings for them.

"A word with you, son?" Karl said, sitting himself down next to Rick and offering him a beer. An actual beer, which was unexpectedly cold.

Karl smiled delightedly at Rick's surprise.

"We got a cooler we can run off the engine in the Land Rover," he explained. "It's supposed to be for fresh meat and such, but Damo usually finds room for a coupla beers in there. So, to your health."

"And yours," Rick said, accepting the chilled can of League Night Lager.

They did not speak immediately.

The mid-afternoon sun was warm on their faces, but an easterly breeze promised a long, cold night. The pleasant radiant heat would soon enough leak away as the shadows lengthened and night came in hard. For the moment, though, the two men, who were still strangers to each other but strangely bonded by the events of the day, sat quietly, enjoying the scene.

The three kids added to the small horde of children in Rick's caravan had blended in seamlessly. The boys—Rick did not know

their names yet—were trying to teach the younger ones a form of
football, which Rick had to assume was some barbarian code from
Down Under. The squeals and the screaming seemed louder than
usual, and the running about a little more frantic and wilder, which
all made sense given everything they had witnessed earlier. It would
be a good thing that the children ran themselves ragged before night
fell.

Rick sipped at his beer. "The air here, it feel like the sandbox to
you, brother?"

Karl nodded. "Yeah, around Mosul in November. It's all the desert
out there, I guess."

The older man looked around with slitted eyes and sighed. Something changed his mind. "No, now that I think on it," Karl Valentine
said, "It reminds me more of Baghlan on the Ring Road."

The Ranger nodded. "You're well-travelled."

Karl shrugged. "Everyone needs a ride, son."

The men sat silently with their beers, the memory of the call to
prayer, the echoing *adhan* hovering between them. Across the other
side of the park, James O'Donnell stood with his hand around
Michelle Nguyen's shoulder, and they both laughed at some story the
Australian was telling. It involved a lot of acting out and cartoonish
gestures. Peter Tapsell was over there, too, sharing a beer with
Ramona Tilley and a heavily bandaged Sparty Williams.

They were all laughing at Maloney's performance.

It was Karl who broke the silence between the two former
soldiers.

"These people I'm with," he said. "They're good people, Rick. You
can trust them."

Rick said nothing, but he did not disagree. Not out loud.

Laurence Bloomfield ran past, holding a football, trailed by a
swarm of happily screaming children and one barking black dog. He
meant to talk with Laurence a little bit later. Nomi had saved the boy,
James said. But it had been a hard save. He did not want the kid to
have to deal with that alone. Rick had tried to deal with things by
himself after his first tour. It did not go well.

He searched for what he wanted to say. For what needed to be said.

He cleared his throat.

"James tells me you did good work this morning, Karl. All of you. I have to thank you all for that. These are my friends. Family, I guess."

Karl sipped at the beer. He looked uncomfortable.

"Hell of a thing, using people like that," Karl said. "The way that preacher did. I feel bad we hurt so many innocent ones."

"He's no preacher," Rick said. "Just another killer, I reckon."

Karl nodded. "Amen to that, brother. And I say to Hell with all the holy killers."

They clinked the beer cans together.

Rick Boreham imagined that it would be hard, looking on without context, to tell this scene apart from any holiday weekend. The RVs and sports utilities. The ladies working the barbecues. A pack of rowdy children tear-assing around a park with a football. A couple of gents sharing a beer.

But context was everything.

Those vehicles, those people, had all been on the road for months and not for the pleasure of it. Not for the adventure of a lifetime but because they were all running from the reality of adventure. That was just another name for when terrible things happened to everyday people, far from the safety of home. The small western town, picturesque and a little enchanting in the golden afternoon light, held fast within its borders to all manner of darkness. The townspeople hailed them as liberators, but that would not last. Even now, they held back from the outsiders. The postman, Clark, had visited their little picnic not half an hour ago, enquiring about their needs and plans.

He seemed relieved that they would leave sooner rather than later.

Working bees toiled here and there to return Bachman to its former amenity. Rick could hear hammers and saws in the distance, and while that might seem to fit with the repairs he could see underway to the sheriff's office and council rooms, he knew that the workers were not raising a town hall or stands and seating for some community event.

They were putting up the gallows from which their former tormentors would swing.

"So..." Rick started to say before he knew what he wanted to ask.

He fell silent.

"Go on, son," Karl Valentine urged him.

"So, do you mind if I ask... how come you decided to ride in and help?"

Karl finished his beer and smiled, but whether at the question or the pleasure of his cold lager, Rick could not say.

"That was Miss Jodi," Karl said.

"I'm sorry, which one is she?" Rick asked.

Karl pointed at the beautiful woman with ice-blond hair. She stood at the barbecue plate with her arm around the waist of the shorter, darker woman from Karl's group. The cook with all the tattoos.

"Miss Jodi couldn't abide the idea of leaving those children to whatever was about to happen," he said. "She convinced us it was well past time for the cavalry to ride on that hill again."

He seemed pleased with the allusion and nodded as if recognising the historical echo.

"And you? And Maloney?" Rick asked.

They sat on a park bench. Valentine tried to turn around to look Rick Boreham in the eye. He was in his late forties, and the years had stiffened him up.

"Well, son, we didn't know you then—none of you. We didn't know what we'd be getting into if we decided to make that ride. There was a good argument for leaving you to it."

Rick nodded. The man's face was open and honest.

"But you didn't leave us to it."

"Nope. There was another argument, and Miss Jodi made it. In not so many words, she said that given our current difficulties—what with so many folks turned one against another—it was a laydown certainty that those who would go to the effort of caring for so many children would not likely be the sort to turn against others for selfish advantage."

Rick Boreham took a moment to weigh all of it.

Karl smiled and nodded.

"Bottom line, son. She figured you for good folk. So we had no choice but to ride in."

THEY RODE out as night fell.

Evening came early and fast, with the sun falling below the dark line of low hills to the west in the late afternoon. Home – James's home, which had become some form of a Promised Land to the group – was somewhere ahead of them. Another two weeks away, maybe three, depending on the road.

They did not bury Lew Gibb or Bruce Goldie.

"We would consider it an honour if you would leave their care to us," Ray Clark said.

James and Rick stood a short distance from the Sierra, the lead vehicle in the convoy, which was now larger by one car. Damien Maloney's Land Rover.

They each shook hands with the postman.

"We would appreciate that very much," James said. "They were good men."

"We have our people to lay down to their rest," Ray Clark said. "And Mister Gibb and Mister Goldie will rest with them. It's only fitting."

They said thank you again.

Few of Bachman's other inhabitants were there to see them off, but James was glad.

It was strange. The whole thing was strange, and James would be glad to leave it behind.

Ray Clarke waved them off as they drove away.

"You think they'll make it?" James said.

He wasn't asking anyone in particular.

They rolled slowly past the gallows in the second, smaller park at the other end of town.

"I don't know," Michelle answered.

18

TURDS IN THE HOT TUB

The Sacajawea Hotel blazed with warmth and light in the wintry dark, a beacon shining in the cheerless gloom. An elegant chateau of white clapboards and deep verandahs, it had been one of the finest historic hotels in the West. In 2011, after careful restoration work and a successful relaunch, it was recognised by the Historic Hotels of America with a Preservation Award of Excellence. There was a polished brass plaque and everything. The Sacajawea had boasted one of the best steakhouses in all of Montana —quite a boast when you thought about it—and its twenty-nine guest rooms were renowned among connoisseurs of luxury frontier travel.

Jonas had moved in for the winter with some bitches.

He had the best rooms in the house, of course. And first pick of the quality gash headed to the Officers' Club. It should have been the perfect fuck-you to Montana's gathering snowpocalypse, but he could tell he wasn't gonna be allowed to enjoy it.

Not today, and certainly not by Mathias Runeberg.

The Legion's Chief of Operations—a bullshit title Runeberg had insisted on taking for his own—had just wheeled in an electronic whiteboard from somewhere. This was not good. They'd already sat through a two-hour presentation from him on the Bozeman siege, and Jonas was nearly tripping balls from the tedium. But as bad as that'd been, at least it hadn't needed a fucking whiteboard.

And not just that, but an *electronic* whiteboard with an inbuilt printer.

Jonas Murdoch could feel his cock shrivelling in anticipation of all the spreadsheets Runeberg was about to crap out into his day. This tedious shit was why he'd stashed the admin dorks in that shithole motel across town. But the tedium followed him everywhere.

He caught Leo Vaulk's attention across the room. Leo, who was way better than Jonas at this sort of management bullshit and admin-istrivia, rolled his eyes – but only while Mathias had his back to them, filling the smart board with dense blocks of writing in his small, precise script. It was too small to read, but that's why he'd brought in the smart board. They were about to get buried in printouts.

"You gonna be long, Matty?" Jonas called out.

Runeberg stopped scribbling and half-turned around. He looked almost hunchbacked to Jonas, an effect not helped by his shaved head, narrow features, and long, spindly arms. Everything about this guy seemed awkward and just slightly distorted.

There was no denying his brainiac cred, though. Dude totally had a dose of screeching autism, but that was the price of being a fucking human supercomputer, Jonas supposed.

"Three minutes," Runeberg said, and Jonas did not doubt he would fill that whiteboard with text in as close to one hundred and eighty seconds as made no fucking difference.

"Gonna grab me some white-man crank," Jonas said. "Coffee," he added when Runeberg frowned. "I'm gonna take five and grab a cup of Joe."

He could feel the relief washing around the room at the announcement. Most of the Legion's top guys were not like Runeberg or Leo. Before all of this, they hadn't sat on their asses for a living.

"You keep on trucking there," Jonas said. "But don't give yourself a hand cramp. Everyone else should take five," he called out.

The collective groan of relief was loud, and the clatter of chairs followed almost immediately as everyone stood to stretch and refuel.

Everyone but Tommy Podesta, who was already at the coffee machine, putting in his order. Runeberg bent back to his task.

More than a dozen men and two women sat on the Legion's War Council, convened today in the largest conference room of The Saca-jawea Hotel - a generous space warmed by two roaring log fires to hold back the chill from the long wall of French windows. These afforded a pleasant view of the manicured lawn surrounded by a mini-village of tiny white cottages where most of his guards were billeted. Two guards from the Cohort stood out there in winter gear, stamping their feet and smoking to stay warm. Inside the room, a long table was filled to the edges with fresh sandwiches and little cakes, while a sergeant of the Cohort—formerly one of Starbucks' finest—stood ready to fill any hot beverage orders.

Jonas checked his watch, the same timepiece he'd been wearing since bugging out of Seattle, a Swiss analogue model he'd stolen from work and still got a kick out of winding up every day. It reminded him what he'd got away with.

10.34 AM.

Jesus Christ. He'd woken up early for this thing, too. So early that the two smokin' hotties he'd left back in his bed had probably turned gay waiting on him to return.

He started to stir, thinking about them macking on each other's sweet little pussies, while he was trapped down here cosplaying competence at managerial chickenshit. Maybe if he stretched the break to fifteen minutes, he could dash upstairs for a quickie?

"Hey, boss?"

Fuck.

It was Leo, of course. Like the dude had a sixth sense or something.

"Yeah, man," Jonas sighed. "What is it? As long it's not logistics. Or ops. Or anything that can wait until this fucking snooza-palooza is over."

Jonas could see from the look on Leo's fat face that whatever it was, it was snooze-adjacent, but the big guy ploughed on anyway.

"I got the mayor and his engineer outside," he said. "They been waiting an hour."

"That's not a good use of their time," Jonas drawled. "Maybe they should fuck off?"

Leo chuckled.

"Yeah. Good one. But no. They're not going anywhere. Said it's real important they see you."

And for some reason, Leo had decided it was even more important that Jonas be bothered by it. He wondered whether this was why Travis, his douchebag boss back at the Amazon warehouse, had been such a prickle dick. Because of the stress of dealing with one whiny asshole after another.

Nah, Jonas decided. Travis was just a natural-born asshole.

But he would admit it was super fucking stressful, having to sit still and listen to the whiny asshole parade, day after day. No denying that.

No escaping it either, it turned out.

"Alrighty then. But at least let me get my fuckin' cup of coffee, Leo. Runeberg's giving me fucking semi-narcolepsy."

"Haha. Good one, boss," Leo chuckled dutifully again.

The Cohort barista fixed him a long black coffee with just a dash of creamer. Another weakness that had crept into his diet, but surely nobody could blame him for that. Not if they saw the shit he had to put up with these days.

Leo led the way through the small crowd at the buffet, snow-ploughing them aside to stop anybody from way-laying Jonas. A couple of guys tried—he was always in demand—but Leo forged on into the smaller adjoining room where the mayor of Three Forks and his city engineer sat waiting for them. They stood up as soon as Jonas appeared and nodded but didn't salute.

Salutes were only for Legionnaires.

"Mister Mayor," Jonas said in a loud, welcoming voice, psyching himself up for this. "And Mister... Sewage and Water! Hail fellows, and well the fuck met. What can I do for you today?"

Neither man looked happy to see him, but the little engineer seemed the least happy of the two. Jennings deferred to him.

"You go first, Dan."

Dan McNabb. Yeah, Jonas recalled. That was this runty little asshole's name.

"Mister Murdoch," the engineer said. He did not try to shake hands. "Your man Runeberg, is he here?"

"Matty? I wish I could say no, but yeah, he is. This is pretty much his show this morning. Why?"

McNabb, a small, wiry man with rapidly receding hair, pursed his lips and knit his brows together as though contemplating something deeply unpleasant.

"You may want to get him out here for this. Just to be fair."

"He's busy," Jonas said. "And I was already bored, so maybe step on the gas here."

The two city officials exchanged a look. McNabb went on.

"I don't know how much you know about the city's water and waste management infrastructure—"

"Nothing," Jonas said. "And I really fucking hope you're not about to try and change that."

If he'd hoped to cower McNabb, he failed. The engineer carried on regardless.

"I am because you need to understand what's happening unless you want to be knee-deep in human effluent by this time next week."

Leo Vaulk leaned forward and muttered in Jonas's ear, "He's talking about the generators at the sewage processing plant."

"Jesus Christ," Jonas muttered loud enough for all of them to hear. "I didn't think this morning could get any worse, but I was wrong."

"Mr Murdoch," Ross Jennings said, "Please."

The man seemed genuinely butt hurt, and McNabb beside him was almost shaking with anger or from the effort of containing his anger. Either way, this looked like one of those horror shows that seemed to take up virtually all his time now. He had assumed that the conqueror's life would be all about pumping and munching his way through heaps of tribute pussy, with the occasional night off to watch his gun wagons dismantle a rebel village or two.

Instead, it was death by PowerPoint and municipal infrastructure. Hell Week, every week, from this day to the heat-death of the fucking universe.

"Just get to the point," he sighed.

"Runeberg wants to pull the Siemens generator out of the sewerage plant," McNabb said.

He stared at Jonas as if this explained everything.

"So?" Jonas shrugged.

McNabb squeezed his eyes shut and opened them again. Jonas was still standing there and looking no better informed than he had been a second ago.

"He wants to replace the Siemens with another generator salvaged from Livingston," McNabb went on. "But with all the extra people in town, we need the higher capacity genny running around the clock."

Jonas turned to Leo.

"Why am I here?"

Leo organised his features into what Jonas always thought of as Leo's Serious Face.

"Actually, boss," Leo said. "I can confirm what Mister McNabb is saying."

"Which is what?" Murdoch said, noting how Vaulk had carefully referred to the engineer as 'Mister'. Leo was one of those guys who kissed up and kicked down. And McNabb was definitely the bottom in any relationship with anyone from the Legion. So, there was something else going on here. No doubt.

"Mathias wants the Siemens unit for the siege works around Bozeman," Leo said. "And Mister McNabb can't really give it up because he's worried that swapping in the Guangzhou model is a shit idea. Like, literally. If it can't keep up with the extra demand on the processing plant because of all the guys we got billeted here in town on top of the refugees they already took in, the genny will fry, the plant will shut down, and we'll end up with turds in the hot tub. For real. I think he's right."

Leo Vaulk, mission accomplished, folded his arms.

Jonas looked at McNabb.

He was nodding.

"Go on," Jonas said, weary of the charade.

"We need that Siemens unit up and running twenty-four-seven," Leo continued. "I told Mathias if he wanted more capacity for Bozeman, there's a whole goddamn country out there with this shit just lying around waiting to be salvaged. He should send a crew out. But he doesn't like that because he's got other priorities for heavy salvage. But boss, unless you want to pull on the hip waders..."

Leo showed Jonas his open palms.

Jonas rolled his eyes.

"Fine. The Siemens generator stays online here. But Leo, you're logistics. If Runeberg needs a bigger generator for Bozeman, that's your job. You send a team out."

"Sure," Leo said so quickly and happily that Jonas couldn't help but imagine he'd just been played off a break.

"Is that all?" he said.

"One more thing," Mayor Jennings went on. "It's... well, it's delicate."

"Oh, for fucks sake. What now?" Jonas asked. "Leo?"

But Vaulk shook his head.

"I just needed the okay for the salvage team."

Jonas finally caught on. "Because Runeberg wouldn't release one?"

Leo looked as though he'd just been caught with his hand in the cookie jar.

Jonas decided he would deal with that later. Or not. He turned to Jennings. "Er, what's your issue, Mister Mayor?"

Ross Jennings shook his head.

"It's the... the officer's club or whatever you call it that you've got running at the motel. At The Continental Divide."

Jonas couldn't help grinning. Finally, a diversion.

"The comfort station," he said.

"It's a brothel," Dan McNabb objected.

"Meh. Tom-ar-to, tom-ay-to," Jonas shrugged.

This, at least, he could enjoy, watching this pair of cucks get their panties in a bunch just because some real men copped a blow job and a cold beer.

"You didn't flag any of this with us before we agreed to sign on to your Legion," Ross Jennings said.

"And I didn't discuss my preference for folding over scrunching when I take a shit because it's none of your goddamn business," Jonas countered.

McNabb's jawline bulged as he ground his teeth together but said nothing. Ross Jennings wasn't about to be cowed, however.

Okay. Good for him, Jonas thought. Finally, showing some spine.

"It is unacceptable," the mayor insisted. "We don't do things like that in this town."

Jonas snorted.

"Roscoe, everyone does it. It's perfectly natural, man."

"You know what I mean," he shot back.

Jonas wiped the smile from his face and any trace of friendliness from his voice. He liked a guy who could stand up for himself, but there were limits to his indulgence. He was in charge here, and it was past time for Jennings to understand that.

He stepped up into the other man's grill.

"You got your way on the generator because that was city business. The comfort stations are the Legion's concern, not yours. My men go into harm's way to protect you people. They take casualties. If you want a say in the Legion's business, you take the oath and take the same risks they do fighting bandits and gangsters and shit. Until then, I suggest you shut the fuck up. None of your women are working at the Officer's Club or the Enlisted Men's Rec Centre here in town. That's not how we do it. But if any do volunteer for comfort duties elsewhere," he added, "It's not your fucking say so whether they go or not. This is the twenty-first century, Mister Mayor. A woman's choice is her own to make. You need to get woke to that new reality or get fucked. We're done."

And with that, Jonas turned on his heel and stalked away, primarily so that nobody could see the smirk spreading across his face or how much trouble he was having not laughing.

That was almost as much fun as an old-fashioned internet pile-on.

He grinned openly as he pushed through the doors back into the conference room.

His temper had improved so much that not even Mathias Runeberg, standing at his smart board, impatient and vibrating like a giant vertical ass polyp fit to fucking burst, was enough to sour his mood.

THERE WERE MOMENTS, and increasingly whole days, when Jonas Murdoch preferred memory to reality. He wasn't going crazy. It was just that reality sucked. Back in the conference room, his ass growing numb as he sat through another presentation by Mathias Runeberg, this one about the siege of Bozeman, Jonas wondered what might've happened if he hadn't lost his shit and punched Omar in the face. You know, all the way back on the very first day.

Runeberg was gibbering about the need for more earthmoving equipment, drone surveillance and generators outside of Bozeman. Jonas was trying to concentrate because people would expect him to at least lead the discussion afterwards, but his eyes gradually unfocused. His thoughts slipped back to that day in August when he realised that Omar and Yolanda had fucked him by concern-trolling management with a lot of bullshit sexual harassment complaints. He could feel his old rage rising as he thought on it, even though the whole thing could've happened a thousand fucking years ago for all it mattered now. That world was deader than Elvis.

And Hell, he probably owed them anyway. If he hadn't lost his rag, hauled off and broken Omar's jaw, he would never have had to flee the warehouse, steal his roommate's mountain bike and bounce the fuck out of Seattle to dodge an arrest for assault.

He chuckled at that. It drew some confused looks as everybody wondered why the boss was so tickled by this punishingly detailed briefing on the crucial need to apply rigorous audit and risk management protocols to a quarantine cordon around the besieged city of Bozeman. But Jonas had knocked the hell out of that uppity black prick, and as good as it felt at the time, he could see now how crucial a moment it'd been in his life.

Most people never got that, Jonas knew. Most people were sheep, and if they ever reached a fork in the road, it would never occur to them to take the path less travelled. Mostly, they'd stand around chewing on the grass and enjoying the occasional dump. But Jonas Murdoch hadn't, and that's why he was here, and they had all gone to the slaughter.

Runeberg droned on, "If you turn to appendix 5 in the second volume of the first report on estimated—"

Jonas tuned him out and went back to his happy place.

Usually, that would be the hot tub back in his room, but for now, he retreated to a chillout zone inside his head where he congratulated himself on how he'd smoothly managed to pull all of this shit together. A little murder. Some light treason. And a lot of smooth talking.

Getting out of Seattle, he would mark down to good luck. He hadn't known what the fuck he was doing other than bailing on a bad situation at work. It hadn't occurred to him for another day or two that the motherfucker of all traffic jams that locked up the city's road system was part of something much bigger. He hadn't even noticed the collapse of electronic payments or the cell phone network. After all, he'd ditched his phone so the cops couldn't track him, and he'd broken into his roommate's piggy bank to steal about a thousand bucks in cash. Another stand-out decision.

He quickly covered his mouth as he snorted in amusement.

How was Mikey, he wondered.

Chances were Mikey Summers never even made it home to discover his roommate's treachery, Jonas decided.

Asshole probably died defending the Supermall Burger King from food rioters.

Jonas composed himself and looked around the room as if making sure everybody was paying extra close attention to Matty Runeberg's fascinating fucking thesis on whatever the hell he was talking about now.

And just like naughty children, all his eager little beavers bent to their notepads and scribbled harder.

All of them except Tommy Podesta, who was sipping coffee from one of those tiny little cups over by the window. And Luke Bolger, whose natural state of being was random rage in search of a focal point. Even Leo Vaulk, who could be a lazy fuck, was hard at work, but Jonas figured he was just scheming for some way to shit-can Runeberg and take over his turf. Those two were always looking for a chance to blade each other.

It was a good thing he'd done, putting together this pirate crew. At first, it was just a bunch of assholes like Brad Rausch and Leo Vaulk, and Jonas didn't even know what he was building at the time. He was just keeping his options open and making sure he had locals to speak for him while he was holed up in Silverton. But he could see now that those guys, especially the late Dale Juntii, had formed a beta version of the Legion with him. A dependable crew, and each man with something to offer. Rausch had the vehicles they used to escape when the time came. Leo had his stockpile of weapons and, just as importantly, the weakness of character to make a really dependable sidekick.

As for Dale, he was just a champion ass-kicker. The ex-Marine was another reason Jonas was still around. He'd saved his life more than once in Silverton and on the road afterwards.

Not for the first time, Jonas found that he really missed Dale Juntii. Not in any kind of homogay way. It wasn't like they were Canadian wrestling buddies or anything. But Dale was solid. And a dude who kept his opinions to himself most of the time. But when he shared them, they were worth hearing; if he didn't, they were usually worth seeking out.

Hell of a shame what happened to him, Jonas thought.

His eyes narrowed slightly, and sought out Luke Bolger. The Legion's military commander, dressed as usual in a spanky mix of surplus army camo and urban warfare chic, had sat himself down at the end of the table so he could study Runeberg's whiteboard without having to crane his head around.

Jonas wasn't a hundred per cent sure that Bolger had killed Dale, and the guy had straight up denied it. But it was a righteous certainty that Bolger had hated the guy. It was just one of those things when two men instantly disliked each other. Dale had been all in on taking Wenatchee. They needed food and shelter. But for once, he'd spoken his mind when Luke had said they should hang the town's leaders as a warning to others.

Dale Juntii had not approved.

Bolger looked up from the notes he was taking, saw Jonas staring at him, and raised both eyebrows as if to ask, "What's up?"

Jonas blew out his cheeks as though he was bored, which he was, and Bolger nodded in sympathy before returning to his notes.

If you're going to bullshit somebody, Jonas knew, the best sort of lie is always wrapped around a sweet little candy corn kernel of truth. It was an undeniable truth that these briefings were hard work, and everybody knew that they bored the hell out of him. He shifted his gaze away from Bolger, but he couldn't help but tease the question, like probing a broken tooth with the tip of his tongue. Did that guy kill Dale? He was more than capable of it.

Mathias, meanwhile, had moved on from Bozeman to talking about the bigger picture, which Jonas could follow without any immediate danger of face-planting into his coffee with extreme prejudice.

"Signals intelligence –"

Runeberg meant listening to the radio.

"– indicates that another three of the former regime's so-called stronghold cities have collapsed," he said. "Kansas City, Boulder, and

Portland have all gone dark. This leaves Sacramento as the largest concentration of Federal forces in our area of responsibility."

Jonas blinked the sleep from his eyes and sat up, immediately causing a ripple around the table as everybody noticed him paying attention.

It was Bolger who spoke up, though.

"Any further or better particulars about the feds in Sacramento?"

Runeberg looked annoyed to be interrupted, but he always had the relevant information to hand. Consulting a clipboard, he picked up from the table in front of him, he replied, "Intelligence indicates that additional forces from the Pacific Northwest have redeployed to Sacramento, adding another ten to fifteen thousand active-duty personnel to their order of battle."

That called forth a buzz of worried murmurs. It'd been a while since anybody heard of the Feds being able to move those kinds of numbers. Nobody expected the literal fucking cavalry to come riding down on them any time soon. If ever. But everyone in this room had done things that could be counted not just as crimes but as crimes against humanity.

Not just killings, but murder. And not just murder, but atrocities.

It was unlikely any judge would countenance a defence that rationalised ends over means when the ends had been the survival of a few, and the means had been the extermination of so many.

"Hey, Matty," Jonas called out, cutting off the rising unrest. "Remind me about Sacramento, man. Why are the feds hunkering down there?"

Everybody turned back toward the Chief of Operations. He answered without consulting any briefing notes.

"Sacramento is an inland port surrounded by a couple of thousand square miles of productive agricultural land. Even during the so-called Great Drought, the hinterland was well watered by industrial-scale irrigation. They can grow enough food to keep at least one million people on subsistence rations, and inefficiencies at the Port of Sacramento meant that large stockpiles of stable nutritional resources were held in store."

"But it's not sustainable, right?" Jonas said.

Runeberg shook his head.

"I don't believe so, no. My modelling predicts that Sacramento, like the other designated strongholds, will exhaust its stockpiles and replacement capacity before the end of winter. They will starve, and they will collapse."

"Sounds good to me," Jonas declared, looking around the room. "So, you can all just suck up that little bit of wee you just made in your pants…" this earned a few wry laughs, "…and get back to worrying about what's really important. Getting our shit together in the here and the now. The Old Republic is dead. We're gonna build a new one. Matty, carry on."

Jonas's intervention visibly eased Runeberg's disgruntlement at the interruption. He returned to his briefing, which moved on to a summary of what they knew from overseas.

Short, because the answer was 'not much.'

China and large swaths of Asia were a vast open grave filled with billions of corpses piled up by the virus – an *actual* fucking virus, not some bullshit computer thing – that had run wild there and almost nowhere else. Europe wasn't much better, although it was the first horseman of the apocalypse who'd got loose over there when the Russian Federation sent its massed tank divisions west. Fat lot of good that had done them.

"The Russian Federation is now functionally extinct," Runeberg said.

That was a bummer, Jonas thought.

Vladimir Putin had been one ironclad motherfuckin' badass.

He tuned out again. There was no doubt the world had been remade, or at least that the old world was gone, and if it was gonna be remade, the job would fall to small bands of hard-core fucking samurai, just like the ones he had knitted together into the Legion of Freedom.

He checked his watch and stifled a sigh. Hours to go until lunchtime and the chance to sneak away to his room for a quick threesome with his apocalypse hotties.

19

THE SURVIVAL ENVELOPE

When James O'Donnell studied economics at Montana State in Bozeman, he and his friends often drove five hours east to party in Billings. They joked that Billings was three times the size of Bozeman and at least half as much fun. James had no idea how many times he'd made that run along the I-90. Dozens? Maybe a hundred or more? Enough that he knew not to trust it for the last leg of their trip to his parent's ranch. It wouldn't be a thousand-mile wrecking yard, like the freeway system of LA, but there would be more than enough breakdowns and crashes and chokepoints and fortified towns that they'd be a hell of a lot better off diverting along the minor, less travelled state roads to the north. Especially if it meant avoiding whatever happened to Billings.

It was Michelle, of course, who first suggested they route around the city. With a population topping out well over a hundred thousand, there was no way it could have survived. There was a size above which urban centres could not endure when the hyper-complex supply chains upon which they depended failed. Billings wasn't a federally designated stronghold city. It had no access to large nutritional stores, no significant military installations, and no strategic value worth protecting. Like every other place that couldn't feed itself when the Chinese pulled the plug, it would have collapsed. Too many souls living within the city limits and not enough food, medicine or power to sustain them.

"We need to give it at least a fifty-mile swerve," Michele warned as they planned the last leg of their journey. "And a hundred would be better."

James directed the caravan north, his fears about what he might find when they arrived home growing with every hour. It had been a long time since he had spoken to his parents. He'd managed a quick call on Michelle's sat phone just before the satellite networks went dark, so they knew he was coming, or at least they had known. And James had warned them it might take a few weeks to make the journey.

He had been nearly three months on the road.

Would they be all right?

James hoped they were far enough away from any big population centres to ride out the collapse. But there was Livingston, ten miles upriver, and it was on the edge of what Michelle called the survival envelope. Twice as large as any small town they had seen pull through but nested within a rich, rural hinterland with plenty of nutritional sources and social capital.

Michelle Nguyen was a big believer in the value of social capital. Stuff like trust and understanding and simple neighbourly concern.

James's fears and hopes chased each other like dogs in accelerating, diminishing circles as he drove through Montana's eastern plains, and the land gradually rose towards the foothills of the continental divide.

They had to negotiate roadblocks run by local folk at Musselshell, on the river, and a couple of hours further along State Route 3 at a crossroads town called Roundup. His old Montana driver's licence got them through the first one, and ten pounds of Eliza Jabbarah's deer jerky bought passage through the second. They had to abandon Bruce Goldie's RV just outside Shawmut when it ran out of gas. But by then, James knew they were less than a day's good driving from his parent's ranch and maybe less than that if they had good luck.

Their luck nearly ran out in Livingston.

The county seat had been a small but thriving gateway to Yellowstone, a couple hours' drive south of US 89. James was at the wheel of his SUV when the remains of the city came into view. It was not the first burned-out ruin he had seen, but it was the first one that meant anything to him. He decelerated so quickly that Karl Valentine in the Land Rover behind them had to swerve sharply to avoid rear-ending him. James had led the convoy down Willow Creek Road, and apart from weaving around a couple of abandoned pickups and sedans, the back road into Livingston had been clear. It had been many years since he had driven it, long enough that the little bridge across Ferry Creek snuck up on him. It was late in the day when they crossed the tree-lined waterway, and James had forgotten about the sharp bend in the road on the other side. He handled the sudden course correction, but he wasn't ready for the sight that greeted him when he wrenched the wheel through the ninety-degree turn. Half of Livingston was gone. Just... gone.

"Holy crap!" James said as he pumped the brakes.

The big SUV skidded on loose gravel. Dozing in the passenger seat, Rick Boreham came awake with a startled shout.

Sitting between Michelle and Melissa, Nomi squealed and barked in the back. Like Rick, Mel had been dosing. On the other hand, Michelle was wide awake, but her head was buried deep inside a Kindle. It flew out of her hands as the vehicle slewed to a stop.

"The fuck, James?" she cried out.

He started to apologise.

"Sorry, sorry," he said. "It's just, I know this place. It's... it shouldn't be like this."

His voice was shaky and a little too loud.

The other vehicles slowed and stopped behind them. Doors opened and closed along the line of the convoy. Rick took the AR15, his preferred personal weapon, from the gun rack on the dashboard.

"Wait. Are we getting out?" Michelle asked.

James said nothing. He just stared at the archaeological ruins of the town he had always considered home.

Livingston sat on the interstate just outside Paradise Valley, a long, wide, fertile plain running north-south between the Absaroka Range in the east and the higher, fiercer ramparts of the Gallatin in the west. The valley was ten miles across at its widest spot but much narrower for most of its length and neatly divided into three by US 89, the Yellowstone River, and a quieter two-lane state road that everybody just called the East River Road. His parents' ranch was about nine miles down that road in a secondary valley, carved from the granite and bedrock of the Absaroka by two streams and hundreds of springs over a couple of million years.

O'Donnells had worked the rich volcanic soils of the valley for more than a century. And the Livingston of his memory was his hometown. It was where he had gone to school, kissed his first girl, drunk his first beer, and passed out face down in the sawdust behind the Stockman Bar. All on the same night. James stepped out of the Sierra on legs that had gone rubbery. He tried to make sense of the burned-out buildings and piles of shattered rubble in front of him.

"You okay, man?" Rick asked.

Michelle came up beside him and took his hand, threading her arm through his.

"Hey baby," she said. "Come on. This is not the ranch. I can give you a hundred different reasons for something like this happening. None of them involving barbarian hordes or Chinese drone strikes."

He squeezed her fingers gently.

"It's just... a shock is all," James said.

More members of the caravan joined them. They had been driving for at least five hours, and everyone was grateful for a chance to stretch their legs. Children spilled onto the grass by the side of the road, whooping and yelling as they chased each other through the knee-high greensward. They had all seen so many burned-out towns that another one meant nothing to them.

"I don't reckon we're getting through there," Karl Valentine said. "Leastways, not your big motorhome. Looks like that road is blocked to any kind of traffic."

"How far away from your oldies' place are we, Jimbo?" Damien Maloney asked.

Michelle warned him off the question with a shake of the head.

"No, no, it's all right," James said. "I just wasn't ready for this."

He turned his back on the ruins of the town. Nearly two dozen people waited on him.

"We can work our way around Livingston," James said, getting his nerves under control. "Or what's left of it, which isn't much, I'd say. We cut across the interstate and down into the valley. There's no way the river road will be blocked. We're not that far from home. My home. And yours too, for as long as you need."

"We should probably scope out the road ahead anyway," Rick said. "Might be we can leave Sparty's RV here and come back for it later."

Sparty Williams agreed. His leg was bandaged and splinted, and he didn't want to prolong the journey by another day.

"Okay," James said. "Okay. You're right. We should check it out."

He didn't get his rifle from the car, and maybe that saved him. When he started walking toward the burned-out wreckage of his hometown, he was unarmed.

The bullet that dug up the soil in front of him was a warning shot. It cracked out of the deepening cool of late afternoon like thunder on a clear day. James was so surprised he didn't immediately dive for cover. Maybe that saved him too.

Behind him, everyone else scrambled. Somebody screamed, and the children dived into the thick, tall grass, hiding themselves as they had been taught.

"James, get out of the damn way," Rick Boreham cried.

James did not need to look around to know that his friend was already scanning for a target and would return fire in just a second or two. Everything was happening so quickly, but his mind was moving with almost glacial slowness.

It wasn't right that he had led them all the way across a dying continent only to fall here on the doorstep of his family home. Why would anybody in Livingston turn a gun on him?

A voice called out from somewhere in the rubble.

"O'Donnell? James O'Donnell? Is that you?"

James did not recognise the voice, but he recognised his name, of course, and he took a step towards it.

"No, James!" Michelle cried out. "Don't be an idiot."

But he raised his hands and walked towards the voice, calling out his name.

"Yes," he called out. "It's me. James. Senior Class of '07. Park High. I asked Laura-Marie Lawson to go to the prom. She said no. Very publicly."

Everything went quiet.

Until he heard laughter from somewhere in front of them. The voice called back, "That's because you were a nerd, O'Donnell. And too stupid to know it."

Michelle appeared at his side again. She was carrying her Glock but held down by her side.

"Who is this asshole?" she said.

James thought about it. He almost grinned.

"I think it's Mark Lawson," he said. "Laura-Marie's brother. He promised he was gonna kick my ass down East Park Street for even asking her."

"Yeah, well, I'm gonna kill them both," Michelle said. "You're my nerd, and nobody disses you like that."

The uncertain smile on James's face had cracked wide open into a genuine grin.

"No, don't do that," he said. "If I'd gone to the prom with Laura-Marie, I might've ended up staying here. And we would never have met."

He leaned down and kissed her, and the look of surprise on her face was so profound that he couldn't help laughing.

"So, we're good here?" Rick Boreham asked. The tension in his voice had unwound, but only by one notch.

"We're good," James said.

But they were not.

20

A GOOD DOG'S THERAPY SONG

James did not recognise Mark Lawson. Not at first. It wasn't just that they had not seen each other in fifteen years; Lawson had changed. He'd been as big as a refrigerator back in high school and played defensive tackle for the Bozeman Hawks. Measured against the memory of that hulking giant, the man who emerged from the rubble of Brad Taylor's bait and tackle shop was almost wraith-like. Still tall but shockingly thin, with loosened skin, sunken cheeks and a strangely vacant yet intense stare, which he fixed on everybody behind James.

"You brought some friends," Lawson said.

James nodded.

"I did, Mark."

He remembered that he was still holding Michelle's hand.

"This is my... partner. Michelle Nguyen," he said. "And my friend Rick. And Melissa Baker and..."

He trailed off. There was no point introducing everybody. Nobody would remember all the names, and Lawson did not seem interested.

"How's Laura-Marie?" James asked instead before common sense could get the better of him.

"She's alive," Lawson said. His voice was flat. His eyes hooded. "Legion couldn't kill her."

By now, pretty much everyone from the convoy had gathered around James. Except for the children, who had gone back to chasing each other through the grass.

"Did that bloke say something about a legion?" Damien Maloney asked.

"Fuck those guys," someone else spat. A tough, News Yorker's accent. Eliza Jabbarah. The tattooed chef.

It occurred to James that his little motorcade must look like a travelling circus to somebody like Mark, who had never left the county, let alone Montana, as best as James could recall.

Lawson, dressed in a filthy, ragged hunter's cloak, shouldered his rifle and gestured behind him for somebody else to come forward. Two more figures emerged from the tumble-down piles of masonry and scorched timbers. James did not know the younger boy, but his heart leapt to see Pablo Bruh. He let go of Michelle's hand and hurried forward, unable to keep the surprise and delight from his expression.

Looking tired and much thinner than James remembered, Pablo grinned hugely and threw wide his arms, gathering the younger man into a warm embrace.

"Oh jeez, man," James said. "It is good to see you, Pablo. And... my parents... How are they?"

He was almost too frightened to ask. Part of him expected Pablo to suddenly lose that smile, which had been such a large part of James's childhood, and to shake his head slowly.

Instead, he nodded and squeezed tighter.

"They're good, Little Jim. Both of them, they're good. Big Tom's been holding things together here."

Pablo straightened his arms, pushing James away to better look at him.

"They will be happy to see you," he said. "But you better have your story straight, boy. They've been worried to death about you. We all have. We thought you were done for when all the cities went up back east. They said you were in Washington."

"I was," he said, and remembering himself, he turned and motioned Michelle forward.

She wore a lopsided grin but was obviously basking in the reflected warmth of his meeting with Pablo.

"Pablo, this is Michelle Nguyen. She's my girl," he said, with more confidence than he'd shown with Lawson. "We got out of DC together. Michelle, this handsome brute is Pablo Bruh. He's been the leading hand on my parent's ranch since I was, like, this big."

James pinched his thumb and forefinger together.

Pablo swept back the camouflaged hood still covering his head and performed an oddly formal bow.

"Miss Nguyen," he said.

"Michelle will do fine," she said, extending her hand. "Pleased to meet you, Pablo."

James heard footsteps crunching up behind him. There was a lot of grit, broken glass, and shattered, pulverised brickwork on the road. He turned slightly and gestured for Rick and Mel to come and meet Pablo. He was surprised to see Maloney had come up with them. Everybody else hung back.

"And these are my friends, Rick and Mel. My best friends, Pablo. They're why I made it home."

More handshakes. More greetings.

And Damien Maloney's loud, nasal voice cutting through it all.

"Mate, did I hear you right? Did you say the *Legion* had been through here?"

Pablo and Lawson exchanged a wary glance.

"You know them?" Lawson asked.

James saw the subtle tension in the line of his shoulders. His fingers, where they gripped the stock of his rifle, had turned white. His voice was not friendly.

"Yeah," Maloney said. "They're a bunch of cunts. We drove about a thousand miles out of our way to avoid them."

Mark Lawson relaxed perceptibly. His head bobbed up and down, ever so slightly.

"You should have kept driving," he said.

THERE WAS NO SQUEEZING SPARTY WILLIAMS' Winnebago through the devastation of James O'Donnell's hometown. But Pablo whistled up more hidden figures from within the wreckage of demolished shops and homes, and they set to clearing a path through for the rest of the convoy. The speed with which they cleared certain large pieces of debris spoke to a plan in the arrangement. The fallen telephone poles and burned-out vehicles were roadblocks, not just random obstacles and wreckage.

"Doc Matheson can see to your wounded," Lawson said as everyone returned to their vehicles for the last ten or fifteen minutes of their long trek down through the valley to the O'Donnell Ranch.

"Old Doc Matheson is still alive?" James said, astounded. "Man, that old codger was grizzly even when Babe Ruth was in Little League."

Mark Lawson smiled with his eyes for the first time.

"Old Doc Matheson passed away five or six years back. You must have missed that in the big smoke. It's young Doc Matheson now. You remember Dave?"

"Dave?" James said, even more surprised.

Lawson nodded.

"Dude, the last I saw of Dave was his hairy ass hanging out the back of Rhino Ross's Pontiac when he drive-by mooned the Neptune," James recalled.

Lawson nodded sadly, "Yeah, good times."

"Are they..." James started.

"Both gone," Lawson said.

Everything was gone.

Michelle took the wheel, and James sat in the back with Mel and Nomi as they weaved through the remnants of Livingston. It was impossible at first to find anything he recognised, so total was the destruction, but eventually, he spied the half-demolished wreckage of Neptune's Taphouse. With a start, he realised that their winding course had taken them off the main strip and two blocks over to East Clark. They moved at barely better than walking pace, escorted by half a dozen armed men and women in hunting cloaks and strange, foliage-covered overalls that Rick called out as 'Ghillie suits.'

"Serious shit," he muttered.

Everyone was wide awake now and scoping out the damage, but only James could put it in context. Only he knew what had been lost here.

"Man, I loved this place," he said quietly as they rolled past the burned-out shell of Wilcoxon's Ice Cream Company. "I worked so damn hard to get away from here; I can't even remember why I left now."

"Because Laura-Marie Lawson pulled a backwoods Snooki on you at senior prom," Michelle said drily. "With first-degree Facebook burns and a promissory beat down from Deliverance Bro back there."

He snorted.

"Oh yeah, now I remember."

Mel Baker reached across Nomi and squeezed his arm.

"And cattle fisting, James. Someone told me there's a grievous amount of cattle fisting when you work on a ranch."

"That too," he agreed.

Nomi lay her head in his lap and made a sound close to a cat's mewing, except deeper and less needful. It was her therapy song. Nomi was trained to comfort Rick when he was spinning down, but she had now adopted almost everyone in the convoy as her responsibility, and she sensed James's distress. He scratched behind her ears, and her tail thumped against the seat. She nuzzled in closer.

"Good girl," he said quietly.

The southern end of town, where US 89 crossed the I-90, was virtually untouched by whatever cataclysm had befallen the other half of Livingston. Here, the streets were clear, the buildings intact, and they could've sped up were it not for the escorts on foot leading them through.

This part of town had survived, but it had been abandoned.

Nobody other than the camouflaged fighters and the vehicles of their caravan moved through the empty streets. A few places were boarded up. The Pizza Hut and Chrysler dealership were clad all over in plywood shutters, but the pharmacy and compounding lab stood open, and two guards flanked the front door.

James recognised them.

Katherine Bates and Kevin Savage, from the year just ahead and behind him at school.

He almost waved as Michelle drove past, but something stayed his hand – the blank hostility on their faces.

Rick turned around in the front seat. His face was deeply creased with worry.

"This Legion your friend told us about," he said. "They used heavy machine guns and goddamned mortars on this place. For no tactical justification that I can think of."

"It's a strategic play," Michelle said from behind the wheel. "Not tactical."

The skin on James O'Donnell's forearms puckered into goose-flesh. He had that reaction sometimes when Michelle turned cold and analytical. Time and again, her threat detectors had saved them from blundering into the shit, but this was his home she was feeding into her mental algorithms.

"Maloney said this group was establishing dominance and excluding competitors in an AO stretching from Washington state down into northern Oregon," she went on. "It's why they detoured so far west. The Legion cut Route 93 before they could use it to get to his salmon farm up in Canada."

"He could have told us earlier," James said, feeling ill-disposed towards the Australian and his fellow travellers for keeping such vital information to themselves.

"James," Michelle scolded. "Don't. This militia group was one of about a hundred problems they had. We've never bothered telling

Damo about Tammy's cannibals or those rapists we hanged outside of Kearney. It's all just shit that happened. I'm going to interview them properly now we know it's relevant. But don't go blaming them for what happened here. There's no connection. We're lucky we have them to debrief at all."

He felt his cheeks heating with the embarrassment of her smack-down, but she was right.

"Sorry," he said quietly.

Mel squeezed his arm again.

Nomi burrowed in deeper.

"We need to plan for this," Michelle said as they approached the intersection with the I-90. "We need to gather intelligence, work the data, and make some hard fucking calls. But first," she said, slowing to a stop and turning around to look at him directly, softening her features with a smile, "You need to take me home to meet your parents."

21

GOOD NEIGHBOURS, NEWLY FOUND

Michelle brought the Sierra to a stop as they reached the crossing. Maloney's Land Rover idled to their rear, with the rest of the convoy strung out nose-to-tail behind them. James leaned out of the window and shook hands with Mark Lawson. Both men had a tight grip.

"It's good to see you, O'Donnell," he said. "It's good you got some people with you. Things are bad around here now. We need good folk, but your old man can tell you all about it. I sent word ahead. They'll be waiting for you."

"Thanks, Mark," James said.

After a brief pause, when neither man let go, Lawson added, "It would be good after you get settled if you called on Laura-Marie. She would appreciate that. Me too."

Lawson's grip strengthened for the briefest moment as though he was trying to force some sort of understanding into James through the power of his grip.

"I'll do that," James promised.

He returned the squeeze and let go of the handshake.

Lawson signalled to a young man across the highway, who might have been Shane Chisolm or maybe one of his younger brothers.

Whoever it was, he spoke into a CB radio unit hooked up to a car battery and waved them through.

"You're clear to go through," Lawson said. "Sentries been notified all down the valley, but don't go off the river road, James. Just drive straight to your parents' place. Okay?"

"Okay," James said. "We got it."

He saw Michelle and Rick exchange a loaded glance, but neither said anything as the convoy moved forward.

It had been three years since James O'Donnell had last visited home. That was the Thanksgiving after he'd cleared out the loans the mortgage broker signed his dad up to as the drought dragged on. Punishing, high-interest loans that compounded like a bastard. It had been an awkward trip.

His parents were more than grateful for his help saving them and the ranch from the repo men, and James had resolutely made nothing of it – even though he'd been sleeping in his car to make their repayments. Just for a little while. But the whole time he was home, James felt the slow burn of his old man's humiliation. Not just around the house but whenever he ventured into town or met up with old friends who might know how close Tom O'Donnell had sailed to the rocks of financial ruin.

James never did tell his dad about having to move out of his apartment and bunk down in the Camry. Indeed, Michelle was the only human being he'd ever told. James never imagined returning to the ranch or the valley for anything more than a family visit. Now, he didn't know if he would ever leave.

"It's beautiful," Michelle said as she steered the big SUV through the narrow pass that opened into the valley's northern end. The Yellowstone River had cut deeply into the steep-shouldered hills on either side of the road, their slopes densely forested with evergreens and dusted white with the first snowfalls of the coming winter. She rolled down the window, and the cold air brought the strong scent of pine and fir trees and the rush of clean water over sandy riverine island shoals to their left.

"Observations posts," Rick said, squinting up into the hills and seeing something that eluded James. Everything looked normal to him except for the greenery. They'd obviously had good rain of late for the first time in years.

"I feel like we should be bringing something with us," Mel said from the back seat. "You know, instead of just more mouths to feed."

"The problem won't be a lack of nutritional resources," Michelle said. "It'll be having the labour to harvest, prepare and distribute them. You can relax, Mel. We're not just extra mouths. We're bringing more hands, too."

She waved briefly at a group of twenty or more people bent to work in a field of dark black soil lined with rows of some leafy green vegetable.

"And more fingers to pull a trigger," Rick added. He did not sound happy.

"I'm sorry," James said. "I thought coming here was a good idea."

"It was," Rick said, gently cutting him off. "Still is. But the situation has changed. All of the trouble we had getting here, that trouble's been waiting on us to arrive, too."

Michelle fed more power to the engine, and their speed picked up on the open road. James checked behind them to make sure everyone was keeping pace. He saw Karl Valentine grinning like a happy fool at the Land Rover wheel and Damien Maloney giving them two thumbs up. No breakdowns or burned-out wreckage were piled up, blocking their passage through the valley. A couple of dead SUVs pushed off the shoulder and a motorhome lying on its side in a drainage ditch near where the East River Road split from US 89 spoke to an organised effort to keep the transport corridor open.

The head of the valley was heavily cultivated, with all the flat land up to the river's sandy banks given over to farming. That hadn't changed, but the crops had.

"Used to be all cash crops through here," James said, raising his voice over the passing roar of the wind. "Alfalfa, malt barley, wheat, corn, sugar beets."

"Looks like they switched to subsistence," Michelle called back.

"I'm guessing onions, potatoes, cabbages and pumpkins. Shitload of pumpkins."

James did not ask how she knew or guessed all of that. Food security had been her particular kink for the National Security Council. It was how they met, why they were still alive.

"Good fishing here, James?" Rick asked. He was looking out the window at the broad blue course of the river. The banks were thick with grass and wildflowers, and the water ran higher than James had seen for years. More evidence of recent rains.

"Best fly fishing in the world, man," he said, and he felt an unfamiliar warmth in his chest.

With a small start, he realised that it was pride. He was both humbled and excited to be able to show off his home to his friends. He was almost pathetically grateful that they had a place in the world where they might be safe.

The warm inner glow clenched into something harsher and less agreeable when he recalled the devastation of his hometown.

Mel Baker suddenly cried out with absolute pleasure at a small family of elk grazing on wild grasses in the gentle hummocks of the riverbank.

"Oh wow, wouldn't Nomi love to get in among them!"

Hearing her name, Nomi barked and sat up a little higher, looking around for a treat or the offer of a ball to chase. Luckily, she did not see the elk. James fell quiet for the next few miles, content to take in the changes he could see and wonder at those he could not.

Michelle commented on the number of people working the fields, wondering how many had been forced from the city by the Legion's attack.

"Did you have many migrant workers in the valley, James?"

"Me? No. Pablo was born in Bozeman."

"No, dummy," she said. "I didn't mean your family. I meant the local economy. Was it dependent on itinerant labour? Did the landholders have the infrastructure in place to house them? I'm just wondering where all these field workers came from and where they go at the end of the day."

He shrugged.

"There's always need for seasonal labour on a farm, but we're a long way from the Rio Grande up here. Most of the harvest was mechanised. But those big rigs would all be in the sheds now. No fuel."

That seemed to appease her. She went back to scoping out the passing fields.

The closer they got to Deanna Canyon, where the O'Donnell Ranch sprawled across six hundred acres with a dozen lakes fed by two permanent streams and an unknown number of natural springs, the weirder and more unreal James felt. He'd just had his head turned inside out by the destruction visited upon Livingston. For three long months, since he and Michelle had sprinted from the grounds of the White House—the actual goddamned White House— they had fought and fled and sneaked and stumbled their way through the vast, collapsing tomb of the American republic. But here, as Michelle turned off the river road and drove up the winding, unsealed track to his family home, it was as if nothing had changed. They stopped at the first gate, and Rick climbed out to unlatch it.

"You go on ahead," he said. "I'll catch a lift with the last one through. Make sure the gates are closed properly."

"Thanks, man," James said. He had just assumed everyone would know to close the gates behind them. But Rick was right. They wouldn't.

Michelle drove on, and bighorn sheep scattered from the edge of a pond where they had been drinking. Mule deer, startled by the engine noise of so many vehicles, darted into the tree line where James and his cousin Simon had spent their first night out under the stars many years ago, camping on a grassy hill overlooking the Yellowstone River. His father's rudimentary barbecue pit would almost certainly still be there. A thin column of woodsmoke rising from the higher slopes beyond a windbreak of native maple and birch trees marked the location of their homestead.

"It's lovely, James," Mel Baker said.

"Rick will love it," Michelle nodded. "It's defensible."

"Plenty of room for Nomi to run around, too," James said, but he wasn't following the conversation closely.

They had enough elevation as Michelle turned the wheel into the first of half a dozen switchback turns that he could see out across the way to the sheer granite cliffs of the Gallatin ranges. The valley floor was only five miles wide at this point, and he could easily make out the Lawson and Tuer family homesteads on the far side of the river. There seemed to be more vehicles parked around them than James recalled and more people working in cultivated garden beds around each house. Laura-Marie's mom had grown prize-winning Alpine lilies and rein orchids in her front yard, but he supposed they had given way to onions and potatoes.

"Much further?" Michelle asked.

"No," James said. "Just follow the road around the next plateau, and we'll be there in a couple of minutes."

MICHELLE TOOK the last bend slowly. She had enjoyed the drive down the valley and the minor challenge of navigating the gravel track as it climbed through the lush alpine pastures. The prolonged drought did not look nearly as severe in this part of the country as it had beyond the Rockies. Verdant fields blazed with late-blooming wildflowers. Half a dozen small lakes caught the rays of the late afternoon sun and cast them back into the world as a vast mural of brilliant blues and golden sunbursts. She could imagine escaping everything up here. It was a landscape of redemption and forgetting.

The dirt road – a flat, well-maintained track of bluestone gravel – emerged onto a small plateau from the thick band of alpine forest. The dark, closely planted stands of pine trees would offer both privacy and some protection from the winds that must roar along this valley when the weather turned spiteful. James had told her many stories about growing up on his family's ranch, but Michelle was still not quite ready for the Rockwell panorama that greeted them on the other side of that alpine screen.

"Oh, it's so pretty," Mel Baker cooed from the back seat.

But it was more than that.

The ranch house was a long, low, wooden structure surrounded by deep verandas on all sides. Three stone chimneys poked up through the pitched roof of dark wooden shingles. Tendrils of blue-grey smoke curled away from the largest. She could see the original structure of split logs, and river stone was old, but generations of the O'Donnell clan had added to their ancestral home over the years. The newest annexe looked strikingly modern, a glass and steel box that seemed to serve no function beyond affording the occupants a grand and sweeping aspect down the length of the valley and over the serried, snow-capped peaks of the far ranges.

"James!" she said, punching him in the arm and pointing at the glass cube. "You didn't tell me about the architecture!"

"Ow!" he said, rubbing at the spot where she had hit him. "It's not architecture. That's a kit home. A tiny house that my dad converted by adding some glass. He got it cheap."

"Well, your dad could kick Mies Van der Rohe's ass," she said.

"You can tell him yourself," James said. "There he is."

An older, stockier version of James O'Donnell had appeared from beneath one of those wide verandas and carefully navigated the three stone steps from the porch down to the low-cut grass. He was slightly bandy-legged but still tall, with a strong, unbent back and an open, sunny face upon which a smile of untempered joy was spreading like a sunrise after a long, occulted night. He turned and called out to somebody inside, and a woman in blue jeans, a faded, red-checked shirt, and a floral apron hurried out to join him. They both waved, and she heard James make a slight sound in the back of his throat.

His eyes were moist, and he rubbed at them.

"Oh, they're lovely. Just look at them," Mel said.

Nomi barked and thumped her tail on the seat.

Michelle drove the last fifty yards as carefully as she had ever driven, pulled up in front of James's parents, cut the engine, engaged the parking brake, and reached across to take his hand.

"Go on," she said.

He fumbled at the door, missing the handle once, before getting it open and almost falling out of the Sierra. He had run the short distance to his mom and dad and fallen into their embrace before Michelle had left the driver's seat. Behind them, five more vehicles pulled up, but for the moment, nobody else got out.

Michelle was dressed in jeans, a thick corduroy shirt and a sheepskin jacket for the cold weather. She tied her thick black hair, filthy and unkempt, into a loose knot as Mel Baker hopped down from the back seat, and Nomi landed on the grass with a thump.

James and his parents were hugging. They all seemed to be in tears, but his mother most of all. Tom O'Donnell wiped his eyes and sniffled a little, but he looked the sort to hold his feelings close. Michelle's feelings were a little frayed and unmoored. Her mouth was dry, and her heart beat fast beneath her ribcage. She was annoyed with herself for being so nervous. She had briefed presidents and given evidence in secret and in front of the whole nation in both Houses of Congress. Nor had she always been a desk analyst. Meeting her boyfriend's parents should not be the scariest thing she'd ever done. But waiting to be introduced, she felt herself stupidly jittery and skittish.

The O'Donnells emerged from their group hug, and James pointed down the sloping garden to the two women.

"Oh, this is delicious," Mel Baker said beside her.

"Huh? What?" Michelle asked. She was all at odds with her own thoughts.

Mel dug a knuckle into her ribs as James waved them to come up.

"You better go first, girlfriend. Those humble mountain folk are probably wondering which minority they're about to marry into."

"Huh," she said again and then realised what Mel meant. "Oh, fuck off."

Mel pushed her in the small of her back, propelling Michelle forward. James broke away from his parents to hurry down and take her hand. He was grinning like a small boy.

Nomi ran in circles around them, barking with delight, her paws digging up small divots of turf.

"Come on," James said, almost hurrying Michelle back up slope. "Come meet my folks."

Tom and Mary O'Donnell were still red-eyed and shiny-cheeked, but they were also beaming at their son and her.

"This is Michelle," he said.

"Thank you, thank you," Mary O'Donnell repeated, almost like a prayer, and before Michelle could awkwardly try to shake her hand, James's mother had enclosed her in a deep and nearly smothering hug. Michelle was overcome with the smell of butter and strawberries and was suddenly aware of how bad she must smell. It had been many days since they had bathed. She still had blood under her fingernails from the fight at the Bachman Cav memorial.

"I didn't do anything," Michelle said, her voice muffled inside Mary's embrace.

"Nonsense," Mary said. "Here, let me get a look at you." She leaned back a little but held on to Michelle's arms. "You saved my little boy. You brought him home. You all did," she added for the sake of Mel, who had come up close enough to be included in the magic circle.

Michelle looked at James and smiled at his obvious embarrassment.

"Oh, he played his part, don't let him get away with any of that aw-shucks bullshit," she said before blushing and cursing herself for swearing in front of them.

Shit-shit-shit. Why was she always like this?

But Tom O'Donnell threw his head back and laughed with a rich, rolling baritone.

"Yeah, you got his number," he said. "Good for you, young lady. And yes, thank you all."

O'Donnell senior turned to the rest of the group, who were just alighting from their vehicles and holding back to give the family some privacy.

"Please, everyone," he said with a voice she could easily imagine echoing down the valley, "come join us at the table. Our boy is home safe, and he has brought good friends. You are all welcome here for as long as you need to stay, and if that should be as long as our family has lived on this mountain, then I will say a prayer of thanks for good neighbours, newly found."

JODI HAD sixteen shots left on the little disposable Kodak, and she spent them freely at the welcome feast. They were still getting used to being around other people, having been so long on their own. But the children loved having the company of so many kids. Damo, of course, just loved company because that was his nature. Ellie put herself forward to help James's mother with the cooking for so many unexpected guests, and Karl—as was *his* nature—quietly offered to help her.

That left Jodi to wander the grounds of the O'Donnell ranch and document their arrival.

That's what it felt like to her.

Arrival in a promised land.

But they were not done with their journey. Damo's farm was still hundreds of miles north, over the border with Canada, and although the elder O'Donnell was very generous, inviting everyone to stay as long as they wanted, Jodi could not imagine how that would work out.

So many people had just rolled up on them.

For now, however, she felt herself unclenching for the first time in months.

For one thing, she had showered, and it was glorious. There wasn't much hot water, not for so many people needing a good scrub down, and she'd shared her time with Ellie. Just a few minutes. Not long enough to get down to anything. But it felt fantastic to have clean hair and skin, to strip off the filthy clothes they had been wearing, and dress in fresh jeans, tee shirts, thick, fleece-lined hoodies and woollen sweaters. Mary O'Donnell provided all those things, sending word up and down the valley that she had people in need.

A procession of vehicles drove up the switchback track and

through the screen of dark green pine trees all through the afternoon. They delivered food and clothes and helped set up long trestle
tables and propane heaters. A man who introduced himself as the
acting principal of the elementary school asked if she would like to
send Maxi, Pascal and Beatrice for lessons while they were in the
Valley. Jodi did not know how to answer, unsure of what Damo had
planned.

But Principal Edmonds was persistent, and eventually, she agreed
that the children probably could use some classroom time, given the
long, forced excursion they'd been on.

Mostly, though, Jodi did not throw herself into the social whirl.
She much preferred to wander by herself, content that everyone was
safe and she had the luxury of looking at the world like the photographer she had once been.

Jodi took pictures of the following things.

Ellie rubbing down a pig's carcass with a paste of herbs and garlic
she had picked from the glass house behind the main homestead.

Ellie laughing at some story Tom O'Donnell had just told her and
Karl while they hoisted the pig onto a rotisserie. The muscles in
Ellie's arms bulged, making the sinuous tattoos on her biceps move as
though the ink was a living thing.

Maxi and four other children all rolling down the gentle slope of
soft grass in front of the old homestead, while Nomi the dog jumped
over them, barking and wagging her tail so fast that Maxi said she
was about to fly off down the valley like a helicopter dog.

Damo, standing with his back to the spitted pig, holding a can of
beer in his gigantic paws, warming the backs of his legs on the
glowing coals. He was deep in conversation with Rick Boreham,
Michelle Nguyen, Tom O'Donnell and a younger man who looked a
bit like James.

A close-up shot of four pies, freshly baked from the wood burner
in Mary O'Donnell's kitchen. A blueberry pie, two strawberry-
rhubarb and one apple, all wearing golden crusts, dribbling hot fruit
filling, and venting small columns of steam from knife slits in their
pastry lids.

Maxi hugging a squirming chicken that totally did not want to be hugged.

Karl and Rick, standing a little away from everybody else, sharing a beer and staring off down the valley as the sun set over a distant mountain, frosted with snow that blazed with a rich bronze radiance.

And finally, three long tables full of people eating a full-blown feast, quite amazing after the privations of the long road. A banquet, hours in the preparation, and hours more in the consumption.

That photo would eventually sit in a simple wooden frame over the fireplace in the house where she lived the rest of her life. Jodi Sarjanen would often find herself standing in front of it, losing track of time in the memory of that good night. At least fifty faces turned towards the tiny lens of her shitty cardboard camera. More than half of them were the people she met when they joined the convoy after the terrible fight at the Memorial. Many were unknown to her when she took the shot. They were local people, residents of the valley who had come to the O'Donnell ranch when invited by Tom in celebration of his son's return. Others he had summoned to take the counsel of those men and women entrusted with securing the valley against all dangers and enemies.

The photograph was surprisingly good for the simple camera. Jodi had purposely not triggered the shutter when anyone was looking directly at her, avoiding the curse of red-eyed subjects. She had positioned herself to capture almost everyone at the tables in good light and had composed the shot so that the subject areas—the long tables, the glowing fire pits, the candlelit interiors of the frontier-era homestead—balanced each other across the entire composition. Within that simple frame, she had juxtaposed her subjects such that all the forms, tones and colors carried the same visual weight. Every face, every element, and each surface and line commanded the viewer's attention equally.

But that was not why she often found herself transfixed before it.

The photo was simply the only document she had, which gathered in one place all the people she had loved so much, some of whom she would soon lose forever.

TAMMY KOLCHAR COULD NOT RECALL ENJOYING a barbecue so much. Turned out that Ellie, the tattooed lesbian lady, was as handy with a baster as she was with a shotgun. Woulda been good to have some nice soft bread rolls to fix herself up a loose pork sandwich, but there was such a sufficiency of roasted hog and golden crackle that it didn't matter that she couldn't have everything she wanted.

She had more'n enough.

"Ain't so much like Dillonvale, is it?" Roxarne said.

They were sitting on a log by themselves, taking advantage of the warmth from an open fire pit set by Jim O'Donnell's old man. You couldn't see nothing down the valley after the sun went down. Just a few spots of light here and there, all of them twinkling golden yellow because they were natural fire light, just like the flames they were sitting over. People had electricity here; those with solar panels and batteries did anyway, but they saved it for refrigerators and such like. Not for lighting the dinner table, which could be done just as well with candles.

"This is a damn sight better than Dillonvale," Tammy said. "Fuck that dump."

"Fuck it twice and backasswards," Roxy agreed, cutting into a big wedge of fruit pie with a spoon.

They had been at the ranch for seven or eight hours, but the time had not dragged on the way it can. They had their children to attend, of course, but there was plenty of others in the convoy that James and Rick had put together and seen safely across the country. It was a minor revelation to Tammy how much satisfaction you could take from something as simple as wrangling a bunch of kids when you didn't have another bunch of angry cannibals and fuckin' perverts chasing after you.

Her young ones, Bobby Jr and Wynona were lost in the pack of laughing, squealing kids charging up and down the big, wide-open lawn in front of the homestead, chasing after Rick Boreham's dog, which had a deflated football clamped firmly between its teeth.

Nomi, the dog, would tear away from the children, gaining a good thirty or forty yards of open space before laying down her prize and waiting for the kids to catch on up with her. Just as the first of them would get close enough to have a chance of snatching back the ball, Nomi would bark, grab it, and dash away in a four-legged sprint again. Tammy had snorted beer through her nose the first time she'd seen it.

"You did the right thing," Roxarne said.

"What? Going back for more pork?" Tammy said. "Cos I am saving room for pie, you know. Unless you ate the lot."

"No, dummy, I mean getting us out of Dillonvale. That was your call, and it was the right one. I reckon we'd be dead as, if we'd stayed back there."

"Well, sure. Thanks," Tammy said. "But we wouldn't have made it here without you, Rox. You kept us going plenty of times I just wanted to give up."

Roxarne chased the last piece of pie crust around her paper plate with the spoon. She shrugged, "Once you get started on something, it's best to finish," she said. "And this trip turned out all right."

Taking her old roommate at her word, Tammy finished the last of her third helping of spit-roasted pig and slid down off the log so she could lean back against it and lightly drum her fingertips against her painfully distended belly.

"Sure did," she said.

Neither spoke again for a while, simply enjoying the freedom to watch the children play and let their dinners settle. Tammy had no idea how many people had come up the dirt track to join the festivities, but if she had to lay money on the table, she'd have put the crowd at maybe seventy or eighty strong.

"Helluva turnout," she said. "I don't reckon you'd find a crowd this big anywhere in the country at the moment. Maybe the whole world."

"What, not even China?"

"They're all dead, they reckon. Army gave them the flu as payback for computer hacking us."

"I know," Roxanne said. "It's weird, isn't it? Kind of sad, you know. I try not to think 'bout all the people who died, but I reckon it'd have to be heaps of them."

"Most of them," Tammy nodded.

"In Dillonvale, you mean?"

"Nope, everywhere," Tammy said.

She thought about getting up and returning to the big table to try and find her some pie like Roxy had, but she was too full and tired. She would probably have slept out here by the fire tonight, except it would go out, and she would freeze to death. Still, Tammy thought it was nice just to plant her ass and enjoy a little T-time.

"Do you think she is pretty?" Roxarne asked, confusing the hell out of her.

Tammy tried to sit up, but it was too hard, and in the end, she gave up.

"Huh? What you mean?"

"Jodi, the blonde one who looks like a supermodel," Roxarne said, pointing at the tall woman with icy blonde hair who had joined their party back at Bachman.

"You thinking of going gay for her?" Tammy teased. "Because her girlfriend looks pretty tough if you ask me. And she's a chef. She's got knives."

Roxy elbowed her in the ribs. Almost knocking her over.

"No, asshole. I was just wondering, is all. How she keeps herself looking that good. It's hard. I ain't got no beauty routine left to speak of."

"Testify to that one, sister," Tammy said. Since they had been on the road, she'd had no time for make-up or hair care or nothin'. All of her nails were chewed to shit, too. It was, then, a mystery worth her contemplation, how that pretty blonde girl managed it. After all, neither she nor Rox had a man they could call on right now, and they were unlikely to find themselves one, looking like a pair of fuckin' free-range wilderskanks the way they presently did.

"She used to be a photographer, they reckon," Roxarne said as if passing on a secret. "And I wondered if she was a model before that, and she had to do photography after she had a kid and lost her figure."

"She still got a pretty good figure, Rox."

"Oh, so maybe you'd go gay for her," Roxarne teased right back.

They both fell about laughing. Tammy had half a dozen beers under her belt, and she was plenty drunk. Roxy had been drinking less, but she was a cheap date. Especially after months on the road. When they had recovered from their shared and secret joke, Tammy looked again around the large gathering of people.

James O'Donnell was talking with his mom. James's girlfriend Michelle, who they reckon used to be a spy or something, was standing a few feet away, deep in conversation with Rick and that massive Australian dude, Damien. Or Damo, she reminded herself. They called him Damo. Tammy shifted her gaze back to James.

Roxarne leaned over and whispered in her ear.

"Michelle is gonna catch you looking at him, and she is going to cut your throat while you're asleep."

"Fuck off," Tammy giggled, but Roxy had her number, all right. She *had* been checking James out. She did that sometimes, even though she knew he was hooked up with Michelle.

"He's cute, is all," she said.

"He's got a cousin," Roxy suggested.

"Married," Tammy lobbed back.

"Damn, girl, you checked already."

"I got all the gossip, girl," Tammy said.

"What about that big Aussie guy?" Roxarne said.

Tammy gave her the side eye, "He's okay, I suppose if you like your beef aged."

"Well-aged," Roxy said.

DAMO WAS ENJOYING the split-screen sensation of the fire's warmth on his arse while the bracing chill of the evening tightened the skin of his face. He chatted with Pete Tapsell, the pommy bloke from James

O'Donnell's mob, who'd travelled through a heap of the same shit-holes and backwaters as Damo over the years.

Damo was having a grand old time, the two of them bullshitting each other with tales of their adventures, reminding him of so many nights in the field as a young geologist. The beer helped too. Some local piss called River Nymph Golden Ale. It was heavier than most American beers - or at least the big commercial brews you tended to get at corporate functions. They'd had to carry some of them at the restaurant because there was always some complete numpty who wanted his fucking Bud or whatever. Still, Ellie had insisted on stocking the fridge with proper craft drops from a bunch of arse-kicking microbreweries. It'd been one of his favourite things about owning a restaurant, being able to pinch a few mystery froths from the cool room whenever he felt thirsty.

"Worst bastards I ever had to make a deal with out in the boonies were definitely the Chechen mafia," Damo assured Tapsell, nursing his golden ale. They watched Sparty Williams, surrounded by excited children, setting up his telescope a little ways off.

"Chechens are soft cocks," Tapsell replied. "Lord's Resistance Army, guvnor. I reckon they'd take the prize for the worst cunts in the world."

And he launched into a long and winding story about smuggling a bag of conflict diamonds past the LRA in Uganda.

Tapsell, many beers into the wind, eventually meandered off to have a gander at the stars through Sparty's telescope, which was now a bona fide sideshow attraction. Even some adults had lined up for a peek at the night sky. This left Damo to enjoy a few quiet ales on his own, a situation in which he was delighted to indulge himself until Rick Boreham and this bolshie little Nguyen chick bore down on him with a battery of questions about his encounters with the Legion, back west.

Boreham was quiet and reserved, as always, but she was relent-less and frankly a bit hard to take after indulging himself in the froths.

"Mate, we never really met them," Damo tried to explain, "We just heard about 'em a couple of places. Enough to know they were blokes to avoid running into."

"Where did you hear about them?" she asked.

Rick, who had looked legitimately ready to shoot him back at that servo in the ghost town, was now leaning forward as though intent on memorising every word. He was a massive unit with a close-cropped beard and the lines of a man who'd always done physical work for his living. Soldiering in Boreham's case. Damo recognised the type. The wilder fringes of the mining industry were filthy with security contractors. Most of them were ex-special forces blokes who couldn't get over the fact they weren't quite so fucking special anymore. They were a cost of doing business in some of the shittier holes he'd gone digging up rocks and drilling for oil. Rick Boreham didn't look to be anywhere near as unsavoury as some of the private military guys Damo had hired in places like Nigeria and the Russian outback. But, he didn't doubt the bloke would slot you as soon as look at you if he had reason to.

He recognised Michelle Nguyen's type as well.

Ex-government, for sure. But not your friendly civil servant from Parks and fucking Rec.

Interrogating him, she gave off the undeniable vibe of a high-functioning sociopath. Reckoned she'd worked for the National Security Council and still had the laminate to prove it. But she reminded him of another unsavoury type of character you also met out in the boonies. Damien Maloney would bet dollars to donuts that she was ex-Agency, or military intelligence or something like that. It was almost surprising she was partnered up with young O'Donnell.

To his eye, she was much more of a sort with Boreham. There would be no denying or escaping her questions, and to be honest, if anybody had to front up to some redneck chimpenfuhrer and his Hitlerotica fanboys, Damo would prefer it was them, not him.

"I reckon we first heard about these militia numpties a couple of days after getting past Sacramento," he explained. "That was one of those federally designated strongholds, you know."

"Yeah, I know," Nguyen said. All business. She wasn't knocking back the River Nymph Golden Ales. She was sipping black coffee and writing down everything he said in a small, battered Moleskine notebook. She had some boss-looking tatts on the back of her hand, and he wondered where she'd been to get them.

"We went as far upriver as we could get in my boat," he said. "Got off at a place called Shasta Lake, sold the boat. Or traded it, I guess, to a bloke who wanted to go downriver, back the way we'd come. He got my fucking four-million-dollar yacht, and I got his shitbox Land Rover. But it was a fair trade."

"That's great, Damo," Michelle said. "But the militia. The Legion, when did you encounter them?"

Damo finished off his beer.

He turned around to toast himself on the other side. The heat from the fire stung his frozen face. Boreham and Nguyen both moved around to the other side of the firepit. The soldier gave him another beer.

"Don't get him drunk, Rick. This is important," Nguyen said.

"Mate, I'm not getting drunk on this lolly water," Damo snorted. He knocked the top off the ale and took a long draw. A screaming horde of sugar-crazed children ran past, and he wondered for a moment how his son, Andy, was doing. Damo knew he'd made it back to Oz and was heading down to Tasmania, to the family farm outside of Hobart. Whether Andy ever made it there, Damo didn't know. The phones, the internet, they were all gone. Hopefully, fucking Hobart was still there.

Probably, he told himself. Tasmania was overrun with billionaires who were too slow to buy up all the five-star bolt holes in New Zealand. The place would be...

Michelle Nguyen reached over and removed the beer from his grip. He was so surprised he let it go.

"Focus, Damo. The Legion. Tell me what you know."

"I didn't say it was the Legion, not at first anyway," Damo said, realising the fourth or fifth ale had hit him a touch harder than he'd thought.

He really wanted that beer back, but the quickest way to get it would be to answer Nguyen's questions. She reminded him a bit of Ellie in that way. A bitch with scary focus when she had to be.

"Soon as we had wheels, we got off the main transport corridors," he said. "Stayed right the fuck away from the interstates, avoided the smaller highways too, snuck around any kind of settlement with more than two or three thousand people, and eventually, we just avoided towns and villages altogether. Wasn't worth the hassle, mate. By this time, if they hadn't fallen apart or eaten each other, they'd turned into bloody fortresses, and half of them were shooting at anything that moved outside the wall."

"Ha! You don't need to tell us, man," Rick Boreham said. "A road trip that shoulda taken a week took us three months with all the backtracking and go-arounds."

"Mate, I'd say cheers and raise my beer to you, but your scary little friend here stole that off of me, and frankly, I'm frightened that if I try to get it back, she'll have me terminated with extreme fucking prejudice."

Rick gave Michelle Nguyen a look and a smile, and she rolled her eyes but returned Damo's beer.

"That beer is 5.5% alcohol by volume," she said. "It's not lolly water, you dopey convict. Unless you want to do this again with a hangover tomorrow, I need you to put your big boy pants on and answer my questions. You've seen what those assholes did to James's hometown. They've withdrawn from this area for some reason, but they'll be back. We need to be ready."

"No. *You* need to be ready, mate," Damo corrected her. "We're just passing through. I've got my farm to get to and those two Canadian little ones to get home to their old man."

The young woman raised one eyebrow at him.

"And you think the people who did *that*..." she waved into the dark, in the direction of the ruined township they'd driven through earlier in the day. "You think those people are going to pay any attention at all to the border? As far as they're concerned, the border doesn't exist. The law doesn't exist anymore. They intend to make themselves the law."

Damo said nothing.

She might have a point. His farm wasn't that far over into Canada and was a long way from any major towns or cities.

"I don't think the Mounties are coming to help you," Rick Boreham said.

"Maybe not," Damo conceded. He paused to sip at the beer and think over the situation. "Yeah, fair cop, you might be right about that. But I'm not gonna make any calls without talking to my guys. We been through a lot to get here, and I promised them they'd all be safe at my place. I can't just say, 'new plan' we're gonna hang around here waiting to punch on with a bunch of actual fuckin' Nazis."

"Nobody's asking you to," Rick said. "We owe you. Not the other way round."

Damo waived that away.

"Fuck that for a contractual obligation, mate. I reckon you'd have stopped and helped us if the roles had been reversed."

"Maybe," Rick said.

"Definitely," Michelle corrected. "And you can pay us back by letting me finish my debrief. So. Your first encounter with the militia? Any militia. Organised or otherwise."

Damo looked for a place to put his beer down. There was none, so he drained half the bottle and carefully put it on the ground. He folded his arms. Burped. Ready to get to work.

"First lot we ran into were a bunch of pretenders," he said. "Woulda been just over the state line, southern Oregon. We were coming up on a place called Coleman Lake, I think. A nice long stretch of road and we came over a hill and saw this roadblock about two or three miles up ahead. Karl pulls over, and we get my binoculars. I've got a really kick-arse pair you can use for stargazing and shit."

Boreham looked interested, but Michelle Nguyen did not.

"Anyway, we had a look at these blokes, and they did not look like they wanted to talk and cuddle. They were all tooled up. There was a heap of vehicles pulled over by the side of the road, too. Very suss."

"You re-routed?" Michelle said.

"Too fucking right we did," Damo snorted. "I didn't need Karl to tell me that was a set-up. They were obviously pulling people out of their cars and probably slottin' them for stale Twinkies and chocolate bars."

Rick Boreham shook his head.

"No way. Twinkies never go stale."

"Sure, mate. So I reckon that was the first time we saw anything looking like a militia. You know, a bunch of fat blokes all dressed for the same Rambo fantasy, pretending to be soldiers. Shaking punters down. We kept a lookout for that sort of shit afterwards. About a week later, we ran into these other blokes who said they were in a militia unit based out of Seattle. Reckoned they'd lost contact with their mates when everything went pear-shaped, and they had to strike out on their own. They were okay, I guess. We traded a bit of food and a bottle of bourbon with them. A week after that, we found this town on the other side of the Oregon Badlands. Completely buggered. Like somebody had stood off and just shot the shit out of it. There were bodies everywhere, just lying out for the crows, and more of them hanging from telephone poles. There were all these signs, too, on the road into town and out."

"What did the signs say?" Michelle asked.

Damo frowned.

"Here lies Carthage. Learn from history. Bullshit like that."

"Jesus Christ," Michelle sighed, suddenly looking very tired. "A psychopath with a history major. That's just awesome."

ELLIE JABBARAH WAS TIRED. Closer to exhausted, in fact, but it was honest fatigue, well-earned and deeply satisfying. She lay wrapped in a blanket on a comfortable old rattan chair on the veranda, nursing a vodka and tonic with ice, marvelling at the fact that anybody still had access to vodka and tonic water and, most amazing of all, to actual goddamned ice cubes. But, for all the rustic charms of the O'Donnell ranch, it did boast some modern amenities, including a big ass Tesla battery and a large bank of solar cells to feed it.

She swirled the ice in her double-strength drink.

The party was winding down, but she estimated there were still just over a hundred people gathered at the trestle tables or standing around the open fire pits and scattered across the garden in small clumps of three and four, their breath steaming in the cold night air. Ellie had a lot of experience quickly guesstimating numbers on a restaurant floor. This was a hundred-cover gig, for sure.

She heard boot heels on the deck planks and spied Mary O'Donnell coming out of the kitchen, steam trailing from an old enamel mug she held in both hands as though to warm them.

She smiled at Ellie.

"I must thank you, Eliza," the older woman said. "I don't know if I could have pulled this off without your help."

Mary gestured at the gathering.

Ellie scoffed.

"Mary, I bet you're one of those women who could crank out a feed for two hundred cowboys before turning around to do a garden party for the PTA. I just helped. That's all."

"Nonsense," Mary O'Donnell insisted, taking the empty chair next to Ellie. She was dressed lightly for the cold, protected only by a woollen shirt and a sleeveless puffer. But she would be used to the cold up here, unlike Ellie, who had spent the last decade in hot kitchens on the West Coast. "You absolutely must give me the recipe for the spice rub you put on that pork," Mary said. "Everybody is talking about it."

"It's a French rub," Ellie said. "Escoffier via Julia Child. The secret is the fresh herbs, which is all down to you and your glasshouse. But I'll write it out for you before we go."

Mary sipped at her drink. Hot chocolate, Ellie thought, with a dash of rum.

"Are you sure you want to keep moving?" she said. "It's very dangerous out there now."

"It's very dangerous everywhere now," Ellie said. "We drove through Livingston."

A shadow flitted over the other woman's pleasant features.

"It was terrible," she said quietly. "They did that, and then they left. Like they were just making a point."

"They were," Ellie said.

"But what?" Mary asked.

"The point," Ellie explained, "was to show that they could do it, and you couldn't stop them."

They fell silent for a minute, watching everyone else enjoy themselves. Most of the children had disappeared, frogmarched off to bed by a phalanx of grown-ups led by Tammy Kolchar and Ramona Tilley. A few of the older kids gathered around a fire pit to finish whatever remained of the dessert. Ellie knew the name of the eldest one, Laurence, who was playing checkers with Pascal while Maxi looked on. She grinned at that. Maxi was officially one of the 'little ones' as the youngest of the children were collectively known, and he should have been in bed already.

"He's a lovely boy," Mary said, seeing Ellie's attention settled on Max. "Is he..." she started to say before trailing off. "I mean, did you and Jodi..."

Ellie smiled to see the bright red flush coloring Mary O'Donnell's cheeks and quickly spreading down her neck.

"No," she smiled. "Jodi was with a guy in San Francisco when she had Max. A personal trainer. Complete douchenozzle."

Mary's confusion was evident.

"He worked in a gym, shouting at people," Ellie said. "He was a terrible human being."

And probably dead, she thought.

The last time she'd seen Chad Moffat, he was running away from them, and Karl Valentine was standing over the body of his dead roommate.

Jesus Christ, that felt like a thousand years ago.

"Well," Mary said as if all her questions had been answered and the matter was settled. "Your Max is a very polite little boy. You and

Jodi have obviously raised him properly before all… this." She waved one hand around. "And you've done very well to keep him safe since it all happened."

"Thanks," Ellie said. "But we had help. Karl and Damo are solid men."

She nodded to where the two of them had taken up position near the spit roaster.

Mary nodded. "They must be."

She put down her mug of hot chocolate and reached over to squeeze Ellie's arm.

"You will do what you think best, but Tom and I want you to know how grateful we are for you helping to get James back home."

Ellie shifted uncomfortably. She was still having nightmares about that day.

"No problems," she said.

Mary shook her head.

"No. James told us what you did. He would not be alive…" Mary O'Donnell searched the small crowd for her son with eyes that had suddenly gone glassy and wet. "None of them would be alive if you hadn't stopped to help."

She turned her red eyes back on Ellie.

"So, thank you, and know that you'll always have a place to stay here."

Ellie thanked her, but her throat was tight, and her own eyes were a little blurry with tears.

RICK BOREHAM DROPPED into the seat next to Laurence Bloomfield. Laurence played checkers with the French kid while Jodi Sarjanen's little boy watched. That wasn't going to last. It was well after ten o'clock at the end of a long day, and Maxi Sarjanen was almost asleep, his eyelids drooping and his head nodding forward, no matter how furiously he tried to fend off the Sandman.

Rick's arrival woke him for a few seconds, but Ellie Jabbarah swooped in, gathered him up despite his yawning protests and carried him away, warning Pascal that he was next.

The two bigger boys rolled their eyes.

"She's right, boys," Rick said. "Everyone needs to get to bed soon."

"Not us," Pascal said, moving a piece across the checkerboard as if that was the perfect answer to Rick's challenge.

"Oh, are you offering to stay up and help tidy?" Rick said. "That's good. Because there is a heap of washing and cleaning to be done."

Pascal's eyes went a little wide.

"I'm sleepy," he said, quickly standing up from the table and pointing to the checkerboard. "I'll beat you in the morning, Bloomfield. Don't move any of those pieces. I have a photographic memory."

And with that, he was gone, running off to catch up with Ellie and avoid enlistment in the clean-up crew. Small groups were already picking up the leftovers, and Laurence sighed and started to gather the dirty paper plates from which he and Pascal had been picking at bits of pie crust.

"Don't worry about that," Rick said. "I just wanted to talk to you before you went to bed."

"Oh," the boy said. "Okay. What's up?"

Rick shook his head, a discreet movement.

"Nothing's up," he assured the boy. "I've just been meaning to see how you were doing after the fight at the cavalry memorial. James told me you did really well."

Laurence was very still. His shoulders might have lifted a little, or they might not.

"Was okay," he said. "I had my karate."

Rick chuckled at that, but not unkindly.

"Well, your karate was strong, Laurence. James and Michelle said the guy you were fighting was twice your size."

"Not that much," the boy said quietly. "Maybe one and a half times. But he was slow. And I kicked him in the knee like my sensei taught me. Knees break easily."

"They sure do," Rick said. "And Nomi, she jumped in and finished this guy, right?"

Laurence looked around as if searching for the dog. She was asleep by a fire pit full of glowing coals, her tummy noticeably fatter from all the pork she'd eaten. The boy looked troubled. He nodded uncertainly.

"It was kind of gross," he said.

"Not like shooting a man from a distance. Or even kicking out his knee?" Rick suggested.

"No," the boy agreed. Reluctantly. "It was different from that."

Rick slowly rubbed his hands together against the creeping chill. It was getting icy cold, and the fires had all been allowed to burn right down. The background roar of conversation and revelry had subsided to a buzz as everyone still awake pitched in to help tidy up.

"Yeah," he said. "It's a hell of a thing, coming through a fight like that. A terrible thing, Laurence, in some ways, because the fight keeps going on in your head. Even when you're done with it in the real world. Does that sound right?"

"Yes, sir," the boy said in a small voice.

"You don't have to keep fighting, though," Rick said. He leaned over and lightly punched Laurence in the shoulder. A supportive gesture. "You can leave it behind. I promise you that, Laurence. I've walked out of a lot of fights. Bad ones. And it took me a long time to learn how to walk *away* from them, which is a different thing. But it can be done."

A shudder ran through the boy's shoulders, but only one before he stilled again.

"Okay," he said.

Rick reached over again and tousled his hair.

"You did good, son. People here tonight are still breathing because of you looking out for them. But now you gotta look out for yourself. You go see Mrs O'Donnell and get yourself a glass of warm milk. I know she's got some. It'll help you get to sleep and digest all that food you ate. And I want you to take Nomi with you tonight. You can bunk down with her in your sleeping bag. She looked after you before. She'll look after you now."

Laurence Bloomfield blinked at Rick as if he didn't quite understand.

Rick leaned forward to impart a grave secret.

"She gets a little shook up after a fight, too. And she likes a cuddle. Calms her down. So, could you do that? Take care of my good girl tonight?"

The boy nodded, unsure at first but then with more confidence.

"Yeah, I guess," he said.

"Good man. Her farts are terrible, but I'll bet yours are worse," he added, drawing a laugh from the boy. "Now, unless you want to stay up and wash dishes, I suggest you make yourself scarce," Rick said in a low, conspiratorial voice before whistling to Nomi.

She came awake slowly from a roast meat coma but dutifully answered her master's call.

"Nomi! With Laurence," Rick said, clapping him on the shoulder.

Nomi grunted and trundled off with the boy, her legs slightly splayed to make room for a bloated tummy.

Rick was about to get up when Mel surprised him, slipping her arm around his neck from behind and kissing the top of his ear.

"Hmm, what's all this 'ere, then," she teased, kissing him again.

Rick pulled Mel around and sat her down on his lap.

"Just checking up on him," he said. "He's been quiet since Bachman."

Mel watched Laurence disappear inside the house, heading for the lounge room where some of the older children were sleeping on the floor.

"You constantly surprise me, Sergeant Boreham. He gonna be okay, you think?"

"I think so," Rick said. "I guess. I don't really know how any of these kids deal with it. What a world we've made for them."

"We didn't make it or unmake it, love," Mel said. "We're just doing our best." She ran the tips of her fingernails through his short-cropped beard. "And your best is very good."

She leaned in and kissed his ear again, keeping her lips against his skin, sending a low-grade electrical charge through his system. "And Mary's given us a room to ourselves."

"Oh," he said, catching on. "I see."

She pulled away and smiled. A slow burn.

Rick frowned.

"But I was supposed to talk with Tom and the other fellas about this Legion thing."

"In the morning," Mel said.

"But Michelle said…"

Mel placed her hand over his mouth, shutting him up.

"Michelle and James have their own room, too."

22

THEY TOOK HER

Ross Jennings was sitting down to a steak dinner when the front doorbell rang. He didn't slam his knife and fork in annoyance, but he didn't lay them down gently either.

"I'll get it, Dad," his youngest daughter Amy said. "You just got back from work."

Whoever was at the door rang the bell again, adding a rapid series of loud knocks for good measure.

"Oh, good grief," Jennings said. "What now?"

He waved at his daughter to sit down. She did so, but reluctantly. Coming on twenty years of age, she was growing into her mother's wilfulness, God rest her soul.

"You stay here, Amy," Jennings said. "Whatever this is about, I don't want you involved."

The young woman frowned but did as she was told. Jennings took the small flashlight he used for moving about the house at night and clicked it on. The batteries were getting old, and the beam from the LED bulbs was weak. He adjusted the focus to provide a smaller, brighter light circle.

He heard a man's voice at the front door, muffled.

"Ross, are you there? It's me, Dan. Come on, please."

He recognised his caller immediately. Dan McNabb, the city engineer. Jennings managed to feel both relieved and slightly pissed off. At least with McNabb, the problem would be something serious but conventional. Broken water mains. A malfunctioning sewerage processor. Issues with the diesel generators at one of the medical clinics. It wouldn't be another shit sandwich from the endless buffet served up by Jonas Murdoch and his goons.

Jennings tried to set aside his resentment as he felt his way down the darkened hallway. Behind him, the kitchen was dimly lit by candlelight, and it was dark enough outside that he couldn't see McNabb's outline through the frosted glass of his front door. The further he got from the wood-fired stove, the colder and darker it got. But not nearly so much as it was outside, of course. There was minimal street lighting in Three Forks these days, and Murdoch's people had 'requisitioned' all of the solar cells and batteries around town for their so-called strategic priorities.

"I'm coming, Dan," Jennings called out as the knocking continued. And more quietly to himself, "If you would just hold your damn horses."

He was seized by a moment of guilt just before opening the front door. The smell of his dinner was powerful. Amy had cooked the two steaks in a cast-iron skillet on the wood-burning stove. She had baked biscuits, too and made gravy. It was a feast, even in Three Forks, where they had done better than most places, but he knew it wasn't the sort of meal that regular folk could look forward to.

McNabb banged on the front door again. Less of a hammering this time and more of an urgent rapping. Ross Jennings pointed the flashlight's beam directly at the frosted glass to let Dan know he was coming. McNabb pressed the doorbell again. What on earth was wrong with him? Jennings got over his guilt at enjoying a decent home-cooked meal – after all, nobody in Three Forks would begrudge him the indulgence, knowing what he had to put up with these days – and he hurried to unlock the door.

McNabb was a slight man with thinning hair and a stooped posture. But his appearance belied an iron core. That curve in his spine had been much worse, Jennings knew. A childhood disability corrected by more than a dozen surgeries over his teenage years. Dan McNabb had studied for his engineering degree lying on a hospital gurney. His postgraduate qualifications he collected in a wheelchair. And during his first year working for the city's engineering department, McNabb got about with a pair of crutches. If Danny McNabb was any tougher, he would rust. Ross Jennings had never seen the man looking so distressed as when he opened his front door to him that night.

The city engineer was lightly dressed, wearing a thin windbreaker over his office clothes. He must have been freezing. But he was so agitated by whatever had brought him to Jennings' door that he seemed not to notice the wind chill and the sleet outside.

"They took her, Ross. They took my little girl," he said, his teeth chattering so hard that Jennings had trouble understanding him at first.

"Good Lord, Dan, get in out of the cold right now," Jennings said. "You'll freeze to death out there."

He held the door a little wider, even as the warm air inside his house rushed out into the night, but McNabb made no move to enter. Instead, he sort of jumped up and down on the spot, more out of frustration than any attempt to keep warm.

"Ross, you don't understand," he shivered. "They took her. Murdoch's men, they took my Nicky for their... comfort station."

He had trouble getting the last words out, as though they were caught behind his teeth. Quickly looking up and down the street to see if any of Murdoch's men was watching them, Ross Jennings took his friend and colleague by the arm and dragged him inside, quickly closing the door behind them.

"Nicky?" He said. "But she's only sixteen."

"Fifteen," McNabb said. "She's still fifteen, Ross. And they took her. They're not supposed to do that."

Amy's voice reached them from the other end of the hallway.

"Dad, is everything alright? Is that Mr McNabb? You want me to set another place?"

"Sure, honey," Jennings said, waving her off. "Do that. And go and have your dinner in front of the TV. We have some city business we need to discuss."

The TV didn't work, of course. But Amy didn't protest. She might have inherited her mother's wilfulness, but she had also been gifted with Maureen's intelligence. She would know that something was up.

Now that he was inside where it was warm, Dan McNabb seemed overwhelmed, possibly even suffering from shock. Or maybe hypothermia. He blinked slowly and looked around as if he wasn't quite sure where he was. Jennings took him by the elbow again and pulled him gently towards the kitchen. Amy was fussing around at the bench by the oven, fixing their guest a small meal from their own provisions. Jennings didn't interrupt her as he sat McNabb gently at the table, but he went to the cupboard and pulled out two shot glasses filled with a couple of decent slugs of rye. That was one thing they had plenty of since the Legion took over. The bars all over town were well-stocked for those who had the means to drink there.

"Thank you," McNabb croaked. He threw down the shot in one go. His eyes, already watery, teared up, and he wiped at them with the back of his hand, but otherwise, he showed no ill effects from having just slammed down a double measure of Knob Creek.

Jennings sipped at his with care. More for the sake of form than because he needed the libation. His dinner was getting cold, but he ignored it.

"Tell me what happened, Dan," he said, taking the chair next to him.

McNabb breathed out, and Jennings could smell the whiskey on his breath. He shook his head, but more as though he couldn't believe what he was saying.

"Well, you know we've been having trouble with that Runeberg fella," he said, looking directly at Jennings with his bloodshot eyes.

"I remember," Jennings said. "The generator at the sewerage plant."

McNabb nodded.

"That's right. They wanted to swap out our Siemens unit for some rinky-dink Chinese thing they pulled out of Livingston when they shot that place to hell. They said it would do the job and needed our genny for their camp outside Bozeman. Well, I told them no. You pull out our generator and drop in a lower capacity model, and you'll have raw sewage coming out of everyone's kitchen sink in less than a day."

"I remember. Go on," Jennings said. Had Dan forgotten they'd had a meeting with Murdoch about this?

"Well, I was dealing with that mechanic fella they've got running a lot of their machine shops. Rausch, his name is. And he was about as reasonable as any of those guys. I think he understood the risk they'd be running if they plugged the underpowered generator into the treatment plant, given we got so many extra people in town for the winter. I thought I might have even turned him around on it. But the next thing I know, Runeberg is in my office with a couple of goons, and he's yelling at me, screaming at me, Ross, to get it done and get it done today, or I'd regret it. It was like Murdoch never talked to him after he said he'd sort it out."

Jennings poured another round of drinks. Just a few drops for him and a modest measure for his old friend. He didn't want him getting drunk, and Dan McNabb was not one for bending the elbow. He threw that second drink down just as quickly as the first one, though.

"Well, of course, I didn't do as he wanted. That's not something I would do without consulting you or the rest of the council. That would be a helluva thing, wouldn't it?"

"Yes, it would. You did the right thing, Dan. But what happened next? What happened to Nicky?"

The mention of his daughter's name hit McNabb like a slap.

"When I got home," he said, swallowing awkwardly. "I got... I came home, and she was gone. She wasn't there, Ross. They took her. I know they took her, and I know where. To that... place they have."

He couldn't go on, and Ross Jennings patted him on the shoulder, sparing him the effort.

"That's enough," he said. "I'll go see Murdoch right now and sort this out."

The engineer squeezed his fists into tight little balls.

"I'm coming, too."

"No, Dan. You're not," Jennings said. "Stay here and have dinner. Keep an eye on Amy for me. I will bring your Nicky back with me. Okay? Can you look after Amy for me?"

McNabb agreed, if reluctantly.

Jennings thought about telling him there was a .45 in the top drawer of his dresser in the bedroom but decided that three belts of rye whiskey would not mix well with Danny McNabb's fear and rage, and a loaded firearm wasn't likely to help with that.

He told his daughter he was going out for half an hour to make sure Mister McNabb ate something and to keep his dinner warm as best she could.

JONAS MURDOCH WAS in the dining room of The Sacajawea Hotel, enjoying slow-cooked beef ribs with Leo Vaulk and Tommy Podesta and wondering if it might be worth sending a scouting party to Idaho to search for potatoes when a lieutenant of the Cohort approached the table. They were the only people in the room beside a couple of waiters dressed in the hotel's livery, nervously awaiting a summons to top up a drink or deliver another round of smoky beef ribs. Chad had the night off and was probably in a gym somewhere, racking up weight plates.

Jonas probably should have been there with him.

He hadn't done any training worth a damn in nearly a month, and he was getting soft around the edges. Very soft.

The Cohort lieutenant, a former rent-a-cop at the North Town Mall in Spokane, marched up to the table and saluted.

"Sir, the mayor wishes an audience."

"Dude, send him in," Jonas said. "Old Ross'll turn into a fucking popsicle if you leave him outside too long."

Another salute and the man spun around with machine-like precision before marching out of the dining room again.

"Bolger's really got those guys wound up tight," the Tripod said.

"A little too tight, you ask me," Leo replied, sinking his fork into a steaming slab of dark meat that came apart at the touch.

Podesta grunted.

"Just saying is all," Leo shrugged.

"You worried about Bolger?" Jonas asked Leo.

"You should worry about the hundred triggermen he's got answering direct to him," Podesta put in before Leo could say anything. "Or maybe not *worry*. But don't *forget* about them, boss. My old boss, the Mooch, he always said power don't come from the barrel of a gun. That's just bullets. Power comes from the guy who says to put one-a-them bullets in another guy, and everyone goes, "Yeah sure, boss," and starts pulling fuckin' triggers."

Jonas grunted but said nothing.

The Tripod would never win first-class honours from Harvard, but that wasn't a bad explanation of the theoretical difference between power and violence.

None of it was helping his digestion, which had not been good of late. Truth was, Jonas did sometimes worry about Bolger and the Cohort. The Legion was ten times as big as Bolger's elite guard unit. But that was the thing, wasn't it? The Cohort was the elite. Lots more ex-military guys. More than a few cops. And the rest with National Guard or legit militia experience on their resumes.

He pushed the plate of meat away, suddenly not so hungry.

None of this shit was easy. Jonas had done a pretty good job, he thought, pulling everything together after Silverton. And who could argue with the results? Here he was, sitting in a fancy fucking steakhouse, scarfing down slow-cooked beef rib, despite the end of the fucking world. It wasn't just him, either. All his guys got the good stuff. He was the only reason anybody enjoyed anything nice these days.

Jonas looked around the cavernous dining space as Mayor Jennings appeared through the French doors at the other end of the room, escorted by Bolger's lieutenant.

He was alone in here, save for Leo and the Tripod.

Every other table was empty.

He felt something that might have been indigestion or worse starting to burn a hole in his guts.

It put him in a poor frame of mind to listen to Roscoe Jennings' whiny bullshit.

"Mister Mayor," he sighed. "What can I do for you?"

ROSS JENNINGS HAD NOT BEEN to the Sacajawea Hotel since Zero Day. He struggled to remember the last time he actually had been here and thought maybe it was for Dean and Hope Folkvords' silver wedding anniversary. That had been quite the party. Probably the biggest night at the Hotel since it reopened back in 2010. He tasted bile at the back of his throat when he saw Jonas Murdoch and his cronies sitting across the room, tucking into enough food to keep a family alive for a week.

For a small mercy, the giant Aryan ape-man he kept around as a bodyguard was nowhere to be seen. Probably because they couldn't trust him not to inhale the buffet. Jennings worked hard to keep his expression neutral as he approached. He needed something from Murdoch, and there was no sense getting the man offside. Jennings didn't know whether to be relieved that Runeberg wasn't eating with them. It would be quicker to get to the truth of the thing if he had been here. But possibly dangerous, too. Mathias Runeberg was a much more intelligent, nastier customer than this second-rate Mussolini. On the other hand, the presence of Podesta and that fat degenerate Leo Vaulk was, on balance, a positive.

Podesta was obviously a mobster of some sort and no intellect, but he had street smarts and had taken a liking to Marion Bates, Jennings' secretary. Marion said he was quite the gentleman when he wasn't hanging around Murdoch and glowering at people. It set Jennings' teeth on edge, to be honest, but who was he to judge Marion for keeping company? And Vaulk? He was one of those characters you met more often than you'd imagine in the small business world, a fellow with an overly large opinion of himself but a man to whom there was so much less than met the eye.

"Mister Mayor," Jonas Murdoch sighed as if already bored. "What can I do for you?"

Not a good start, then.

"I'm sorry to interrupt your dinner, sir," Jennings said. He had never taken to calling Murdoch 'Centurion', but the rote deference came quickly to him now, and he dipped his head to Vaulk and Podesta. "Mister Vaulk, Tommy."

Vaulk nodded but was too busy shovelling meat into his mouth to say anything.

Podesta smiled pleasantly enough, "Mister Mayor."

"What's up, Ross?" Jonas said. "You can't be hungry. Mathias said the ration allotments went out to everyone today. And you're on the A-List, man."

"It's not the rations, no," Jennings said. "But it is to do with Mister Runeberg."

"Oh yeah," Leo Vaulk said, suddenly interested. The fork hovered just in front of his open mouth. There was barbecue sauce smeared all around his lips. "What's Runeberg done now?"

Jennings maintained his poker face but filed that away. It was apparent that Leo Vaulk had some issues with Mathias Runeberg. Made sense, he supposed that the Legion's logistics manager and operations boss might rub up hard against each other.

"Well, I don't know that he has done anything," Jennings explained, in as reasonable a tone as he could, "but I worry that there's been a mistake."

Murdoch was already looking bored and ticked off, but Vaulk's attention had shifted from his dinner plate to whatever Jennings had just brought to their table. Jennings pushed on.

"My engineer, Dan McNabb, was working with Mr Runeberg to sort out the issues with generators and power supplies. You might remember we discussed them a few weeks ago. Dan is concerned..." Jennings chose his following words carefully, "... He is very worried that Mr Runeberg has..."

God, there was no way to say this without just saying it. All three men stared at him, none bothering to hide their feelings. Vaulk looked like somebody had just placed a second hot dinner in front of him, and he had realised he was still hungry. Murdoch looked angry, but the anger was free-floating and could just as easily fall on Jennings as on Runeberg. And Podesta had gone blank. He did that when things were undecided. Waiting for his orders, Jennings presumed.

"Look," he said, deciding to plunge in with both feet. "Dan had that blow-up with Runeberg over the distribution of diesel generators. Bottom line, you told Runeberg no, and now Dan's daughter is missing. He is terrified that she's been grabbed and put to work in one of your damn brothels. As a threat or... something."

There, he'd done it.

It felt both terrible and a blessed relief to get the words out. Now, he just had to wait and see what happened. Leo Vaulk was smiling, and it looked like the smirk of a man who's just rolled a hard six on his last five dollars. Tommy Podesta was still unreadable. If anything, his expression was more of a blank slate than before. Jonas Murdoch, however, rolled his eyes.

"Oh, for fuck's sake," he muttered. "This again? You sure about this? About all of it?"

Ross Jennings allowed a small flame of hope to flicker in his chest.

"Yes," he said. "I am. Dan just came around to my place, and he was in a state. Nicky, his daughter, is only fifteen years old. She's still at school, Murdoch. She's just a kid."

"So, what do you want me to do about it?" Murdoch said, and that small flame flickered out inside Ross Jennings' heart. "A lot of women volunteer to serve in the comfort stations. Conditions are good there, Jennings. Much better rations, for one thing. Maybe she volunteered?"

Jennings stared at him.

"She's fifteen."

This had precisely zero effect, so he hurried on. "And Dan is classified as a tier one essential worker, so his ration allotment is very generous."

"Maybe she got bored," Murdoch shrugged. "Women get bored. My ex-wife did, for no fucking reason at all."

"Ha, amen to that, boss," Podesta said, seeing where this was going.

They all could, including Leo Vaulk.

"What do you want us to do about it, Mister Jennings?" Vaulk asked. There was no challenge or impatience in his voice. It seemed a genuine inquiry, and Jennings was convinced then that if he was to have any leverage in this exchange, it would come from leaning into Runeberg's rival, not his boss.

Politics, he thought. It never ends.

"I would expect you would get her out of there," he replied.

"Out of where, Jennings?" Murdoch asked. His tone was still shaded toward belligerent. This was obviously going to be a problem, and he didn't want to deal with it. "You don't know where she is, do you?" Murdoch went on. "Did you even bother checking out the Officer's Club before you came at me?"

"As you know, the... Club is for Legion personnel only. Even if I wanted to go in there, I couldn't get past the front door."

"She might've had a fight with Daddy and decided the way to show him who's boss was to open her legs," Murdoch said.

Oh, this was not going well.

Jennings felt his temper getting away from him. He took a deep breath before he said something stupid. He needed a result, not a fight he couldn't hope to win. Jennings glanced at Vaulk, who was eating again but watching him closely.

"Mister Murdoch," he said. "I don't need you to get between Dan and your man Runeberg over the generator issue. They're both big boys. They know their jobs, and I'm sure they will sort it out. But this... This business with his daughter. It cannot stand. If it gets around town that your people are taking children and making them work in brothels, you will have a revolt on your hands. A revolt you could easily avoid."

Jennings looked directly at Vaulk before adding, "A revolt anybody who was half competent could have avoided."

"Jesus fucking Christ," Murdoch muttered, shaking his head and staring at the table.

"Mathias is in charge of operations for the whole of the Legion," he went on. "He makes sure that everybody we promised to look after is looked after. Food, shelter, power, medicines. Security. He is making that happen across a four-state area. Your guy is way out of line making accusations like this."

Leo Vaulk carefully placed his cutlery aside and turned toward Murdoch.

"Boss, this could be a real problem for us. One we don't need."

Murdoch rubbed a hand down his face, pulling his features into a grotesque mask.

"Fuck, Leo. I just wanted to enjoy my dinner."

"It's a good dinner. But the mayor is not the one fucking it up. That'd be Mathias stepping out of line again. You were the one who said we never put the local girls into the local brothels. It just gets folks stirred up. Volunteers only, and they gotta work at least a hundred miles from their hometown. But you know what Mathias is like. Dude likes to cut through a problem. Remember those guys he hung back in Missoula? Turned out they were the only ones who knew the combo to the bank vault where they'd stored all the medicine in town. This'll be his way of not fucking up that badly again. He might have put that kid in the whore house, or he might have stashed her at his office. But he took her. For sure. That's just classic Runeberg."

Murdoch sighed. Exhausted by it all.

"Tommy," he said, half turning to Podesta. "Can you check this out? And if the kid ended up in the Club by accident or by mistake or whatever the fuck went on, just deal with it, would you?"

"Sure, boss," the mobster said.

Ross Jennings could not contain his relief. He felt like he was levitating just an inch or two and could have hugged Leo Vaulk. Instead, like Podesta, he waited to see what happened next. Sometimes, shutting the hell up was the smartest thing you could do.

Murdoch's head was in his hands now. There was no moral universe in which Jennings could find even the merest sympathy for the man, but he did understand the pressures of leadership. And that's what Murdoch was feeling. He was demonstrably unfit for the office he had assumed or seized to be more accurate, and it was crushing him.

"All right, Tommy," Murdoch said through his hands. "Go now. Get it done."

"I'm on it, boss," Podesta assured him. He folded his napkin and placed his knife and fork next to each other on the plate. His dinner remained largely uneaten.

"You oughta come along with me, Mister Mayor," the mobster said as he stood up and slid his chair back under the table.

Jennings felt his balls try to crawl up inside his body at the suggestion. He did not want to get involved in whatever messy, low-rent conflict was playing out here. But nor did he fancy the idea of confronting Mathias Runeberg by himself. And Runeberg had to be confronted.

He bid good night to Murdoch and Vaulk and followed Tommy Podesta out of the dining room. Leo Vaulk was happily carving into his beef rib again. Jonas Murdoch just sat there staring at his meal, shaking his head.

Tommy 'The Tripod' Podesta had seen how fast this shit could go sideways. The Tripod hadn't ever been a made guy when he was collecting the vig for Paulie Milano, but he wasn't no fucking zip neither. When the LA crew went to the mattresses over that thing between the Milanos and the Franchinas, the Tripod was right in the thick of it. The Milano administration trusted him. They let him see things. And as he walked Mayor Jennings down the street to the former real estate office where that little shitweasel Runeberg had set himself up, the Tripod could feel things slipping sideways here, too. Didn't mean they were going to start throwing down with each other, but when the bosses got ideas into their heads, it could be a hell of a job changing their minds.

It was deathly fuckin' cold on the night-time streets of Three Forks, which was one of the dumbest names for a joint Podesta had ever heard. And although he figured it was because of the rivers they had out the back of town, because rivers had forks in them, whenever he thought about it, he couldn't help but see a plate set out for dinner, with three forks instead of your more conventional silverware arrangements. This fuckin' place, it messed with a guy's head.

Mayor Jennings, who was as big a log of fuckin' stale mortadella as Tommy Podesta ever met, had a flashlight, which he used to guide them along the icy footpath. For this, the Tripod was grateful, it not being on his list of things to trip up and fall on his ass in the dark. That sort of foolishness could kill a guy these days. Seriously. And the sidewalks were starting to ice up as bad as Chicago. Another cold-as-hell cow town. He'd been to that particular shithole for two weeks back in '08, chasing down a guy who thought he could skip out on the forty large he owed the Milanos. And hadn't that been a helluva thing, having to tiptoe his way around the fuckin Chicago outfit because they were still pissed at Paulie for some shit he pulled on them back when Frankie Breeze was doing the numbers on the south side before fuckin Frankie Jr took a wire for the feds and ratted out his old man. Or so they said. Only being an associate of the Milanos rather than a properly made guy, Tommy Podesta was not privy to *every* fuckin' thing that went on, but he knew his way around the outside of most of them. And that's why he was worried about this Runeberg thing.

Shit like this was likely to get out of hand if you let it.

And he did not care to imagine what that would look like, given all the camouflage gimps and Johnny fucking Rambo wet dreamers walking around this joint like redneck fuckin' Taliban.

He burrowed deeper into his coat, a really lovely coat that he had picked up from an outfitter in Livingston after they dealt with those jamooks, and stepped out onto the road to cross the street behind Jennings. The mayor was bundled up in one of those ugly-looking puffy jackets all the ski faggots used to wear, and his breath was pluming out of him like Old Faithful as he hurried along.

"Slow it down there, Speedy Gonzales," Podesta warned him. "It's getting slippery with all the ice and shit."

Jennings was jumping around like a guy with a chilli pepper up his ass, but he did slow down.

"I'm sorry, Mr Podesta," he said. "But this is really very urgent. Nicky is just a child. I need to find her. I'm sure if you had children, you would understand."

"Ha!" Podesta laughed. "Don't you worry about me, Mister Mayor. I know all about that kinda trouble. Before all of this happened, I was paying all the alimony in the world plus two sets of school fees to this fancy fuckin college for my kids in LA. And if the school wasn't ringin' me to chase up the fees, they was ringin' me to chase up the kids because neither of those little shits knew the value of a dollar or how hard I had to work to keep them in that stupid joint."

Jennings had stopped in the middle of the road, but it didn't matter because there was no traffic. In fact, they were the only people on the streets. Even the Legion's foot patrols, which randomly wandered around the town centre looking for people breaking curfew, were off busting somebody else's chops right then. Not that they woulda dared bust a single chop belonging to the Tripod.

In the Murdoch organisation, he wasn't *just* a made guy. He was a fucking capo.

"I'm sorry," Jennings said, sounding like he meant it, which surprised the Tripod. "I didn't know you had family in LA. Or anywhere. You must be worried about your children."

To be honest, which was a new thing for Tommy Podesta, he hadn't really thought about his kids in months. They didn't like him much, probably on account of their mother, and apart from bitching about the expense of keeping them in that stupid school, he hadn't given them much thought since Valerie had up and walked out on him. Jesus Christ, had all that been twelve years ago?

The thought left him standing in the middle of the road. Just like Mayor Mortadella here.

It was amazing how time got away from you, especially since everything had gone to shit when the Chinese virus, or whatever the hell it was, put all the computers on the fritz. Including the machines at the track out at Los Alamitos.

Tommy Podesta chuckled at that memory, and his chuckle grew into a rich, happy, genuinely runaway laugh.

The mayor of Three Forks stared at him like he'd gone bananas.

And maybe he had, standing there in the middle of the road, freezing his nuts off, while the whole fuckin' world fell apart. But the truth of it was he was a lucky guy. If he hadn't bet Paulie Milano's four grand on the ponies at Los Alamitos, and the Chinks hadn't done whatever it was they did on that same mad fuckin' day, putting the zap on everyone, including the fuckin' bookies holding his winnings —for once in his goddamned life, his *actual* goddamned winnings— well, it was a lay down that Thomas Vincenzo Podesta would not be alive to enjoy the frozen bite of Montana's mountain fresh air. His fuckin' corpse would be feeding the desert worms in a shallow grave somewhere between LA and Vegas.

He laughed and kept on laughing until he saw the look of genuine distress on the dial of Mayor Jennings. Finally, he turned it down again, wiping away a tear of mirth.

"I'm sorry, Mister Mayor," he said. "But you brought up some things, and they wouldn't normally be counted among the happiest of memories, but you know what, you and me, sir, we are alive tonight when plenty are not, and that makes us winners at the crap table of life. D'you see what I mean?"

Jennings did not, but the Tripod chuckled again.

Nothing had improved except for his mood.

"Come along, Mister Mayor. Let's find your friend's little girl and sort out this unfortunate misunderstanding."

It was not a misunderstanding.

Mathias Runeberg was very clear about that. The Legion's Chief Operating Officer—that's what he called himself, and he had a plaque on his desk in the old Keller Williams real estate office to prove it—Runeberg was one of those fellows who always looked like he was sucking on something extra sour. He had taken over the bright yellow, two-storey clapboard offices of Keller Williams, tucked in between the Frontier Club and the Three Forks Saddlery, most likely because it had solar panels and a big battery. The main office, where four secretaries still tapped away at keyboards, was lit by Coleman lamps, but those keyboards were all plugged into computers, and the computers ran off a big Tesla battery. It was altogether more commodious than the cheap motel they had commandeered when the Legion first took over the town.

"Yes," Runeberg said. "I assigned the young woman to Comfort Station 13. Personnel assignments are the prerogative of Operations, and Station 13 is understaffed. I will admit I also calculated it would encourage the city engineer to rethink his recalcitrant attitude to the greater needs of the Legion as a whole."

Runeberg's shaved head glowed in the lamplight. Shadows pooled in the sunken hollows of his cheeks as he jutted his jaw at the two men.

The bile, burning at Ross Jennings' stomach for nearly an hour now, threatened to leak out through his clenched teeth.

Murdoch was an oaf, but this man was a monster.

A quiet and efficient monster.

Jennings had avoided him whenever possible, but thankfully, Jonas Murdoch's trained gangster seemed to be unfazed by Runeberg's defiance and even scorn.

"Matty, Matty, Matty," Podesta said, "You know the boss don't want no trouble with these folks, and I can't think of a quicker way to make trouble than putting some guy's daughter onto the auction block at a fuckin' discount whorehouse."

"Personnel assignments are the prerogative of Operations," Runeberg repeated.

"She's not yours to assign," Jennings said, and Podesta turned around, placed an open hand on his chest and patted him like a dog.

"Just let me handle this, okay, Mister Mayor."

"I don't suppose you want to handle the power shortage at the Bozeman siegeworks, too?" Runeberg asked. "Because that's what I'm trying to do, with precious little help from anybody, especially Mister McNabb and his so-called engineering department."

"Your siege works are not Dan's problem to deal with," Jennings said, pointedly ignoring Podesta.

"No, they are not," Runeberg shot back, "but Mister Murdoch has tasked and empowered me to deal with them, and your engineer is refusing to assist in the quickest and simplest solution to that problem."

"Matty," Podesta said, "there ain't no point solving that problem over there by making a bigger problem over here, and from what Leo tells me..."

Runeberg rolled his eyes at the mention of Leo Vaulk, but Podesta pushed on anyway.

"From what Leo tells me, that generator you want to slot in here just ain't up to the job."

"I have reviewed the documentation and warrant that it is."

"But you're not an engineer," Jennings protested. Podesta turned, laid his giant paws on Ross Jennings' shoulders and forced him to sit in the cheap, plastic school chair in front of Mathias Runeberg's desk. When Jennings was thus dealt with, Podesta turned back to Runeberg and folded his arms, looming over the little rat-faced man.

"Well, the boss says, it is what it is, Mathias. Find another generator, and give the little girl back."

"If I had another generator, I would have used it," he protested.

"Runeberg," Podesta said, lowering his voice an octave and leaning forward to loom over the much smaller man. "The boss says it is what it is."

He held the man's gaze, staring him down.

Muscles bunched in Mathias Runeberg's jawline, but eventually, his eyes flitted away.

He snatched a notepad from across his desk, scribbled a few words on it, tore off the page and thrust it at Podesta.

"Fine! Go get the little bitch, and don't blame me for Bozeman."

"Pfft," Podesta smiled, passing the paper back to Jennings. "Nobody's blaming you for anything, Matty. Which would not be the case if we started getting toilet water out of the drinking faucets here in town."

Runeberg spun around in his office chair, deliberately showing Podesta his hunched-over spine. He started typing furiously at his computer.

Jennings could only wonder what sort of bizarre and tangled power play he had just watched.

"Let's go, Mister Mayor," Podesta winked. "Time to rescue a princess."

23

AN UNFORTUNATE MISTAKE

He was too late. For as long as he lived—and Ross Jennings would defy the foreshortened life expectancies of the seven or eight decades after Zero Day by living well into his nineties—the mayor of Three Forks was never able to forgive himself for that. He was simply too late.

There was nothing sluggish or laggard about how he busted out of Mathias Runeberg's offices and hurried up the street to where the Legion had established its so-called Officers Club in The Continental Divide Motel. Nor did Murdoch's henchman slow him up. If anything, Podesta seemed as determined to settle the matter as Jennings. Undoubtedly, for his own reasons, but what did it matter? In the end, they were too late.

The motel sat at the northern end of Main Street, between the abandoned Conoco gas station and Wayne Oddy's *Stagecoach* pizza restaurant. The *Stagecoach* was still hanging in there, open for business three nights a week, thanks to supplies provided by Leo Vaulk's logistics operation. Your money was useless there, of course. But a ration card, signed by Vaulk, would get you a hot pizza pie with all the toppings for the equivalent of three hours of manual labour on approved public works for the city or two hours if you volunteered for a project under the direct control of the Legion. Something like digging trenches at the siege works around Bozeman, for instance.

The restaurant was closed tonight, and Jennings hurried past with his hands jammed deep into his pockets. Winter was coming in hard, and he could tell the evening temperature had already fallen below freezing. Podesta hastened alongside him, looking much more comfortable in his overcoat, long scarf, and hat. An armed patrol called to them as they crossed the intersection near Sacagawea Park, but they backed down when the mobster growled at them to 'fuck off.' As a few scattered flakes of snow started to drift down, Jennings hurried across the road and up the front steps of the Continental Divide, another one of those few buildings in town with a permit to run off batteries and a generator after dark. It was well lit up, and he could hear music inside.

Two sentries stood at the top of the stairs, but seeing Thomas Podesta, they stood aside and let both men through. The blast of warm air in the entry hall was a shock after the brutal chill of the night. Jennings felt sweat begin to prickle under his layers of clothing. Not all of that was the sudden temperature change. He was profoundly uncomfortable setting foot in this place, outraged at an almost organic level by how these hooligans had turned a perfectly decent place of business into a house of ill repute. There was no other word for it. Well, actually, there was. There were plenty of different words for what had happened to the Continental. Bordello, brothel, whorehouse. They would all fit.

At first glance, the reception desk looked the same as ever, even down to a box of fundraising mints for the Elks Lodge and the pamphlets advertising local businesses and spots of interest for travellers. But Chrissy Trotter, who used to welcome everyone to the motel with a bright smile and a friendly word, was nowhere to be found. She died two months ago from complications relating to her diabetes. Instead, a young woman from somewhere out of state staffed the front desk and looked like the sort of floozie you might expect to find guarding the entrance to a strip club. She wore a leather miniskirt, knee-high boots and a very low-cut top that would have ensured a quick death from hypothermia were it not for the heating having been turned all the way up. She looked surprised to see Jennings come through the door but smiled when she saw Podesta behind him.

"Hiya, Tommy," she said. "Didn't expect to see you in here. What's the matter? Your lady got a headache?"

"Not a time for jokes, Varna," Podesta said, all business. "You woulda had a fresh fish dropped off here by some of Runeberg's boys," he said before turning to Jennings. "You got that chit he signed for you?"

Jennings was still holding it in his pocket. He passed it to the other man, crumpled and a little damp.

"We need to take this woman with us," Podesta said. "There's been a mix-up in assignments, and she shouldn't have ever been sent to you. You wanna go get her for me, darlin'," Podesta said.

It was not a question.

The young woman's eyes went a little wide when she read the slip of paper, and Jennings was sure that had she not been wearing so much makeup, he would have seen all of the color drain from her face.

"She's in with Mr Bolger at the moment," Varna said.

She did not look like some intimidating big-city nightclub vixen now. She looked petrified.

Jennings didn't know what to feel, but that hardly mattered because his feelings had got entirely away from him. His head was light, his mouth dry, his heart beating like a trip hammer inside his chest.

"This little girl," he said, pointing at the slip of paper held by Podesta, "isn't even out of school yet. She is the daughter of a very good friend of mine and the man who keeps the power running to this... this... abomination of a place," Jennings spat as the doors to the motel's small restaurant and bar swung open. Two men emerged, both of them holding drinks. They wore the grab bag of vaguely military clothing favoured by Murdoch's gun thugs. Camouflage this and tactical that, leavened by personal touches such as the *Duck Dynasty* tee-shirt gracing the one who looked more than a little the worse for wear. He carried a beer in one hand and an oversized glass of some brown liquor in the other. His belt was undone, and the fly on his sandy-coloured army pants was only half-buttoned.

"You got some trouble out here, V?" The second man asked, registering Jennings before realising that Murdoch's right-hand man was also standing there.

"Go and get yourself another drink, Johnny," Podesta said. "I'm on the boss's say-so to clean up a messy pile of Runeberg's shit. Unless you want me using your face as a rag to wipe it all up, you should fuck off back inside."

'Johnny' opened his mouth to say something and even took a step, if somewhat uncertainly, towards Podesta. But before anything could happen, his friend, the two-handed drinker in the Duck Dynasty tee-shirt, hooked an arm around his elbow and pulled him back towards the dining room.

"You don't want a piece of that, man," he said. "Come on, the bitches are going to be getting cold on us."

Podesta said nothing.

He stared into the eyes of the other man, never once dropping his gaze.

"Go on, Johnny," the woman behind the desk said. "I'll comp you and Rog a couple of free ones. On the house. Go on."

That seemed to mollify him, and he backed off, allowing himself to be pulled through the swing doors. Jennings caught a glimpse of the goings-on and was quite frankly shocked. It looked nothing like the old restaurant. Somebody had filled the space with lounge beds and strange, circular couches in which three or four people could stretch out all over each other. Many of them had, and they were not even dressed.

"Sweet Jesus," he muttered.

"Avert your eyes, Mister Mayor," Podesta said. "There's nothing for you to involve yourself with."

Podesta turned back to the girl on the desk.

"What room is Bolger in?"

She didn't have to check.

"The big suite," the woman said. "Up on the top floor. With the hot tub."

Jennings started to say something, but Podesta reached over and grabbed his arm, digging his fingers in. It was like getting caught in a piece of farm machinery. The man's grip was inhumanly solid and unyielding. Jennings almost gasped.

"The smart play for you is to shut up," Podesta said. "You got no authority here, so don't go acting like you do. Just leave it to me."

He turned his attention back to the receptionist.

"Varna, I'm going up there and getting that girl because that's what the boss told me to do. I suggest you do two things and you do them in this order. You ring ahead, and you tell Mister Bolger I'm coming on Mister Murdoch's say-so. You tell him there's been an unfortunate mistake, and he's going to have to find himself another piece of pussy. And then, Varna, you put that phone down, and you go find him some pussy. Not just any old stale fish taco, neither. The best in the house. That's what I'm talking about. Premium gash. Yours, if that's what it comes to. Me, I'm gonna take the stairs. The Chad says I need more exercise, but my knees are not what they used to be, so you probably got a minute to make it all happen. If it don't happen and I gotta clip this mope when I get there, it's gonna be you explaining how all-a-them bullets ended up inside of Mister Bolger, who, despite being a giant asshole, is also an inexplicable fuckin' favourite of your boss and mine, Mister Jonas Murdoch. *Capisce?*"

She nodded quickly, already fumbling for the in-house phone.

Jennings could only stand in front of the desk, his mouth open, his head turning inside out, and his moral compass spinning around as though deranged by a sudden magnetic storm. Podesta, true to his word, started trudging towards the stairwell. He unbuttoned his overcoat and drew out a handgun with all of the ceremony and significance that Jennings might attach to fetching himself a piece of cold chicken from the refrigerator. It was just another immaterial task on a very long to-do list in the middle of yet another workday for Thomas 'The Tripod' Podesta.

THE TRIPOD TRUDGED up the stairs of the Continental Divide, half-wondering what kinda shit show he was gonna find when he got to Bolger's room and half-cursing his luck at being so good at his job that he was always the guy who got sent to do it. Always. He'd been a glorified janitor for Paulie Milano in San Francisco, too, forever cleaning up little piles of shit for that no-good ingrate. And now it seemed he was gonna be sweeping up after Jonas Murdoch the same way. His polished leather loafers creaked on each step as he climbed towards the top floor. The Tripod had to wonder what he'd ever done to deserve this. It wasn't like he was the mope with the statutory fuckin' rape kink banging some local yokel's precious princess in this cheap fuckin' flop house. He was just the guy expected to clean up the mess.

He sighed heavily, pausing at the turnaround on the first floor to light himself a smoke. Luke Bolger was not a guy you went bursting in on, even when you had your rod out and he was distracted by nailing some piece of jailbait. Bolger was the sort of weirdo who would definitely wear an old-fashioned gun belt when he was getting his end wet. Fuck that. He probably couldn't get it up unless he had some sort of weapon to stroke his Johnson. Guns and knives were just instruments to a guy like the Tripod. Tools of the trade. But he'd seen Bolger all but creaming his pants whenever they opened fire on those places that didn't roll out the welcome wagon. The guy was a fucking twist, for sure.

Tommy fully intended to let Varna make the call and give him the bad news first. Let him get used to the idea.

He took a moment to enjoy a couple of long drags on the cigarette before resuming his slow trek upstairs. On each floor, he heard doors opening and closing. On the second floor, one woman was laughing, and another was screaming. He heard country music. The raucous voices of what had to be a room party getting out of hand. And as he made the landing on the top floor, a telephone rang, and a man's voice answered. He stopped and listened. Bolger. Could it be that

Miss V was only getting through to his room now? Sure. So it was worth waiting a little longer.

He had some sympathy for Jennings, who was a bit like him in some ways. Just a guy doing his job. Cleaning up other people's messes. Helping to keep the joint running. But he wasn't about to get clipped on Jennings' behalf by storming in on some angry cock-shrivelled twist like Bolger.

It was a pity about the girl, he supposed, lighting a second cigarette off the first. The Tripod had a daughter, even if she was a bit of a skank and probably dead or running with some fucking gang now. He wasn't the complete deadbeat his ex-wife had made him out to be in divorce court.

Hell of a thing for a man to put up with, the idea that some other guy could just come and take his daughter, his own flesh and blood, and have his way with her. Of course, nobody coulda done that with Tommy Podesta's daughter unless they were lookin' to dig a shallow grave out in the Mojave and fucking beggin' to be put into it after he'd finished with them. But these mooks like Jennings and the engineering guy from the city weren't like that. That's how Jonas had rolled on them in the first place. They didn't have the nuts to stop him.

Still, the Tripod knew it could be a helluva thing, pushing a man. Whether that was a man like Bolger or a man like Jennings. Better idea was to plug them first before they knew you were even coming. He turned to the right at the top of the stairs and started walking down a red-carpeted corridor with light blue walls. Bolger's suite, the biggest in the place, was at the end of the hallway. Double doors and everything. The Tripod could hear him inside, arguing with somebody, almost certainly Varna.

That was good.

At least she got through to him. Stopped him from doing whatever he was doing. And now there was no chance that the Tripod's visit would be a surprise. He didn't holster his pistol. He slid the Smith & Wesson into the pocket of his camel hair coat. It would be a hell of a shame to ruin the fabric by shooting through the pocket, but he knew where he could easy find another one, and it wouldn't do to walk in on this guy with a gun in his hand. Not so that Bolger could see it, anyway. He knocked on the door and stepped to one side, just in case.

"Luke, it's me, Tommy P," he called out. "The boss sent me over to collect the girl."

He heard footsteps thumping towards the door. They were heavy but soft. The footfall of a man not wearing shoes. Podesta prepared himself. Bolger would likely be angry. He sure as shit sounded it. He could be in a mind to lash out. He might even be pissed off enough to focus that anger on the Tripod.

That's how guys were sometimes. Especially about pussy.

And it was why, even after he got the kid out of this room and back home to her old man, he knew his work would not be done. Because as dangerous as somebody like Luke Bolger could be in the usual run of things, a man who had been humiliated and made to feel worthless could be even worse. Which meant Podesta would have to keep a close eye on both Jennings and his friend, the engineer, after this. At least a couple of weeks.

The door flew open, and the commander of the Legion's Cohort stood before him, wrapped in a tiny towel.

That was something, the Tripod thought. He wasn't sure what, but it was definitely something. Jonas Murdoch, for instance, was a guy who loved to get his cock out and wave it in your face. And not in no figurative sense of the thing, neither. He did have kind of a donkey dick, and he liked showing it off. Bolger, it turned out, not so much. At least wearing that towel, the Tripod could see that Bolger didn't have to hand a gun or a knife or anything.

"What the fuck, Tommy?" Bolger snapped.

"Nothing for you to get your nuts in a twist over, Luke," Podesta replied as evenly as possible. He had both hands jammed into his overcoat pockets, but he could tell he wouldn't have to shoot anybody. This didn't feel like that. He took his hands out and folded his arms, standing foursquare in front of Bolger and using the advantage of his height to lean down a little into him.

"Runeberg made a mistake sending the girl over here, is all," Podesta said. "She shouldna been here. It's his fuck up, not mine, not yours, not nobody's but Mathias. So, I gotta take the girl back. Murdoch's orders."

He put some extra power into the last two words. Growled them at Bolger. That should have been enough. The Tripod's presence and the boss's authority should a been enough to bring any man to heal. However, Tommy Podesta was this close to slipping his hand back into the pocket of his expensive camel hair coat because it seemed to make no difference in this case. It seemed to him that this ignorant fucking redneck was gonna give him some pushback.

"The fuck does Jonas care who I screw? He gets first pick of the best pussy. He didn't want this. It's mine now."

Bolger jutted out his chin as if inviting the Tripod to take a swing at it. And Podesta woulda done it too, except they both heard the crying of the girl coming from behind Bolger at that precise moment. She had wandered out of the bedroom – these rooms being more like an apartment than a hotel set up, and her wandering being more in the way of staggering.

The Tripod could see she was in a bad way, banged up and shit, and he favoured Luke Bolger with his most ill-favoured scowl. More fucking mess to clean up. Bolger had the balls to roll his eyes like it was no big deal, and he almost did get himself cold-cocked for that because disrespecting Thomas Podesta was a big fucking deal. What saved him was the timely appearance of these two Fuck Me Barbies out of the elevator just down the hall. They were dressed as schoolgirls from a porno. Uniforms and everything.

They spilled out of the doors carrying six packs and waving a bottle of champagne, and they giggled up such a storm that the Tripod couldn't even hear the crying of the girl in the room no more.

"Hiya, Tommy," they both called out at the same time.

"V said there was a party up here," the redhead went on. "You gonna hang out and party with us, Tommy?"

He had no fucking idea who they were, but he swept off his hat and gave them a bow anyway. They were playing their part. He would play his.

"I am afraid that duty calls, ladies. But I am sure Principal Bolger here will be happy to give you a spanking for one of those beers."

They squealed with delight.

These two women were good at their jobs. Good enough that it gave Tommy Podesta reason to wonder what they had done before all of this. They didn't have the hard-faced look most women got on the game. They looked like local girls, he thought. Like the kid in Bolger's room had been.

They wouldn't be local girls, though. Not from around here, anyway. That's not how things worked. The same way that the Legion didn't have its recruits standing guard over their hometowns, it didn't recruit women to work in the O Clubs where they had lived neither. Nothing good could come of that. This pair was probably from Idaho or Oregon.

Not that the Tripod could give a shit. The only thing he cared about was that they got told what to do, and they got their tight little asses into gear to do it.

That was the sort of professionalism that Tommy Podesta liked to see in an organisation. He would note these two and ensure they got some kind of bonus for making his life easier. Because that was a smart play, too.

He turned back toward Bolger, and the next thing he had to get done.

"I'm gonna need the girl now, Luke," he said. "She got any clothes in there?"

Bolger was distracted. He was already focused on the arrival of the school girls.

"Huh?"

"The girl, she got any clothes? Cos if she don't, I'm gonna need a bathrobe or something for her."

"Yeah, whatever," Bolger said. "Why don't you sort it out, Podesta? None of this is my fault. Runeberg told me I was good to go. And he said I should give it to her rough."

Huh. File that tidbit of information under 'U' for 'Useful', the Tripod thought. But he didn't have time to pull on that thread. The two naughty schoolgirls had arrived at the door, and Bolger stepped aside to invite them in. Podesta followed, looking for the girl.

"Nicky," he called out. "Nicole McNabb, you in here? I'm here to take you home to your dad."

He couldn't see her anywhere, and Bolger was already heading for the bedroom with his new playmates.

"For fuck's sake," Podesta grumbled.

He started searching for the girl. It didn't take so long. Found her curled up in the corner of the tiny kitchenette. She was naked and shivering, even though Bolger had the thermostat cranked up to the max. Tommy Podesta had seen some piss poor things in his life. Occupational hazard in his line of work. But few of them were as pitiful as that little girl trying to squeeze herself into the corner with the dust devils and dead cockroaches.

The fucking degenerates he had to put up with.

Podesta undid the buttons of his overcoat and shrugged it off his shoulders. He removed the gun and wrapped the warm, heavy camel hair coat around her.

"Come on now, Princess," he said. "I'm not gonna hurt you. Not like that other asshole. I'm just here to take you back to your old man. To your dad, at home. Would you like to go home?"

He didn't think he would get anything out of her until he mentioned her home. She didn't stop shaking or shivering, but she did manage to nod her head.

"Alrighty then, kid. Let's get you moving. We'll find you some new threads, but we'll do that downstairs. Get you outta this dump. Pretty sure you want to get gone from here, eh?"

The Tripod could have been some sort of shrink, he was such a good reader of people's minds. That little girl was hugely invested in getting gone from Luke Bolger's room. She dug deep and found enough of herself left to get her ass up off the floor and out of that little kitchenette wrapped in Tommy Podesta's nice new coat.

Well, it had been nice.

He would need another one now because this one had blood all over it.

———

TWICE, Jennings almost followed Podesta upstairs. Twice, the woman behind the desk stopped him, the second time threatening to 'get a couple of guys out here' to beat him down. Jennings didn't think it should take this long to walk up three flights of stairs and get Nicky McNabb. He didn't think there was much point in repeatedly calling the room when Bolger was obviously not answering the phone. And he hardly knew what to think when the young woman at reception dived into the bar to retrieve a couple of prostitutes dressed as schoolgirls.

This was all some sort of nightmare.

But it got worse. Podesta eventually returned with Nicky, and Jennings' horror at the girl's condition was such that he was rendered utterly speechless. Grim-faced but businesslike, Podesta ordered the receptionist to find Nicky some warm clothes and to hurry up about it. Jennings tried to comfort her, but Podesta advised him to 'just fuck off for now.'

They had about ten minutes of people going back and forth, with Nicky stashed away in the manager's office, from where Chrissy Trotter had once run the legitimate business of The Continental Divide. Finally, the poor thing emerged from behind that door, swaddled in athletic sweats, running shoes, and Thomas Podesta's pale tan overcoat. She nodded robotically to Jennings but seemed to truly respond only to the gangster. She was clinging to him and would do whatever he said, and Jennings supposed her to be in shock. He would have to get a doctor over to Dan's place.

"We can't walk her home like this," he said to Podesta. "Dan McNabb lives ten minutes outside of town. She'll catch her death of cold if we make her walk."

"She's lucky she didn't catch her death from Bolger," Podesta said out the side of his mouth. But he seemed to take Jennings's point.

"Hey, sweetheart," he said to the receptionist. "I'm gonna need your car keys."

The woman nodded and dug them out of a handbag she kept under the desk. The bag, Jennings noted in a moment of bizarre inconsistency, was the sort of thing his youngest daughter might have taken to school a hundred years ago. A bright pink clutch covered in Disney princesses.

"Here you go, Tommy," she said. "It's the grey Civic out the front."

Podesta took the keys and shepherded Nicky McNabb towards the front door.

"Come along, Mister Mayor," he said. "Miles to go before we sleep."

24

COME THE THAW

James O'Donnell awoke to the smell of his mother's cooking. He floated in that strange, liminal space between waking and dreaming, where he knew he imagined things, but he didn't care. James indulged himself in the imagining anyway. He was eight or maybe nine years old, and it was the first day of vacation. Incredible vistas of gloriously empty space and time stretched out ahead. His mom was cooking up a storm in the big kitchen they used to feed all the ranch hands. He could smell bacon frying, eggs, flapjacks with maple syrup and coffee in the pot, and distantly, the smell of the cheap cigarillos favoured by Pablo, the leading hand.

It could not last. Reality pressed in, and soon, way too soon, the world crashed in, and James remembered everything. He was home, and although he was happy and relieved to have made it, his return was not without regrets. James made a groggy but mindful effort to push aside the memories of the last three months. The fact was they had made it. He was home. His parents were alive, and his friends were safe. At least for now.

He reached out for Michelle, realising that she was already up as soon as he did. She had probably been up for hours. She had that rare gift of being able to go for days at a time on only a few hours of sleep snatched here and there from the chaos of both day and night. He sometimes wondered whether she had learned the skill, had it imposed upon her, or had simply been born that way. He was naturally an early riser, but that was after years of being turned out of bed to get an early start on his chores around the ranch.

His room was still dark, and he blinked, bleary-eyed, looking for the old electric clock, which should have been glowing in the corner. He found it, but the display was dead, the unit unplugged from the wall. That made sense. His parents would have more pressing needs for their solar panels and battery than running an old digital clock.

Swinging his legs out of bed, he pulled on the jeans that lay in a pile on the floor. They smelled faintly of smoke, but compared to the filthy clothes he had been wearing day in, day out on their long trek across the continent, the Levi's were minty fresh. It didn't seem right to fetch a new pair from the dresser in the corner. He did change his shirt, however. He had spilled barbecue sauce on the one he wore to dinner last night. James vowed to wash it himself rather than simply tossing it into the laundry hamper, as he would have done when he was younger. His mom didn't need the extra work. He pulled on an old and favoured hoodie from Montana State, laced up his joggers, and went to breakfast.

Padding down the main hallway, lined with family photos from generations past, he could already tell there were people in the house. Not just those he had brought home but others who had stayed over. He recognised some of the voices immediately. The loud braying laugh of Damien Maloney and the sharp nasal interjections of Ellie Jabbarah, the chef. He heard Michelle's measured, educated vocals in answer to some question about Washington and the singsong laughter of Mel Baker teasing Sparty Williams about being too lazy and hungover to join her on a morning run. Sparty shot back that he would have run her into the ground when he was a young adventurer.

"But then I took an arrow in the knee."

There were other voices, which he thought might be familiar. He caught a couple of words from his cousin, Simon Higgins, and couldn't quite believe it when he heard his old school friend Stephen Collins reply. James was sure Stephen had left the valley and moved overseas for work; not long after, he had also left the valley.

His face lit up with a dawning smile when he saw that he was right, and Collins was sitting next to his cousin about halfway up the long table. He hadn't been at the barbecue last night, but he was happily tucking into an old camp plate full of scrambled eggs, sausages and bacon. He seemed twice as big as James remembered. Not fat, just thick with densely packed body mass. His arms looked like ham hocks and....

Yes. There it was.

His grin spread wider when he saw the compound hunter's bow leaning in the far corner of the breakfast room. The smile faded a little when it occurred to him that his old friend had probably been using that weapon for more than hunting deer and elk of late.

James experienced a moment of discontinuity. Probably just from walking into a room full of people, eating and talking together. It hadn't been all that long since he'd last encountered such a picture of normality. There'd been at least three or four times as many people at the barbecue the previous evening. But he had watched that event come together over many long hours. Stepping into his mother's kitchen and finding all of these people sitting here, the morning light streaming in through the windows, Ellie banging away at pots and pans on the old wood-fired range, wearing one of his mother's aprons, but also a chef's hat – an actual chef's hat! – James suffered a brief but powerful sensation of free fall. It was almost as though he'd stepped into the past, where people still met for breakfast. Or anything. The clinking of knives and forks, the thump of a thick enamel mug hitting the hardwood tabletop, the sound of laughter and forgetting... After everything that happened, it was almost make-believe.

Michelle saw him, or rather, she saw Stephen Collins pointing at him, and she turned and winked. He smiled and waved back just before his mother appeared before him, carrying a plate piled high with breakfast fixings.

"Where in the hell did you get all this stuff, Mom?" James asked, genuinely perplexed. He had seen the neighbours coming in with food and offerings yesterday but not this morning.

"Don't curse, James," his mother said. "Reverend McKreel is here," she whispered.

James stood, slightly dumbfounded, and took in the crowded room. There had to be thirty or more people squeezed in there. It seemed louder than last night, with voices bouncing off the stone floors and hard surfaces. He hadn't seen the ranch this busy since he was a boy before his father had sold 500 acres and the cattle that ran on them to Darren Tuer across the valley. Recovering slightly and taking a spare seat at the end of the table, he nodded to Maz Jovanovich, who had taken over her father's crop dusting business about the same time James had gone off to college. He said a quick hello to Adam Edmonds from the high school and Dave Matheson, reminding himself that it was Doctor Dave now and that he was a pillar of the local community, not Rhino Ross's drunken co-conspirator.

Tom O'Donnell held court at the other end of the table, surrounded by his contemporaries, older residents of the valley who had not changed nearly as much as James's peers. That made sense, he supposed. Most of the familiar faces looked thinner and greyer, more worn out than he would have normally expected, but these were not normal times.

Outside, children ran about on the lawn, leaving tracks in the silver netting of early morning frost. More grown-ups sat out there, eating breakfast rolls and watching over them. He saw Jodi Sarjanen laughing with Roxarne and Tammy. Karl Valentine was chopping wood for the stove. Seeing James arrive, his dad started to tap a spoon against the side of his coffee mug. The repetitive clinking sound soon brought quiet to the room.

"Thank you, everybody," Tom O'Donnell said, climbing to his feet. His voice was slightly hoarse, and he coughed to clear his throat. "I think everybody is here now, and I know my hangover isn't going anywhere soon—"

He got a few laughs for that.

"So, I think we should convene."

Convene what? James thought. He didn't have a hangover, but he was still groggy and slow.

"Michelle?" Tom said. "Would you like to begin?"

Michelle Nguyen thanked James's dad and got to her feet.

Wait, what?

"Good morning. My name is Michelle Nguyen," she said, "and until three months ago, I was a threat assessment analyst with the National Security Council."

James was instantly thrown back to the first day he had met her.

No, that's not right.

It was the second day after she had recruited him and dropped him headfirst into a long train of crisis meetings full of admirals, generals, and nameless spooks from an alphabet soup of agencies. They were freaking out as the digital infrastructure of America collapsed under Chinese attack and took the rest of the country with it.

Michelle reached into her shirt pocket and plucked out a small plastic rectangle. Her laminated ID. She handed it to Damo, said something James didn't catch, and he passed it on to the next person down the table.

"I apologise to all of you who are familiar with the reality on the ground here, but if you will excuse me, I need to brief in my people," Michelle said.

She reached under the table and pulled out another object, larger and heavier this time. James recognised it as her satellite phone.

"And for those familiar with the situation beyond the local area, I also apologise, but it's important we all end up on the same page this morning."

She held up the chunky black handset.

"This is an Iridium Extreme 9575 satellite phone."

It might have sounded cool, but James knew it didn't mean anything. He'd thrown away his laptop three months ago and thousands of miles behind them. Michelle's sat-phone hadn't worked in all that time. The network on which it depended had disappeared or been shot down or something. The whys and the what-the-hell-of-it hardly mattered anymore. The bottom line was that her expensive piece of tech was just a useless slab of plastic and dead silicon. But she had kept it.

"I was assigned this phone on the orders of Admiral David Holloway," Michelle said. "My supervisor at the NSC in Washington."

It was as though she had invoked some magical incantation over the phone. Everyone leaned forward to get a closer look. A few local boys had been staring at the intricate swirl of tattoos on her forearms, but Michelle's gorgeously inked flesh had now lost its fascination for them. They were all staring at the device she held aloft.

"This phone allowed me to directly plug into the national command architecture via a secure encrypted channel. A certain combination of numbers and letters keyed into this unit would light up a similar handset on the desk of the president of the United States."

James and maybe Rick were the only ones who didn't quietly gasp or murmur in awe. James quickly stuffed a forkful of scrambled eggs into his mouth to cover the smile that wanted to run across his face. A certain combination of numbers and letters keyed into any phone anywhere in the country would get through to whichever bunker they had hidden the president in. You just had to have his contact deets. Still, he nodded in quiet admiration at Michelle's stagecraft. With this performance, he could easily imagine her enthralling a roomful of those generals and admirals. She hadn't lost her edge. Not a bit of it.

"The phone no longer allows me to do that," she said, and silence descended on the room as though she had thrown a weighted blanket over it. "The satellites which carried the encrypted signal are gone. As best I know, the National Command Authority is gone. James, whom I'm sure you all know, will confirm that we haven't been able to get a signal on this thing for months. It's not dead, but the system it plugged into is dead. The country which built it is dead."

She let the low murmur of protest and dismay run around the

room and back. When she had waited long enough, Michelle raised her voice and said, "We are on our own. The government is not coming because the government no longer exists. It has ceased to exist in Washington. It has ceased to exist in your state capital. It no longer exists in Livingston."

More protests, but she did not allow them to run on this time. She slammed the phone down on the table with a loud bang. Everyone jumped, but they also shut the hell up. When Michelle spoke next, she looked everybody in the eye, scanning the room from end to end.

"When the thirteen colonies declared independence," she said. "And secured that independence through force of arms, they held certain truths to be self-evident and certain rights to be inalienable. To secure those rights, they instituted a new form of government, deriving just powers from the consent of those governed."

The silence in the room felt like it was swelling as she spoke.

Michelle had the entire room focused on her now. James had stopped eating. The quiet was too pregnant with meaning to fill it with the clatter of cutlery on his plate.

"You have not declared independence. You have not sought it, but I am afraid it has been thrust upon you, and if you wish to secure those rights you have always taken for granted, there are necessary measures that must now be taken."

James looked across the table at Rick. He was watching Michelle intently, but his face was unreadable.

"Unlike some of you," Michelle Nguyen went on, allowing a softer, more playful tone to carry her voice to them. "I do not have a hangover this morning. I spent most of last night talking to people. In my old job, we would have called it debriefing or assessing or some hundred-dollar consultant's term like that. But mostly, I just walked around and talked to everyone who would talk to me. There is a lot of raw intelligence floating around this valley. Some it derived from travellers and refugees. Some from direct contact with the Legion's scouts and emissaries. This morning, at Tom O'Donnell's request, I will synthesise what I have learned."

James couldn't help himself. He had forgotten his breakfast and been drawn completely into Michelle's performance.

"The Legion which attacked and destroyed your county seat, the town of Livingston, has used similar tactics to establish control across a swathe of territory covering at least four states in the Pacific Northwest. They send so-called ambassadors to a town, usually officials from nearby population centres who have already surrendered, offering simple terms. Submission and protection under the rule of the Legion, or destruction. Livingston chose not to submit."

A few of the men around James's dad shifted uncomfortably. He did not have to wonder whether they had been involved in that decision. Russ Chatham and Tom McGuane were two of the most powerful men in the valley.

Michelle, rolling with her presentation now, had started to walk up and down the room.

"The Legion is led by a man called Jonas Murdoch," she said. "He seems to have been a lawyer in an earlier career before pivoting unsuccessfully to online media work in the last couple of years. I'm sorry I can't be more specific. If I had that intelligence, I would share it with you. But you know, the internet's a bit flaky these days."

Chuckles.

"What we do know about Murdoch," she went on, "is that he leads a militia force rumoured to have more than three thousand fighters. The equivalent of a U.S. Army brigade or cavalry regiment."

James saw the expression on Rick's face go from neutral to disturbed. A furrow appeared between his brows, and the corners of his mouth turned down.

A couple of other people around the table appeared to be similarly upset.

"Some of these fighters will be veterans," Michelle said. "Some may have law-enforcement experience."

A low murmur rose at that.

"However," she said, dialling up the volume but also dropping her tone, putting enough bass into her words to cut across the commotion, "*after* its initial victories, the Legion, as a whole, has never massed in one place. I estimate that at least two-thirds of its strength is devoted to maintaining internal control in those territories under its domination, leaving a smaller battalion-sized force to deploy into the field for operations. The paramilitary unit which invested Livingston and reduced it in a punitive show of force most likely topped out at seven to eight hundred men," Michelle said, before adding almost as an afterthought, "and women. Murdoch seems to be an equal opportunity fascist."

She got a few more chuckles for that, but they were in no way light-hearted.

"Significantly, the Legion did not attempt to take your county seat through close combat—"

"But they shot the hell out of it," someone objected.

"That's right," Michelle confirmed. "They did. They stood off with long-range weapons and poured fire on their objective until they judged all organised resistance had collapsed. That is not heavy infantry taking ground. It is murder by artillery."

A heavy silence filled the room again.

She did not let it rest there.

"Having demanded submission, the Legion withdrew. Without explanation."

Rick Boreham stared out the window into the bright morning light, but his face was deeply shadowed. James wondered whether he and Michelle had discussed any of this before she stood up to speak, but he dismissed his naïveté. Of course, they had.

"Why do you think they did that?" Tom O'Donnell asked.

Again, James did not imagine that question came from nowhere.

"I would defer to local knowledge of seasonal weather conditions," Michelle said, "but we can all see the first snow flurries in the valley. Your valley. The simplest explanation would be that the fighting season is over. The Legion stretched itself to come this far, but having neutralised the last significant resistance to its rule in the area of operations, they withdrew to barracks for winter. They will return in force, come the thaw, to reclaim the ground they have already prepared."

25

THREAT ASSESSMENT

Michelle was on her feet for nearly an hour. By the time she finished speaking, her voice was cracking. It had been a long time since she'd done a lone-handed briefing like this. Hell, Michelle had never done a briefing like this for a roomful of scared and angry farmers. Because that's what these guys were. They weren't fighters. They weren't killers. Their only experience of actual violence was watching this Murdoch asshole demolish their county seat with heavy machine guns and mortar fire. A performative mass atrocity that, she would admit, had the desired effect. It had frightened them into passive compliance. They didn't even realise it, but she could see they were just sitting around waiting for this guy to come back and finish the job in the spring.

"Here you go," Eliza Jabbarah said, handing her a chipped enamel mug. "Cinnamon tea with a spoonful of honey."

"Thanks," Michelle said.

"No worries," the tough-looking chef replied. Michelle could hear all of the time Eliza had spent with that big Australian doofus in those two words. 'No worries' seemed to be his personal Zen koan.

Michelle sipped gratefully at the steaming hot beverage as the meeting recessed for a ten-minute coffee and cigarette break. She saw James coming for her, looking worried. He threaded his way through the room, stopping briefly to say something to Rick Boreham before fixing his radar on her and ignoring everybody who wanted a little piece of him. Michelle understood. She had not flagged this morning's effort with him. She hadn't wanted to worry him or ruin what had been a wonderful homecoming. But it was his old man, Tom O'Donnell, who had taken her aside at the start of the evening and asked if she would be willing to talk to a few people 'from here and abouts' and get back to him with her thoughts about 'these militia characters.' They'd apparently brought order to the northwest states through the simple expedient of killing everybody who stood against them.

"What's going on?" James said as he finally reached her.

"I'm sorry," she said. "Your dad asked me to talk to a few people last night."

"Yeah," James said. "I know. I was there. But this isn't that. What the hell is this? It's like you're back in Washington again."

She did not bother denying it.

It was noisy in the big, open kitchen, with the voices of two dozen people bouncing off the hardwood floor and riverstone walls. She gestured for him to follow her outside. She had spoken for so long that the sun had climbed over the snow-capped peaks and spilled into the valley to glisten on hundreds of tiny lakes and ponds and the long, sinuous course of the Yellowstone River. It was cold, and Michelle shivered, but she did not go back inside to fetch her fleecy-lined jacket. James saw the gooseflesh on her arms and took his coat off, draping it over her shoulders. She tried to object, but he insisted. He was used to the cold up here.

"I'm sorry," Michelle said, picking up their conversation. "But, it didn't take long last night to figure out that your parents and their friends are in trouble, James. Real trouble."

The thing she liked about James O'Donnell, the thing she loved about him, was how his ego never ever got in the way of his considerable intelligence. He frowned, but he did not arc up and make it all about him the way so many of her previous boyfriends would have. Or some of her former colleagues, for that matter.

"You talking about Livingston? About what happened there?" he said.

"Not just there. It's been happening across the state and back in Idaho, Washington and Oregon," Michelle said. "There are lots of people hiding out in this valley, James. A lot of refugees who've been running from these guys."

She saw Damien Maloney talking with Rick and Mel while inhaling one of the sausages from the breakfast buffet that Jabbarah and James's mother had made up. The nutritional resources concentrated in and around this valley were prodigious. Nobody else seemed to understand what that meant.

Well, nobody except Murdoch and his cronies.

"Even those guys," Michelle said, pointing at Damo and Ellie and the others, "even they went about a thousand miles out of their way to avoid tangling with this Legion group. They didn't even know they were doing it at first, just that they were avoiding trouble. Turned out that most of the trouble in Oregon and Washington State was down to one guy and his band of douchebros."

She could see that James was still pissed off with her for not discussing it with him before he walked out of the bedroom and into the crisis meeting his old man had called, but she could also see when he bit down on his disappointment and put his feelings aside.

"So, they asked you to do a threat assessment?"

She nodded.

"Your dad also spoke to Rick this morning. He was up early. They both were."

"Somebody could have come and got me," James said, the closest he got to complaining about being left out of the loop.

Michelle smiled and took his hand, squeezing it gently. She rubbed one finger against his palm where nobody could see the small, intimate gesture.

"Baby, you earned your sleep-in this morning."

He blushed.

"I'm sorry I didn't wake you," she went on, "but this was something I could do that would go a little way towards paying off what I owe you for getting me out of the capital."

The expression on his face was confused. Almost hurt.

"You don't owe me anything for that."

She squeezed his hand again.

"Yeah, well, I have a lot of karmic debt."

A small band of rowdy children chased each other across the lawn, waving sticks like swords. The sort of thing anxious parents would have stopped them doing a couple of months ago. Not now, though.

"You're forgetting, James," she continued. "We didn't really know each other back then. We'd just met. You had no reason to ask me along with you; to be honest, I could give you a bunch of reasons why you'd have been better off leaving me behind."

"That's crazy talk, Michelle," James said.

But she shook her head.

"No," she said. "It's not. A lot has happened since then. Between us, to us, to everyone. And it's not over, James. It's not even close to being over. It doesn't matter how much we want it to be or how much we thought it would be when we finally got here. This thing is not done with us. You saved my life when you invited me to come here with you. Now I will try to save these people's lives, or most of them anyway, so we can finally stop running."

Somebody started ringing a dinner bell, signalling that the meeting was about to resume. The children ran past again, whooping it up, not at all concerned with the tiresome business of grown-ups. Some of the adults were just as disinclined to rejoin the world of real things. Tammy Kolchar had somebody else's little girl on her back and was racing away, pursued by a pack of squealing children. Karl Valentine appeared to be shambling after another host of screaming little ones, his arms held out in front of him as he moaned theatrically, "Brains, brains, feed all the little brains to Zombie Kaaarrrl..."

Michelle could not help but smile.

"What are you going to do?" James asked.

She held his hand as they started walking back into the house. "My job," she said.

JAMES'S COUSIN Simon was waiting for him just inside. Simon Higgins and James O'Donnell had gone through school together, all the way from kindergarten to college. Their paths had diverged then, with James leaving the valley and Simon staying behind to help out on his family's ranch, which he had eventually taken over when lung cancer had taken his old man many years before his time.

"Hey, buddy, this scary lady the one you brought home?" Simon grinned, winking at Michelle to show he meant nothing by it.

"No," Michelle said flatly. "I brought him home."

She winked at Simon, but she didn't smile.

"I'm back on," she said to James. "We'll talk later."

"Damn," Simon said as Michelle marched away. "She really is scary."

"Only if you cross her," James deadpanned.

Simon nodded, "Uhuh. Been married ten years now, and I have found there's two theories to arguin' with a woman. And neither one of 'em works."

James didn't smile, but he did offer his hand. "How are you, cuz? I didn't see you last night."

They shook hands, and James noticed how much harder and more calloused his cousin's grip was than his own – and it wasn't as though he'd spent the last three months working a keyboard and moisturising every day.

Everyone returning to the meeting was inside now, and Simon had to lean in close and raise his voice to be heard over the buzz.

"Sorry I couldn't get here, but I had the watch along Trail Creek Road last night," he explained. "Rode out most of the way to the interstate with Chris Paolini and Ed Garcia. Made a camp in the hills above where the two creeks meet up."

"You take quad bikes or horses?" James asked.

Simon gave him a look.

"Horses of courses."

An old joke between them.

His cousin was famously reluctant to invest in modern technologies for the Higgins Ranch, and James had to assume it'd paid off in the months since those technologies had mostly died. Or been killed from afar.

The meeting of long-time locals and new arrivals put itself back together with a lot of chair scraping and conversation, which died away as Michelle banged a spoon on the edge of her coffee mug.

"We have a lot to get through," she said, projecting her voice to the furthest corners of the room. "And I'm sure there is some delightful cowboy aphorism appropriate to getting on with the job—"

"Talk slowly, think quickly," somebody called out.

"Behind every successful rancher is a wife who works in town," another voice shot back.

Laughter rolled around the table.

James cringed a little inside, wondering how Michelle would handle it. This was not a conference room full of admirals and spymasters. She quirked her lips into a half smile, tapped the spoon against the edge of her coffee mug again, and waited for quiet.

To James's surprise, she got it by sweeping the room with a level, no-nonsense stare that fixed her attention, however briefly, on every man and woman present. As Michelle Nguyen locked eyes with each of them, they fell silent.

"Thank you," she said. "In our last session, we reviewed the facts on the ground, which did not give rise to many reasons for optimism. In this session, I will give you several options for taking action. Rick Boreham, a former Army Ranger with three tours of Afghanistan and one in Iraq will take you through what each of those options entails. None of them will be pleasant to contemplate or simple to execute. All of them require that we gather more intelligence, and I don't imagine the Legion has a liberal policy as regards the treatment of captured spies."

All of the levity which had just filled the room was gone.

Michelle gave it a moment before speaking again.

"With that in mind, and never deluding ourselves about what we are actually discussing today, let us begin," she said. "Option one. Targeted assassination of the enemy's leadership cadre."

ONE OF THE mysteries of life, Damo thought, was the way that as a bloke got older, everything hurt more, except for his arse, which would go numb within a couple of minutes of planting it on any hard surface. The chair he sat in was probably some sort of antique. But that merely meant it was fashioned from butt-numbing hardwood with none of the comfortable ergonomic design and expensive materials to which his tender, aging arse had grown accustomed over the last couple of years. He started shifting uncomfortably in his seat when Michelle Nguyen laid out her second option – sending envoys to cut some deal with this bed-shitting fascist. By the time she moved on to what she had called 'conflict options', Damo was ready to walk the hundred miles or so to this Three Forks joint; there to plant his boot so deeply into Jonas Murdoch's arse cleavage that the fuckwit pocket Nazi would be able to taste shoe leather and old socks at the back of his throat.

Instead, he made do with clenching and unclenching his buttocks through the thirty-minute briefing. At least Michelle didn't go for the whole hour like before. And Rick Boreham, who followed her, was even quicker. He spent about ten minutes talking through some pretty gnarly projections for casualties connected with each of Michelle's options. In the worst of them, hunkering down and trying to hold the valley by force of arms, everybody died.

Damo could tell nobody liked hearing that, but he couldn't find it in himself to disagree with Boreham. The quarter-hour they'd spent weaving their way through the ruins of Livingston told him everything he needed to know about how Jonas Murdoch did business. He might, just might, be talked around to some form of a negotiated settlement if the costs of laying siege to the valley could be made prohibitive. But those costs would be imposed on both sides.

When Rick was done, and Tom O'Donnell took his place to lead the discussion, Damo quietly pushed his chair back and excused himself, saying he had to duck out for a slash. He did, as it happened, but when he'd finished, he avoided the crowded cookhouse and made his way outside, where he found Ellie smoking with Karl.

"You been following any of this?" He asked them as he shaded his eyes to take in the sweeping view of the valley.

"That's why I'm smoking again," Ellie said. "I figure, what does it fucking matter anymore?"

Karl, as was his way, kept his own counsel.

"What about you, mate? What d'you reckon?" Damo said, trying to draw him out.

Karl shook his head.

"Can't say I have an opinion, Damo," he said. "Unless it's to say none of it sounds good. But what does these days?"

Ellie stubbed out her cigarette on the heel of her boot. She blew a thin stream of smoke at the ground. Damo had seen her do that many times out the back of the restaurant when things were not going well.

"You want to get going again, Damo?" Ellie asked, her voice tense and clipped. "Had been kinda hoping we could hang out here for a little while. Jodi was too. Maxi has really enjoyed all this."

She waved at the gently sloping lawn where some of the children were playing with a football under Pascal's supervision. Jodi was down there with the kids, following them as they ran up and down the big, open, grassy area. He could see she was still carrying that little cardboard camera they'd salvaged for her birthday from a looted pharmacy back in California.

"Mate, I figured we'd hit the road again pretty quickly," he said. "Get up to my place before winter shuts everything down."

"Sounds like there is a but coming," Karl said.

"Yeah, but," Damo continued, "I don't reckon we've got Buckley's chance of getting there."

They both looked up at him from where they sat, but Ellie's stare was the more searching.

"Buckley's?" Karl asked.

"Sorry, mate. A bloke whose luck ran out. I meant that I don't reckon we got much chance of dodging trouble much longer."

"Because of this Murdoch guy?" Ellie asked.

"Yeah," Demo said. "You were in there, El. You heard what Michelle was saying. This bloke and his crew have locked up the better part of four states, and she reckons they'll be hungry for more once the snow melts next year."

Damo reached around and massaged his butt cheeks which were still tingling with pins and needles. He could hear Tom O'Donnell inside, still talking away, batting off the occasional question, while he worked his way toward whatever point he intended to get to.

"You think we'd have trouble getting through their territory?" Karl asked.

"I wouldn't know," Damo conceded. "But they don't sound like people who'd be reasonable. About anything. And to be honest, even if they let us through, I'd be concerned about them turning up at my place six months later and saying it all belonged to them now. That's how they roll, and I don't see the Canadian border making any fuckin' difference to them."

Ellie lit another cigarette, took a shallow draw on it, frowned, put it out on the heel of her boot again, and flicked the rest of the smoke away. She looked pissed off, but not with him.

"Man, this blows chunks," she said. "Why do people gotta be like this?"

"That's just how people are, some of them anyway," Karl shrugged. "Probably been that way since Cain and Abel."

She smiled thinly at him.

"You've never been much of a Bible thumper, Karl," Ellie said.

He shrugged and grinned almost shyly.

"A fella's creed is his own business. And I'm not one for making a big noise about anything," Karl said.

"Yeah, well, I am," Damo said. He clenched his fists and

knuckled them into the small of his back, cracking the kinks out of his spine. "I'm gonna head back there in a minute and start saying my piece, but I need to talk to you and Jodi first. I want to know what you think about staying on here for a little bit."

He paused, and they both shrugged and nodded. They'd all been living in each other's pockets for so long that neither Ellie nor Karl had to speak. He knew they were cool about extending their stay in the valley.

"... And, if you would have any problems with me putting my hand up to go on this diplomatic mission Michelle was talking about?"

Karl, again, said nothing, but a shadow passed over his face.

Ellie was not so reluctant to share her thoughts.

"The fuck are you talking about?"

"You heard the options. One of them was to send a bunch of people over to try and talk a bit of sense into this bloke."

"No, Damo. That was only half of the reason to send people over. The other half was to poke our noses where they're not wanted and gather as much information as possible."

"Spies," Karl said.

Damo shrugged.

"A lot of diplomats are spies," he said.

"And you'd be shit at both," Ellie said, her voice growing hard. "You're not a diplomat. You're not James Bond. You're a big-mouthed clumsy bullshit artist on a good day."

"Those are all good points, Ellie," Damo admitted with a cheeky grin. "But you forget what I used to do for a living. It wasn't spying, and it wasn't diplomacy, but it wasn't a million fuckin' miles away from either of those things."

Ellie folded her arms and glared at him.

"Rolling into some sketchy African dictator's palace with a fruit basket full of blood diamonds or paying off a bunch of former KGB goons to grab up drilling rights in Siberia is not the same thing... *mate*," she said. Ellie leaned into that last word just as Jodi, who had walked up from the football game, finally joined them on the veranda.

"What's up?" she said, her expression betraying an immediate wariness.

She could probably tell from looking at Ellie that her partner was deeply unhappy and that Karl, who was closely examining the mud at the end of his boots, was just as uncomfortable.

"Nothing's up, darlin'," Damo said. "We're just talking through a few things, is all."

Jodi Sarjanen frowned.

"What things?"

Ellie stood up in a hurry, throwing a hand up in Damo's direction.

"This fucking idiot wants to go off and get himself killed, that's all," she snapped.

"Damo?" Jodi said, instantly on guard. "What's going on?"

Damien Maloney stuck his hands in his pockets and furrowed his brow. Inside, the discussion looked as though it was well underway, with one speaker after another getting to their feet to make their case. He had no idea what path they would choose in the end, but having sat and listened to Michelle Nguyen for over an hour, he'd become convinced that they would have to do whatever it took to shut down this little prick who'd set himself up as some bush league Emperor. He'd seen enough of that shit to know how it ended.

"Jodes," he said, "you remember how we had to divert around that militia ambush back in Oregon? Just after Coleman Lake?"

She nodded. Still wary.

"And then we had to keep going further west because we started running into towns that had been shot to shit?"

Another bob of the head, this time with a slightly haunted look in her eyes. She quickly glanced back over her shoulder, probably looking for Max.

"Yeah, well, the people who did that were a bit more organised than we thought. They weren't just bandits, or criminals, or whatever. It was this mob calling itself the Legion. Like one of those militias you'd see on the news sometimes."

"I don't understand," Jodi said.

Ellie, who had been drumming her foot on the floorboards, stomped past Damo to the edge of the veranda. She stood with her back to them, hands on her hips.

"Long story short," she said. "This fucking superhero wants to charge in swinging his dick around."

"Damo, no!" Jodi protested. "I thought we were going to Canada. To the fish farm."

Damo threw up his hands.

"And we are, mate. Or we will. But I'm worried we'll never get there if we gotta drive through these blokes. And if we do make it, I'm even more worried that they might turn up sometime next year and try to kick us out, or takeover, or something."

Ellie spun around.

"Jesus fucking Christ, Damo, just listen to yourself. They *might* turn up. They could *try to* kick us out. Maybe they'll take over, or maybe they won't. If you'd come to me with a business plan like that four years ago, I would have told you to go fuck yourself. It's all what-if, and perhaps, and maybe. None of it is real, but I'll tell you what is real. The one hundred per cent certainty of you getting yourself hurt or killed or even worse if you charge off on some dumbass schoolboy adventure."

"What do you mean 'worse'," he joked, not all that successfully.

Before she could see the trap he had laid for her, Ellie Jabbarah pointed through the big glass windows to where Michelle was addressing the room inside again.

"You heard what she said about those people. They're animals. If they catch you spying on them, or if they just feel like it, they'll hang you by your fuckin' heels from a lamppost or something."

Even as Ellie was saying it, Damo could tell she realised she had made a mistake.

"What?" Jodi said.

Jodi had missed the entirety of the morning's presentation, preferring to spend her time outside with Maxi and the other kids. Even on the long trek here from San Francisco, she had usually deferred to the judgement of the other three when deciding matters of high policy, like whether to divert around a fortified town or engage with the occupants for a few items of trade. She had Max, Pascal and Beatrice to take care of.

"Who are these guys?" she asked.

Ellie closed her eyes and let out a long, exasperated breath.

"Like Damo says," she explained. "They're some sort of militia. They've been... Taking over places."

"What do you mean taking over?" Jodi said.

Damo did not miss the opportunity.

"Capturing them," he said. "Or destroying them if they don't feel like being captured. That's what happened to Livingston. This Legion rolled up and gave them a choice between doing what they were told or getting fucked hard in the arse with zero lube. That's what they're talking about inside now, Jodes. What to do when they come back. Because they are coming back. And that's what we have to deal with. There's no pretending we don't because, as Ellie just said, they're not very nice people. If you get in their way, or if they just feel like doing it, they'll kill you."

Nobody said anything. The children playing nearby had all been herded away, probably for breakfast somewhere else in the homestead. It was enough that they could hear Michelle talking about various options for gathering intelligence. A woman called Maz stood up and offered to fly her crop-dusting plane over Three Forks to do aerial reconnaissance.

"What do they want?" Jodi asked.

Damo almost snorted but caught himself at the last moment. It was a simple question, but it did sort of cut to the heart of everything, too.

Ellie surprised him a little by answering before he could.

"Michelle says they're after three things. Territory, food, and manpower."

"Well, that doesn't sound too bad when you think about it," Jodi ventured.

"It doesn't," Damo said quickly before Ellie could speak again.

"But it's not like here, mate. The bloke who runs this outfit is a bit of a warlord. You cross him, and he'll kill you. You look sideways at him, and he'll kill you, or his goons will. And he's got a whole heap of goons. Thousands of them, they reckon. Which is why he needs all the food."

"And the manpower," Karl Valentine put in. He had not spoken for a few minutes, and Damo had almost forgotten he was there. As he had back at the cavalry memorial, however, once Karl had made up his mind, he spoke it.

"Seems to me we backed ourselves into a corner. Or got backed in. Doesn't really matter," he said. "Cos, here we are. Damo, if you go on this job with these envoy fellas, and you need a lift, I'll drive."

"Thanks, mate," Damo said.

Ellie shook her head. Even less happy than before.

But she said nothing.

It was Jodi who had the last word.

"You two need to be careful," she said. "Do whatever you have to. But be careful."

WHEN THEY GOT anxious and fucked up, some people liked to eat. Liked it so much they couldn't stop. Ellie Jabbarah was not like that. She broke the other way. When she felt everything was spinning out of control, she cooked. She always had, even as a little girl. When Damo slipped back inside the cookhouse to rejoin the meeting, she found Mary O'Donnell in the big, walk-in pantry and asked if she needed some help.

"Maybe some bread or cookies or something needs baking?" Ellie suggested.

"You are a kitchen dynamo, aren't you," Mary grinned. "I wish I'd had your help back when we ran the big herd and had all the extra hands to feed."

"I just like to keep busy," Ellie said.

Mary nodded, "I understand. Sometimes it helps."

The two women set to work at a long stone bench in the preparation area that Ellie recognised as being something close to a commer-
cial-grade space, at least in terms of capacity. She guessed that Mary
had probably catered for up to a dozen ranch hands at a time in this
kitchen. She wondered if the prolonged drought that had made life
so difficult in the restaurant trade also accounted for the O'Donnells
having to sell off most of their herd and a good portion of their land.

She didn't ask, of course. That was none of her business, and she
was just happy to be able to keep herself busy.

Mary set her to make a couple of loaves of bread while she cooked
up a batch of choc chip cookies. The timeless rhythms of sifting flour,
mixing eggs and milk, kneading the dough, and packing it into old,
battered baking tins helped calm Ellie's restless soul.

She was pissed at Damo, but mostly because she knew he was
right. And that made her even angrier. That's how it always seemed to
go. They had settled into a quiet, almost tranquil routine on the boat
back on the Sacramento River. Then a bunch of assholes charged in
and messed that up. They'd kept to themselves on the road, avoiding
any entanglements they didn't absolutely have to deal with. And to be
honest, it had been awesome. Even though they'd been living in each
other's back pockets, she and Jodi had never spent so much time
alone with each other. Damo and Karl had said nothing but done
everything they could to ensure they got that time and the privacy
they needed. It was a form of bliss. Until they ran into those suppu-
rating assholes at Bachman, and they'd been forced to step up and
step in.

And now, she thought, working the cookie dough, they would
have to risk everything all over again. It didn't seem fair.

She punched the dough hard.

Damo and Karl were probably going to get themselves killed.

Punch!

And it probably wasn't going to make a damn bit of difference.

Punch!

They were going to lose everything this time. For sure.

Punch!

Because of some dipshit militia cosplay motherfuckers...

Punch! Punch! Punch!

"Whoa, sweetheart! Whoa there!"

Mary O'Donnell's fingers, covered in flour, closed over her wrist.

"You must work the dough, not beat it for the world heavyweight crown."

Ellie stopped.

The whole room had stopped.

There was not a sound to be heard anywhere.

Everybody was staring.

"Oh. Sorry," she said. "Just, uh, don't mind me."

"Come on," Mary said, gentling her away from the bench and outside into the fresh air.

Ellie, who was not used to being pushed around a kitchen, allowed herself to be led by the elbow.

When they were free of the room, the conversation inside restarted.

Ellie felt the flush of embarrassment warming her face.

She was surprised to see Mary offering her a long, thin cigarillo.

"I didn't know you smoked," she said.

The older woman smiled.

"One a day," she said. "It's all Tom will allow since my brother died. Lung cancer."

"Oh," Ellie said, even more embarrassed. "I'm so sorry. I didn't... I just."

She fumbled for the right thing to say and failed.

Mary O'Donnell waved it away.

"It was ten years ago. I still miss him sometimes, but it would be wrong to dwell on past sorrows when we have such a sufficiency of them in need of attention right now."

Ellie turned down the offer of the cigarillo, but she did fetch another of her smokes from the dwindling packet of Chesterfields in her shirt pocket.

"That's a tough guy smoke," Mary grinned mischievously.

Ellie returned the smile. "I like to pretend I'm a tough guy," she said, examining the cigarette. She had liberated it from a roadhouse a day earlier. Eventually, she supposed, they'd be too stale to smoke. "Jodi wants me to give them up," she said, lighting the end and taking a deep, calming drag.

She blew out the smoke.

"Well, they say it's like kissing an ashtray," Mary teased, and they laughed just a little. Probably at their weaknesses and addiction.

"I sat down in the shower," Mary said then, for no apparent reason.

Ellie looked at her, "Sorry? You what."

Mary smiled sadly.

"When it all fell apart. Back in the summer. After the Chinese or the Russians or whatever launched their damn cyber-attack. James managed to call us and said he was going to come home. He said he was bringing friends. Including someone special."

"Michelle."

"Yes. And he's right. Michelle is quite special. But not at all what I imagined."

Ellie said nothing.

"Oh, not because of the tattoos or because she's, you know…"

Now Mary seemed slightly flustered and at a loss for words.

"Because her family's from Vietnam?"

"Yes, that, but no. She's just very… I mean *very* strong-willed. And James, in his own way, can be very stubborn too, you know. Like deciding to study economics. And go east. I always thought he'd end up with someone much more… conventional and, I don't know… quieter."

Ellie laughed out loud. So loud that a few heads turned in their direction from the meeting inside. She didn't care. She kept laughing because it felt good to let out whatever had been building up inside her. She took another drag on her cigarette and blew the smoke high into the sky.

She smiled.

"The first time I saw Michelle, she was… look, to be honest, she was killing a guy. And, uh, she was not being quiet about it."

"No," Mary said. She looked uncomfortable.

"Oh, don't worry," Ellie hastened to add. "He was desperately in need of being killed. They all were."

"James told us," Mary shuddered. "Things are terrible out there, aren't they?"

"Yeah. They are," Ellie confirmed. Unhappily.

"What are we going to do?" Mary O'Donnell said.

Ellie blew out more smoke before snubbing out the butt end of the Chesterton.

"I think I'm gonna quit smoking," she said, making the decision as she spoke and suspecting she really fucking meant it. "And make some bread. You got any olives or rosemary?"

Mary O'Donnell took a moment to consider her own thin, brown cigarillo.

"I didn't finish before," she said.

"What do you mean?" Ellie asked.

"The shower, when I thought we'd lost James, lost everything, I just sat down in the shower one night, and I couldn't get up again. I couldn't see what the point was. I couldn't make my legs work. I couldn't make any of it work."

She looked at Ellie, and their eyes locked. Mary's hand was shaking a little.

"This thing," she said. "It catches up with everyone differently, Ellie. It caught up with me, all but crippled me for a while. I think maybe it caught up with you before. Inside."

Ellie nodded. "Yeah. Maybe."

"But it didn't cripple you. It didn't even stop you, really. I do believe you may well have punched a hole right through my stone bench top if I hadn't caught a good hold of you."

Ellie blushed again. But she snorted too.

"Sorry," she said. "I do have a temper in me."

"No," Mary said. "Don't apologise. You're a fighter. That's a good thing. I fear we're going to need them. But you're right. What we need right now is to cook up a storm."

They went back inside and resumed.

Working in the kitchen meant listening to the rest of the meeting, including Damo lobbying for the diplomatic mission, which he volunteered to be a part of.

"I don't really know any of you except for young James and his mob," Damo said. "But we've been travelling with them for the last couple of days, and I know they're good sorts, and they'd make good neighbours. I got a place not too far north of here, so I'm keen to help out if you'll have me."

One of the ranchers asked him what he was offering to do and why they should trust him.

James jumped to his feet.

"Because Damo and his friends saved the lives of everyone in our caravan, including all those kids running around out there. And they did it because it was the right thing to do. So, you take that back, Mister Quaid. Right now."

The man who had questioned Damo's trustworthiness and, by extension, asked whether any of them could be trusted threw up his hands in mock surrender.

"I didn't mean anything by it," he said. "Not like that. We need to be certain, is all."

An argument broke out then over whether the valley would mind its business or call for help from outsiders. A few people even argued that Murdoch's issue had been with Livingston, not the valley. And they were not the same thing. Michelle brought that to an end after a couple of minutes of increasingly noisy contention by banging her mug on the table.

"You already decided these questions when you asked Mr O'Donnell," she pointed at the elder O'Donnell, "to come to me for the threat assessment. The fact is, unless you want to go under the yoke, you will have to fight. And you will be fighting alongside the refugees and outsiders you already have in the valley. If you decide to reach out and touch them first, I'm afraid some of the skillsets you need are best found in people from outside. People like Rick and Damien."

Ellie kept kneading a fresh batch of dough. She searched for

Damo in the crowd. He was standing over by an old-fashioned pot belly stove, warming his ass and deliberately avoiding her gaze.

"The other thing I need you to keep in mind," Michelle went on, "is the need for operational security. Whatever you decide here, whatever course of action you take, you will need to move quickly. This isn't the CIA or Special Operations Command. Whatever you decide to do *is* going to leak out. Guaranteed. The information could get to Murdoch and his people. That's got nothing to do with whether somebody grew up here in the valley or came in after Zero Day. It's just the reality you must deal with now."

That set off more arguments, but they were quieter and contained within several smaller groups. They went on like this long enough that Ellie and Mary baked up two batches of cookies and a half-dozen loaves of various sorts before the meeting took a final vote. It was utterly fucking incongruous to Ellie Jabbarah that a roomful of cowboys had to vote on this madness while the smell of baking bread and freshly made cookies filled the room.

Who knows, she thought. *Maybe it grounded them or something.*

She was gratified to see that they rejected out of hand any suggestion that they would dispatch assassins. There was something so fundamentally sick and wrong about such an idea that it gave Ellie pause to wonder what the hell sort of thing Michelle had been into for the National Security Council back in Washington. But there was no mandate for surrender either. The destruction of Livingston killed off any idea that they could live under the guns of someone who would do that. But nor was there much confidence that the valley could hold out against an armed militia as large, well-armed and manifestly vicious as the Legion.

The final vote came down in favour of sending a mission to Three Forks to at least attempt some form of a negotiated settlement.

It was carried on the voices.

26

THE MISSION

They left at night, the better to pass unseen through troubled lands. Mel Baker huddled deeper inside the old Army parka, which Rick had picked up back in Nebraska and worn almost every day since. It smelled strongly of his scent. She was not going with him. She stood on the verge of the highway with Jodi Sarjanen, the young mum who had joined their caravan with Maloney, the Australian. A couple of dozen people milled around saying goodbye, but Mel didn't know many of them. A handful from the long journey over here, like Roxarne and Tammy. A few like Jodi she had met in the last week or so. The rest were all locals. Some of them were old friends of James, and others even he didn't know.

Three vehicles idled in the gathering gloom and creeping chill of dusk. Rick was busy seeing to the weapon loads going into each SUV. They had a small armoury of high-powered rifles and shotguns and the sidearms everyone had been wearing since the collapse. And a second, smaller cache of weapons, which Rick stowed in oilcloth and secreted deep inside the door panels of the three SUVs. These, hopefully, would not be detected and confiscated at the border of the Legion's territory.

Meanwhile, Eliza Jabbarah checked and rechecked their provisions. It wasn't that far on a map to Three Forks, but maps no longer described the reality on the ground. The roads could be blocked anywhere, and nasty weather was closing in for the winter. Already, the wind bit into Mel's cheeks like an ice knife, and a few desolate snow flurries had dusted the road's surface. She stamped her feet and rubbed her arms up and down with thick padded gloves.

"I'm beginning to see why there's no brass monkeys to be had around here, not for love or money," she said.

"Monkeys, what?" Jodi Sarjanen asked.

"Never mind," Mel replied. This bird was from California. She would never get the brass monkey thing.

"God, I hate this," Jodi said.

"Don't reckon anybody likes it, love. But Rick and Michelle both say it's gotta be done, and this sort of nonsense is their bread-and-butter, innit? Or it was, anyway. Before everything turned to shit."

Jodi folded her arms one way and then the other, and her breath condensed in thick clouds of steam as she spoke.

"I said I hated it, Melissa. I didn't say I can't understand it."

Her voice was clipped, and her temper seemed to carry a sharp edge.

Mel regarded her warily. Jodi Sarjanen's face was almost ethereally beautiful in the golden red glow of the taillights. She was, or had been, a photographer, they said. But she looked like a model to Mel, and because of that, she'd probably spent most of her life being thought of as dumb.

"Sorry, love," Mel said. "Didn't mean it like that. I'm not happy about this myself. But I trust Rick. And Michelle. And your mate Damo, too, for that matter. He's a solid bloke, isn't he."

Jodi bobbed her head up and down, her shivers turning it into an almost comically exaggerated gesture.

"Karl is too," she said. "I don't think we'd have made it out of San Francisco without them. There's no way we'd be here if we were on our own. Not two women and a little boy."

Mel heard the clip-clop of horse hooves behind them and turned to see a large group of riders approaching through the gathering shadows. It was a hell of a sight, like old frontier history leaking into the present day. And it meant this thing was really happening.

"I think you'd have been all right," she said. "Michelle told me about your wifey absolutely kickin' off when things got busy with those mad buggers in Bachman. Said your Ellie was a proper fuckin' hard nut. And look at you, bringing them little ones from Canada home. Not many could do that or would've even bothered trying. Not now."

"*They* did," Jodi said, pointing to Tammy Kolchar and her friend Roxarne. Tammy was talking to Damo, which is to say she was flirting like an outrageous trollop with him, which caused Mel to grin hugely. The big fella seemed happy for the attention, but he wasn't leaning into the exchange. There was no way he was gay, so Mel had to figure he was too old and tired to fall for that bullshit.

Good luck to her, though.

Everybody needed someone.

The approaching horses grew louder, and Jodi stood on tiptoes to watch the riders coming up from the river flats.

"Ellie's not my wife," she said. "We're not married. I was once. But that didn't work out so great."

"It's just a saying, mate," Mel said, and Jodi smiled at her.

"Damo says that all the time."

"What? Wifey?"

"No. Mate."

Mel snorted. "Well, most Aussies started out as the dumbest Londoners who couldn't keep ahead of the Old Bill. That's a whole country full of convicts there, love."

"Tammy doesn't seem to care," Jodi said.

They both watched the young woman trying to work the older man. She was putting it right out there. Maloney still wasn't giving her much back, even when she started touching his arm and twirling her hair.

"Your mate's a cool customer then," Mel joked. "He got a missus, too, has he? Cos our Tammy over there is definitely on the pull. Looks like she's just about ready to have him for dinner and dessert."

Jodi grinned, and it was a sly, almost wicked expression.

"He's divorced," she said in a stage whisper. "Happily, too, but he gets lonely. I've seen it. And I told your thirsty girl over there that he was like a really big millionaire."

Mel couldn't keep the confusion from her face. "But he's not anymore," she said. "No one is."

"He's still got plenty to offer," Jodi said. "And Tammy's looking for someone who can look after her kids. I saw her checking Damo out. Saw her scoping out a few gentlemen when we got here. But she'd be good for him, I think. She'd keep him fit, that's for sure. Lots of cardio in that relationship, if it happens."

As they watched the scene play out, Tammy leaned in and kissed Maloney on the cheek.

"Huh," Mel went. "Look at you, scheming like a total Emma."

"A what?"

"That's a Jane Austen shout-out, girl. I'm all about the classics."

"Oh man, I loved *Pride and Prejudice and Zombies*," Jodi said, and Mel couldn't tell whether she was even joking.

They spotted James O'Donnell riding in on one of the horses. He was saddled in a great coat that bellied out over layers of even more warm clothing, and he wore an honest-to-God cowboy hat. He saw them and waved. The two parties, the cross-country riders and the vehicle convoy were both leaving from a smaller canyon that ran west off the central valley. The SUVs would take the interstate, but the riders were supposed to loop around at least a hundred miles north of I-90, attempting to avoid detection.

The horsemen and women coming up behind James were at least twenty strong, and they angled away from the highway and into a field of low grass and clover where the horses bent their heads down to feed. Mel found the jingling sounds of harnesses, the clopping of iron-shod horseshoes and the tearing, crunching noise of the great beasts feeding themselves to be strangely delightful. It was like something out of a fantasy novel. The moment was only slightly diminished by one of the horses cutting loose with an absolute firehose of steaming piss. James swung down from the saddle and led his mount over.

"Hey," he said. "Here to see us off?"

"Here to make sure you come back," Mel said and leaned in to peck him on the cheek. He hadn't shaved. His skin was stubbled and icy cold. "I can't believe you're taking these nags," she said.

"Only way to cut across country," James said. "We'll probably get there before Rick and the others, with all the breakdowns and stuff."

"Probably," Mel agreed.

"Is it going to be okay? All of this?" Jodi asked.

James favoured her with that look, the one he got when he was about to speak some truth that nobody wanted to hear. It always made Mel nervous. She'd seen it a lot in the last few months.

"I can't tell you that for sure, Jodi. But I can tell you we'll do our best."

"I know," Jodi answered after a brief pause. "I just worry."

"I'm sure she'll be fine," James said, nodding in the direction of Ellie Jabbarah, who was chewing out some poor guy who'd put the wrong crate into the wrong car.

Elsewhere along the line of vehicles, Mel saw boxes of ammunition and medical supplies going in last so they could be reached first. Rick saw her watching him, winked, smiled, and held up one finger.

He'd be with her in a minute. Nomi saw her and barked, excited to be along for the adventure.

"I wish Ellie wasn't going," Jodi said. "I wish none of you had to go."

Ellie was one of the last additions to the so-called envoys' delegation. Everything seemed to be up in the air. As the sun fell below the jagged peaks of the Gallatin Ranges, Rick finished resealing the door panels on their hidden weapons stash and re-joined Mel and the others at the rear of the convoy. He was dressed as though for the ski fields, looking like a slimmed-down Michelin Man in a black puffer jacket. Nomi trotted along proudly beside him, her tail wagging in a blur.

"Hey baby," he said, taking Mel in his arms and holding her tight.

They stood, entwined, for at least a minute, rocking a little in each other's embrace. Mel no more wanted Rick to go than Jodi wished for Ellie to leave. But she had been a cop, which meant accepting that sometimes your best people had to put themselves in harm's way. Mel would have gone herself, except she didn't think she had anything to offer on a diplomatic mission and certainly couldn't ride a horse. She could, however, be put to good use back on the ranch, teaching basic but effective unarmed combat. She had her first class ready to go in the morning.

"You're gonna be careful, aren't you, love," she said quietly. Her head lay on Rick's shoulder, and his short, thick beard scratched her cheek when he nodded.

"I figure to let Damo and Michelle do all the talking. I'll stand there looking pretty," he said.

"Oh, that will distract them for sure," Mel grinned.

Rick kissed her forehead, and she leaned into him for one last hug. When they finally separated, with Nomi trying to nuzzle between them, James O'Donnell was there to shake hands with Rick.

"Good luck, brother," James said. "We'll meet you at the rendezvous point if it goes well. And if it doesn't..."

He said nothing more, shrugging off all the possibilities that ended in failure and most certainly in blood.

"If it doesn't go well," Mel said pointedly, poking James in the chest, "I expect you boys to charge in there and get them all out."

"That's the plan," he said.

Rick clapped his hands together and blew into them. He was the only one not wearing gloves.

"We'll do a comms check now," he said. "And another when we've been on the road for an hour. But after that, we go dark. Okay? And we only break radio silence from Three Forks if we need you guys to come in hot."

James nodded.

"Got it. My cousin Simon's got the radio. Can you hold my horse while I go talk to Michelle?" he asked, handing the reins to Mel.

She took them, a little overawed by the size of the horse.

"And you should go see Ellie," she said to Jodi. "They'll be heading out in a minute."

———————

JAMES FOUND Michelle in the driver's seat of the lead vehicle, poring over maps that had been augmented with as much intelligence as she could gather about any potential obstacles ahead. She was sealed up inside the Jeep with the heater running. James tapped on the glass. She sent him around to the other side to let himself into the passenger seat.

"Hey baby," Michelle said, leaning across the centre console to kiss him slowly and deeply. Her lips were warm. His were not, but she didn't seem to mind that.

The cabin light was on, and James couldn't help but wonder who was watching, but he didn't much care. They broke apart only after a good few long moments.

"I'm going to miss you," he said.

"You'll be seeing me soon enough and seeing enough of me to keep any good cowboy happy," Michelle teased, kissing him even more deeply.

He was a little breathless after that one.

"Yeah, but this is the first time we'll have been apart since DC," he reminded her when he recovered.

That seemed to give Michelle a moment's pause. She leaned back in the driver's seat, looking out into the dark.

"That's all the more reason to get this done quickly and properly," Michelle said.

"And what is it exactly that we're doing?" James asked. There was the stated plan, but he couldn't help feeling that Michelle and maybe even Rick had wheels turning inside wheels.

She looked at him but said nothing. Not for a few seconds, anyway. Just as the moment started getting loaded down with significance, Michelle leaned forward.

"We will reach out to the Legion and determine their intent

regarding the Valley," she said. "And Rick and I will assess their capability regarding those intents."

"And that's all? Right?" James said. "Like, you wouldn't be thinking about walking in there and putting a bullet between Murdoch's eyes."

She favoured him with a small, wintry smile.

"I'm an analyst, James. Not an operator."

"You haven't always been an analyst, though, have you?"

She didn't answer that question. Instead, she said, "Neither have you."

"Yeah, but before I wrote my newsletter, I was just a researcher at Chase. And before that, a student. And before that, I was from here. Michelle, I just... I don't want to lose you."

"James, if we sit on our asses and wait for this guy to make his play, whatever it is, we will lose everything. I guarantee you."

Another awkward silence.

"Is that why you suggested that I go with the riders?" James said at last. "Were you trying to keep me out of harm's way?"

She surprised him by leaning forward and taking his hands in hers. Michelle's touch was soft and warm.

"James, we are not going in there to throw down with this jerk. Promise. We're gonna check him out. Stall him. Dazzle him with bullshit. Whatever it takes. Maybe we have to throw down at some point soon. If you ask me, I don't see how we avoid that. But any negotiations with these assholes will go better if they're not talking to the people they just fucked over in Livingston. Your dad was part of that. He was on the council, which told them to pound sand. If they figure out who you are, they'll totally grab you up as a hostage. I would, in their position. I don't want you in that room."

Before he could reply, she wrapped one hand around his neck, pulling him in for a much longer and more torrid kiss.

"I just want you in me," she whispered when they were done. "But when we get back. Right now, you need to fuck off and let me work."

ELLIE DIDN'T KNOW what the fuck she was doing or why the fuck she was even doing it. She stood yelling at some poor fucking mope who'd tried to load the dozen hot chicken rolls she'd cooked for their dinner on top of the frozen breakfast burritos they were supposed to have tomorrow morning. This was not the first packing error she had encountered. None of these hicks knew a goddamn thing about *mise en place*.

"Just... look, just fucking let me do it," she snapped at the guy.

He scuttled away from the rear of the Toyota, and she rearranged everything to her liking.

Except nothing was to her liking.

She still wasn't sure why she'd decided to put her hand up for this bullshit job. The whole thing had got entirely out of control, what with this posse full of actual fucking cowboys riding off over the range, Damo's dumbass secret squirrel mission growing like topsy, and Karl insisting he be the one to lead the convoy and...

What the hell was everyone thinking?

Were they even thinking? Or were they just charging in like fucking morons after so long sitting around, letting shit happen to them?

"Honey?"

Ellie spun around.

Jodi was standing behind her, almost lost inside a fur-lined ski jacket. The curse that had boiled up out of Ellie's foul mood died before reaching her lips.

She shook her head, opened her arms, and they fell on each other.

"Do you want me to stay?" Ellie found herself asking. "Cos I can just... I can..."

Jodi hugged her tighter and kissed her neck.

"I don't want anybody to go. I don't want anyone to get hurt," Jodi said.

They came apart and looked at each other. Ellie knew what came next. They'd had this conversation before. It'd been going on all day in one form or another.

"But if we just sit here and do nothing, peeps are gonna get hurt?" she said.

Ellie had said that hours earlier when she began worrying about sending Damo and Karl off alone.

They had been through so much that it seemed impossible to imagine anything turning out right if they didn't all do it together.

And yet, there was no question of Jodi going anywhere. She had the kids to look after; only a dumb ass would say that wasn't important. In some ways, it was even more important. All the shit people used to say about children being the future wasn't just feel-good warm-'n'-fuzzies anymore. It was the literal fucking truth, boiled down to its essence. Jodi would stay right where she was and make sure that Max, Pascal and Beatrice were safe, even if that meant loading up the Land Rover and peeling out for Canada if everything went sideways.

Damo and Karl were also right to insist that they had something to offer on the mission to Three Forks. Ellie initially resisted this suggestion because she didn't like the idea of breaking up their odd little family. It seemed a chance taken too far, a challenge to the gods of shit luck and payback. But when Ellie Jabbarah finally asked herself where she could be of most use, she had to admit it wasn't pounding out loaves in Mary O'Donnell's kitchen. It wasn't curled up in a warm bed next to her lover, letting somebody else cover her shift. It was, unfortunately, on the road with Damien Maloney and Karl Valentine.

"You just make sure those boys don't do anything stupid," Jodi said. "Especially Damo. He's not as young or as badass as he likes to think. And he's got Tammy to think about, too."

"Wait. What?" Ellie frowned. "That redneck hot one?"

Jodi giggled.

Ellie's mouth unhinged and fell open.

"You fucking didn't! Get out!"

"I did," Jodi confirmed. She looked over her shoulder as if checking for anyone watching them. The last of the twilight succumbed to full darkness, but the road was well-lit by headlights and dozens of flashlights. There were even a few cell phones. Ellie looked, too, but Damo was nowhere to be seen in the small, constantly moving crowd.

Ellie took Jodi's hands. She was wearing thick gloves and started peeling them off, but Ellie squeezed and said, "No. It's too cold."

Around them, everybody was hurrying through the final moments of preparation. She pulled Jodi into a hug, a fierce clutch she wished could go on forever. But it couldn't.

When they let each other go, Jodi said, "I still have one shot left on that camera you guys got me."

She pulled the little cardboard Kodak out of a pocket in her ski jacket. But she put it away again.

"I was going to take a photo of everyone before they left, but I'm going to save it for when you all come back."

"That's good," Ellie said. "Because I look like crap right now."

Jodi smiled and held Ellie's face between her hands. Her gloves were made of soft leather, and they were lined with fur that tickled Ellie's cheeks.

"You look beautiful," Jodi said. "You always have. And I don't know whether you know this, but I'm a professional photographer, so I know about this stuff."

They laughed and kissed a short, chaste goodbye.

They had made love earlier that day, and the memory of it was enough to keep Ellie going for now. Even if that meant going away.

A car horn blared, and Karl's voice, surprisingly loud and commanding, called out, "Time to get rolling."

"Do you think maybe you could set Karl up with the other one? Roxarne or whatever?" Ellie said.

Jodi shook her head.

"Karl is happy in his own company," she said. "Damo's not. He needs someone. Bring him back safe. And you, too."

"I will," Ellie said.

"You better," Jodi warned her.

Up and down the line of vehicles, boots crunched on the tarmac, doors opened and closed. Onlookers and well-wishers drew back.

Horsemen and women called out their goodbyes and guided their mounts clear of the two-lane blacktop. A full moon cast a silvery glow over the valley. They would ride a familiar trail under its watch for a few hours until they got clear of any possible lookouts.

MEL BAKER FOUND Jodi Sarjanen again. They had each circled back around to meet where they had first stood talking. They waved as the short procession of motor vehicles departed. Somebody rolled down a window of the second SUV and leaned out to wave back. Damo. But nobody else. Everyone had said their goodbyes.

"Bye, Damien," a woman called out.

Tammy Kolchar.

Mel grinned and punched Jodi Sarjanen lightly on the shoulder.

"You tricky bitch."

The two women, who did not know each other particularly well, stood by the side of the road until the last of the taillights had disappeared around the foothills of some small mountain a mile away. A dozen or more people stood around with them.

"You hungry?" Mel asked.

"I haven't eaten all day," Jodi replied. "Too nervous, I think. God, this is so hard."

They turned and started walking back towards the central valley.

Mel had borrowed a car from somebody. She couldn't remember who, but she hoped Tom or Mary would know.

"I'm going to make a cup of tea," she said as they reached the car after a short walk. "Do you drink tea? Like, the proper stuff. Not that hippie rubbish."

"Sometimes," Jodi said.

"Well, I'm English," Mel said. "So, I drink it all the time. It has magical powers. Did you know that? No amount of bother cannot be made good with a proper cup of tea. Come on. I'll show you."

"Let's give Tammy and Roxarne a lift, too," Jodi said with a grin.

"Sure thing. Emma."

27

WHAT JAMES MADISON SAID

For once, Rick Boreham rode in the back seat. It was kind of luxurious not having to pull shotgun duty. Karl Valentine, the old E-4, took the wheel, and Maloney insisted on riding up front. That suited Rick just fine. They were in friendly territory for now and wouldn't hit the Legion's outposts for at least another day or so, not moving as slowly as they were likely to.

Karl had scrounged up a pretty good set of wheels for them, too. An eight-seater Expedition, straight off the lot, he joked. The old dog had liberated it from a dealership in Livingston that hadn't taken any fire when the Legion reduced the city. There were six of them riding in the big Ford. Maloney and Valentine upfront. Ellie, the cook, stretched out on the very rear seat, listening to music on an old iPod. Michelle sat in the middle, just across from Rick, staring out the window for the first twenty minutes or so, and Nomi, stretched out between them, with her head snuggled into Michelle's lap and her tummy presented for all the rubbing she was due.

James was out there in the dark. So was his cousin Simon and a troop of twenty-one horsemen and women who had volunteered for what Rick thought of as a ready reaction force, but the locals called 'the posse.' Rick wasn't entirely sure how he felt about that. It was always good to have backup, and the riders were as close to actual cavalry as made no difference.

But Michelle had been forced to talk half of them out of just riding down on Three Forks with guns blazing. Given the Legion's firepower, there was no guarantee those guys would have been riding into anything but an early grave.

Nomi picked herself up, turned around and dropped her head into Rick's lap.

She could read his mind or at least his heart's feelings.

He stroked her head and scratched behind her ears, and the dark thoughts that had been welling up started to break apart and drift away.

Nobody said much for that first leg of the trip, the drive up a narrow country road that almost but not quite paralleled the interstate about twenty miles to the north.

Twenty miles on a map, Rick reminded himself. If you were fool enough to try to walk there in a straight line, you'd be climbing a whole bunch of densely forested mountains. Assuming such a trek was even possible, it'd take weeks.

After a while, James and Co. disappeared north, probably cutting through some canyon trail that only a local would ever know. Rick was sure they were gone when Michelle turned away from the window, opened the roadmap sitting on her lap and immediately started backseat driving.

"Karl," she said. "They told me there was a major pileup about four miles after the intersection with I-90, and I'm just wondering whether we could work around that by taking this fire trial near Billman Creek and—"

"I know all about it, Miss Nguyen," Karl Valentine said. "I got that map stored in the best GPS unit the good Lord ever put on this Earth."

He tapped the side of his head with two fingers.

"I do appreciate the offer to navigate," he went on, "but we will do fine if you just leave me to do my job – at least for this first little ways. I spent most of this afternoon talking with a bunch of local fellers who've been all over these roads, and they gave me all the good news. Once we get to Three Forks, I'll be somewhat less useful than fake boobs on a mechanical bull but rest assured, I won't be offering nego-tiating tips and such while you go about your business."

Damien Maloney turned around and winked at her.

"Told you, didn't he, mate?"

Michelle said nothing, but she folded the map up with a snap and put it away. Nomi whimpered and switched her attention away from Rick toward Michelle. Rick leaned over and said quietly, "James is gonna be fine, Michelle. He rode all over these hills when he was a boy. They all did. Even the girls. There's nothing we need to do for him. And there's not much we can do until we get up in Murdoch's face."

She drew in a small, sharp breath, and he prepared himself for the smack back that he was sure had to be coming. But Michelle collected herself. She let out that breath, leaned forward and said to Karl, "Sorry, man. I'm not much of a passenger."

Karl Valentine snorted softly.

"Most people aren't," he said. "Not in my experience. But have some faith, Miss. I'm a pretty good driver. It's possibly all I'm good for. Let me have that, and I'll get you where you need to go."

"Everybody needs a lift, man," Rick said.

"Testify, brother," Karl nodded.

The Jeep ahead of them was running spotlights, throwing a wide, bright cone of halogen light up the sides of the foothills, which drew ever closer to the road as they motored up the canyon. Peter Tapsell was behind that wheel, riding with Lawson, the guy who'd almost shot them when they rolled up on Livingston, and Pablo, Tom O'Don-nell's leading hand, who'd stopped him.

Rick had met the three people in the Toyota behind them, all locals, two of them mechanics, and the third, Katherine Bates, an ER nurse, had a sister who worked for the council over in Three Forks.

She was their introduction if they needed to plug into what was left of the local power structure.

With Michelle gently demoted to commuter, they rode in silence until Ellie reminded everybody she was there by passing forward a packet of brownies wrapped in greaseproof paper. Nomi was instantly alert at the first crinkling of the paper.

"Not for you, Scooby Doo," Ellie said. "These are full of chocolate."

Nomi whined a little until Rick fetched a dried liver treat from the baggie he kept in his pocket.

The unexpected snack broke through the vaguely stricken mood that had seemed to come over them when they'd finally left the shelter of the gorge and turned onto the interstate.

"You sure these are legit, young lady?" Karl said over his shoulder. "I can't afford to have my driving skills impaired by those drugs you young people are always putting into innocent baked goods."

"You wish," Ellie scoffed. "Nothing in here but an honest block of couverture chocolate that Damo didn't even know he had on his boat. Fucking barbarian was just eating it like broken bits of Hershey bar."

Rick took the packet of brownies, teased out one for himself, and offered it to Michelle, who gladly accepted a small square before passing it to Maloney. The Australian claimed one for himself and passed another over to Karl.

"Bugger me, these are good, Ellie," Maloney said. "What are you trying to do to me?"

"You can't fatten the pig on the way to market, Damo," Ellie replied, which seemed to amuse him much more than warranted. Rick assumed it was some private joke between them. He turned around to talk to her over the back of the seat.

"Did you always want to be a cook?" he asked. They had a long, hard road in front of them, and it would help them to know each other better than they did.

Damo laughed, pulling Rick's attention back to the front of the car.

"Don't call her a cook, mate. She's a chef. She'll fuckin' cut you for less."

"My apologies," Rick said. "Did you always want to be a *chef?*"

Ellie rolled her eyes, but not at Rick.

"Don't listen to that wanker," she said. "He wouldn't know the difference between Chateaubriand and a shit and anchovy sandwich. Yes, Rick, I pretty much always wanted to cook for a living. Even before I knew the difference between being a good cook and a chef."

Michelle unfolded a little and turned to Ellie, hanging over the back of the seat.

"Where was it that you guys worked in San Francisco?"

Ellie laughed. "I worked." She pointed at Damo. "He sat around squeezing his dick and scarfing up all the free food."

"Fuck me," Maloney roared in theatrical mock outrage. "It was hardly fucking free, you dodgy Afghan trader. I had to pay for everything. Including your famously failed experiment riffing on pigs in blankets. Fucking gourmet hogs in truffle hoodies, for Christ's sake. I almost had to sell my boat to pay for that spectacular fucking debacle."

Ellie just grinned at him, a quirky half-smile.

"Damo is just a cashed-up bogan who wouldn't know good taste if it jumped up and bit him on his enormous ass," she said.

"A bogan?" Michelle asked.

"It's like a Down Under barbarian with a mullet and a jet ski."

Maloney didn't seem too put out by that. And if he was, he salved any wound to his ego by inhaling another brownie.

"We had a restaurant in Temescal," Ellie told Michelle. "Fourth Edition. The drought made things hard, but it was a pretty good bistro. Mid-Pacific menu. Lots of French technique and Asian influence."

Michelle nodded, her brow furrowing as if she was trying to recall eating there. Ellie smiled; a genuine smile this time.

"We won a couple of awards," she said. "Got some nice reviews in the *Times*."

That got Michelle's attention. She sat up straight.

"Ooh, which one?"

"Both of them. LA and New York," Ellie said. She tried to be cool, but Rick could tell she was proud of the achievement. It was funny the lives people had led and the things they had most valued in them.

"Man," Michelle said. "I used to love restaurants. I rarely cooked for myself at home."

A scowl darkened her expression.

"It's gonna be a hell of a long time before we do that again," she said. "It's hard to believe sometimes, isn't it? All of the stuff that's gone now."

They left behind a winding stretch of road with pine forests crowding in close on both sides, and Karl fed the wheels some speed as they hit a stretch of open road.

"You're supposed to be a bit of a brainiac," Maloney said, twisting around to address Michelle directly. "How long do you reckon it'll take before things get back to normal, at least in places like the Valley and Livingston?"

Michelle did not answer immediately, indicating she was taking the question seriously.

Eventually, she shook her head and said, "It'll go differently in different places. Like, I've got no idea whether any of the stronghold cities made it through or just fell apart when they ran out of food. The idea was that they wouldn't go under, and the government would push out from those sanctuaries and re-establish control."

"That sounds like a plan that didn't survive contact with reality," Maloney said.

Michelle shook her head.

"Maybe not. But who'd know? We don't even know what's happening a hundred miles west of here. Just that some pissant warlord cosplay nut has set up shop and declared it the new Rome. God only knows what's happening in places like Kentucky or Florida once you get away from the big die-off zones around the cities."

Maloney nodded and appeared to think it over.

"I worked in some pretty rugged shitholes over the years," he said.

"People are resilient. That's what always surprises me. Just how hard they cling to life, even in the worst places."

He jerked a thumb back over his shoulder.

"That valley where your boyfriend James and his parents lived. That's no shithole. That's a bit of a bloody paradise, mate. It's a pity what happened to the town, but I don't see any reason that everyone left over couldn't pull together and rebuild. They got plenty of food. There's fresh water. And with a bit of salvage and tinkering, you could rig up a decent local power grid with renewables and storage. Take a couple of months at worst. And I dunno how they'd go with the tech over the medium term, looking out to, say, a ten-year horizon. But there's no reason a place like that couldn't make a decent go of it whether or not the feds turned up. And there'd have to be plenty like that scattered all over America. It's a bloody big country, after all."

Rick considered what Maloney had just said and found himself reviewing his opinion of the man. If he was honest, he hadn't warmed to him after Bachman. Rick was grateful for the help there, desperately thankful if you wanted the truth of it. But he never really got past his impression that the loudmouthed, blustering foreigner was anything more than ten pounds of shit in a five-pound bag.

The fact he owned a restaurant or earned a lot of money digging things out of the ground didn't impress Rick much. It was obvious that Ellie Jabbarah had run their business in San Francisco. And it didn't take a genius to make money from stuff like oil and gold. Sometimes, Rick knew, all it took was a crude ruthlessness of thought and deed.

But Maloney was possibly a little more thoughtful than he'd given him credit for.

"What do you think the best way of coming at this problem is, Damo?" Rick asked. The first time he could recall using the man's preferred nickname. "This guy we're going to see in Three Forks, I mean."

Maloney looked out of the window for a second. There was nothing but darkness outside now.

"To be fair," he said carefully. "I'd probably defer to Mishy on that."

He pointed at Michelle Nguyen, who looked very surprised and not a little unsettled at being referred to as 'Mishy'.

"She's the one who's got the goods on him," Maloney said. "But, since you asked me, in my experience, these sorts of blokes have a lot of trouble understanding the difference between violence and power."

Michelle leaned forward.

It wasn't a sudden movement. She didn't leap up or anything. But Rick could not help seeing how she had switched, quite abruptly, from leaning back, almost slumping in the absurdly comfortable seats, to focussing solely on Damo and whatever he was about to say.

"What do you mean by that?" she asked, almost challenging him.

He blew out his cheeks.

"This bloke's got, what, three thousand shooters he can call on?"

"Give or take a few hundred," Michelle said. "Best guesstimates."

"Yeah, well, that sounds like a pretty powerful outfit, on the face of it. But only if he *can* actually call on 'em."

Rick frowned.

"What do you mean? If he can put them all in the field at once? Because we know he can't do that. Or he won't."

Damo smiled.

"Too right, he can't. And that's the difference between power and violence, isn't it."

"Go on," Michelle said. She wasn't about to let this go.

Eliza Jabbarah was still leaning over the back of Rick and Michelle's seat. She rested her chin on her folded arms as if settling in to listen to bedtime stories. She obviously thought whatever her old boss had to say on the matter would be worth listening to. Karl Valentine said nothing, but Rick was getting used to his quiet presence. He focussed on the way unwinding ahead of them. They were passing through open pastureland, and the full moon glittered like millions of silver coins on a lake just north of the road.

The dashboard lights illuminated Maloney's face from below,

emphasising how much weight he had lost during the last few months. The skin under his chin hung down, and his cheekbones stood out prominently over shadowed hollows.

"That business at Livingston, blowing up half the town because they wouldn't do what he wanted. That wasn't the choice of a powerful man. It was precisely the fuckin' opposite if you ask me. Power is given. It's not taken at gunpoint. You can take a life at gunpoint, no fucking worries about that. Take as many lives as you got bullets, mate. And you can get compliance, for sure, that way. But it's not power. That's just payback or a judgment day waiting for you down the track. Power is something else."

"Yes. It is," Michelle said. "Go on."

She leaned in further and took another brownie, patting Nomi on the head as consolation for not getting one.

Rick's dog agreed to make do with that for now. But she was not happy, sighing deeply at the injustice of it.

"I don't really understand, Damo," Rick confessed. "Most of my life, I watched men use guns to take what they wanted. You're saying that's not power?"

Maloney shook his head, looking for some way of explaining himself.

"Let's say that a crim walks into a bank with a gun. He gets what he wants. A bag full of the folding stuff. He gets compliance. Obedience, right? He dominates."

"Yeah," Rick said. "I guess so."

He was still missing something, but at least he could tell he was missing it. Michelle wasn't. She was nodding and seemed to know exactly where Maloney was going. She had lost interest in the darkened world outside the windows of the speeding Ford. Michelle was all in on wherever Damien Maloney was taking them.

"But your bank robber doesn't have the *support* of the bank staff or the customers, does he?" Damo said. "He can't bank on their allegiance."

"No," she smiled. "No, he doesn't, and he can't."

"You're saying this Murdoch is like a bank robber, then?" Karl

Valentine asked, still watching the road ahead. "With a gun pointed at everyone's head?"

"That's exactly what he is, mate. And the Legion are his accomplices. But like most crims, he can't really trust them, can he, Mishy?"

"No. Not all of them," she said. "And don't call me Mishy."

"No worries, mate. You see where I'm going, though, Rick?"

"Starting to, maybe," Rick admitted. "Are you saying the Legion is like some sort of regime we gotta knock over?"

Michelle surprised him by answering for Maloney.

"No, he's saying more than that. A lot more. He's saying that the power of a state or an institution isn't manifest in the weapons it deploys. It is the support of the people, their collective will that lends power to a leader. It's like James Madison said. All governments rest on opinion. And that's as true for monarchies and dictatorships as it is for democracies. Even more so. It's why dictators fall so hard when they do go down. Because in the end, as their power ebbs away, they have nothing to substitute for it but violence. Murdoch's power is not his own. It belongs to everyone, not just in the Legion but everywhere the Legion occupies. I wonder if he's figured that out?"

Michelle sat back and looked out of the window again. She appeared to Rick as though she could see something out there clearly for the first time.

"Is that what you meant?" Rick asked. "That this guy only thinks he's powerful because nobody's told him otherwise."

"Close enough for government work," Damo said.

"So, what's it mean but?" Ellie put in from the back seat, looking from Damo to Michelle and back again.

"It means," Damo said, "that although we're going to see this Murdoch arse-clown, he's not the most important bloke we'll meet over there."

"Who is?" Ellie asked.

"Everyone else," Michelle said thoughtfully.

IT HAD BEEN a long time since James O'Donnell had been on a horse, longer still since he had ridden the trail from Dry Creek Road to the North Fork. After three months of the Sierra's luxury seats gently cupping his butt cheeks and a decade of office work before that, he would feel this in the morning. Nonetheless, it was almost glorious to be out under a full moon, riding with friends he had not seen in years.

Almost.

There was no avoiding the reason they were out here and moving under cover of darkness. Twenty or so mounted riflemen and women could not move through the countryside in silence. They did not try. For now, this was their land, and although the Legion had come into it and done great damage, they had not stayed. Michelle seemed convinced they had razed Livingston to secure their flank and that they had bigger concerns elsewhere. Probably at Bozeman, which they had surrounded and placed under siege.

James did not really understand any of it. His father told him that more than half of Bozeman's population had poured out of the city in the two weeks after the Chinese attack. More had followed in the following month as starvation set in. Why this Murdoch fellow had decided to surround it and starve out the few remaining survivors, nobody could say. Perhaps Michelle would ask him.

He shivered under his layers of clothing as his breath steamed out of him in thick white clouds turned almost silver by moonlight. The moon was high above them, bathing the smaller canyon in a magical light. He knew the vast glimmering band of the Milky Way would shine out of the northern skies with almost stunning clarity but for the rising moon's brightness. He wasn't complaining. He was gratified at how quickly the muscle memory of how to sit a horse had resurfaced for him, but his confidence would be a few days coming back.

"Not much trail riding to be had around Baltimore," his cousin said.

"Not much, no," James agreed. "Got some kick-ass art museums, though."

Simon laughed. He was cloaked in a dark all-weather duster on the horse next to James, his face hidden under the brim of an old hat. It was unmistakably his cousin, however. The voice, the ramrod straight posture, the way he swayed so easily with the motion of his chestnut brown stallion. It all put James back in mind of their teenage years in the valley.

They were placed about halfway along the string of riders.

Ahead of them, Steve Collins's silhouette bobbed up and down in the saddle of his bay gelding. Collins wore a fleece-lined rancher coat, but he was not as extravagantly swaddled as some others. James recalled him having worked for years in Alaska and supposed he was even more desensitised to the cold than almost everyone else. Collins carried a Remington pump as his saddle gun, but the distinctive span of a hunting bow stuck out over his left shoulder.

"Must have been a hell of a trip getting back home," Simon said as they steered their mounts with a press of the knees to tack a little further to the north. This trail, which James fondly remembered from his childhood, was an easy course, well favoured by tourists on pony-riding day trips. It would carry them another five miles from the road where Michelle and the others moved at much greater speed towards the I-90 intersection.

"Man, you have no idea," James said before he could catch himself.

Simon and Stephen and everyone in the valley had seen more than their fair share of horror. Hard times didn't even begin to describe it.

"Sorry," he hurried on to add. "That was a dumb thing to say. Things have been just as bad here."

"Livingston was pretty bad," Simon agreed. "But we'd already moved a lot of folks out to help with the harvest, and we knew they were coming. They straight up told us what they were going to do."

"Jesus," James said and regretted that too.

He'd grown used to easy profanity in the East, even though he was not much given to it.

Nobody called him out, though, for which he was grateful. An owl hooted nearby so loudly that it caused James to jump a little in his saddle. He was very glad of the darkness. He didn't doubt his old neighbours and friends would rib him without mercy for jumping at every little hoot and bird call in the forest.

"Your old man made sure the town was evacuated," his cousin explained. "As best he could, anyway. Some folks, you know, they just won't be budged."

28

___

IF YOU SEE TROUBLE COMING

Ross Jennings did not get much sleep that night. It was only a few minutes' drive from the motel to his small bungalow on East Cedar Street, overlooking the park. Podesta drove, and Nicky rode up front. Jennings squeezed into the back seat, pushing aside a gym bag, two heavy coats and a couple of six-packs of apple cider that clinked against each other the whole way back. Podesta kept up a line of chat, promising the girl that she'd be with her father soon and she could have a big hot bath.

"You got hot water, Mister Mayor?"

"I'm not sure," Jennings said. "We don't have power."

"Then you boil some up any way you can. Give this girl a hot bath. If that's a problem, you come get me. I'll get you all the hot water you need."

Nicky McNabb didn't say much besides, "I couldn't stop him."

She'd keep repeating that, and in an unexpectedly gentle voice, Podesta would say, "I know that, Nicky. Everyone knows that, sweetheart. Wasn't your fault."

"I couldn't stop him," she would say again.

"No one could," Podesta would say quietly, which was such a

bald-faced lie coming from someone like him that Jennings expected Nicky to say something like, 'But you could have. Where were you?'

But she didn't. She seemed comforted by the lie.

The mobster drove them south on Railway Avenue, past the medical clinic and the hardware store, before turning left into West Cedar at Landrigan's Machine Shop. He drove slowly, hunched almost comically over the tiny steering wheel, his eyes focussed on the icy road surface, but his attention never slipping from the young girl in the passenger seat. He seemed so adept at soothing her with his murmuring guttural drone—"Wasn't your fault, kid. Nothin' you coulda done different. But you're safe now. We ain't gonna let that happen again"—that Jennings wondered if tonight was his first time around this particular block. There were many rumours about what Thomas Podesta had done for the Milano crime family in LA and San Francisco.

They encountered one of the Legion's foot patrol, and this time, Podesta did allow them to flag him down, but as soon as he rolled down his window and they saw who was driving, they lost interest in the traffic stop.

Nicky shied away from them, turning her face down into the darkness so they could not see her.

"Who's that?" one of the patrolmen asked.

"None of your fucking business, you mook," Podesta growled. "But if you wanna sit in the fucking latrine trenches at Bozeman all winter, keep asking."

They did not keep asking.

Podesta pulled up outside of Ross Jennings' home without being told where that was, and turned off the engine.

"Nicky, your old man is inside waiting for you and seeing you home safe is gonna be the best thing that ever happened in his life, let me tell ya," Podesta said. "You want me to give you a hand inside, or are you gonna be right to go in with Mayor Jennings?"

"I'll be okay," the girl said in a voice so small, it was hard to hear over the ticking of the engine block, cooling down in the frozen night.

"You're a good girl, Nicky," Podesta said. "Don't let nobody tell you different, and don't you ever think different, neither."

She nodded. The nervous twitch of a small, frightened animal.

"Hey," Podesta said quietly. "I mean that. I know people. Good people and bad people. Me. I'm a bad guy in lotsa ways. A really bad guy. You know that. Everyone knows that. But that means I can see you're a good girl. And, Nicky, if anyone says different, you come to me. You tell Tommy Podesta. And I promise you, nothing good is gonna happen for them. You promise to come to me?"

She nodded.

"Good girl. Now you go see your old man. He's a good one too. Just like you. Okay. I'm gonna lean across and open the door. Okay?"

She nodded, and he did as he said he would.

She thanked him in her tiny, broken voice and got out.

Jennings was about to follow when Podesta reached into the back of the tiny car and stopped him.

"And you, Mister Mayor, you come to me too, okay? If you think there's gonna be trouble outta this. You come to me, and I'll sort it out. That's my job. Not yours."

"Then it's a pity you didn't do that a couple of hours ago, isn't it?" Jennings said bitterly, not caring at all if he had angered the man.

But Podesta merely nodded.

"It is a pity, yeah. Be good if we could avoid any more pity and sorrow coming out of this, too. So you come to me if you see trouble coming."

THE FIRST TROUBLE he had was convincing Dan McNabb to stay overnight. Jennings closed the door on Podesta and felt his way down the darkened hallway to where Amy was already boiling three big pots of water on the wood-fired stove in the kitchen.

"I'm running a bath. For Nicky," she said when Jennings entered the room.

But the way she said it made him look for McNabb.

"He says they're leaving now," Amy whispered, just before Dan appeared from the sitting room, with Nicky trailing behind him, wrapped in a blanket. She was crying again. Quietly.

"Dan, why don't you stay here?" Jennings asked.

The city engineer could not look at him. He was patting down all his pockets as if doing that little dance everyone did before leaving the house. *Car keys. Wallet. Phone.*

None of which would be of any use to him.

"Dan," Jennings said, trying to imitate Tommy Podesta's oddly gentle but unwavering tone. "Dan, I insist. It's freezing outside, and you don't have your car. And there's patrols out everywhere. We ran into two of them."

McNabb kept patting his pockets. Not looking at Jennings.

Car keys. Wallet. Phone.

"I'm taking Nicky home," he muttered.

"Dan. If they stop you without a pass, they'll lock you up. And they'll take Nicky away again."

Car keys. Wallet...

But that got his attention at last.

"I've got water on for a nice hot bath, Mister McNabb," Amy said. "We had some hot water left in the solar tank, but Nicky can really get a good clean soak in this. And we've got plenty of room here. Nicky, would you like a hot bath?"

The girl nodded. A small twitchy bob of her head.

"Dan," Jennings said, "let her have a bath. We'll keep boiling water all night if that's what she wants. She's safe here. You both are. But out there..."

He shook his head and let the lack of any conclusion speak for itself.

McNabb let go of a long, shaky breath he'd been holding.

"All right. Fine. I'll take the couch."

"Nicky can sleep in my room with me if she likes," Amy said. "I've got a big double bed. Nicky, would you..."

But Nicky was already nodding in answer to that.

The water was soon hot enough to pour into the bathtub, and

Jennings left Amy to supervise all of that. He thought about a drink and realised he was starving. His dinner was still waiting for him, under foil, in the warming rack of the old oven. He was desperately grateful to his daughter for thinking of that, but he didn't feel he could eat alone.

"Dan, I need to have some dinner. Can I get you something? Anything? We've got a big piece of boiling bacon in the cold locker. I could make you a sandwich. Amy made some sourdough this morning. Gonna have one myself."

But McNabb was not hungry.

Jennings didn't think it a good idea to pull a cork either, given the man's dark mood.

"I'm gonna kill the sonofabitch," he said.

"What?" Jennings asked.

"Runeberg. I'm gonna kill him. And Murdoch. I'm gonna kill them all."

"Not tonight, you're not, Dan. You go out there now; they will shoot you down as soon as they look at you."

"It wasn't your daughter," McNabb said. His voice was low and dangerous. "It was my Nicky."

Jennings almost said something trite and political like, 'It's all of our daughters, Dan,' but he caught himself before he could be so damned foolish.

Instead, he said, "I know. And it won't stand. We won't let it, Dan. There'll come a reckoning for this, but not tonight. Tonight, you have to look out for your girl."

"What? Like I did when they took her? Fat fucking lot of good that did," he snapped.

Jennings was almost as shocked by the use of profanity as he was by the sudden change in tone. He had never once heard Dan McNabb use a curse word before. Dan wasn't an especially religious man, but he was always careful to say exactly what he meant, and that precluded despoiling any message he had with unnecessary swearing.

Jennings supposed it was necessary in this instance.

"It wasn't your fault," he said, taking a leaf out of Thomas Podesta's book. And, now that he thought back on it, from Leo Vaulk's performance earlier in the night, too.

"It was Runeberg. It was all Runeberg," he said. "And we will settle with him on Nicky's behalf. When we go after him, we must do it right the first time because we won't get a second chance."

It was enough to still the other man's constant nervous movement around the kitchen.

He stopped patting himself down, looking for the keys, wallet and phone he hadn't carried in months.

"And the other one," Dan said. "Bolger."

"Of course. Him too," Ross Jennings assured his friend. "We'll get them both, Dan."

"No, we'll get them all," McNabb said through gritted teeth.

"Yeah. We'll get them all," Jennings agreed.

But he thought he would probably need the help of Thomas Podesta and Leo Vaulk to do that.

He got to his dinner after Dan McNabb took himself off to the couch with a blanket to bunk down for the night. Jennings quietly retrieved the .45 pistol from the dresser drawer in his bedroom and checked it, never letting Dan see what he was doing.

It had been years since Jennings had been to the range, and the gun felt much heavier than he remembered. It had an almost malign heft to it, as though it was possessed of purely dark and cursed possibilities. He stashed it in the dresser next to his bed and returned to the kitchen to find Amy cleaning up. Without saying anything, he went to his daughter, folded her inside a hug and kissed the top of her head. His thoughts went to his older child, Chrissy, but he shut down any such contemplation. Chrissy was an Air Force captain. He did not know where she was, but he had faith in her. She was tough and resourceful. Amy was his sole responsibility right now. In a weird and quite unsettling way, she seemed smaller and lighter to him, where his old Colt automatic had felt impossibly dense and weighted with malevolence.

Ross Jennings realised for the first time since this all started back in August just how close they all stood to the shifting veil between this world and the great silence.

"Thank you," he said, kissing her again on top of her head.

His daughter returned the hug but eased out of it, pushing him away. It was almost as though she was the grown-up who had to take charge.

"She had her bath, got into my bed and fell asleep straight away," Amy said. "I think she was exhausted."

"Okay, thanks," Jennings said. "She might have... nightmares and... you know."

"I know," Amy said. "I remember from when Mom died. I'd keep waking up inside that car, crashing. Every night. I'll look after her."

Jennings had never been prouder of his daughter or loved her more.

"I'll finish tidying up out here," he said. "You try to get some sleep while you can. I don't think this is over. And Nicky won't sleep well all night."

Amy looked at him. Her eyes were haunted.

"What's going to happen to us, Dad?"

"I don't know, pumpkin," he said, and she managed a small smile for him.

He never called her that anymore.

With everyone down for the night, Jennings cleaned the kitchen as quietly as he could. As he wiped down the table with a damp cloth, he tried to think of a way out of this or around it, but no answer came. It wasn't just tonight. It was everything. Murdoch had brought a sense of security to the town and a supply chain that had otherwise disappeared months ago. But with that came fear and the certainty they were hostages to the whims of the men they'd let into their home.

He shook his head.

But what was the alternative?

He had seen what they had done to Manhattan.

He also knew there were deep fault lines and divisions within Murdoch's camp. It was obvious that Vaulk and Runeberg were rivals and would take each other down in a heartbeat. They could probably be set against each other without much effort. But this wasn't like counting numbers for a vote on some municipal budget line item. If he got this wrong, people would die. Or worse.

His own daughter could be taken from him.

But there would be no denying Dan McNabb some form of vengeance, either. He knew the man too well. Dan's will was such that it would not be bent from the course of retribution by impossible odds or the certainty of his destruction. And Jennings could not allow that.

He stopped his incessant wiping. He'd been absently scrubbing at the same small circle for ten minutes. His eyes felt hot and prickly. His back ached.

He heard McNabb tossing and turning on the couch and did not feel he could turn down for the night until he was sure the man was not about to do something stupid.

He wondered if he might be able to enlist the mobster in some scheme.

Podesta had asked Jennings—no, Podesta had *told* him—that he was to be informed of any trouble that might boil up out of this.

Maybe Jennings could use that? The man seemed ready to gun down Luke Bolger a few hours ago.

But try as he might, the mayor of Three Forks could not imagine how he might yet best these animals. They were not the opponents he was used to facing in primaries for the local Republican ticket, and even less so in any contest at the ballot box with the half dozen or so woebegone Democrats in town. It was enough to drive a man to despair and even to recall with surprising warmth and some fondness the futile efforts of Alyson Roberts to unseat him from City Hall last November.

God, how he missed the times before... all this.

Hanging the wet washcloth over the oven door handle to dry, he tip-toed to the living room and checked on Dan.

A quiet snore assured him that, for now, at least, the man was resting.

He did not call in on Amy, as he usually did, to kiss her goodnight. He did not imagine that Nicky would take well to the sudden appearance of any man at the bedroom door.

Instead, he added a few logs to the wood-burning stove and put water on for coffee.

He dug up a pen and writing pad from the drawer where they had once kept all of the household admin, pausing for a moment to smile at the last unpaid phone bill he had received from AT&T. They had threatened to cut off his landline, but by then it was already dead, thanks to the Chinese.

Hell of a testament to the way they'd run their business, he thought, that the last part of the company to die was accounts receivable.

Fatigue passed over Ross Jennings in a wave, leaving him dizzy and nauseous.

He ignored that and poured himself a long cup of joe. Black. No sugar.

The mayor of Three Forks pulled up a chair at the kitchen table and started to write.

29

A POWERFUL SENSE OF WHAT'S THEIRS

The Legion checkpoint, a herringbone blockade of four pickups, straddled the road as it passed through a long valley about twenty miles west of Bozeman. James observed the encounter from a forested ridgeline about two miles north. The binoculars he peered through were nothing like the massive astronomical pair Damien Maloney had carried away from his yacht. They were almost dainty in comparison but heavy, too, their manufacture predating modern materials science by at least a couple of decades. James remembered them well from his childhood.

They had once belonged to his grandfather, who had handed them off to Tom O'Donnell with instructions that James should have them when he took over the ranch. That had never come to pass, obviously. But, his dad had insisted he take them on the long ride to Three Forks, and James was glad of them now. They were powerful enough for him to recognise Rick and Michelle as they got out of the Expedition and approached the roadblock with their hands raised in the air. He saw Nomi jump down and trot after her master and found that even more unnerving. He hoped the dog would not bite anybody. James lay on a soft mat of damp, rotting maple leaves, and he distinctly felt his balls try to crawl away from the forest floor and into his body, as armed figures manning the checkpoint raised their weapons at his friends.

"Be cool, James," Simon Higgins said quietly.

His cousin lay belly down on the soft ground next to him. "This is how it goes. We've sent people into their territory before, usually to trade food for medicines and batteries and stuff. They just got a powerful sense of what's theirs, is all."

"I know," James said. "Doesn't make it any easier to watch from up here, though."

'Up here' was the crest of a meandering line of hills that roughly paralleled the back road along which Rick and Michelle's little convoy had been travelling. The vehicles had abandoned the interstate not far west of Livingston, and over the following days, the outriders had roughly matched their westward course a few miles to the north. It was surprisingly slow going, with a lot of backtracking and workarounds required to avoid washouts, two bridge collapses and all the usual pileups. James had seen plenty of those on the long journey home, but he was surprised at how quickly nature had started to reclaim her dominion.

"Yeah, when the drought broke, it broke hard," Simon explained when he'd asked about it. "Some real bad storms and a whole lotta flooding."

None of that had been of any concern to the outriders. The small troop of mounted men and women negotiated their path through the backcountry with relative ease. It caused James to wonder about the future of transport, at least for the next couple of years. It seemed like the horse was about to make a real comeback. Perhaps he should send out an email, he thought sardonically.

Most of the riders and their horses waited in a gully a couple of hundred yards shy of the crest. A freshwater stream ran through a hollow, and the horses ate well from the thick, verdant grasses that grew at the edge of the watercourse.

As James watched, one of the militiamen patted down Rick, looking for concealed weapons. Or at least that's what James assumed he was doing. Three others kept their guns trained on both

Rick and Michelle. When they were done searching his friend, they moved on to Michelle. James forced himself to chill out. To let go. Otherwise, he was apt to shatter his teeth by grinding them together so hard. Even with the binoculars, it was difficult to tell, but Michelle seemed no more troubled by the pat down than Rick had been. He knew she had served in overseas posts in some pretty hairy parts of the world, and he had to assume she'd been given all sorts of training to deal with the shit you had to expect on a posting like that. But it was still hard to watch.

"She's brave," his cousin said next to him.

Simon watched the confrontation through a hunter's scope, a sort of fat, short-barrelled telescope that he had mounted on a small tripod. It was undoubtedly a lot more powerful than the antique binoculars James had inherited.

"She is," James agreed. "Among other things."

"She used to be a spy or something, right?" Simon said, his eye still glued to the viewfinder.

"Nah," James scoffed. "She was an analyst. Keyboards and screens, just like me."

"Yeah, cool story, bro," Simon deadpanned.

And James wasn't entirely sure he believed it either. He had seen enough since they'd left Washington to have his doubts.

A heavy figure suddenly appeared on the ground next to him, and he jumped a little in surprise. Stephen Collins had come up on them without making a sound that James had noticed. Not a single broken twig.

"How's it going?" he asked. "Enquiring minds want to know. "

"Looks like the usual shakedown at the border crossing," Simon Higgins replied. "They'll have them out of the vehicles in a minute for the weapons check."

And almost as though speaking the words spurred events to follow them, a detachment of the militia moved to surround the other vehicles. They were no longer pointing their weapons at the occupants as though they intended to murder them in broad daylight, but James's heart was still beating fast as he watched everyone climb out and place their hands behind their heads so they could be searched as well. It reminded him immediately of getting bailed up on the outskirts of Livingston, but this looked a lot more dangerous.

What the hell had happened to everyone?

Why were people like this now?

It was a stupid question, of course. James knew exactly what had brought them to this pass. He'd been there and even played his own very minor role at the start. This might have started with China, with the virus or computer hack or whatever the hell it was, but they were all responsible for what happened after that. As he watched through his grandfather's old binoculars, he saw one of the fighters remove what had to be a handgun from Damien Maloney, but he did so without unduly abusing or assaulting the Australian. The man appeared to empty the pistol of ammunition before placing the gun into a locker in one of their patrol vehicles. More weapons came out of the three SUVs, long arms and handguns, and all went into the same locker. A woman supervised the confiscation. When it was done, she approached Rick with a clipboard and offered it to him. He signed whatever papers she had given him, and everybody returned to their vehicles within a minute. The roadblock opened up, and the convoy drove through.

"So, what just happened?" James asked.

"There's no Second Amendment in Legion territory," Stephen Collins explained.

"And they're not too fond of the First, either," Simon remarked dryly. "Come on. Let's saddle up. We got a long ride ahead of us."

"I GUESS it wasn't the worst checkpoint I've been through," Rick said.

"Same," Michelle agreed.

"Didn't even put their hands out for a bribe," Damo said. "What sort of a tin pot operation is this Murdoch bloke running?"

As they rolled slowly through the blockade, Rick noted the weapons and the dress of the Legion fighters.

First thing to note, nothing was uniform. Everybody was attired and equipped as they pleased, and it seemed to please most of them to play dress-ups.

"What d'you see, Michelle?" Rick asked.

"Fifteen strong unit," she said, staring out of the window as they cleared the last of the herringbone. "Call it half platoon strength. Inconsistent, non-standard loadouts. I got seven different flavours of AR-15, weapon of choice for your ammosexual crisis actor. Three pump action shotguns of eccentric calibre. Four hunting rifles. One museum piece..."

"The Winchester?"

"Yeah, and a lucky dip of side arms. Nine mil, mostly, but some .45s and a .38 special on the bitch with the clipboard. I made her as a Leo."

"You what, mate?" Damo said from the passenger seat up front.

"Law enforcement officer, Damo," Karl explained from behind the wheel. "Not a star sign. She was more of a Sagittarius, I'd say. A very blunt lady."

"Oh, right. A narc. Gotcha."

Karl increased their speed as they left the roadblock behind.

"They reckon there's clear running all the way to Three Forks now. But we gotta stay off of the I-90. Can't go through Bozeman at all."

"How long 'til we get there? To Three Forks, I mean," Rick asked.

Between him and Michelle lay Nomi, her head resting in his lap, grumbling. The encounter with the Legion still aggravated her.

"Not long now," Karl said. "Traffic won't be an issue, the route is signposted, and they reckon the road condition is good. But there are two more checkpoints. Call it two hours on these back roads. Three if there's shenanigans at the roadblocks."

Damo grunted thoughtfully at that.

"They seemed, I dunno, pretty well behaved. For a bunch of wankers," he said.

"Yeah," Michelle said. "I'd have been happier if they'd tried to shake us down. They look like a bunch of ass clowns, but it takes real discipline to deny yourself the undeniable fun of fucking with people at a checkpoint like that."

"Agreed," Rick said. "On the whole, I prefer my enemies to be an undisciplined rabble. Those guys weren't that. But they weren't the A-Team, either. Don't know if it even occurred to them we might've hidden more weapons somewhere besides the ones they confiscated."

"They took inventory and issued us a receipt for the guns. That was interesting," Michelle said. "It implies a bureaucracy of command and control."

"Interesting, maybe," Damo said. "Worrying, fuckin' definitely."

They were at the front of the convoy, leading the three vehicles through a patchy landscape of forested hills, open fields and occasional hamlets or villages. Some were obviously deserted. Two had been destroyed, and Rick was in no doubt the Legion had done that. They were less battle-damaged than devastated by stand-off weaponry. He'd poured enough fire from a safe distance into Taliban and ISIS-held settlements to recognise the signs of a one-sided exchange.

"What're you looking for, mate?" Damo asked as Karl leaned forward over the steering wheel to peer up into the sky. Lowering clouds, bruised and scalloped with dark leaden tones, obscured the tops of the higher ranges and promised snow before long. It was the sort of drear winter an old friend of his from Missouri used to call 'the grey, lingering, waking death.'

"Drones," Karl replied. "Them fellas was pretty fierce on the matter of not stopping or deviating. They didn't say we'd be watched, but they seemed mighty confident they'd know if I got fancy with the route."

Rick squinted into the sky, too.

There was nothing up there that he could see.

"They'll probably have two or three-man observation points every couple of miles," Michelle said. "Tactical radios for comms, or even old CB units from busted long-ass haulers. And there's not many points you can pull off and go cross country anyway."

"No, there's not," Karl conceded. "But I just like to know when I'm being snooped on, is all."

"Amen, brother," Rick said quietly.

He felt keenly the press of hostile intent all around them. The countryside was empty, yet it seemed laden with ill will and belligerent potential. The same way it sometimes felt as if the rocky heights of the Hindu Kush would bare themselves hungrily at outsiders, like broken teeth in the vast open maw of a mountain giant.

Nomi whimpered and nuzzled in closer. She could sense the darkness creeping up on him.

He scratched behind her ears, concentrated on settling his ragged breathing, and decided to let Michelle do all the threat assessment.

He would observe because he could not help doing that and would answer any question she asked. But this was her realm, not his. And it was probably best that he ceded it to her. Instead, he patted his dog and gazed out and up into the wooded slopes.

James would be out there, somewhere. Keeping up with them. Avoiding the enemy. Moving unseen through the wilderness.

Or at least that was the plan.

Above them, the winter clouds pressed down heavy and grim.

Now that Karl had raised the possibility of aerial surveillance, Rick had trouble getting it out of his mind. He stared into the void, but there was nothing out there. Just the grey, lingering, waking death.

30

NO JUSTICE, NO PEACE

The smell of porridge and maple syrup woke him.

"Dad?"

Ross Jennings came awake and quickly regretted it. His daughter had cooked oats on the stovetop and sweetened them with a heavy dollop of maple syrup, one of the precious condiments he was allowed as a first-tier recipient on the Legion's rationing system. He had fallen asleep in an armchair in the living room, and he knew even before he opened his eyes that he'd put his neck out and would suffer for it the rest of the day. Jennings blinked the sleep out of his eyes and was surprised to find Amy standing over him, waving the bowl under his nose. He shouldn't have been. She often woke him in the morning by doing the same thing with his toast and coffee.

"They're gone," she said without explanation.

It wasn't needed.

He could see that Dan McNabb no longer lay on the couch. Jennings had settled in to sit and watch over him at about four in the morning. He had been up until then, trying to work out how he could make good on his promise to Dan that they would somehow settle with Murdoch and his men for what they had done.

To be honest, and Ross Jennings was nothing if not an honest man, he could see no way around it other than leaning into Murdoch's Bozeman project. The Legion's weirdly hipster-fascist strongman had fixated on taking the small city and establishing his capital there. And sometime around two in the morning, it had occurred to the mayor of Three Forks that the sooner Murdoch achieved his ends, the sooner he would get the hell gone out of Jennings' hometown.

That would be a hell of a hard sell to Dan McNabb. But perhaps, once they had rid themselves of the suffocating presence of the Legion and specifically of Murdoch's Praetorian guard, the so-called Cohort, the sooner they'd be free to plot a course that might rid them of their tormentors for good.

"Thank you, darlin'," Jennings croaked to his daughter.

He took the serve of sweetened oats and carefully rearranged himself in the armchair. His lower back hurt almost as much as his neck. This was going to be a tough day.

"How was Nicky?" he asked. "When did she and Dan go home? Er, they did go home, didn't they?" he added anxiously.

Amy nodded.

"Yes," she said. "I drove them."

Instantly, Jennings was alert and more than somewhat alarmed.

"But the curfew..."

"Dad," she said. "It's 9.30 in the morning. I drove them when the curfew lifted. You were snoring. I didn't want to wake you."

He saw that she had added a couple of logs to the small fireplace on the other side of the room. The whole house seemed so agreeably warm that she had to have banked up the wood-fired oven in the kitchen, too.

"I made coffee. I'll get you a cup."

"But it's late," he said, starting to rise out of the chair and nearly spilling his breakfast in the process. His back spasmed, and he bit his lip against the pain. "I have to get to work. I have to check on Dan," he said, gritting his teeth.

"You have to eat your breakfast," she said, brooking no resistance.

"I will drive you to work. Nobody is going to complain about you being a little late. Not after last night."

He paused when he was just about to scoop out a spoonful of oats.

"What do you mean?"

Amy looked as though she regretted saying anything.

"Amy," he said. "Nobody but us knows what happened last night."

She looked pained.

"That's not exactly... true," his daughter replied.

THEY HIT the second checkpoint seven or eight miles north of Bozeman, on a back road Damo imagined had been cut through the forest by loggers. It was a dirt track, really, meandering, poorly surveyed, and badly corrugated. It reminded him of any number of primitive backwoods tracks he'd travelled all over the world. At least the checkpoint was well-signed. They started to get warnings about five miles out. Karl dropped their speed to a sedate thirty miles an hour. The off-road vehicles could have safely handled twice that, even in the foul, sleeting weather, but Karl was adamant they didn't want to come roaring around a bend in the forest road into the guns of a bunch of unhappy rednecks.

"Better five minutes late in this life," he started to say.

"Than fifty fuckin' years early in the next," Damo finished for him.

They had grown accustomed to each other on the long road from San Francisco.

The mood in the big Ford was tense as the hand-painted signs on the trail counted down the miles to the checkpoint. Nobody said anything for the last two miles until they crested a small hill and saw another blockade through the light mist and falling sleet.

"Bloody hell," Damo grunted. "That thing looks like they stole it from Saddam's car lot."

Rick Boreham leaned forward, pulling himself up between the two front seats. He glowered through the windscreen.

"That's an MRAP," he said. "Mine Resistant Ambush Protected. An armoured patrol vehicle. Possibly ex-army, but some asshole thought it'd be a good idea to gift a bunch of them to a lot of dinky little police departments over the last ten years or so. More likely, that's where they got it. Not a military base."

Karl dialled down their speed even further, but not enough to cause suspicion up ahead. The weather thickened up, and he flicked on the wipers.

"Damo," Michelle said. "Pass me back your binoculars, would you?"

She took his oversized Skymasters and quickly scanned the vehicles blocking the unsealed road.

"This looks like a much tighter unit," she said, handing the glasses back to Damo. "Better uniforms, standard load out. And somebody has probably been trained in the operation of that big-ass armoured car."

Ellie Jabbarah spoke up from the back seat.

"Is this bad? It sounds pretty bad."

"Yes and no," Rick Boreham said.

"If they have good unit discipline, the chance of them blowing their wad in our faces is less than last time," Michelle explained. "But it's bad because..."

"It looks like they have good unit discipline," Rick said. Like Damo and Karl, those two had also started finishing each other's thoughts over the last few months.

Armed sentries were already flagging them down. Karl pulled up at least a hundred yards short of the roadblock. Besides the oversized military vehicle, salvaged from the Portland City School Department, which was odd, the checkpoint was secured by a couple of pickups with heavy machine guns mounted on tripods in the back.

"Fuck me pink. It's like Mogadishu or something," Damo said.

A man in forest camouflage was walking towards them through

the slush and sleet. He had not drawn his sidearm and carried no rifle, but the three men with him were all packing military-style carbines. They approached cautiously but with confidence that could only come from having all that heavy artillery backing them up.

"You know, they ain't as good as they think they are," Karl remarked drily. "If they figure to hose us down with ol' Ma Deuce up there, they're gonna have to shoot through their own guys. Make a helluva mess."

"Nicely observed, Karl," Michelle said. "I'll compliment you on your excellent analytic skills now because I won't have a chance if they turn us into loose meat with those gun trucks."

The officer in charge of the roadblock gestured for Karl to wind down his window. His troops looked pretty miserable, but he seemed unfazed by the cold, wet weather.

He wore a name tag – CREIGHTON – on his uniform and took a notebook out of his breast pocket.

"You'd be Mister Karl Valentine out of Paradise Valley?" he said.

"Of late," Karl answered.

Creighton scowled at him.

"And which one is Maloney?"

Damo leaned forward a little.

"That'd be me, mate."

Creighton ticked off a name in his book.

"And you're one of the designated negotiators for this group?"

"Yeah, that's right."

"What are you, British or something?"

"Australian. Like the Crocodile Hunter."

"He's dead," Creighton said.

"A lot of blokes are," Damo answered back.

Creighton seemed to consider that and found it an acceptable rejoinder. He stepped back to peer into the rear of the vehicle. Consulting his notebook, he took a roll call.

"Richard Boreham?"

"Here," Rick snapped back.

"Michelle Nguyen?"

He mangled the pronunciation, but Michelle answered anyway.

"That's me."

"And I'm Eliza Jabbarah," Ellie said from the very rear of the Expedition. "And this is Nomi, a very good dog."

Creighton was not much amused by her attempts at cheeriness.

"You got the Chinese flu?" He asked Michelle. "I thought you people all got the flu and died."

Michelle stared at him.

"Not even a sniffle," she said. "I'm not Chinese."

"A slope's a slope," Creighton said. He bent forward to get a closer look at Ellie and did not much like what he found.

"And what are you? Some sorta towel head?"

"Hey," Rick growled. "She's a chef. And a damn good one."

Creighton stared at him. Rick refused to drop his eyes.

It was Creighton who finally stepped away, but only because he had another card to play.

"Everybody get out of the vehicle. Now."

"What's the problem, mate?" Damo asked.

Creighton looked at him for a full second before answering.

"The problem is you're not getting out of the vehicle. Mate."

He put his hand on his sidearm. The men behind him raised their weapons.

Their attention suddenly shifted to a point behind the Expedition. Damo heard a door open, followed by Peter Tapsell's English accent, but inflected with an unfamiliar upper-class tone.

"I say, chaps," Tapsell cried out. "Is there some sort of bother up there? I'm ever so keen to get to a civilised toilet and have a decent whiz".

One of Creighton's spear carriers, Damo wasn't sure which, muttered, "What the fuck?"

Creighton glowered at Tapsell.

"You get back in your vehicle now, asshole. We'll get to you."

"Righty oh, then," Tapsell called back. "But please do hurry. I don't think I can cross my legs much longer."

Creighton shook his head as if he couldn't quite believe the exchange.

"Just get out," he said to everyone in Damien's car, most of the animosity drained from his delivery by the bizarre exchange with the Englishman.

Damo smiled discreetly, recalling Tapsell's story about Uganda and smuggling the briefcase full of conflict diamonds past a whole company of the Lord's Resistance Army.

Karl and Damo got out first, followed by Michelle and Rick, who pulled his seat forward for Ellie. Nomi hopped down after her and joined her master in the mud at the side of the road. Creighton spoke into a small walkie-talkie he pulled from his utility belt.

"Hey, Miranda, you need to come up and do the vehicle inspection. Bring Ed and Mikey, too. Got a travelling comedy troupe up here."

A woman's voice crackled back from the handset, "Sure thing, Adam."

Damo's balls retracted just a little. They'd sailed through the previous vehicle inspection without incident, but this mob looked like they might know what they were doing.

"You seem pretty well informed about our movements, mate," Damo said. "So, you probably know we already handed over our weapons and had a vehicle inspection back at your first border post."

Creighton didn't even look at him when he answered.

"Not by my guys, you didn't," he said. "So far as I'm concerned, that never happened, and now we gonna do it properly."

Damo shrugged as if he didn't care. It was an effort to appear so calm.

He resisted the urge to glance at anybody, but especially not at Rick, who had broken down and hidden a second cache of weapons inside the door panels of the Expedition and the Jeep that Tapsell was driving. He prayed Pete wasn't trying to retrieve one of the guns and rebuild it on the fly. They couldn't hope to win a fight with these bastards. They were completely outgunned.

Instead, he turned towards the crunching footsteps of the three people, two men and a woman, approaching from the main body of the roadblock. The men were dressed like Creighton in forest pattern camouflage uniforms. The woman was either a state trooper, or she'd found a Smokey the Bear hat somewhere.

Miranda, he presumed, with the famous Ed and Mikey.

She inspected the vehicle with their help while Creighton's three riflemen kept the occupants under guard. They removed everything from the inside and piled all the contents on the muddy, unsealed road. She looked under the seats and in the various nooks and crannies that modern luxury vehicles offered for storing or hiding bits and pieces. Nobody spoke much. Damo tried to engage Creighton just once, but the Legion overseer told him to shut the fuck up, "Or I'll shoot the dog."

Damo could feel a cold fury coming off Rick Boreham at that comment. He didn't doubt that Boreham would try to kill the man if he drew his gun on Nomi. Nor did he doubt the rest of them would die in the next few seconds, shot down by the other dress-up Nazis. So, he did as he was told and shut the fuck up.

The inspection took ten nerve-wracking minutes, but Miranda did not get around to breaking down the vehicle into its constituent parts. It started to snow for real after five minutes. Perhaps she might have been more thorough if they hadn't been on a country road and it hadn't been so cold and wretchedly unpleasant. Even the Legion troopers were stamping their feet and blowing onto their fingers after a few minutes. They didn't say anything, but it felt like everybody was pissed off and wanted to be somewhere else.

Creighton wandered back to the command post to get himself a cup of coffee. He returned with the Thermos just as Miranda finished her inspection of the sunken well that housed the spare tire.

"Good to go here, I reckon," she said.

Creighton seemed disappointed but accepting of her call.

"Okay," he said to Karl. "Pack your car but sit your ass here while we do the others."

"No worries," Damo said, waiting for a beat before adding, "Mate."

JENNINGS DID NOT DRIVE to work. He had a petrol ration, another privilege of his elevated station, but he lived close enough to the city office to enjoy and benefit from a brisk daily walk. The mayor had also quietly been using his ration allotment to build a small reserve supply of gasoline just in case it became necessary to get Amy out of Three Forks. Now, he had enough to get to Canada and quite a bit further.

But he also wanted to walk because he needed to take the pulse of the streets.

And the streets, as it happened, were angry.

He could hear the crowd gathered outside The Continental Divide two blocks before arriving on-site. He quickened his pace, hurrying towards the disturbance, a sick feeling twisting in his guts. He'd decided to leave his sidearm at home – was that a mistake? The Legion had banned residents from carrying firearms and had confiscated hundreds of them. But most folk still had a piece somewhere.

It took another block before he could make out what they were chanting.

"No justice, no peace. No justice, no peace."

"Oh my God," he muttered to himself. "Please, God, no."

All his fears were confirmed as he bustled around the corner of First Avenue on the main stem of State Route 2, known locally as Railway Avenue. As he rounded the corner, Jennings saw the adjacent siding where that refrigerated goods train full of frozen beef had been stranded back in August. At the time, it had seemed such a godsend. Now Jennings cursed the random stroke of fortune which had drawn Murdoch and his damned Legion down upon them.

At least a hundred, maybe a hundred and twenty people had gathered outside the motel. Many of them carried quickly made and crudely fashioned handmade signs. He couldn't read most of them from a block away—his eyes were not what they had been—but he didn't need to. He already knew what they denounced.

Three Forks was a respectable town, peopled by decent folk.

Nobody had been happy about Murdoch's goons opening a couple of brothels on the State Route through town as if to announce that they would remake all that was left of the world however they chose. But nobody had been foolhardy enough to openly object, either. The destruction of Manhattan had done its work of kindling an exemplary terror among the citizens of neighbouring Three Forks. And to be fair, none of the women working at the Legion's O Club or their Enlisted Men's Rec Centre was from here. Mathias Runeberg shipped them in from the far reaches of the Legion's remit. So, everybody had put their heads down and done their best to ignore what was plain to all; they had let barbarians inside the gates, and now they must live with the consequences of that moral failure. Buy the ticket and take the ride.

Having toured the ruins of Manhattan, Ross Jennings still regarded the decision to yield his town as the only correct and ethical one. He had no stomach for pointless sacrifice, which was why he felt so nauseous seeing what was happening in front of The Continental.

Dan McNabb was there, looking drawn and grimly furious, and the leaders of all the town's houses of worship supported him. Strikingly, the overwhelming majority of those in attendance were women. He was relieved to see Nicky McNabb was nowhere to be found. He wondered where Dan might have hidden her away. But she was present in spirit and likeness. Many women chanting "No justice, no peace" held placards emblazoned with her image.

Two images, to be precise.

A smiling portrait obviously taken some years ago, when she still wore braces and pigtails and a more recent picture. Very recent indeed, taken after Luke Bolger had abused her. The poor girl's face carried the fresh bruises and swelling of that assault.

The placards were crude. The images produced on a photocopier and blown up for effect.

But the effect was powerful.

Recognising what he was looking at transported Jennings back to the darkest hours of the long night he had just gone through.

He slowed as he approached the edge of the rally.

But it did not matter.

A protester recognised him, and he heard his name called out.

And cheers.

They were cheering him.

Ross Jennings despaired.

31

EXECUTIVE TIME

"Lot of folks about," Rick Boreham said from the back of the big Ford.

"Not for much longer," the militia man said.

They were negotiating the last of the checkpoints on the edge of town. It was, if anything, the most relaxed of the three inspections they had undergone by the Legion's enforcers. State Route 2 curved gently around a golf course before entering Three Forks from the north. The fairways and greens had been allowed to grow wild, but the town looked orderly and peaceful. Except for all the hillbilly Taliban on the streets.

A police cruiser sat parked at the side of the main road, and two uniformed officers waved them down as they approached. They were backed up by a squad of heavily armed Legion fighters, but the encounter was much less hostile. Even the Legion's squad commander was more chilled out, albeit distracted.

The cops asked them what business they had in town, and the Legion guy answered before Maloney or Karl could tell him.

"They came over from Livingston," he said, checking a notebook. "Here to negotiate a surrender or something."

Someone called ahead, Rick thought.

The cop suddenly lost interest in their business.

"Alrighty then, you'll need to talk with these fellows here," he said, handing them over to the officer, whose name tag read Wilson. He wore the silver bar of an Army lieutenant, but Rick had no idea whether he'd ever served. At a guess, no.

"Enjoy your stay in town," the cop said. "Curfew runs 6 PM to 6 AM."

He stepped away, and Lieutenant Wilson took his place at the window.

"We're not from Livingston, mate," Damo said. "You blokes shot the shit out of that place. We're from the valley a bit to the south. A delegation. We'd like to chat with your boss about not getting the shit shot out of us if that'd be cool."

"All very cool and very legal," the officer grinned.

Quite the laid-back junior warlord, Rick thought. He looked again at the man's shiny Lieutenant's bar. It seemed very new and wasn't pinned correctly on his collar.

"You need to take the first left up ahead," Wilson said. "Go down five blocks, take a right back out on the main drag, down another block, and you'll find yourself outside an old real estate office painted bright yellow. You can't miss it. That's the Op Centre. You check in there, tell them what you're here for, and they'll tell you what next."

Karl looked confused. "Why not just drive straight there?

'Lieutenant' Wilson shook his head.

"Oh, you don't want to do that, old-timer. There's some sort of protest down there," he said, pointing to where Route 2 curved around. "Just follow my say so. Go to the Op Centre. Check-in. Tell them what you're here for, and somebody will give you a billet and a job to do while you wait."

"What sort of a job?" Damo asked.

Wilson grinned again.

"Poorly paid with terrible benefits. But everybody works here, sir. If you're going to be in town for more than twenty-four hours, you'll have to pay your way. But the op centre guys will sort you out."

Wilson stepped away from the window and waved them on, pointing at the intersection where he wanted them to turn.

"Hey, Karl," Rick said when they were underway again. "He remind you of any living, breathing officer you ever met in your life?"

"Not really," the driver said. "Seemed kinda like he hadn't even figured out how to put the pants on one leg at a time."

"His name was Wilson, right?" Michelle said.

"Yeah," Rick confirmed.

She nodded, her eyes narrowing just slightly. Rick could almost see the cogs turning in her head, committing the single data point to memory.

"I'll check him out," she said. "It's a problem for elite units..."

She sketched air quotes around the word 'elite'.

"That once they get a reputation, over time they attract pretenders."

"Well, this crew ain't hardly your elite, Miss Michelle," Karl said. "And they ain't had so much time for recruiting, neither."

She smiled.

"I'll take your first point, Karl. But time is relative, and it's been compressed and accelerated since all of... this."

She waved her hands to indicate their immediate surroundings and the wider world.

"Anyway, take it slowly, buddy," she said to Karl. "I'd like to get a look at this protest, even from a distance."

"You got it, Miss," Karl said.

Damo turned around to face her.

"How come you never chip him for calling you Miss?" he said.

"Because he's charming," Michelle said. "And you're a fucking vulgarian."

Damo took that in.

He nodded.

"Fair enough then."

They drove slowly into Three Forks.

It was uncanny, in the true sense of that word, as Rick understood it. It had been many months since he had been in an ordinary, functioning American town or city. Once they were past the checkpoint, apart from the occasional foot patrol by Legion soldiers, Three Forks looked almost normal. People were out on the streets and hurrying in one direction – perhaps towards the disturbance Wilson was talking about. But you could just as easily imagine them in happier times hastening towards Friday night football, the county fair on a Saturday morning, or something, anything that didn't involve violent chaos and madness.

"There they are," Michelle said, pointing up a side street where Rick could see a sizeable crowd spilling over the road. Karl slowed down, but he couldn't stop, and before Rick could get a handle on what was happening, they lost sight of the crowd again.

He could hear them, though. They were chanting.

"No justice! No peace!"

Over and over again.

"I'm not sure whether we got here at just the right moment or way too late," Michelle said.

Another glimpse of the crowd at the next intersection was no more informative. There were a lot of people up there. But other than being pissed off about something, they gave away no intelligence about their specific intent.

At the next set of crossroads, he could see that the numbers were petering out.

"That crowd occupied two city blocks," Michelle Nguyen said. "I could be off by half, but I'd bet there were at least a thousand people. Out of a population of two thousand, maybe three with refugees and occupying forces."

"There's no prize for guessing the number of jellybeans in the jar, Mishy," Damo said. "But you're right, mate. It's a solid whack of punters."

Michelle had given up trying to get Damo to stop calling her Mishy.

"Okay," she said. "Let's check in at this Ops Centre. We might find out what's going on there; if not, we can do recon."

She rolled up her window. Karl did too.

JONAS HAD an excellent start to the day. Spectacular, even. He came awake in his king-size bed, like literally. The two hotties he was currently banging woke him up with a tongue bath and a double blow job that turned his fucking brainstem inside out. Probably because he had a lot of stress to get out of his system. He felt so good after that wake-up call that he nailed the blonde one doggy-style while she muff-dived the ever-loving fuck out of her friend Kimmy.

He was pretty sure the blonde was Gwen and the brunette was Kimmy.

Not that it mattered. All that mattered for real was that he woke up in a much better mood than he'd been in for weeks, determined to seize the day and shake the shit out of it. Jonas even knew where to start. He was gonna call up Chad and program a couple of hours in the Box. He hadn't done a CrossFit session worth a damn since getting out of Seattle. There'd been plenty of hard labour in Silverton and not much easy living that first month or so on the road. But after he'd pulled together the band of dudebros that became the Legion, he had to admit that the siren song of an easy life had called to him. And, since they had decided to winter over in Three Forks, he'd gone soft. That was why things had started to slip. That was why he didn't feel like he had his usual iron grip on things anymore.

Jonas Murdoch had let himself get soft.

Jonas chuckled as he lay in bed with Gwen and Kimmy languidly rubbing themselves against his flanks.

"What's so funny, baby," Gwen asked.

She had that slow, lazy, Just-Fucked-By-The-Centurion glow about her. Jonas patted her deliciously firm little ass almost fondly.

"I thought I was getting soft, baby," he said. "But I guess I was wrong."

"Oh baby, you'll never go soft with us," Kimmy said, gently wrapping her hand around his dick. He started to stir, but he pushed her away.

"You ladies get yourself a hot bath and some breakfast. You'll be needing your energy later. But right now, I'm gonna go work out. You be here when I get back. Make yourselves nice."

He was gratified when they promised they would, even though it wasn't like they had much choice. Where the fuck else were they gonna go to find three hots and a cot? He owned that market.

Jonas all but leapt out of bed and rolled into the bathroom, where he ran a hot shower.

He was used to the amenities, the luxuries even, of the Sacajawea Hotel, but Jonas took a moment to breathe in the steam that filled the room and luxuriate in the hot water that stung his skin as he washed off the residue of their sex. He might have been the only man in America, maybe even the whole world, who had woken up in a luxury hotel this morning, fucked a couple of hotties, and could now look forward to getting in a workout with his personal trainer before inhaling a breakfast buffet full of macros. He resolved to take a moment to stop and suck up the awesomeness of that.

He had done this. It had not been easy. At times, they'd come close to disaster, and there had been pain. Losing Dale? Jonas would cop to that being some real pain right there. But if CrossFit had taught him anything, it was that pain was temporary. Quitting was forever.

He had not quit after Silverton. He, Jonas Murdoch, had built the kick-ass Legion of motherfucking Freedom. And whatever difficulties lay ahead, he would kick the shit out of them too. Jonas used a whole bottle of hotel shampoo and conditioner on his thick, shoulder-length hair and thought about the day ahead. *Today*, he promised himself as he worked the suds, *I will do what others won't, so tomorrow I can do what others can't.*

Fuck yeah.

He was gonna have to deal with Runeberg. No way around that, and no reason he should try to get around it. That stunt Mathias pulled last night, that was out of line. It could've easily gotten out of hand if the Tripod hadn't grabbed that girl back from Bolger before he totally fucked her up. But the girl wasn't the problem, of course. Nor was her old man, that half-crippled toilet engineer. Not even Mayor Jennings. Once you started adding them all together, though and throw in a bunch of other pissed-off citizens, that's when you got problems. That was the whole fucking reason they didn't let any chicks work at the comfort stations within a hundred fuckin' miles of their hometowns. And why they had to be volunteers, sort of. Any other way was just asking for trouble.

Jonas had repped more than enough dumb-ass motherfuckers who got themselves jammed up over some skank to have insisted on the hundred-mile pussy policy himself. He hadn't needed Leo or Mathias to suggest it.

Now he thought about it; maybe *that* was the problem.

Maybe Mathias had been looking to fuck with the hundred-mile rule because Jonas had come up with it. Mathias would never front Jonas himself, so he'd scammed dopey fucking Luke Bolger into breaking it.

Huh, Jonas thought, as a little cartoon lightbulb went on over his head. He almost laughed out loud at the sneaky little shit.

That theory was worth some quality pondering time when he got a chance.

Until then, however, Mathias was just gonna have to apologise. He was a rigid, uptight little prick and being forced to admit he'd made a mistake and to say sorry for it would probably be punishment enough to make sure he never did anything so fucking stupid again.

Yeah, that was some hairy balls-out leadership right there, Jonas told himself as he rinsed a thick lather of suds out of his hair. He was on a roll today. What the fuck else was he going to do to seize this day?

CrossFit workout? Tick.

Egg white omelette? Tick.

Some hot, pussy-pounding action to get him back on focus when his mind started to wander, about two or three this afternoon? Double tick.

Yeah, these were all excellent ideas. But what Jonas really needed was to stop wallowing in his bad moods of late and take charge of this machine. He stepped out of the shower and reached for a towel, resolving to talk with the Tripod. Podesta never said shit about it, not really, but that dude had definitely been a made guy. So, he would know how to run an organisation full of testosterone and ambitious motherfuckers.

First thing Jonas was gonna ask him was what to do about Bolger. Luke had been pretty good at running the military side of things when you looked purely at the results.

But, when you really thought about it, he had those results because of Jonas and his policies. Number one was never to get into a stand-up fight. Luke, and the Legion for that matter, had never had to wage a legitimate campaign. The guy was a fuckin' prison guard, after all. He was used to piling on with overwhelming force, and he'd just scaled up that model with the Legion.

Mostly, what Luke Bolger did was give the order to open fire when Jonas decided it was time to make an example of some dumbfart podunk town that was getting in the way. As best he could, Jonas tried not to let things get to that point. It was always Luke pushing for another massacre.

Jonas wasn't about to tell Bolger he had to apologise for knockin' that girl around last night, though. That wasn't his fault. That was down to Mathias. But something Podesta had said was bugging him and had been bugging him since the Tripod had brought it up. He couldn't recall the exact form of words but seemed to remember it'd been a pretty good point.

Something about the bosses in his old outfit having all the power because when they told their guys to pull a trigger, the trigger got pulled. Standing in his big-ass, white-tiled, super luxe hotel bathroom, drying his nuts with Egyptian cotton waffle weave, and thinking about what would happen if he did tell Bolger he had to say sorry, Jonas Murdoch realised he wasn't entirely sure.

He could order Luke Bolger to pull the apology trigger, but he had no guarantee that trigger would get pulled.

And that was a fucking problem.

Jonas had made a mistake, he slowly realised, letting Bolger run both the Legion and the Cohort for him. It was a dumb play. The Cohort was supposed to be *his* Praetorian Guard, and they should answer to *him*. Directly to him. Not to Luke fucking Bolger. Last night had made that clear.

He finished drying himself and wrapped the towel around his waist. It was a moment of vanity. Weakness, if he was being honest about it, and Jonas was trying to be honest with himself now. He had gone soft around the middle. So sure, the towel.

But he was gonna get on top of that motherfucker this very day. He would get back to his CrossFit, and he would take charge. He would reverse the drift of the last few weeks, or even months, which more and more found him sitting around on his increasingly fat ass while other motherfuckers did the running.

That's not who he was. That's not what The Centurion had been about.

It was time to start kicking ass again. His own, most of all.

He marched back into the bedroom and fetched a fresh pair of jeans from the dresser. Pulled on a black tee shirt. Smacked Kimmy on the ass because it was a fine American ass in desperate need of some spanking.

She giggled and tried to entice him back to bed, but he was strong. Only the strong would survive.

"Gonna take care of my shit. Then I'll see to you sexy fuckin' bitches. Promise," he said.

A loud rapping at the door interrupted him.

He heard Tommy Podesta, muffled, out in the hall. He sounded... tense.

"Hey, boss. It's me. Sorry to interrupt executive time, but you're gonna wanna come deal with this."

32

LET'S MAKE A DEAL

Tucked in snug between a saddlery and a frontier-themed bar, the bright yellow building had once been a real estate office. The neighbouring businesses were shuttered and dark, but a constant stream of people flowed through the administrative hub of Jonas Murdoch's Legion of Freedom. You couldn't just walk in and take a number, though. Damo counted seven armed guards out front, warming their hands around a big-arse propane heater. He had a couple of them on the deck of his farmhouse down in Tasmania. As Karl pulled in across the street, two men strode over, looking like they'd be more than happy to shoot you for a parking violation.

"You want me to do the happy talk?" Damo said.

"Speak slow and use small words," Rick Boreham muttered from the rear seat.

"Pardner," Karl said in a cautionary tone, "I dunno that you should be takin' the lead with these fellas. You ain't from round here after all."

"None of us are," Damo reminded him.

"Damo, you deal with these losers," Michelle said. "I want to try to get a look at that demonstration. Rick, you wanna come with?"

"Sure," Boreham replied as the two Legion militiamen stepped up to the driver-side window and settled the question of who would do the talking.

One of them consulted a notepad.

"Looking for a Damien Maloney," he said, leaning into the vehicle.

"That's me, mate," Damo said.

"You the designated representative for this... ah, diplomacy business?"

"That's a fancy way of putting it, but yeah, if you like."

"Either you is, or you ain't. Which one?"

"I'm Maloney," Damo said, trying to keep his voice neutral.

This felt familiar. Almost reassuringly so. Like dealing with moronic border guards and chickenshit bureaucrats in all the former Soviet shitholes he'd blagged mining leases for BP and Shell.

Rick spoke up from behind.

"We wanna stretch our legs and get something to eat, too," he said. "Anywhere we can do that around here?"

The Legion guy bent down and peered into the back of the Expedition.

"You need ration chits to buy anything in town," he said. "But you can trade for them at the commissary... if you got anything worth trading."

"Where's that?" Damo asked.

"Two blocks over on Railway Avenue. But you're expected inside, Maloney. The rest of you are free to move around. You have been cleared. But I'd stay the hell away from that shit show at the O Club if I was you. Unless you're looking for a beatdown, of course. You can have that for free; you go sticking your nose where it ain't wanted."

The two Legion guys stepped away and returned to their posts.

"So, they have a pretty good C3," Michelle Nguyen said. "After that first stop, they knew who we were and what we wanted, and the information propagated all the way here."

"Yep," Rick agreed. "I was kinda hoping for something a little more bush league."

"I dunno," Damo said. "Your well-regulated militia over there looks like they've mostly been regulating themselves extra fuckin' Twinkie rations if you ask me."

He pointed at the goon squad outside the old real estate building; all crowded around the propane heater. The officer they'd spoken to had a half-threatening air of malicious competence to him, like a trolly car ticket inspector with a sawn-off shotgun. But the rest of his crew plumbed new depths of motley. Damo wasn't trained to look for these things – not like Rick and Michele – but even he could see how they'd patched their uniforms together. And, he'd bet good folding money the average body mass index over there was one hundred per cent jelly donuts... not that anybody was still taking bets in good folding money these days.

"I'll go talk to this operations bloke then," Damo said. "And suss out what the go is with these ration cards they got. See if it's just here, or they're doing it all over Legion territory."

"Yes, please," Michelle said. "That would be useful to know."

"What about me?" Karl Valentine asked.

Damo grinned and punched him lightly on the shoulder. "Put some Netflix on. Get a beverage, dawg. Be the best you can be."

"I'll hang with you, Karl," Ellie called out from the very rear of the Expedition.

"Thank you, Miss Ellie," he called back.

"I'll send Tapsell and the others up here," Michelle said. "Stay close, though. Like that guy said, don't wander off where you're not wanted. Leave the secret squirrel shit to us."

"How about Ellie 'n' me check out this PX store they got?" Karl asked. "See what they're willing to trade for? Tells us what they're short of, I reckon."

"Outstanding," Michelle said. "You're a natural-born spy, Karl."

They all climbed out. Nomi, last of all. Damo didn't even have to make a show of stretching after the long drive. His back ached, and his bladder was full to bursting. It was cold enough that his breath steamed in front of him.

"Damo, I'm gonna need you to distract those Legion assholes in a minute," Michelle said. "When we get down to Pete and the others. Get us enough cover to slip away."

"Sure, mate," he said.

The other two SUVs in their convoy had parked a block and a half down, and Tapsell's group was ambling towards them, taking everything in as they came. Michelle Nguyen did make a show of waving to Pete and taking Rick by the arm to lead him and Nomi off in that direction.

Damo didn't know if it was tradecraft or simple play-acting, but it did the job. The Legion's goons watched the reunion without enough interest to stray far from the gas heater. It wasn't bitterly cold in Three Forks, not by Montana standards, but there was a damp and miserable chill to the morning. Iron grey clouds hung low, and it looked like sleet, even a few flurries of snow, might fall soon.

"Borrow you for a second, Karl? You too, Ellie," Damo said.

"Sure thing, man," Karl replied.

They followed him across the double-wide street. He timed the walk as best he could to arrive out front of the Op centre just as Michelle and Rick disappeared into the huddle of travellers from the other two cars.

"Hey mate," Damo said as they approached the cluster of guards. "That commissary you mentioned? Where was that again? We got some road food we might trade for fresh if we can."

The goon squad underboss repeated the directions from before, adding, "It's an old marketplace. You can't miss it."

Karl and Ellie broke away to run their errand, and Damo said, "So, who's this bloke I'm seeing?"

"Runeberg," someone said.

"Mathias Runeberg," their squad commander added. "But I suggest you call him 'sir.'"

A couple of underlings snickered, but it didn't seem like a joke.

"Whatever he wants," Damo shrugged. "I just go in?"

"You're expected," the man said.

He might have been expected, but he still had to wait. Damo was sitting on an old plastic chair for twenty minutes in the waiting room of the former real estate office. It didn't help his back pain much.

It did give him plenty of time to take inventory, though.

They had power here. Good, old-fashioned electricity and enough of it to run space heaters and all the computers and lighting. Damo counted nine women typing away on a fleet of those giant Microsoft surface things, which was weird. He wondered if they'd looted a nerd warehouse somewhere, whether they were networked, and if the network extended beyond this building. There were a couple of blokes in the place, but neither of them Runeberg, he judged. They looked too deferential to the woman he picked as the office manager.

She ran the joint with a sharp tongue and a liver-frying stare that would've put Sister Mary Angela to shame back in primary school. Damo copped a red-hot taste of it when he asked if he could use the toilet. She wasn't a complete monster, though. Not like Sister Mary Angela. She did at least order one of the men to escort him to the bathroom. Damo tried to engage him in conversation, but he wasn't having any of it.

"The head's in there," he said. "You got two minutes. Don't make me drag you out."

Damo noted his use of maritime jargon.

Occasionally, the dragon lady disappeared into a separate office behind a frosted glass door, and Damo had a bet that Runeberg was back there. Confirmation came when a balding, bat-faced little git stuck his head out and nodded.

"Mister Runeberg will see you now," the woman said. She nodded at one of her male colleagues, the sailor boy who'd shown Damo the way to the crapper. He took up station just outside Runeberg's offices and adjusted his coat to show off the shoulder holster he was wearing.

Wanker, Damo thought.

But he kept it nice as he walked past.

The first thing he noticed about Runeberg's office was the view. There was none. He could've had a view. There were offices with windows looking over the street and a pleasant little park, but this bloke was so focused on work that he didn't look up from his desk much. Or maybe he was paranoid about getting sniped. The armed guard suggested sniperphobia.

But Damo went with option number one.

Runeberg had squeezed two desks into the confines of his office, and they were both piled high with files, dossiers, printouts, laptops and external monitors. But it was orderly – almost painfully so – reminding him of a complete knob he used to report to at BHP Billiton in Melbourne. That fucking nimrod would build a whole world in miniature on his desk every day, but it was a rigidly policed world, with not a paper clip or a sticky note out of place. He was getting the same sort of vibe in here.

"G'day," Damo said. "My name's Maloney. Damien Maloney."

"You have two minutes," Runeberg said. "Don't waste them."

"Jeez, mate, no pressure. Right. I came over with a delegation from Paradise Valley. It's about an..."

"I know what it is and why you're here. Is there a good reason you're talking to me? Because we have a standard agreement you can sign if you are so authorised, incorporating your administrative region into the Legion's cooperative alliance. Miss Stokes can provide you with the documents on your way out. An advance team will escort you back to your settlement and make arrangements for occupation and merger."

Runeberg did not glower, smirk, or reveal his feelings in any way. He was simply telling Damo how it was.

Damo smiled.

"Don't piss in my pocket and tell me it's raining, mate, and I won't feed you a dog turd on a toothpick and pretend it's a fucking cheerio."

A whole second passed before Runeberg reacted. Then his eyes got a little wider.

"What?" Runeberg gaped.

"A cheerio, mate. It's a little party sausage from Australia. Where I'm from."

Runeberg's voice, when he replied, was flat, devoid of affect, but not of implied threat.

"Perhaps we'll put you in a bag and send you back there?"

"Prefer not," Damo said. "Just like I reckon you blokes would prefer not to have to fight your way into the valley and take it by force after the thaw next spring."

A slight flush of color reddened the other man's neck.

"Do you have any idea who you're talking to? Of where you are?"

"Yeah," Damo said. "And I know that one word from you and your mate outside the door will pop in here and shoot me in the back of the head."

Damien Maloney was matter of fact.

Like Runeberg, he was a businessman. Simply telling it how it was.

His heart did thump a little when the door to Runeberg's office opened, and the guard asked if there was a problem, but the Legion's operations man waved him away.

"No, thank you, Gerald. I will need a few more minutes with Mr..."

"Maloney."

"With Mister Maloney, thank you."

The door closed, and Damo was glad Runeberg couldn't see his arsehole unpuckering. Always a dead giveaway in a tense negotiation, that.

"Who are you, Mister Maloney?" Runeberg sighed.

"I just told you that, mate. I'm from..."

"No," Runeberg shook his head. "I don't imagine you're a representative of that community. We tried negotiating an offer of merger with them, and they rejected it."

"No," Damo corrected him. "You negotiated with Livingston. They rejected your offer. And you blasted the shit out of the place and straight up murdered a couple-a-hundred people doing it. But I'm not from Livingston."

"And you're not from the valley, either," Runeberg countered.

This bloke was a little sharper and faster on the take than Damo cared for.

He stalled for time to organise his thoughts, asking Runeberg, "Why do you say that?"

Runeberg sketched the outline of a smile on his ratlike features, but it was only a sketch. A facsimile.

"Many of the town's leadership live, or lived, in the Valley. We would have encountered you earlier if you were a part of that community."

Damo performed a large, endearing grin.

"You got me," he said. "I'm a blow-in. I rode in late with a local boy. Name of O'Donnell."

He wasn't entirely confident, laying down that revelation. He wasn't sure how young James would feel about being played as a card in this two-handed poker match, but he needed this little prick to engage.

Runeberg did.

"Ah," he said as if that explained everything. "Yes. I do recall the elder O'Donnell. A difficult character. In large part responsible for the reduction of the town."

Damo said nothing.

Runeberg, unreadable, was just as quiet but in no apparent haste to move on.

"How is Mister O'Donnell?" He asked at last. "O'Donnell senior, I mean."

For a mad moment, Damo was tempted to bullshit him. He almost told Runeberg that Tom O'Donnell was dead. Killed by the Legion's attack on Livingston. It might be a solid favour to old Tom, having this mock Dickensian villain thinking he was six feet under.

But he couldn't be sure that Runeberg didn't know full well that Tom O'Donnell was still alive and kicking.

"He's tickety-fucking-boo, mate," Damo said.

"What?" Runeberg frowned.

Damo grinned again, more genuinely this time.

"He's good. Hard as a nut."

"I see."

Mathias Runeberg did not seem well pleased to hear that. Time to lean in on him.

"So, here's the thing, *Matty,*" Damo said. "You blokes made your point in Livingston, and it was a sharp point too. But now you gotta live with it jabbing you in the arse."

Runeberg stared at him.

"Please explain."

Got him.

Damo leaned back in his chair.

"You've put together this... business of yours by arbitrage. I'm gonna guess you know what that means. Before all this, you woulda been, what, an accountant, a lawyer or something?"

Runeberg shifted uncomfortably in his seat.

"I was the chief financial officer for Walmart Neighborhood Market in Oregon."

"Brick and mortar retail. Good for you. That's a tough business. Razor-thin margins. A metric fucking shit ton of competition."

Runeberg nodded carefully in acknowledgment.

"It's probably why you're the bloke running this show for Murdoch, right?"

Runeberg said nothing.

"I'll take that as a modest yes. And I'll clarify my earlier comment. I reckon you're doing a yeoman's job of holding it together, but some other bloke came up with the idea of standing over a bunch of two-buck tiny towns to put all this together. They would've sold it as a risk-free investment. Am I right?"

Again, another careful nod.

"So, here's where the fancy arbitrage comes in, mate. Whoever came up with that idea thought they were taking advantage of a price difference between the two markets. The price to be borne by some backwater shithole for providing its own security in a completely deregulated marketplace and the marginal cost of inviting you blokes in to replace the previous federal regulators with your more aggressively, ah, laissez-faire offerings. Do you follow me?"

"I can, but I don't see where this is going?" Runeberg said, furrowing his brow.

Damo nodded.

"Into the shitter is where it's going, buddy, because whoever designed this fucking shakedown racket did not factor in a third market type of the sort you'll find in the Valley the next time you roll up there – say, a couple of weeks after you take Bozeman?"

Runeberg was quiet, but the sudden lift of his eyebrows spoke volumes.

Damo went on.

"What you got in that Valley is the Legion's maximum address-able market of pissed-off punters who are now highly fucking moti-vated to resist any merger or threats of a hostile takeover and who, more importantly, are well set up to offer that resistance. It's a valley, *mate*. A big fucking valley full of fresh food and water, surrounded by unclimbable fucking mountains. Your Legion boys could have a legit-imate go at getting in there, of course, but they'd have to fight their way through a bunch of smaller valleys that are the perfect setting for long, leisurely ambushes. The locals will reduce your blokes to sausage meat and red food coloring before they get within cooee of the main valley, and after Livingston, they'll enjoy doing it. And, of course, it's not Livingston. Or Manhattan. Or any of those joints you demolished from a distance. If by some fucking miracle you boys do get in there, you'll be on the valley floor while about eight thousand snipers up on the high ground decide whether to shoot you in the face or the dick. Or both, of course. They could shoot you in both, just for fun."

Damo finished with a shrug.

Runeberg was staring at him with his mouth slightly open. A single strand of spittle stretched between his lips.

It had probably been a while since anybody had spoken to him like that. Damien Maloney waited for two heartbeats before adding, "Of course, it doesn't have to go like that."

"What do you mean?" Runeberg croaked.

Damo grinned.

"Mate. You're a businessman. Let's make a fuckin' deal."

"W HERE'D you get your field experience?" Rick asked.

"In the field," Michelle answered.

"Uhuh. Figured," he said as they used the cover of the brief meeting with Peter Tapsell's group to duck down a side street, heading towards the demonstration.

Fact was, Rick thought, James O'Donnell's girlfriend was way too comfortable with all this spooking around for her to have been merely a desk analyst. Michelle didn't even look back to see whether Maloney and the others had provided the distraction she'd asked for. She didn't tell Tapsell much beyond letting him know, briefly, that they were going to check out the shit show a couple of blocks over, and everybody else should keep their heads tucked in.

Michelle walked briskly but with no more sense of urgency than you'd expect from somebody hurrying through a cold, unpleasant morning. Anybody watching would assume she had some small errand to run and was hoping to get it over and done with as soon as possible. With his much longer stride, Rick did not have to hustle much to keep up, but Nomi's claws clicked rhythmically and rapidly on the sidewalk as they hastened towards the disturbance.

"No justice, no peace."

The chant grew louder as they approached.

"We won't stay long," Michelle said. "I just need to find out what this is about."

"Copy that," Rick said.

They turned onto the main street, and he was surprised, almost shocked, to see the crowd which had collected there. It had been months since he'd seen so many human beings gathered together. They did not look like the sort of people Rick used to see on the news at things like this. They were dressed for the bad weather, the men in dusters and cowboy hats, the women herding children. There were a surprisingly large number of children.

Next to him, Michelle slowed a little, and he saw her scoping out the numbers, making a rough calculation inside her head.

"I make it about one and a half thousand people," she said. "You?"

"Hard to say," Rick admitted.

"Compare it to something you know," Michelle suggested. "How many companies of soldiers could you make out of the crowd? Would they fit into the basketball stadium at your old high school? To me, that looks like a big enough crowd to fill this bar I used to go to in college when a band would tour. Easily a thousand people and a few more lined up for beers."

"I'll take your word for it," said Rick.

He reached out and took her gently by the arm.

"Seriously, Michelle," he said. "I need to know who I'm working with here. Before you took a desk in Washington, you acquired some other skills. Where?"

The young woman looked at him, and he did not recognise her. She had not disguised herself. She was the same tattooed Asian-American he had met after the shootout at the Harris Teeter on Darnestown Road. Short of stature but fierce in aspect. Her skin was covered in a dense pattern of sinuous tattoos. They had travelled together for nearly three months, struggled, and fought for survival. She was his best friend's lover. And he looked into her eyes and realised he did not know her at all.

"You can trust my skill sets, Rick," Michelle Nguyen said. "Like I trust yours."

Rick nodded.

"I guess that will have to do then."

"You guess right," she said. "Come on, let's get this done and get out of here before it turns to shit."

For once, Tommy Podesta was wrong. Jonas totally did not 'wanna come deal with this.' If Podesta had looked in a mirror and seen the sick and worried expression on his face, he might have figured that out. Instead, he'd hurried upstairs and grabbed hold of Jonas as soon as he got word of this situation down at The Continental Divide. That's what the Tripod called it. This situation.

"We got this situation down there, boss," he said. "Looks like it could turn into a riot or something worse."

"Something worse than a riot?" Jonas said. "Like what?"

It was an honest question, and Podesta answered honestly.

"Leo says there's a bunch of Cohort guys headed there cos the local cops can't handle it," Podesta explained as they hurried down the main staircase and into the foyer of the Sacajawea Hotel.

Okay. A massacre would probably be worse than a riot, Jonas conceded.

"Jesus Christ, it never fucking ends, does it," he said.

"Not in my experience, no, boss," Podesta replied.

They hurried outside, and Jonas was struck by how fucking terrible the weather was. Grey, freezing and threatening to rain or sleet at any minute. He realised he hadn't left the hotel in three days, not since this cold front moved in. He experienced a fleeting nostalgia for Florida, for the painfully bright sunlight and steam press humidity. For the color and movement. For the promise, the open possibilities of the place.

And then he told himself to stop being such a fucking idiot.

He'd been disbarred in Florida. His wife had fucked his boss back there and stolen his children away. As tough as things had been later in Seattle, nothing had been as bad as his last few weeks on the redneck Riviera. Pining for that shit and those days was weak and crazy. This here was his future.

Chad was waiting for him outside, packing his giant dumb ass sledgehammer, and Jonas was glad to see him. A squad of the Cohort stood ready to ride escort wherever Jonas might lead them. No doubt about where that might be. He could already hear whatever was happening. It was a noise he hadn't heard in a while. The roar of a crowd. A large and pissed-off crowd.

Instinct almost got the better of him.

Standing in front of the hotel, resisting the urge to shiver in the cold, he faltered.

"Wait a minute," he said to no one in particular. "What the hell are we doing here?"

"We gonna break some heads and kick some fucking ass, that's what," Chad Moffat declared.

"Uhuh," Jonas went. Unconvinced. "Is that just gonna make it worse?"

"No boss," Tommy Podesta countered, glaring at Chad. "We ain't gonna do nothing like that unless we have to. But this could get out of hand. And, you gotta take charge of things, cos if you don't, someone else will. Maybe Jennings. Maybe Bolger. Neither of them is a good result."

Jonas Murdoch stood irresolute at the edge of the top step, caught between a couple of shitty choices that didn't seem to be much in the way of choices at all. He could hear a chant growing louder, maybe half a mile away. He recognised it immediately.

No justice. No peace.

Jesus Christ, how long had it been since he'd heard that bullshit? He would've bet a good, old-fashioned Benjamin it had never been popular around these parts.

There was a second, just a second, while everybody waited for him to decide. They were all looking at him. His bodyguards. Podesta. Moffat. And he didn't know what to do. Or maybe he just wasn't sure...

The hotel doors crashed behind him, and Leo Vaulk came bustling out, loaded for bear. Jonas hadn't seen Leo so heavily tooled up since the bikers attacked Silverton. He was carrying a shotgun and an assault rifle, and he'd strapped a couple of handguns and a hunting knife to his utility belt.

"Alrighty then," Leo declared. "Let's roll."

It was almost comical, and Jonas couldn't help but smile. It did help lift his mood. If this asshole was able to pretend at martial prowess with such conviction, he should surely be able to do his bit. Jonas forced some steel into his spine and gravel into his voice.

"Okay, fellers," he said. "Let's not go shooting ourselves in the ass, but Leo is right. Let's roll on these fuckers."

They marched down the steps to the waiting vehicles. Jonas wasn't taking the Beemer this time. They were travelling in Cohort gun wagons, just in case. Podesta shooed away some Cohort guy who had meant to drive, relegating him to cattle class in the other vehicle. Jonas climbed in the back seat with Chad while Leo rode up front with the Tripod. They pulled out of the Sacajawea's driveway with the other weaponised SUV leading out.

"So, get me up to speed, Tommy," Jonas said. "What do we know?"

"All I know is that things have gone sideways after last night. You got a bunch of angry fuckin' God botherers preaching up a storm downtown, and Mayor Jennings is down there as well."

"Jennings," Jonas said, confused and maybe even worried. "What the hell is he doing? Making trouble?"

Leo turned around in the front seat.

"No, man," he said. "Jennings is trying to keep a lid on things."

They drove out through the entrance to the hotel and onto Ash Street. The other gun wagon accelerated away, and Jonas imagined that the poor bastards huddled together in the open tray must be freezing their nuts off. Dark grey clouds hung low overhead, and he expected snow to start falling at any moment. Podesta increased their speed to keep up.

"How do you know that, Leo?" Jonas asked. "About Jennings, I mean."

"I had a couple of my guys head over there as soon as I heard it was kicking off," Leo explained. "They been running a relay getting information back to me. I don't want to use the walkie-talkies in case somebody is listening in."

Jonas didn't ask him who he meant.

Because he meant Runeberg. With Leo, it was always Runeberg.

"So, what's going on?" Jonas asked.

They were moving quickly, blowing through the old speed limit. They would be there in less than a minute.

"It's that shit from last night that Tommy cleaned up," Leo said before hurrying on to add, "And Tommy did clean it up. You did good work, man," he assured Podesta. "But people still got pissed off about it."

"Yeah, and how did they find out about it, Leo?" Podesta asked. He did not sound happy.

"I don't know," Leo Vaulk shrugged. "Not hard to imagine, but. Probably the girl's old man. Maybe he was mouthing off to his friends. Maybe she was. Maybe Jennings. Doesn't matter, though, does it? Because here we are. And it's not Tommy's fault. It's not your fault, boss. It's..."

"It doesn't matter who's fucking fault it is, Leo," Jonas said. "The only thing that matters is shutting this thing down before it gets out of hand."

"Boss," Leo pushed back, but gently. "You got a couple of thousand protesters outside the O Club. I reckon it's fair to say this thing is already out of hand."

Jonas rubbed his temples, trying to massage away the headache that was building there. It had come on him quickly. But not as quickly as they were coming up on the crowd's edge. He tried to slow his runaway heart with some deep breaths when he saw how many people had piled up in front of The Continental Divide and how angry they all looked. The other gun wagon pulled up about sixty yards short of the ragged edge of the mob. Protesters pointed and shouted as the Cohort guards leapt from the back of their vehicle and spread out across the road, weapons ready. Tommy Podesta brought them to a halt a bit further back.

Jonas could see at least half a dozen people standing on the front steps of the Divide, among them Jennings and his engineer. The one who'd given Runeberg all the grief. The others standing up there with them appeared to be preachers of some sort, dressed for service.

"Okay," he said. "We don't need a riot or a massacre this morning. That's just a bunch of soft cocks up there. I can talk them down. I know I can."

"Hope so, boss," Podesta said.

"You want to do it quickly, then," Leo cautioned. "Before they get any ideas about how many of them there are and how many of us."

Jonas back-fisted Chad on the bicep. It was like hitting a corned beef bowling ball.

"Stay close, man," he said. "But don't go swingin' that big ass Thor hammer around unless I tell you."

"No problemo," Chad said. Even he looked worried.

Jonas took a deep breath, let it out, and opened the door. His shoes crunched down on the slick, wet road surface before the others followed him. The roar of the crowd rolled over them. It had weight and mass. And the power of so many of them acting in concert only seemed to grow as people recognised him and refocused their anger.

Jonas Murdoch almost jumped back into the SUV and ordered the Tripod to get the hell out of town.

But everybody was watching him now. Even some Cohort guys had turned around and were waiting to see what happened next.

How the fuck did I get myself into this, Jonas wondered.

Nothing for it, though.

He painted a joker's smile on his face and started to walk towards the crowd.

IT DID NOT TAKE Michelle long to confirm the story behind the rally. She asked three separate people what was going on, explaining that she and Rick were travellers passing through. All three gave her similar stories. Not the same story, but obviously sourced from the same inciting incident. A young woman, a local girl, had been taken by one of Murdoch's lieutenants and assaulted. There were, she had no doubt, a thousand variations on that tale. As many versions of what happened as there were people protesting it. But that didn't matter. All that mattered was the kernel of truth at the core of it.

Somebody had fucked up. Badly.

"I think we're good here," she said. "Let's get back to the others."

They were standing well back from the main body of protestors, both of them leaning against a post holding up the awning of a shop that sold irrigation systems. It was closed, but it didn't look abandoned. The front windows had been cleaned recently, and there was even a light on inside. Perhaps the owner was somewhere in the crowd. Nomi sat obediently next to Rick's feet, taking it all in. She looked less troubled by the spectacle than either of her human companions.

"Yeah, this doesn't feel so good to me," Rick said.

He had just clicked his fingers to get Nomi's attention when Michelle reached out and placed a hand on his forearm.

"Wait on a second," she said. "Look. "

She pointed down the road to where several pickup trucks had just pulled over. They were like the technicals they'd encountered at each roadblock on the way here. Makeshift gun trucks.

"Sit, Nomi," Rick said. "Stay."

She plopped her butt down on the cold, damp concrete, whimpering a little.

Michelle swept her gaze over the crowd. The chanting continued, but with slightly less volume and focus, as more people turned their attention to the new arrivals. Some pointed. A couple of small groups started moving uncertainly in the direction of the SUVs. They stopped; their resolve suddenly diminished as half a dozen armed men jumped down from the rear tray of the first vehicle.

A low murmur passed through the crowd as one man emerged from the second.

"I think that might be him," Michelle said.

Rick, a good two feet taller than her, had the advantage, but even he stood on tiptoe to get a better look.

"Maybe," he said.

Michelle took a few steps towards the crowd, straining to pick out individual voices. She heard a few people say the name 'Murdoch'. She heard more saying other things. Asshole. Murderer. Nazi.

"Yeah, I'm pretty sure that's him," she said.

Neither moved toward the man as he started walking towards the crowd. A bodyguard fell in beside him, and Michelle blinked twice.

The second man looked like a nightclub bouncer or maybe a construction worker. No, she decided. He looked like a nightclub bouncer or a construction worker, as imagined by whatever genius put together the original lineup for *The Village People*. He was a caricature of a muscle-douche 'roid ape, and he was carrying...

"Is that a sledgehammer?" She asked.

"No," Rick Boreham answered. "It's a splitting maul. Like a hammer on one side and an axe on the other. Firefighters use them. And forest workers. And this superhero in a book I read once."

Michelle struggled to follow the procession over the heads of the crowd. And it was a procession now. The Legion's militia fighters had formed a solid, protective wedge around Murdoch if that's who this was. They were driving through the assembled protesters, heading towards the front steps of the motel across the street.

"Jesus Christ," she said quietly. "This is gonna get sticky."

TOMMY 'THE TRIPOD' Podesta did not like this at all. Not one little bit. He had a little more faith in Murdoch than he did in any of these other mooks. Especially Leo or Bolger, or Runeberg, for that matter. Jonas did have a way with people. But these were not his people and never had been. Podesta wasn't sure that Murdoch understood that. Still, he had to credit the guy with having a cast-iron pair on him. Jonas was pimp-rolling through this crowd, ignoring all the bad vibes and curses directed at him, and he was smiling. Or trying to. The Tripod knew him well enough to know that it was all an act, but sometimes you gotta put the act on, don't you? That's what fuckin' Shakespeare said, wasn't it? Or something like that. All the world's a stage, and everybody on it is just acting or some shit. Tommy Podesta had never really been a student of the classics. Unless you counted the works of De Niro and Scorsese.

The chanting had stopped.

So that was something.

It trailed off when the Cohort boys jumped into the scene. Or maybe it was Chad and that monstrous fucking strongman sledge-hammer of his. He gave the impression of desperately wanting to start swingin' it at everybody's melons, and whenever he glared at someone, they tended to shut the fuck up and back the fuck down straight away.

There were still heaps of people here, though, and there was no silencing them altogether. Not when they were this fucked off. You could feel that coming off them in waves. The Tripod patted the pocket where he kept his gun to reassure himself that it was still there. What the hell was he gonna do with it if this mob turned on them? He didn't know. There were a lot more people than he had bullets. Maybe if things went sideways, he'd have to grab one of Leo Vaulk's artillery pieces and shoot his way out.

Or maybe, he told himself, you could keep your fuckin' head down and have some faith in the boss.

Jonas Murdoch didn't look like he was planning on letting this turn into an even bigger goat circus. A lot of guys, they woulda been stomping through this crowd, beating their chests and talking shit. But Jonas was smiling. Podesta wasn't sure how he did that, how he kept that stupid grin on his face as they marched up the steps outside of the hotel where they'd rescued that girl from Bolger's room, but there it was, he supposed. That's why some guys like Jonas got to lead, and other guys like Leo and Mathias and, to be honest, Tommy Podesta got to follow. Some guys just had it.

The Tripod caught Mayor Jennings's eye as he followed Jonas up those steps, and he was more than a little surprised at how grateful he was when the mayor nodded to him. It was kinda... reassuring, having someone on the other side look at him like he was a human being and not just some skull they'd be kicking to actual pieces in a coupla minutes.

But of course, he thought, he *was* the guy who rescued little Nicky, or whatever her name was. Jennings knew that. Maybe he'd even told people about it.

Tommy Podesta hoped to Christ he had. Maybe people wouldn't think so badly of him if things went wrong here.

THIS, just walking up here, was the hardest thing Jonas had ever done. He still wasn't sure what to do when he got where he was going. Jonas tried to keep a neutral smile on his face, even with the engineer glaring at him. For a second, he couldn't remember the guy's name. Goddammit. That would be a piss poor look, turning up here to try to smooth this thing over, and he couldn't even remember the name of the guy he was supposed to chill out.

The Continental Divide loomed over them. He had to crane his head back to look up the steps to where Jennings, the engineer and the priests were standing. At least he had Chad and his Cohort and, for that matter, Leo and the Tripod. They were all armed. Most of them heavily. Nobody in Three Forks was supposed to have guns anymore, but Jonas didn't bank on that. At the very least, there'd be plenty of handguns in the crowd. He moved to get as close to Jennings and the others as he could.

"Mister Mayor," Jonas said in his loudest courtroom voice as he reached out to shake Ross Jennings' hand. "Mister... City Engineer," he improvised, merely nodding to...

McNabb!

Yeah. That was the asshole's name. Andy or Danny McNabb, or something like that. Didn't matter. He had a name now.

Jonas turned to the three... What were they? Priests?

One of them was even a woman. A black woman.

"Padres," he said, hoping that would cover all the flavours. "I understand folks are upset with what happened last night."

McNabb lunged for him, and the crowd's collective intake of breath sounded like the moaning wind of a great storm suddenly gathering its strength. But Ross Jennings put an arm out and stepped between them to hold McNabb back.

"It's not the time or the place," Jonas heard Jennings say.

"Amen to that, brother," Jonas said. "Look. I should probably say something," he said to Jennings.

The mayor of Three Forks shook his head.

"I don't think that's a very good idea," he warned.

The crowd noise was building up. Quickly.

McNabb tried to get around Jennings again. Chad pushed him away with ease.

"The only thing you need to say is that your man Bolger is a goddamned rapist, and he will pay for it," McNabb shouted.

It was as though he had uncorked a jar into which all the demons of the world had been poured. A great howl went up from the nearest part of the crowd and quickly spread.

The Cohort squad formed up, beating back the nearest members of the crowd with the butts of their weapons.

This only made things worse, and Jonas was sure everything was about to spin completely out of control when Mayor Jennings forced his way through the cordon and raised his hands.

"Please! Please now, everyone," he called out in an unexpectedly strong voice. "Let's not have anyone else get hurt today."

One of the preachers joined him. The black woman.

"If we would love life and see good days, we must keep our tongues from evil," she called out. It had a noticeable effect on those nearest to them. They slowed in their struggling and shouting.

"We must turn from evil and do good," the preacher woman said. "We must seek peace and pursue it."

The other two priests followed up with verses about peace, enduring iniquities, and shit. Jonas didn't much care for the content, but he was fucking amped that they also placed themselves between him and the crowd, raising their hands as Jennings had done, calling for calm and peace.

Jonas caught Podesta's eye.

He looked troubled but calm for now. He gestured for Jonas to stay quiet.

Meanwhile, Leo Faulk was waving his assault rifle around. Jonas recognised it as the weapon he'd taken from Leo and turned on Sheriff Muller back in Silverton.

He was tempted to grab it again.

But Ross Jennings and the three Jesus cucks did a fair job dialling everything down.

"We can sort this out," Jennings declared. "This is still a civilised country. We have laws and standards. And we will apply them in this case. Isn't that right, sir?"

Huh?

Jonas realised Jennings was talking to him or about him. Or something. A lot was happening here.

"Oh yeah, sure," he said. "Laws and standards and shit. For sure."

And for a wonder, it seemed to work, if only temporarily. Jennings kept talking to the crowd, talking them down.

"I think this will be okay," Jonas heard Podesta say to somebody, possibly him.

But then Luke Bolger emerged from The Continental Divide, which was not okay at all.

33

STONE COLD

In his 32 years as a registered Republican, Ross Jennings had never been much of a gut politician. He had practised politics the same way he did business, as fairly and honestly as possible, while coming out ahead at the end of the day. Privately, he would admit that the old-fashioned approach had been increasingly difficult for a long time before the Chinese destroyed everything, but he had thought and would argue that it'd proved its worth in the months afterwards. Steadiness, rationality and pragmatism had secured the good people of Three Forks from starvation and banditry. Even after Murdoch and his gun thugs had turned up, Jennings had done his best to negotiate a path through their demands and trespasses. That was why he was so distressed by this eruption in front of The Continental Divide. Jennings understood why people were angry and accepted that something would have to be done. He had been there. He had helped rescue the poor girl. But what Ross Jennings knew of human nature gave him no comfort when he saw the crowd gathering in front of Chrissy Trotter's former hotel. There was a point past which you could not rationally discuss anything with people, not when they got themselves riled up beyond all hope of appeasement.

And seeing Dan McNabb up there, stirring up the masses, did not bode well.

He knew all that as he pushed his way through the crowd. Knew it in his heart and his head. There was anger and division. He was jostled and buffeted, carried forward by supporters, and buffeted by others who were not at all supportive. He was hailed as a hero for saving Nicky McNabb and cursed as a quisling for having allowed the Legion into town in the first place. The crowd was a single spark away from exploding into violence. They were united in disgust and loathing for what happened to Dan and Nicky but utterly divided by what to do.

Jennings himself was at just as much of a loss. But he knew that if he didn't get a bridle on this thing, it would gallop away from them, and people would get hurt.

It took him two minutes to fight through the heaving press of bodies, but as he got closer to the steps leading up to the hotel, people started to help him along. Dan helped with that, yelling at them to let him through. Jennings was desperately grateful to find Father Flanagan and Reverend Bell standing with Dan, preaching a gospel of forbearance and peacemaking. He was even more relieved when Gabi Nikobe from the First Lutheran appeared from out of the seething masses to add her voice to her colleagues' prayers for compassion and concord.

He tried to talk to Dan, tried to get him to see sense and wind this down, but McNabb was not for turning away from the confrontation. The only blessing was the spontaneous and utterly disorganised nature of it all. Dan would harangue the crowds for a few minutes, whipping them into a rage before Gabi would say a prayer, calming them down. The other preachers joined in or spoke directly to their flocks. It was a thoroughgoing mess, for which Jennings was thankful. If this mob suddenly knew its mind and determined to turn on Murdoch's enforcers no matter what... many of them would die. He had no doubt about that score after what he had seen in Manhattan.

He heard his name called, and he stood forward to address the sea of faces without knowing what he was doing.

He could only think of telling them what he knew.

"I was here last night," he started, gesturing to the hotel behind him.

He spoke as soberly and judiciously as he could of what had happened, giving people the information but not using it to inflame the passions that were already running hot. Many booed him when he told of Thomas Podesta's help, but Podesta had helped, and Ross Jennings insisted that people know that. Even Dan McNabb nodded quickly when Jennings asked him to vouch for Podesta's role in Nicky's deliverance.

It felt like he spoke for an hour, attempting to soothe the rage that burned in the hearts of so many friends and neighbours. When he checked his watch, he saw that it was only twelve minutes.

Twelve minutes well spent, however.

Jennings was confident that he might have averted a tragedy – until Murdoch and his goons turned up in one of their battle wagons. Two more of the warlord's SUVs appeared at either end of the block, taking everyone under their guns. He was sick with fear for what might happen next, although he assumed they would not fire while Murdoch and his lieutenants were forcing their way through. And Gabi Nikobe redoubled her efforts at preaching restraint and nonviolence, even as the pack of armed men approached.

Murdoch appeared to be grinning like a loon as he climbed the steps. Jennings locked eyes with Podesta, who looked smart enough to be deeply troubled by whatever was about to happen, and Jennings surprised himself a little by nodding to the man. They weren't friends. They weren't even colleagues. But they had done their best to sort out a messy problem last night, and he felt he could trust the man's judgement, if not his character. Podesta nodded back.

"Mister Mayor," Jonas Murdoch roared. "And Mister... City Engineer," he brayed at Dan McNabb.

Jennings was so stunned by the hubris of the performance that he automatically shook the man's hand when he offered it. Murdoch said something Jennings didn't catch to Reverend Nikobe, and McNabb suddenly launched forward. The crowd roared. Jennings jumped between them and did his best to hold his friend off their common foe and tormentor.

"Not the time or the place, Dan," he hissed.

Murdoch appeared to laugh.

"Amen to that, brother," he snorted before leaning in and shouting over the uproar, "I should say something."

Jennings tried to talk him out of it, but he was still attempting to block Dan from laying hands on the Legion boss, fearful that his phalanx of security would start shooting. The giant one, his personal bodyguard, used the shaft of his ridiculous circus hammer to push Dan away. If he was being honest, Jennings was almost pathetically glad of it. If pushing and shoving were today's worst, he could live with that.

But then Dan yelled something about Luke Bolger being a rapist and making him pay for what he'd done, and everything went sideways. Hard.

The animal spirit of the crowd turned dark, and Ross Jennings felt the hot breath of mob violence blowing over them. Murdoch's men reacted with surprising discipline, forming a shield wall and beating back the nearest protesters. Jennings cried out, desperately hoping to restore some facsimile of good order. It all felt as though it was coming apart... until Gabi Nikobe stood forward and, in a powerful voice, boomed out some line of scripture he did not recognise but which fell into a weird and airless moment, an interstitial space between detonations of raw hostility.

"We must turn from evil and do good," she declared, and perhaps the grace of God was upon her because enough people heard and attended to the message that it short-circuited the accelerating spiral into madness.

She hurried on, assisted by her fellow clergy.

Jennings sensed the danger receding. He called out over the tumult to Murdoch, urging him to turn to law and precedent to deal with the assault on Nicky McNabb.

Murdoch seemed to agree, and Jennings risked proclaiming to the crowd that he had done so. Perhaps he could still get a few things done the old-fashioned way.

Thomas Podesta appeared at his side and said, "I think this'll be okay."

And then it wasn't.

JONAS COULD'VE LEGITIMATELY BRAINSPASMED when he saw Bolger come stomping through the swing doors at the front of the Continental, flanked on either side by a couple of his Cohort lieutenants. He was dressed in tactical camo and a ballistic vest and carried two guns in holsters at his hips. His eyes were hidden behind mirror shades. The effect on the crowd was galvanic. A tremendous howling protest peeled up and away into the lowering, iron grey clouds. Bolger just kept coming.

Jonas understood, way too late, that he had made a terrible mistake. This guy didn't look like a loyal servant. He looked like a fuckin' king slayer. Bolger's guys in the close protection squad, the ones who'd brought him over from the Sacajawea, appeared to be almost as confused as Jonas. Their heads swivelled left and right as they looked to each other for answers. Jonas looked to Podesta. He was shaking his head, too, deeply unhappy. Mayor Jennings was yelling at the crowd now, begging them to chill the fuck out, but they were having none of it. The old familiar chant started up again.

"No justice. No peace."

It grew and grew into a collective roar.

Perhaps emboldened by the bellowing war cry of a thousand voices, that runty little engineer suddenly charged out of nowhere as though he meant to tackle Bolger and beat him to a pulp in front of everybody. Jonas Murdoch distinctly felt his testicles try to crawl up inside his body. His 'nads knew the score.

Luckily, the Tripod was on the job. He swung one great ham hock of an arm around, thumping it into McNabb's chest and knocking the smaller man off his feet. He crashed into a couple of the priests, and they all fell over. Another cry went up from the mob, and Jonas got ready to run.

Before he could get his leaden feet moving, however, Luke Bolger drew both pistols.

"Fuck man, no!" Jonas yelled, but too late.

Bolger started shooting. Not into the crowd. But into the air, one shot after another.

CRACK! CRACK! CRACK!

Jonas flinched away.

Bolger roared an order at his men.

"Form up, you pussies!"

The Cohort guard moved quickly to place themselves between the crowd and their commanders. But by then, it wasn't necessary. Most of the mob had surged away, some trampled underfoot as they tried to escape the gunfire.

It was chaos. Madness and chaos.

Jonas felt his bladder go loose as a much heavier weapon opened up. Leo Vaulk fired a long automatic burst high into the sky, yelling, "Yeah, you better run, motherfuckers."

Somebody pushed Jonas down. The Tripod, his weapon drawn, the pistol looking ridiculously inadequate when ranged against the artillery that Bolger had deployed.

"Get your fuckin' head down before someone blows it off," Podesta yelled at him over the uproar. Jonas didn't need telling twice. He dropped to the ground, kissing the dirt, rub-fucking it.

He had no idea how long he was down there. It couldn't have been long, or maybe it was an eternity. Nothing felt real. Finally, the shooting stopped. The yelling and screaming faded away. And more hands grabbed him and pulled him up again. Chad. Podesta. A couple of the Cohort guys.

He was shaking, and even the Tripod was super twitchy. Everybody looked grey-faced and wild-eyed. The crowd was gone. Maybe a dozen or so people lay on the ground, but whether they had been shot or trampled, he couldn't say. There were still hundreds of people milling around, but they had taken shelter wherever they could. He saw that Jennings was still with them and that fat black chick in the priest's collar, but they were cowering on the ground like he had been. The other two preachers? He had no idea.

McNabb was gone too. Smart move, Jonas thought. Bolger looked ready to summarily execute him if he came back. His men had fanned out and held the raised ground in front of the O Club. They looked just as messed up as everyone else, but at least they were holding it together.

"Jesus, man," Jonas said, addressing Bolger directly. "That was pretty fuckin' hairy."

The Cohort commander shook his head.

"I've seen worse. Maximum security riots. This was nothing. They dispersed."

Bolger had put his handguns away and surveyed the aftermath of the riot, or the protest, or whatever the hell it had been before it turned into a panicked rout.

"I suggest we turn out the Legion, lock down the streets, and round up the ringleaders. We need to make an example of them. We need to strike 'em and fast. We need to dominate the battle space."

"Whoa there, General Patton," Tommy Podesta said. He was still holding his pistol, but down low, as though he'd forgotten about it. "You already gave us one giant clusterfuck. You want to take a breath before you kick off another?"

"The fuck is that supposed to mean?" Bolger said, bristling.

"What it means is none of this woulda happened if you hadn't knocked that girl around so bad," Podesta said. His voice was a low growl, and it got lower and growlier as he spoke, and his anger slipped the leash. "You got a whole cat house full of premium gash in there, but you had to get your end wet with McNabb's kid daughter. And even that wasn't enough. You had to rough her up before you could get it up, you fucking twist."

"The fuck you say, you slimy grease ball?!" Bolger shot back, taking a step towards him and raising a fist, jabbing one finger in the Tripod's face. "What the fuck do you even do for us? You think you're so fucking special. You're just a chauffeur. Not a fighting man. None of you are fighting men," Bolger snarled at them all, including Jonas. "You're just a bunch of parasites, living off our risk-taking and hard work."

Jonas had a bad feeling about this. He wondered how far he could get if he just started sprinting now. The Cohort men had turned around and focused on their boss's anger rather than keeping an eye out for any threats coming from the ragged leftovers of the protest.

"You men..." Bolger ordered, and before he gave the order, Jonas was already moving, his thighs bunching, his core hardening, air whistling in through clenched teeth, and he made ready to run.

"This time has come! Arrest these traitors," Bolger shouted.

CRACK!

Jonas jumped and then froze. Stunned by a single gunshot.

For a fraction of a second, he thought maybe he'd been shot, but then he saw the small round hole in the middle of Luke Bolger's forehead. And the genuine surprise that reshaped the guy's features just before they went slack and his body started to fall away.

He noticed the gun then.

Podesta's gun. A chrome-plated .38 or something. An old-fashioned revolver. A blue-grey tendril of smoke snaking away from the muzzle.

Everything was moving impossibly slowly.

Until time jumped ahead a whole second as the silver gun swung around with starting swiftness and cracked again. Twice.

The two Cohort lieutenants who'd accompanied Bolger from the hotel crumpled and dropped. Podesta took one step towards them, then two, standing over them. He fired twice into each man's head and again at Bolger.

Another headshot.

All three bodies jumped and fell still.

Everything fell still.

Jonas heard a bird somewhere. The rasping shriek of a raven or maybe a crow.

"Jesus man, what the fuck," cried the surviving Cohort officer, the squad leader who had come with them from the Sacajawea. His eyes were wide but filmy with sudden trauma. He shuddered as Podesta calmly emptied the cylinder of his .38 and popped in a speed loader before snapping it closed again.

"He was coming at the boss, kid," Podesta said. "You don't come at the boss unless you wanna go in the ground. That what you want?"

The young officer stared at him.

He shook his head.

"No, sir."

"Solid choice," Podesta said. He turned to Jonas. "What now?"

"Jesus Christ," Rick muttered, crouched low behind a car.

Michelle was hunkered down next to him.

They watched the whole thing from about a hundred yards away. He'd known it was going wrong as soon as the militia guy pimp-rolled out of that hotel with a couple of heavily armed wingmen.

Was that Murdoch?

He'd thought the chunky-looking douchebro who arrived in the SUV was the Legion's boss.

"I think this might have been a wasted trip," Michelle said. "We could have just stayed home and let these guys kill each other."

The horde of people who'd gathered earlier had scattered and fled. Here and there, a few who'd fallen or been shot lay on their own or were attended by frantic friends or relatives.

Rick was strongly compelled to get out there and help them, but they stayed hidden behind cover.

The Legion's command cadre, its surviving leadership, or what-ever the hell those assholes were, still had the high ground out front of that hotel.

He'd expected things to go bad, but he was not ready for that dude in the overcoat and the old-fashioned hat to throw down on his own guys.

"Stone cold," Michelle said.

"What?" Rick said, shaking himself out of the trance he'd fallen into.

"That guy. The trigger man," Michelle explained, nodding at the one who'd shot the militia leader and his two offsiders. "That was a stone-cold execution. He let that other guy work himself into a fit, and then he just dropped him. No warning. Nothing. He shot the other two on general principles. They hadn't even moved yet."

"What's it mean, you think?" Rick asked.

"I'm gonna guess it's not his first rodeo," Michelle said. "Come on. We better get back. This isn't over."

34

I JUST GOT A BAD FEELING, IS ALL

Fittingly, Damo was talking about latrines when everything turned to shit. When Runeberg found out that Damien Maloney had worked in the mining industry, he pivoted from negotiating the terms of a truce to venting about the infrastructure requirements for off-the-grid start-ups.

"That playbook's been written several times," Damo assured him. "If it gives you a stiffy, it'd be no trouble for me to write you an explainer, assuming we can bed down this other stuff first. But do you mind me asking why?"

Turned out Mathias Runeberg was trying to blockade and besiege the city of Bozeman, and he didn't know the first fuckin' thing about any of it. How to provide sustainable utility services. How to roster a workforce that was living rough and getting sick. How to plug into the remnant infrastructure surrounding his camp. None of it. Because it turned out that running Walmart's Neighbourhood Market in Beaver's Butt, Oregon was a pretty fuckin' piss poor qualification for running the medieval siege of a mid-sized American city in the middle of a global fuckin' apocalypse. Runeberg's biggest problem was sanitation and reliable power, neither of which were areas where Damo had any professional expertise, but nor were they complete mysteries to him. Over the years, he'd taken his fair share of dumps in Outback port-a-potties. Just sitting in Runeberg's office, listening to him whine about his troubles, Damo learned enough about the Legion to keep Michelle Nguyen in 007 Heaven for a year. The two men were nerding out on remote logistics when Gerald, the goon who'd been detailed to keep an eye on Damo, burst into the office looking like he'd caught his nuts in a woodchipper.

"Sorry to interrupt, sir," he said through clenched teeth. "But there's been some trouble at that protest rally."

Damo kept his expression neutral. Boreham and little Mishy were spooking around the edges of that thing. He could hear voices outside Runeberg's office. They sounded edgy and fearful.

"Yes?" Runeberg said, looking unimpressed to be interrupted.

"Somebody's been shot, sir," Gerald insisted.

Damo's stomach filled with acid, and his bowels felt loose.

"So?" Runeberg shrugged.

"It was Commander Bolger, sir. He was shot. By Tommy Podesta."

That, finally, elicited an uncharacteristically immoderate response from Runeberg.

"Shit," he spat, rocking back in his chair as though slapped. "What now?"

"I'm ordered to escort you to HQ, sir. Top-level debrief. They're putting the town into lockdown. Immediate curfew. Shoot-on-sight ROE."

"Whoa, hold your fucking horses there, mate," Damo protested. "What d'you mean curfew? And shoot on sight what now?"

"He means precisely what he says, Mister Maloney," Mathias Runeberg said. "You people must turn yourselves into the police and await developments."

"Fuck that for a game of two-up, champ," Damo said. "We haven't done anything wrong. We just came here to negotiate a truce."

Runeberg's man drew the weapon from his shoulder holster and pointed it at Damo's head. Damo felt the floor drop out from underneath him.

"Put that down, Gerald," Runeberg snapped. "It sounds like we've had more than enough guns popping off today. And..."

He looked at Damo as though seeing him for the first time. He even tilted his head a little as though to consider a new angle on him.

"And Mister Maloney here will be coming with me."

"What?" Damo said.

"What?" Gerald echoed.

"I don't know why Podesta shot Bolger," Runeberg explained. "But it was probably personal. I'm dealing with bigger problems here. Much bigger. And Mister Maloney has a solution to one of them. Possibly two. Never let a crisis go to waste, Gerald. You should write that down. It's good advice for a young man in difficult times."

MICHELLE NEEDED TIME TO THINK. She needed more information. She needed context for that information and more time to synthesise everything. But she wasn't going to get any of those things. She and Rick hurried along the cross street back to where they'd left Tapsell and the others. Nomi kept pace with them, trotting along at Rick's heel. Dozens of people were moving in the same direction, all hurrying away from the violence and chaos of the demonstration.

No, that wasn't right, she told herself. The demonstration had not *turned* violent. Only Murdoch's crew had done that, and as best as she could tell, they had turned on each other. No idea why. Listening out for scraps of conversation as they hastened past locals fleeing the scene, it seemed that nobody knew any better than she did.

She needed a source. She needed material. They were blind here.

"This was a bad idea," Rick said.

"No, this was bad timing," Michelle insisted. "But it'd be a terrible idea to hang around much longer. We should get our guys out of Dodge. But I'm coming back."

"The hell you are," Rick Boreham said as they jogged around the corner, past the Volunteer Fire Department into South Main Street.

Two cherry red engines stood ready to roll out from the station, but there was no sign of any volunteers to crew them.

Michelle saw Tapsell and the others gathered closely around their vehicles half a block up. They waved excitedly to Rick and her, gesturing for them to hurry back.

"It's not a negotiation, Rick," she said, jogging beside him, her Doc Martens thumping on the concrete sidewalk. "We need this."

"You're damn right it's not," he grumbled. "No way you're making me tell James I let you get killed."

"Then I guess you'd better come back with me and make sure I don't do anything stupid," Michelle said.

"Jesus Christ," Rick muttered. "How the hell does James put up with this?"

"He's very patient."

They maintained their pace up the broad street, jogging past shuttered shop windows and quiet homes. Small groups of local yokels scrambled to clear the area, fanning out and away from the shooting. Sleet started to fall, and Michelle blinked a tiny, freezing flake out of one eye. Nomi barked and panted as though this was the best adventure she'd ever been on.

They rejoined Tapsell and the others at their vehicles.

"Where's Maloney?" Rick asked. The Australian was immediately evident, simply by his absence.

Looking annoyed, Karl Valentine frowned at the yellow facade of the Legion's front office.

"Some fellers came out of there a few minutes ago and took him away."

"Oh, for fucks sake," Michelle said, not bothering to keep the irritation out of her voice. "Where'd they take him?"

"Dunno," Karl replied. "But Ellie followed them. She took the Expedition, and she's gonna come back and grab us up. We gotta get off the streets. Curfew, they reckon."

"Great. I don't suppose the Little League brownshirts over there said where they wanted us?" Michelle asked.

"Police station," Pete Tapsell said.

Michelle took that in. Nobody said anything. They could all see her turning the combinations in her mind.

"All right. Here's the play," she said at last as they clustered in around her. "Nobody's going anywhere near the cops unless they have to. Where's Katherine Bates?"

The ER nurse, standing behind Pablo Bruh and Mark Lawson, waved a hand. The two men stood aside to let her through.

"Katherine, you got a sister in town, right? Is she solid?" Michelle asked. "Would she take you all in? Keep her mouth shut?"

"She's kin," Bates said as if that ended it. Because it did.

"Okay. Get to her. Hunker down. Get a message to James and the Cav on the radio. Two words. Outcome-Harbinger. Repeat that back to me. Three times. Slowly."

Bates did.

Michelle made Tapsell and Pablo repeat the message, too.

"In case Katherine gets killed or taken," she said without sentiment. The two men seemed more upset by that than either Michelle or the nurse.

"O-k-a-a-a-y," Pablo said, looking at Michelle as if she might suddenly grow fangs and bite him. "Outcome-Harbinger."

"And Pete," Michelle said.

Tapsell repeated the code combination.

"Good. Go now, all of you," Michelle Nguyen ordered. "Do not engage with any of these Legion motherfuckers. Avoid local law enforcement. We'll find you later."

The group started to break up, and Rick reached out one hand to stay Pete Tapsell.

"Hey, Pete," he said.

"Yeah, mate? What's up," Tapsell asked. "Besides, you know, every-bloody-thing."

"Yeah. Look. Take Nomi for me, would you? And look after her. I got a... I just got a bad feeling, is all."

For a moment, Tapsell said nothing, but a lot passed between the two men.

Finally, he nodded.

Rick Boreham laid a hand on Tapsell's shoulder.

"Nomi. Go with Pete."

His dog whimpered, then barked once. Rick crouched down, took her face in his hands and kissed her between the eyes.

"Good girl. You're the best girl."

She growled and barked but wagged her tail and leapt up into the Jeep as Tapsell held the door open.

Rick stood up, let go of a ragged breath, and turned to Michelle and Karl.

"I guess we wait for Ellie then," he said.

THE GUN WAGON slid to a halt in front of the Sacajawea Hotel as Tommy Podesta pumped the brakes hard. He threw open his door and exited the vehicle with his gun drawn. The same gun he'd used to execute Luke Bolger and his two lieutenants. Jonas scrambled after him, patting him on the shoulder and muttering, "Thanks, man."

He had zero doubts that the Tripod had done the right thing. That felt like the opening move of a *coup d'état* back there.

Leo and Chad exited the vehicle, each in their own fashion. Leo struggled to lever his bulk out of the door; Chad crunched his boots down on the tarmac and looked for threats. A spiteful wind blew down from the mountains, and Jonas shivered in the cold.

"Leo," he said. "I need one of your pistolas, hombre. At least until my Legion boys get here."

"Sure thing, boss," Leo said, hauling one of his many handguns out of his numerous holsters, checking the safety, and handing it over.

"Where are those Cohort mooks at?" Podesta asked, scanning the hotel's car park. The other vehicle, the one carrying Jonas's close personal protection squad, had not followed them back. Jonas was not so cut about that. He'd prefer a company of Legion fighters around him, guys he could trust because Bolger's control over them was less direct. Less total.

"Don't know, don't care," Jonas said. "Let's get inside so we don't get sniped. I want at least a hundred of our guys here in two minutes. Make it happen, Leo."

"Already on it, boss," Leo Vaulk said. "I radioed the post commander. Trey Wilson. He's a good guy, and his men will follow him."

"He on the way?" Podesta asked.

"With his guys," Leo confirmed.

"How do you know?" Podesta said. He sounded like a DA cross-examining a hostile witness.

"Well, I don't fucking *know*, do I, Tommy," Leo protested. "Nobody *knows* anything. The same way Bolger couldn't have known you were about to put one in his melon. Why the hell did you even do that, man?"

Leo's tone was whiney and grating.

They had been moving into the hotel but stopped halfway up the front steps. Red spots stood out on Leo's cheeks, but the rest of his face had the complexion of stale porridge. He was shaking. Truth be known, they all were, except for Podesta. Chad was incredibly twitchy. He kept twisting his hammer around in his hands like a giant fucking fidget spinner. He hadn't said anything since bugging out and rushing back here. There were spots of blood on his face and, possibly, now that Jonas looked at it, a few flecks of... other stuff. Blowback from one of the headshots.

The chill, blustery wind lashed at Jonas's face and neck. He wasn't wearing gloves, and he could feel his fingers freezing around the grip of the pistol that Leo had given him.

"We can talk inside," he said. "Let's just get our asses out of the cold."

"Good call," Chad said. "Leo's ass is huge. A tempting target."

"Fuck you," Leo muttered.

Jonas heard the roar of engines approaching, and for a second of freefall, he was back in Silverton, listening to the bikers' approach. The Tripod grabbed his upper arm, propelling him up the steps and through the front door as the first of the Legion's gun wagons turned the corner. Jonas had trouble swallowing and even more trouble holding onto his bladder. He had no idea whether they were coming to save him or take him down.

They hurried inside. Not that the tasteful French doors of the Sacajawea Hotel would be much protection against the heavy machine guns mounted on the back of those pickups.

Jesus Christ, how had it come to this?

"It's Wilson," Leo declared as he bustled in after them. "It's cool. He's securing the perimeter."

Relief flooded through Jonas as he saw five gun wagons reversing into position outside – their guns pointed away from the hotel.

The Legion, *his* Legion, had stuck with him.

Two Cohort men came running from the direction of the dining room, and Jonas felt Podesta tense up beside him, but the men were unarmed and confused.

One of them saluted Jonas. "What happened, sir?"

"Was it the mayor? Did he do something?" The other one asked.

Podesta raised his pistol and pointed it at the one who'd spoken first. Jonas didn't even know the guy's name. Looked like he wasn't going to get a chance to learn it, either. But Podesta didn't pull the trigger.

"It wasn't a riot; it was a mutiny," Podesta said. "Bolger tried to take over. You know anything about that?"

The two men gaped at the Tripod, shaking their heads rapidly.

"No. No sir," they answered in unison.

"Nothing at all?" Podesta said. "No chatter at the O Club about your boss takin' over?"

He thumbed back the hammer on the revolver to add a little pepper to the question, and one of the Cohort guys pissed himself. The dark stain spread out from his crotch and down the front of his pants.

"Oh shit, shit, shit..." he babbled.

"Nothing like that, I promise. Nothing!" the other guy said.

Podesta's Smith & Wesson did not waver, but he did not pull the trigger. Working for Hondo back in Florida, Jonas had met some cold motherfuckers. Killers born and made, but killers one and all.

Tommy Podesta looked cold enough to put a bullet between the eyes of every one of them before sitting down to enjoy a big hot meal and a cold beer. But he lowered the handgun.

"Good to hear," he said.

Nobody said anything. Nobody moved.

They might have stood there like that, staring at each other for the rest of time, had Mathias Runeberg not come bustling in through the front door, flanked by two of his Cohort bodyguards. A fourth man followed them. Late middle age. Weather-beaten. And heavyset. Or at least he had been, say, six months ago. It looked like he'd dropped weight recently, Jonas thought.

"What happened? What's going on?" Runeberg demanded to know.

Before Jonas could answer, Podesta shot both of the Cohort men who'd arrived with Runeberg. Before their bodies hit the floor, Podesta had turned around and aimed at the first two Cohort soldiers, but again, he did not pull the trigger.

A heartbeat full of silence followed.

"Bugger me," said the man behind Runeberg, flanked on each side by cooling corpses. "A bloke could very easily get the impression you're not the friendliest fuckin' town, eh."

WHEN TOMMY PODESTA started working for Pauley 'the Mooch' Milano, he'd been appriced to Tony 'Two Fingers' Maniaty. Fingers was old school. He'd been around long enough to see the Vegas mob build Vegas. In his long and varied underworld career, he'd managed the skim for Meyer Lansky, painted houses for Mikey Rizzetello, and gone to the fuckin' mattresses more times than he could ever remember the goddamn reasons for.

It was Fingers who taught a younger and more innocent Thomas Podesta that as soon as you got the feeling you were gonna have to shoot a guy, you were probably in the shit because the best time to have shot him passed about five minutes ago.

"Tommy," Fingers told him. "If you sit around squeezing your dick and examining your feelings about that sorta shit, you are gonna be the one ends up in the shallow fuckin' grave."

Soon as the Tripod had seen Bolger come rolling out of that hotel and rolling heavy at that, he'd known in his nuts what was about to go down. Didn't need the details. The general fucking principle of it was enough.

With those first two mooks back at the hotel, though, he hadn't got that feeling. Not even a little bit. If there was a move on and they knew about it, no way would they be drag-assing around with their dicks out in the breeze and such dopey fuckin' looks on their faces. And the fact that one of them pissed his pants just because the Tripod pointed a gun at him, that there was reason to believe he was not the sort of guy you would rely on if you decided to move on your boss. Sure, it was a fuckin' lay down you could depend on him *after* you made your move, *and* it paid off. Guys who pissed themselves at the first sign of trouble were good for that, at least.

But those two barracuda who came in with Runeberg? Fuck those guys. Same as he knew when he saw Bolger; he just knew those two was in it up to their fucking necks. Coming through that door the way they did, hands on their pieces, and starting to draw them?

He didn't hesitate to pop the both of them.

"Bugger me..." the new guy said, and the Tripod was surprised to hear in his voice that he was some sort of Brit, like that Thor guy in the movies. But he didn't hear the rest of it because he was already swinging around to throw down again if he had to.

Busy morning was what it was.

The other Cohort mooks were staring wide-eyed and freaked the fuck out, though. They weren't even reaching for no pieces cos they had no idea what was going on. And they had no fuckin' pieces.

Tommy 'The Tripod' Podesta could even find it in his heart to feel a little Sympatico for them. They were just muscle like he had once been.

"What the hell is going on?" Mathias Runeberg squealed.

A legit squeal it was, too, like a schoolgirl.

But the Tripod was too busy keeping an eye on the last two Cohort guys and wondering whether it might be simpler to plug them and be done with it when the boss spoke up.

"They were gonna fucking nail us, look," Jonas said.

The Tripod didn't look because he wasn't a fuckin' idiot, and he knew what Jonas meant anyway. The dead men had tried to draw their weapons. One still clutched his .45, and the other guy's piece had clattered to the hardwood floor next to him. There was a lot of swearing and confusion, and that new guy suggested it might be more appropriate if he fucked off somewhere else. So that guy was not a complete fuckin' idiot neither, the Tripod would concede.

But a minute later, they were all still standing around, and half a dozen of the Legion's fighters had come running, and nobody had any idea what the fuck was going on.

"I'LL JUST BE GOING THEN, eh?" Damo suggested.

But before he could exit, Runeberg grabbed tight onto his arm and tried to pull him in close. Damien Maloney was twice the size of Mathias Runeberg. All the smaller man could do was pull himself in tighter next to Damo, almost like a small boy grabbing at his father in a heaving crowd.

This was not at all how Damo had imagined his day going.

These hapless fuckin' arseclowns couldn't organise a piss-up in a brewery, and it was a matter of honest regret to him now that he'd volunteered to come on this dodgy bloody spy caper wrapped up inside an even dodgier diplomatic mission because he was getting the impression he could've just stayed at the O'Donnell's place, put a couple more steaks on the barbie and waited for these fuckin' morons to step on their dicks and fall on their faces.

Who'd have thought that a bunch of fascist halfwits didn't have the smarts to organise and run a third-rate Reich?

With no idea who any of these people were, except for Runeberg and maybe the fat weightlifter who was most likely to be Murdoch,

Damo had trouble understanding one-tenth of fuck all about what was going on. Some bloke had wet himself and looked like he was about to start crying. There were rednecks in desert camo running around in obvious need of backing music from a hundred-piece orchestra of duelling fucking banjos. And his new best mate Runeberg was arcing up for a shouting match with some bloke who looked like a gigantic hairy man-boob with an untreated Rambo fetish.

Maybe little Mishy could make sense of all of this, but it was beyond him.

ELLIE JABBARAH PULLED the big SUV over to the side of the road. She'd had no trouble following Damo. It was a straightforward run to the hotel the Peckerwood SS had taken over, but there'd be no getting through the cordon of weaponised pickups that now surrounded the place.

Three Forks was an unholy mess. Local peeps and tooled-up militia guys running everywhere like headless fuckin' chickens, as Damo would say.

Except he'd say 'chooks', she thought, frowning anxiously as she watched him emerge from a soccer mom Volvo wagon with some guy who looked like Hitler's bookkeeper and a couple of torpedos with short hair, new joggers and jeans that just screamed ex-cop.

They had their hands on those weapons as they took the steps.

Ellie repeatedly swore to herself.

She needed to get in there. Needed to get Damo out.

She had no fucking idea how.

THEY HAD it out in front of Damo. He tried to make himself invisible, to blend in with all the woodwork, of which there was a metric shit ton in the entry hall to the Sacajawea Hotel. But in the end, he didn't need his mad James Bond skills. These blokes were just a bunch of murderous halfwits. Runeberg was undoubtedly the smartest of them, but only in the way that the smartest guy in the room at a slack-jawed dribblers convention could be confident of taking home the day's Einstein Award.

It didn't take Damo long to pick out Jonas Murdoch correctly. He was the bearded douchebro they all kept turning to for settling their disputes. The other two characters Damo figured to be the hired help. The first, the gunman who'd just straight up murdered Mathias Runeberg's bodyguards, seemed to be some fixer for Murdoch. He looked like a crim to Damo, who wasn't surprised to find out the morning's shenanigans had kicked off when this bloke took it upon himself to shoot some other bloke in the head in front of about a thousand witnesses. He only hoped that Rick and Michele didn't get caught up in that mess. The other dickhead hovering near Jonas Murdoch, whom Damo had initially mistaken to be Murdoch, looked like a nonspeaking bit player in some bootleg muscle porn video. Third-cock-on-the-right. But weirdly, he kept staring at Damo with the intense yet oddly vacant stare of an unmedicated lunatic.

It was pretty fucking off-putting, to be honest, and reason enough for Damo to quietly shuffle away, so he'd at least have a passing chance of dodging that oversized sledgehammer if Rainier Wolfcastle over there decided to start throwing it around.

"Where do you think you're spookin' off to, Casper?" the mob guy asked out the corner of his mouth, and Damo's shuffles ended. Runeberg and his org chart nemesis ignored the byplay to keep dinging away at each other.

"None of this would've happened if you hadn't sent that girl over to Bolger to prove a stupid point," Fat Rambo said.

He was jabbing one of his short, sausage-like fingers at Runeberg, who kept trying to slap them away like mosquitos.

"No, Mister Vaulk, none of this would have happened if you had done your job and supplied me with the generators I needed to progress operations at Bozeman. I warned you, and I warned you, and I warned you that there would be consequences, and here we are, my warnings unheeded, and the consequences upon us."

"Hey! Ladies!" Murdoch snapped. "None of this matters for shit. The only thing that matters is we got a mutiny going on, and we don't even know who's doing it."

"It is self-evident who is doing it, Mister Murdoch," Runeberg said. "It is the Cohort. They need to be disarmed immediately and tested rigorously for their loyalty."

"Ha!" The gangster snorted. "How you gonna do that, Matty? You got a polygraph or something? Leo's right. This isn't some planned operation. If it was, we'd all be dead by now. This was Bolger thinking he was in trouble, thinking he was entitled, and thinking he had one shot at the brass ring. He took his shot. That's what happened, and that's why I had to whack him."

"How can you possibly know that?" Runeberg insisted.

The gangster folded his arms and grinned almost ghoulishly.

"Think about it, Runeberg. I got the McNabb girl out of his room just after midnight. He knew there was a problem then. He had plenty of time to go downstairs and tell his boys they were taking over. Most of the guys in that club are Cohort, not Legion. You want to move on a guy, you don't wait. You just gotta do it. If he was planning to move on Jonas—"

He jerked a thumb at the leader of the so-called Legion of Freedom.

"He wouldn't have fucked around. He woulda gone for it soon as he figured his nuts were on the chopping block. And that was you, Runeberg. You did that to him when you sent the girl up there. But he only really figured that out when a thousand solid citizens turned up outside his bedroom window with pitchforks and nooses. What's he gonna do? The smart play for Jonas is to hand him over. Bolger knows that, so he comes heavy. As God is my fuckin' witness, if I hadn't clipped him, he woulda popped Jonas and me and Leo. Probably not you, though, because you'd-a been no threat to him, and he mighta mistakenly thought you were useful."

"Are you with Mister Vaulk then? Are you saying this is my fault?" Runeberg asked in a voice that grew a little shriller with each word.

Murdoch stepped in between the two men to forestall any further escalation.

"Nothing is nobody's fault if we get this sorted out," he said. He seemed to notice Damo for the first time. "And who the fuck is this anyway?"

The shaved gorilla leaned forward and squinted, tilting his head a little as though the effort of thinking and keeping his noggin on straight at the same time was a bit much for him.

"This is Mister Maloney," Runeberg said. "He is a representative from the survivor community in the valley south of Livingston. You may remember we reduced that town to secure the eastern flank of Bozeman. He came with an offer of a truce."

Jonas blinked in surprise and shook his head.

"Fuck, Matty. I admire your commitment to the bit, dude, but there's a time and a fucking place. Couldn't this wait? I got a mutiny to put down."

The gorilla was staring hard at Damo now.

It was no longer just uncomfortable. It felt dangerous. Runeberg started babbling on about how Damo had suggested salvaging equipment from some of the more significant coal mining sites in Wyoming to support operations at Bozeman. He didn't say anything more about the offer of a truce or the threat of insurgency, for which Damo sent a silent prayer up to God or the Buddha or whatever magical sky friend gifted Runeberg with the good sense not to complicate matters further.

"If we could expedite the transfer of this equipment," he went on to Murdoch, "we could improve conditions at the site and here in town and even begin to cut back on the rostered double shifts that—"

"Hey, asshole."

Runeberg stopped talking; his mouth hung open.

Everyone turned to the muscleman standing next to Murdoch.

"Yeah, you," the guy said, pointing the solid steelhead of his maul at Damo.

"Yeah? What?" Damo asked, trying to hide his nervousness. These were not a bunch of jackals you wanted sniffing even a hint of weakness.

"You're from Australia, aren't you."

It wasn't a question.

Jonas Murdoch looked almost as confused as Damo.

"Chad?" he said. "What's the problem, man?"

Something small but thorny caught in Damo's memory at that name. It tugged at his mind like a tiny, shiny, silver fishhook. He didn't answer the question.

"You worked in mining," Chad went on. "And you're from Australia."

It sounded like an accusation.

"What was your name again?" Chad asked.

Like a small, hungry rat, dread started to gnaw at the inside of Damo's ribs.

Chad, he thought.

He'd heard that name more than once over the last few years, but only after Ellie started working for him.

Chad. The personal trainer.

Chad. Jodi's dirtbag ex.

Chad, last seen running away from Ellie and Jodes after Karl gunned down his roommate for threatening the girls and Maxi back when San Francisco was coming apart.

Shit!

"Your name, pal," the gangster said. "What's your name?"

Runeberg suddenly shifted away from Damo, but he answered for him.

"He told me his name is Maloney. Damien Maloney."

Fark, Damo thought. *Should've made something up.*

He wasn't turning out to be worth a pinch of shit as an undercover operative.

"Yeah," he said, trying desperately to find a way out of this. "Maloney's my name. But I wasn't in mining. I was in logistics, like Matty here. I got a brother who worked the mines, though. Mostly oil and gas. Why? He owe you money or something, mate? He is a bit of a fucking deadbeat, sorry."

Chad blinked and shook his head.

Damo had a brother, but he ran some marketing website back in Oz. They hadn't spoken in years, but his brain was running white hot as he tried to build out an imaginary sibling that might make this protein monkey think he had the wrong bloke.

"You ran a diner in San Francisco," Chad said, slightly less confident. "I know you did. I seen you on the web and shit. You and that dyke."

Murdoch, Runeberg, and Vaulk were all staring at Chad as though he was nuts. The gangster wasn't; he was keeping an eye on Damo and his pistol in hand.

Damo shook his head.

"No, mate. I think you might know my brother. He married an American, moved here about five years ago, and cashed out of the oil business. Reckoned solar and hydrogen were gonna finish off the Saudis and the frackers. So, he got out and bought a bar. Not a restaurant."

Chad's face moved with slow, bovine deliberation as he tried to make the pieces fit.

Murdoch clapped him on the shoulder. "Dude. Seriously, we don't have time. You want to kill this fucker, just kill him."

"Wait! What?" Damo said.

"No!" Runeberg protested. "It is not just the generators. It is the valley. They are offering a truce, and we should take it. Tactically, strategically, it makes sense."

"But this old fuck knows where my kid is," Chad said.

Damo's scalp prickled, and his mouth went dry.

This was him. It had to be. Jodi Sarjanen's ex. What were the fucking odds?

Murdoch turned to Damo.

"Is that true? Do you know where his kid is? A little boy."

"Sorry, mate," Damo croaked. "I don't know what he's talking about. Maybe your mate here knows my brother. But I haven't heard from him since everything went pear-shaped. He's probably dead."

"Uhuh, and what's this about a truce?" Murdoch asked.

"It's important," Runeberg insisted. "Even after this morning. No, especially now, after this business with Luke and the Cohort. We cannot afford to miss this."

For a bright and shining second, Damien Maloney thought he'd done it. He'd somehow snuck through.

The doors of the hotel banged open, and four men came in.

They had Ellie Jabbarah with them.

She was a prisoner.

35

NOT A WOMAN YOU WANT TO CROSS

The streets emptied quickly while they waited on Ellie's return. After ten minutes of standing around, shivering in the gloom, Michelle, Rick, and Karl were the only people left outside, save for one militia guy who kept watch in front of the Legion's Ops Centre in the old, yellow brick real estate office. He stood close to the propane heater, clapping his hands and shuffling from foot to foot. Once or twice, he gave them the hairy eyeball, but without backup, he seemed disinclined to leave the comfort of the burner. After fifteen minutes, Michelle was almost sure Ellie was not coming back.

"Karl," she said, her breath visible in the cold air. "Do you think something's happened to her? Is Ellie somebody who'd get herself into trouble?"

Beyond a recent acquaintance with Ellie Jabbarah's mad cooking skills, Michelle did not know the woman very well. But Karl Valentine did. They had come through the end of the world together.

A deep line formed between his brows as he gave her question its due consideration.

"Yeah, I reckon so," he said, nodding sagely. "For sure, if Damo was in trouble. Those two, they're tight."

"Damn," Rick Boreham muttered. "You think they both been grabbed up, Michelle?"

She nodded, her expression bleak.

"Yeah," she said. "Probably in the last 10 minutes, I'd guess."

"What makes you guess that?" Karl asked. He was dressed lightly for the weather, wearing only three layers: a singlet, a red checked shirt and an old, brown corduroy jacket. Michelle could not understand how he hadn't died of exposure yet.

"Because we're still here, Karl," she explained. "If they had reason to lay hands on Ellie, they'll want to track down the rest of us, too. Things are moving, and we have to get ahead of them."

They made a forlorn scene on the empty street, shivering and stamping their feet to stay warm. The temperature seemed to be dropping by the minute. Dark grey clouds piled up high over the mountains to the north.

"You got a plan?" Rick asked. "Because I don't see a way forward here."

Michelle blew on her fingers, attempting to warm them. She had left her gloves in the Expedition.

"First thing we need is to find cover. A safe place to lay up and plan."

Karl folded his arms and hunched his shoulders forward, almost as though he might be feeling the cold.

"That doesn't sound like we're moving ahead of things," he said. "If you don't mind me saying so, Miss Michelle."

She managed a small smile, even though her teeth were chattering. "I'm not suggesting an all-hands planning week at a spa resort, Karl. We need cover, we need weapons, and we need to know what we're going to do before we fucking do it. But we are gonna do something. We have to. I can feel it."

Rick Boreham scanned up and down the street. His mournful expression grew darker.

"Yeah," he said. "Me too. What about you, Karl?"

The older man nodded slowly, almost solemnly.

"Sure feels like it to me."

Michelle glanced across the road at the lone gunman who remained outside the Legion's makeshift Operations Centre.

"You boys stay here. I'm gonna go talk to our man Cletus over there."

"I wouldn't call him Cletus if that's not his name," Karl cautioned. "Folks can be particular about stuff like that."

Michelle favoured him with a grin that was much warmer than she felt.

"You have a good heart, Karl. Lucky for us, I don't. You two stay here. I don't want to freak him out."

She left her two companions behind and stepped out into the road. It was getting so cold that it felt like her fingers would drop off from frostbite. Michelle slipped both hands into the fur-lined pockets of her ski jacket, but only for a second, to check that she still had what she needed. Having done so, she took them out again because what she needed, even more was for this yahoo to imagine that she was unarmed. She needed him at ease, not on edge. A tall order, she knew, with everything that had happened.

Her Docs crunched on the wet tarmac of the road as she hurried across, attempting to suppress her shivering through willpower. It wasn't easy. The sleet had turned to a constant drizzle, a grey, drifting, sodden shroud that one of her instructors back on the Farm in Virginia had lovingly referred to as Scottish mist. Michelle kept her expression on the bright side of neutral as she approached her mark. As she stepped off the road, the rifleman lifted his head in a wary greeting.

"You and your friends need to get off the street," he said. "Curfew."

"Yeah, I know," Michelle conceded, letting herself shiver at last. Suppressing the urge meant that when she did give in, she shook with an almost deep body spasm. All the better to make herself seem a little more pathetic. She pointed one shaking hand at the propane heater. "Do you mind?"

"Guess not," he said. "But you still gotta get off the street, ma'am. Patrols be coming by soon."

"I figured," she said. "But we can't leave without our friend. He was inside talking to your boss."

The other man snorted.

"Runeberg is not my boss."

"Okay, whatever, but we don't know where our friend is. We don't know how long he's gonna be. You got any idea where he could be at?"

The militia man, late twenties, white, with a few spots of acne showing through a sparse and scrubby beard, shook his head.

"Nobody told me anything but to stay here and keep an eye on the office."

Michelle nodded without saying anything. This kid was not giving off a lot of brainiac vibes, but he wasn't openly hostile either.

"So, you got any idea where we could go to wait for him?" she asked after a moment. "Because we're freezing our asses off out here, and, like you said, there's a curfew. We're not local. We don't have anywhere to go."

He shrugged.

"I just got in here myself. They had me out at Bozeman the last two weeks. That sucked."

"And before that? You a local boy?"

He scoffed.

"As if. Portland. I was road-tripping east with a couple of friends on Zero Day. We had a band. We were heading for New York. Woulda been awesome."

His eyes went far away for a moment. Michelle had seen that exact look plenty of times on other survivors. He was back in the Before Times. A happier place.

"Got close to starving before we ran into the Legion," he said, more to himself than her. "Joined them. Got fed. You could sign on."

"And where are your friends?" Michelle asked, ignoring the suggestion and gathering the information. Assessing the threat.

He shrugged again. He did a lot of that. When he spoke, his tone was sad, almost lost.

"I dunno. They split us up. Dougie and Coz could be anywhere within four states, I guess. It sucks big time. But a gig's a gig, right?"

"It is," Michelle Nguyen agreed. The warmth from the propane burner was delicious, almost uncomfortably hot. In contrast, the back of her neck felt icy cold and damp. "But we still need somewhere to stay. That shit this morning, that was off the leash, man. Is that, like, normal around here?"

He shook his head, but more in helplessness than denial.

"I dunno," he said. "I just... I don't really know how any of this works here. I just wanted to go to New York with my friends, is all."

He looked at her as if for the first time.

"You sound like you're from the east. What's it like back there?"

Michelle shook her head.

"You're not going to make New York, sorry. It's gone. Like we should be. Seriously, man, is there anywhere we can go?"

He seemed to think it over, and this time, he gave it more time and deeper thought.

"The town council handles stuff like refugees. You could try them."

"Okay, where are they at?"

He snickered as though the question amused him.

"City Hall is here on Main Street. Just over there, in fact," he said, pointing north.

Michelle frowned.

"Sorry, where? I don't see it."

"That's because it's not much of a City Hall," he said. "Second down from the end of the street. If anybody's in, that's where they'll be. They might let you sit in the waiting room or something until after curfew."

"Thanks," Michelle said.

She turned around and waved to Rick and Karl, pointing north. They nodded and started walking.

"What's your name?" She asked.

"Kelton," he said. "Kelton Palmer."

She took one last intensely pleasurable moment of warmth from the heater before plunging her hands back into the pockets of her ski jacket. Her right hand closed around the handle of the small-bladed fighting knife hidden there, but only to reassure herself that it remained accessible.

"Stay safe, Kelton Palmer," Michelle Nguyen said.

"WHAT D'YOU think she's gonna do?" Karl Valentine asked.

"With Michelle," Rick pronounced. "There is no telling."

And Rick was deeply uncomfortable with it. He would have given anything to have Nomi with him, but this would end in blood. Of that, he was sure. And as difficult as he found it to send Nomi away with Pete and the others, it was impossible to contemplate going on without her. If either of them was going to get hurt—or worse—this morning, it would not be Nomi.

"You okay, man?" Karl asked. "You don't look real good."

"Hah," Rick laughed, a bitter sound without humour. "Does it show that much?"

"Brother, it is coming off you in black waves," Karl said. "I know what that's like."

Rick sighed, a ragged exhalation of dispirited fear and hopelessness. He and Karl stood on the concrete apron of a corner block occupied by an auto parts business. He looked around. This would not be a good place to die, but where was? Unlike many places in Three Forks, the auto shop didn't look like it'd survived the collapse. Most of the windows facing the street were boarded up, but one was broken, leaving the shop open to the elements. Scrappy weeds grew through cracks in the concrete, and the rooftop guttering was bedraggled by leaf litter and birds' nests.

Rick kept an eye on Michelle, envying her proximity to that outdoor heater. Her body language seemed to be relaxed, and the guy she was talking to looked as though he was cool with whatever story she was spinning him. Rick could not unwind, however, not after that unholy mess at the protest. The streets were clear now, but this wasn't the end of anything. It was just the start.

"Your friend over there, what was she before all of this?" Karl asked. "I mean, I know she worked in Washington. But she's no file clerk. Did she serve, do you know?"

Rick shook his head. Uncertain.

"Not in uniform, that I know of."

"She handled herself well in that business back at the Cav Memorial. She knows how to move through a fight. Pick a target."

Rick nodded slowly.

"I figure most people who are still alive know how to do that by now," he said.

"True that," Karl admitted. "But she was trained somewhere. And she's had more practice than most. Not you, I'll wager. But more so than me. I just drove stuff around."

Rick Boreham kicked at an old, dull-edged piece of broken glass with the muddy toe of his boot.

"She and James were in Washington when it happened, you know. They were right there in the thick of it. With all of the generals and admirals. They even went to the White House."

Karl raised his eyebrows and nodded in genuine appreciation of that revelation.

"Quality scuttlebutt," he said. "I didn't know that bit. I know she worked for the national security people, but James was some sort of banker, wasn't he? An investment guy. Like Charles Schwab."

Rick chuckled at that.

"He was, I guess. But he was in Washington doing some consultancy for the government. For Michelle. But it was nothing to do with…" He waved one hand around. "All of this, you know. They just happened to be in the room when it all went down. To be honest with you, Karl, if they hadn't been and Mel and I hadn't met them, I don't know that I'd be here with breath in my body. The whole thing snuck up on me."

Karl Valentine fist-bumped him lightly on the shoulder.

"The whole thing sort of snuck up on everyone, buddy. Look."

He was pointing across the road. Michelle waved at them and pointed up Main Street.

"I think she wants us to go thataway," Karl said.

"Seems like," Rick nodded. "Best do as we're told then. She is not a woman you want to cross."

They turned north and started trudging up the sidewalk. A minute later, Michelle had jogged most of the way back to them.

"Over here," she said, waving at an almost aggressively nondescript building on the other side of the road. It had none of the frontier charm of so much of the town's architecture. It was a cinderblock bunker. A couple of evergreen trees blocked a clear view of the upper storey, but Rick could see the plain lettering attached to the façade.

CITY HALL.

"Looks more like a bus depot," Karl Valentine said. "For a tiny bus."

Michelle hastened over to them.

"Dude said we should try in here," she said. "Town Council has responsibility for handling refugees, and as far as these guys are concerned, that's what we are now."

"Are they even open?" Rick asked. The door was closed, and the windows were almost completely covered in official pamphlets, community flyers and other printed matter.

"Only one way to find out," Michelle said.

She marched up to the front door, knocked twice, and pushed it open.

———

"WHAT THE HELL?" Ross Jennings snapped as he heard the bell jingle over the front door.

"I'll check," Dan McNabb said, just before they both heard a woman's voice, unfamiliar, call out from the front office.

"Hello? Is there anyone here?"

The mayor and the chief engineer of Three Forks exchanged a look. Everything had gone so terribly wrong this morning. Or last night, Jennings supposed. Although, really, nothing had been right since the Chinese or the Russians had shut everything down back in August.

There were three of them hunkered down in Jennings' office. Himself, McNabb and Reverend Nikobe. After the shooting outside the Continental Divide, they had all sought refuge here. Tom Sharkey should have been here too, but the sheriff was busy trying to disentangle his deputies from Murdoch's mess.

"I'll see who it is," Jennings said.

He stuck his head around the corner into the outer office. Three strangers stood just inside the threshold—a woman of Asian appearance and two white men. The larger of the men was in his late twenties or early thirties. His companion was older. Maybe in his fifties.

Ross Jennings quietly cursed himself for several things, foremost among them forgetting to lock the front door. But he also regretted not bringing his gun.

The three newcomers did not look immediately dangerous. They weren't visibly armed, so they certainly weren't Murdoch's people. The bigger man had a forbidding intensity to him, but it was the woman to whom his attention was drawn. She fixed him with a stare and advanced across the room as though she owned the place.

"Hello," she said. "Are you in charge here?"

"I'm the mayor," Jennings said, almost affronted by the question. "Who are you people, and what are you doing here?"

The woman seemed to consider that for a moment. It was almost as though she was deciding who to be. Finally, she said, "My name is Michelle Nguyen."

Jennings's heart started to race a little as she reached into her jacket, but he blinked in surprise when she pulled out... a laminated identity card and showed it to him.

"I'm from the National Security Council," she said.

36

AM I THE ONLY ONE WHO CARES ABOUT THIS MUTINY

It was not a happy reunion.

"You fucking dyke!"

The steroid Nazi raised his oversized cartoon hammer and charged at Ellie. Of the four-man squad who had just escorted her inside, only one had the presence of mind to reach for his weapon. The others all flinched and dodged away from the onrushing berserker. And the one with the gun didn't get off a shot because Damo stuck his foot out to trip up the angry goon before he could swing on Ellie. Chad went down, face-planting on the polished wooden floor. The impact flattened his nose with a sick, wet crunch. Damo thought about punting a kick into the side of his big, boxy head, but by then the Legion squaddies had got around to drawing their weapons, and it seemed a poor, albeit tempting, choice.

"Jesus fuck," Murdoch cried out, throwing up his arms and sounding like he was entirely at his wit's end. "Get off the goddamn floor, Chad, and chill the fuck out, would you. Who the fuck even is this anyway?"

The bodyguard's voice came back muffled and spluttering as if through a mouthful of blood. With everyone distracted, Damo took a split second to catch Ellie's eye. He quickly shook his head. A fractional movement, but one he hoped she would understand. Deny everything, including him.

"Put your guns away, you assholes," the man they called Podesta barked out. "You're gonna shoot somebody, and I'll bet dollars to fuckin donuts it won't be the right sonofabitch."

The militiamen cautiously did as they were told. They had no fucking idea what was happening. Just like Damo.

Moffat was up on his hands and knees, shaking his head, fat dollops of deep red blood dripping from his swelling lips and broken nose. Podesta hooked a hand under his armpit and hauled him back to his feet. Moffat looked like he'd been poleaxed, but he still managed to launch himself at Ellie a second time. Podesta put him down again. But not all the way. He turned his helping hand into some sort of crude arm lock, leaned forward and said in a low, even tone, "I'm gonna help you back up again, Chad, but this is gonna get old. So do me a solid and knock it off, pal."

That seemed to get through to him. Jodi Sarjanen's ex-husband slowly climbed back to his feet while struggling to clamp down on his rage. Jonas Murdoch patted him on the shoulder and turned a hard, dangerous look on Ellie. "Who the hell are you, and why does my boy Chad here want to fuck you up so bad?"

One of the militia fighters spoke up before Ellie could.

"We found her trying to sneak in through the kitchen," he said.

Damo's mind was racing, desperate to think of some way he might communicate with Ellie and warn her off. If this was one of the dumb action movies he used to love so much or just some stupid airport novel, he probably could've come up with some innocuous remark that would have totally clued her into what was happening here. And she would have served up a delicate Bento box of white lies and half-truths to get her arse out of trouble. But he had nothing because there was nothing. Chad had recognised her as soon as she came through the door. And, of course, these pricks had their names from the three checkpoints they'd been through. Everything was turning to shit.

"She fucked my wife," Chad burbled, sounding full of snot and misery.

"This bitch?" Jonas Murdoch grinned, shaking his head in surprise and delight. "Seriously? You got cucked by this fugly dyke?"

"Hey," Damo said. "Steady on, mate. No call for that shit."

For his trouble, he got a short arm jab in the guts from Fat Rambo. For a butterball, Vaulk was surprisingly strong. The sucker punch drove all the air out of Damo, and he doubled over, gasping for breath.

"She didn't cuck me, man," Chad whined. "She's a liar. She's a whore, and she turned my woman and my boy against me."

Just shut the fuck up, Ellie. Damo prayed to himself, still doubled over in pain as he tried to suck in a mouthful of air. *Just shut the fuck up. Shut the fuck up.*

Ellie, of course, did not.

"Hey, Moffat," she said. "You stupid fuckin' cum pump."

Besides Damien Maloney, eleven men crowded into that elegant hotel lobby, many holding guns. All of them except Damo turned to Ellie, suddenly wearing their what-the-fuck faces. Their eyes only grew wider, and their jaws dropped further as Ellie raised two fingers in a 'V', put them to her mouth and stuck her tongue through, speed-licking a pretend vagina like a lesbian Gila monster on bathtub crank.

Jesus, Ellie. Come on.

Damo shook his head and finally gulped in a mouthful of air.

His head jerked up to the sound of laughter. First Murdoch and then all of his lackeys.

Only Damo, Ellie and Chad didn't think it all piss-your-pants funny.

"Oh man," Murdoch chuckled. "You were fighting out of your weight class there, Chad." And to even more peals of laughter, he made a two-fingered V-for-vagina sign, just like Ellie had, before giving it a serve of super-fast tongue.

"Fuck you," Chad muttered, sullen and resentful. He glared at Ellie, wiped the blood from his face and growled, "Where's my kid, bitch?"

"Nowhere you're gonna find him, you fucking douchebag," Ellie lobbed back.

"I want my fucking kid back, Jonas," Chad said with none of the deference he or any of the others had shown Murdoch so far.

Murdoch patted him on the shoulder again.

"We'll get your boy back, Chad. But these two are not a priority right now. Just put 'em on ice. We got a mutiny to put down first. I promise that when we're done, you can deal with this asshole and the dyke however you want."

He dismissed Damo and Ellie as if they were already dead.

Damo was trying to think of some card to play when Runeberg did it for him.

"Mister Murdoch, please. I brought Maloney to you because he can solve a significant problem for us. Two of them, in fact. The infrastructure issue at Bozeman and pacifying the capital's hinterland next spring. I don't think Mister Moffat's personal *contretemps* should be prioritised over the needs of the Legion as a whole."

"Fuck yeah," Damo agreed. "What he said."

Murdoch raked both hands down his face, theatrically clawing his features into a fright mask.

"Jesus. Fucking. Christ. Am I the only one who cares about this fucking mutiny?"

"We can sort that out for you, boss," Podesta assured him. "We just gotta round up all the Cohort mooks who was in on it."

"How we gonna do that, man?" Murdoch asked.

"This pair," he said, and for one second, Damo thought he meant he and Ellie. She did, too, to judge by her reaction. But Podesta waved his pistol at the two unarmed militia guys from earlier.

"Hey," one of them protested. "We weren't in on anything. You said that yourself."

"Shut up," Podesta said. He put the gun away and turned to Murdoch. "We get them on the radio, and they call up the rest of their crew. That's about a hundred guys, right? We tell them to muster up here, out front, but they gotta come unarmed. Straight up, tell 'em why it's gotta be that way. Bolger was a rat. We gotta find the other rats."

Murdoch shook his head. Confused.

"But how do we do that?"

Podesta shrugged.

"Anybody who doesn't turn up or comes heavy, there's your rat."

Damo risked a glance across at Ellie. She was already looking at him, shrugging as if to apologise.

"Not much of a plan, dude," Murdoch said. "But I guess it'll have to do. What about the others, the ones who don't come?"

Podesta made a showy *fuggedaboutit* gesture with both hands.

"They're rats, boss. Exterminate 'em."

ELLIE COULDN'T QUITE BELIEVE she was caught up in this insane teste-fest. All she'd wanted to do was sneak in to see if she could hook up with any of the kitchen staff. Those guys would know exactly what was going down. But that hadn't worked out so well, and now this.

Chad Fucking Moffat.

There was no God unless she was a treacherous bitch with a sick-ass sense of humour. The last time she'd seen this asshole, it'd been the cursed image of his actual goddamned asshole, puckering furiously in a pair of too-tight gym shorts. That particular vision of Hell had burned deep into her eyeballs as Moffat fled the scene of Karl's totally justifiable homicide of his skeevy fucking roommate.

Jesus Christ, that felt like a hundred years ago.

Chad seethed at her from across the lobby, nose broken, lips swollen, and his teeth stained cherry red with blood. He wasn't listening to any of these other psychopaths. He only had eyes for her, and those eyes were full of knives.

She probably shouldn't have aggravated him like that. But she couldn't stop herself. The red mist came down as soon as she recognised him. This was the man who had tortured Jodi for three years. He had threatened to kill them back in San Francisco if they didn't

JOHN BIRMINGHAM

give him Maxi. She had presumed him dead in the months that followed. Half the world was dead by now, maybe more. And somehow, this gigantic lump of barely sentient man-spam was still stinking up the planet.

"They're rats, boss. Exterminate them," some leftover mafia asshole said while Damo was making eyes at her.

Ellie felt terrible. She'd only been trying to help, but there was no doubt she had made everything infinitely worse. Fuck! If only she'd followed her first instinct and gone back to the others. Karl would have known what to do. Or Rick or even Michelle. They knew about this shit.

The murderous pocket Nazis were all yammering on with some mini-genocidal plan to wipe out some other bunch of backwoods floor shitters and doing it openly in front of her and Damo. That did not augur well for the future.

"There is another problem," some weedy little gimp said. "Mr Maloney's companions."

Instantly, he had Ellie's attention.

"I cannot emphasise strongly enough," he went on, "that we need to consider very seriously the offer he is making on behalf of the occupants of the valley. But it might be a good idea to secure the other members of his party. This woman is only one of nearly a dozen envoys sent to negotiate a truce with the Legion."

"Mathias," Jonas Murdoch said. "There's not gonna be any Legion if we don't lock this rebel shit down and quickly."

Ah. The gimp would be Runeberg, then. The one Damo had gone to meet.

"I would concur," he replied. "Which is why it is important to round these people up. They may be diplomats of a sort, but the situation in Three Forks is now very fluid, and it behoves us to take all precautionary measures."

He actually turned to Damo and apologised.

"I am sorry that it has to be this way, but I'm sure you understand."

Damo rolled his eyes.

"Yeah, sure. Whatever, mate."

"Hey. Jabber," Moffat croaked.

Ellie scowled at him. He had always called her that. Because he knew it pissed her off.

"Is Jodi with you? Did you bring Max?"

"Go fuck yourself, Chad," Ellie said.

"Okay! Enough," Murdoch said, raising his voice. He rubbed at his eyeballs as though he was trying to stave off a headache. "Let's unfuck this mess, one step at a time."

He pointed at Damo and Ellie.

"I want these two locked up. Don't just stick them in a room here. They'll get out for sure. Don't give them to the local cops. I don't trust those guys. Just... I dunno... Throw them in the fuckin' meat locker in the kitchen. Put a padlock on it. They're warmly dressed. They'll be fine. Or they won't. I don't give a shit. I just want them off the board for now. Matty, we will deal with your issue later. Okay?"

Runeberg signalled his acceptance with a bow. He was like a community theatre nerd playing at being a loyal functionary.

"You two," Murdoch continued, turning to a couple of unarmed militia guys who looked like they'd simply been hanging around in the hotel. "Lieutenant Wilson is going to go with you to the radio room, and you are gonna put a message out to the Cohort that they are to muster here in fifteen minutes. They are to come *unarmed*. Not even a pocket knife. Anybody who doesn't comply will be deemed to be in open mutiny and yadda yadda yadda. Wilson? You good with that?"

"Yes sir," said the militia guy who'd captured Ellie. "I'll make it happen."

Murdoch turned to the well-dressed gangster who had suggested murdering all of their colleagues whose loyalty might not be rock solid.

"And you, my friend," Jonas Murdoch said. "I need you to get down to City Hall, put a bag on Jennings, and drag his ass back up here. I don't need him making any more trouble. I need him in my corner doing exactly what I tell him."

"You got it, boss," the other man said. "What about the other ones who came in with Maloney?"

"Put the cops on it. They can at least handle a simple job like that. But make sure they've got one of our guys riding along in every patrol car. We can't spare the manpower for a full search at the moment, but Matty is right. It's better not to have them wandering around."

"We have their names and the plates of their vehicles," Lieutenant Wilson said.

Chad Moffat snuffled up a nose full of blood and mucus.

"I'll take care of these two," he said.

He was looking directly at Ellie when he spoke.

Jonas Murdoch narrowed his eyes.

"Sure. You do that, bro, but you..." he pointed at one of the men who'd brought Ellie in. "What's your name?"

"Ridley, sir," the guy barked back.

"Okay, Ridley," Jonas Murdoch said. "You tag along with Chad here. Secure Crocodile Dundee and his lady friend somewhere. If the meat locker isn't suitable, just, I dunno, chain them to a fucking tree or something. But Mr Runeberg and I want them alive and in one piece each at the end of the day, got that?"

He was looking at Chad as he spoke, but Ridley snapped out the answer, "Yes, sir."

"Matty," Jonas said. "You good?"

"That will be acceptable," Runeberg answered.

"And Chad. We cool now?"

"Yeah," Moffat agreed, staring at Ellie. "We're cool."

THE SACAJAWEA HAD A COURTESY CAR, a white Prius. The tank was full, and the batteries topped up courtesy of the hotel's rooftop solar cells. Tommy Podesta seriously thought about driving it off the lot and out of town, getting as far away from Three Forks as he could. This shit was unprofessional. There was no other word for it. He'd seen some stupid beefs get out of hand in his time with the Milanos, but there was still a code to that. Things might get bloody but in a predictable way. There was nothing predictable about what was happening now.

He nodded to the Legion fighters moping around the gun trucks as he turned left onto Main Street and drove carefully away from the hotel. Every one of those assholes was hauling more personal artillery than whole damned crews he'd worked with for the Milano family. The Tripod didn't fool himself about how dangerous these guys could be, but nor would he indulge in any wishful thinking about their competence or reliability.

Tony Two Fingers used to say that you could tell how a crew would be on a job by how they rolled into it. Guys who were going to be calm and professional, who were going to keep their shit tight on a job, they would be like that before, during and after the show. There wouldn't be any fucking around. No drinking, no grandstanding – nothing. A solid crew; you wouldn't even see them going in. And you would never, ever know they had done the job afterwards.

As he piloted the almost silent hybrid down the deserted street, he could not shake the conviction that he might have thrown in his lot with a bunch of retarded circus clowns. The tactical gear, the fire-power, the dressing up and acting out – none of it meant shit when things went sideways. The boss was perhaps the one exception. Murdoch had his flaws, no doubt about it, but he was a guy who thought things through. You might disagree with him. But there was no denying that he had a plan, and he stuck to it. Or he had, until this shit show in Three Forks. The guys around him, though?

The Tripod shook his head.

Leo Vaulk was a blowhard and a fuckin' snake. In Podesta's opinion, Bolger had always been a sick twist and a coward. Runeberg was a bookkeeper, nothing more. And there was nothing wrong with that. Everybody had to keep at least two sets of books. But to the Tripod's way of thinking, you never let guys like that out of the back room. That's where they belonged, not at the high table making the big calls.

A Toyota pickup full of Legion fighters roared past, pulling

Podesta out of his character appraisals as the other vehicle blasted towards the hotel. He half expected to hear gunfire and was relieved when he didn't. There were no locals around anywhere. They'd all been smart enough to bunker down. He did not doubt for a second that half the goddamned town was in their root cellars right now, breaking out boxes of rifles and ammo they had stashed away for a day just like this. No way these fuckin' cowboys gave 'em all up when Jonas told them to.

He could see Mayor Jennings' office coming up, and it was a hell of a temptation to keep going. He passed a couple of Cohort guys huddled inside the vestibule of a hardware store. They eyeballed him as he drove past, and he fought an urge to stomp on the accelerator and get out of their kill zone. But he didn't, and they returned to whatever they were talking about.

He wondered if they'd had that radio call yet.

Podesta didn't drive past City Hall. He steered the Prius over to the curb and cut the engine. It was eerie the way the electric vehicle didn't make any noise, almost like you were floating down the road rather than driving. He'd seen dozens of Teslas on his way out of San Francisco and later heading north, and they'd all been fucked one way or another. Some were burned-out wrecks; others had peeled off the road at high speed. Some had just died. He wondered why the Chinese had killed the Teslas but not this bullshit halfbreed car.

Maybe some slant general had stock in the company?

He shrugged off the minor mystery. None of it mattered. Not why the chinks had done what they did. Not what'd happened to them because they'd done it. He recalled there'd been a lot of balls out crazy talk on the cable news, at the end, about America's retaliation. Nukes, space rockets, superflu bugs that only killed slants. But none of that mattered now. The president had obviously kicked those assholes back to the Stone Age. Otherwise, they would've already been here. What Tommy Podesta thought about that was – good for him. That useless prick finally came good at the end when it counted.

But it was also why the Tripod did not just drive on. There was always consequences. That's what he told that fuckin' mook who thought he could get away from the forty large he owed Paulie by running all the way to fuckin' Kalamazoo.

"There's always consequences, Jerry. You can't get away with nothing in this world. The best thing for you woulda been to put your head down, do your job, and pay the Mooch what was owed."

Then he plugged the deadbeat—one in the ticker, two in the melon.

Consequences were a sonofabitch.

Best to put your head down. Do your damn job.

And his job meant putting a bag on Mayor Jennings and delivering him back to Murdoch.

He crossed the road, noting the single armed guard standing duty outside Runeberg's office, warming his hands over an outdoor heater. It was bitching cold, and he couldn't help but be a little jealous of that asshole. The Tripod shivered inside his overcoat.

What a goddamned mess.

He didn't think about taking out his gun before he pushed open the door to the ever-so-fucking-grandly-named City Hall. He just did it, the habit of a lifetime, the Smith & Wesson resting comfortably in his grip.

37

BOUND IN SHALLOWS AND IN MISERY

Without Nomi, it was hell.

Rick had trouble concentrating. Michelle was talking to the mayor and his people, which reminded him of the briefing she had done at the O'Donnell ranch. She was, if possible, even more sharply focused and persuasive, but he was much less able to follow the thread of her argument. His hands were tingling. Prickly sweat beaded his scalp and trickled from his armpits, just a few inches, but enough to irritate and distract him.

Had Nomi been there, she would have sensed his distress, smelled it on him and nuzzled him with her big black head until he gave up and rewarded her attention with pats and scratches behind the ear. That simple act of solace, of drawing from Nomi's limitless well of assurance and trust, was almost always enough to right him when he felt the world tilting beneath his feet.

But Nomi was not there because Rick could not countenance the idea of exposing her to the evil that was surely coming.

"Ms Nguyen," the mayor said, "I am grateful for the offer of an alliance, and I do not lightly decline, but it is too late for us. The Legion is here, and we are under the yoke. It would be a bloody and fearful business to throw it off at this late stage."

Rick squeezed his eyes shut for a second and tried to settle his racing heart with the breathing exercises Doctor Cairns had taught him at the VA.

"Mayor Jennings," Michelle said. "This morning was a bloody and fearful business, and I can promise you it will only get worse. I don't know why Murdoch's group has suddenly fractured the way it has—"

"Oh, I can tell you that," the city's engineer said in a bitter tone.

"And I would very much like to know, Mister McNabb," Michelle went on. "But it is more important that you see the opportunity you have right now that you will not have a day from now. And the risk you run of falling even deeper into despotism if you do not act now when you have that chance."

The preacher lady, Reverend Nikobe, a heavy-set black woman of sympathetic demeanour, leaned across Jennings' desk and took his hands in hers.

"There is a tide in the affairs of men and of women, Mister Mayor, which, when taken at the flood, leads on to fortune, but when omitted, leaves us bound in shallows and in miseries. Ross, where are we now if not bound in misery?"

"Amen to that," McNabb muttered.

"Excuse me," Rick said, pushing past Michelle and heading for the door to the larger outer office.

He could no longer stand to be confined in the small, stuffy room. His hands were starting to shake. He had to get moving, or he was going to come apart.

Karl Valentine, who had been leaning against the doorframe, moved aside.

"Easy, brother," he said. "I got you."

"Are you in pain, sir?" the preacher asked, already rising from her seat to follow Rick.

"He'll be fine," Michelle Nguyen said. "Karl, look after him."

"I don't think he'll be fine," Reverend Nikobe said. "Your young man is in distress, Ms Nguyen."

And with that, the preacher was up, too, following Rick and Karl into the reception area.

Everyone else came after them in short order.

He had trouble breathing. Enough trouble that his vision started to grey out at the edges. Karl was there, holding him up, with Reverend Nikobe on the other side. She smelled of vanilla, he thought as they lowered him into an old swivel chair. His thoughts were puzzle pieces, scattered by a sudden jolt.

"I don't mean to be rude, Miss Nguyen," Mayor Jennings said, "But this is not very persuasive of your case. There are just the three of you, and Mister..."

"Boreham," Karl said. "Rick Boreham."

"And Mister Boreham does not seem capable of taking care of himself, let alone taking on Murdoch's gun thugs."

"I'll be fine," Rick said, sounding anything but.

The hell of it was that he would be, eventually. This panic attack would pass, but without Nomi or a heavy dose of valium, there was no certainty about when.

His anxiety over letting everybody down folded back on his fears about being unable to protect and defend them in the first place, accelerating the spiral.

It could have ended in a very dark place if the man with the gun had not come through the door.

At first, Rick thought he was hallucinating, which was even more distressing. As bad as his stress disorder could be, florid hallucinations were not usually part of the deal.

"Podesta?" the mayor said.

"The fuck is all this about?" the man said. His voice was harsh, guttural.

Rick recognised him. He was the one who'd shot the militia commanders.

He was waving the same gun around now. Ordering everyone to get back.

The preacher, Nikobe, refused.

"This man is sick," she said. "He needs an ambulance."

"Yeah, well," Podesta said, "he's shit outta luck. There's a lot of that going around today."

It was the gun that Rick fixed on.

An old-fashioned revolver, maybe a police special. A .38 or a .357 Magnum.

He needed to do something about that gun.

Identifying a tangible threat, an actual, material object on which he could focus, had the effect of flipping millions of chemical switches across his entire cortex. The previous disturbance to the delicate balance of neurotransmitters and hormones, which had so thoroughly unmanned him, was flushed away by an equally powerful adrenaline storm. He felt himself falling, but this time into well-formed patterns of thought and behaviour.

In this heightened state, suddenly alert, hyperaware, hundreds of decision loops running at white heat and hyper-velocity, he saw Michelle Nguyen appear from behind a four-drawer filing cabinet next to Podesta.

Rick had no idea how she had closed the distance from Jennings' office to that particular blind spot, but as the man with the gun passed into her fighting arc, she moved in a chromatic blur – almost a strobing effect in which Rick perceived discrete moments of action as significant links in a greater chain of meaning. Michelle kicking out Podesta's kneecap. Her leading hand C-clamping his elbow joint. The other hand, rigid, open, whipping hard into the side of his neck. Both hands blurring, reappearing far, far away, down around Podesta's wrist, blurring again as her whole body shifted, and for a fraction of a second, the two of them stood hip to hip, shoulder to shoulder. But only for the merest sliver of time, and then she was moving again. Striking, turning, levering, disrupting, destroying.

Michelle's freakishly swift negation of the unforeseen threat must have been impossible for the others to understand. The flow of movement and precisely targeted kinetic effects stripped the weapon from Podesta's grip, robbed him of his balance, and broke at least one rib, his elbow, and possibly his knee.

He collapsed like an ancient brick smokestack, demolished by a master of the explosive arts.

Toppling, groaning, and finally crashing the floor, he lay, shocked and staring up at the small, tattooed woman who had just taken him apart in the space between two heartbeats.

He stayed down, staring and in shock, like everyone else in the room.

Except for Rick.

He took a breath. His head felt lighter but clear of the fog that had undone him.

He stood up. Carefully. He was still a little dizzy.

Michelle kept the pistol trained on Podesta.

"Mayor Jennings," Rick said. "I'm afraid you were mistaken before, sir. There's more than three of us."

A COMMERCIAL KITCHEN is a dangerous place. There is a lot of heat. A lot of sharp edges. But Ellie Jabbarah was as comfortable moving through such a place as Damien Maloney would be sitting in an old armchair with a six-pack. Even when Chad kicked her in the ass to hurry her past an apprentice cutting up pork belly, she was cool. These dumbass motherfuckers had decided to hold her prisoner inside her own world.

The kitchen in the Sacajawea Hotel was at least three times the size of *Fourth Edition's*. She could tell it had been renovated in the last couple of years and perfectly maintained in the time since. There was no patina of age, no compacted layers of grease and history that you found in an older, working kitchen, no matter how well cleaned. Stainless steel gleamed. Edges ran true. The *mise en place* in its entirety was outstanding. Almost peerless. Ellie couldn't help but imagine the focus and rigour it must have taken to maintain such professional standards as the world fell apart. A chef and two apprentices were at work when Moffat pushed her and Damo through the swinging doors. They all looked up, and Ellie could tell they were a little freaked out. She supposed everyone in Three Forks was a little freaked out today. Ellie nodded to the chef, winked at his juniors and scanned the room for weapons, hiding spots, exits, and advantages.

She even assessed their preparation. Duck legs. Pork belly. Stewing lamb. Goose fat.

These guys were making a cassoulet.

The chef, a sad-faced man in his fifties, returned her initial greeting with a nod, but he stared at Chad and Ridley, the Cohort asshole.

"Don't get any stupid ideas, Jabber," Moffat said as he kicked her in the ass. It wasn't a full-blooded punt kick. Just enough to drive her on.

"Hey, Champ, why don't you try that with me? See where it gets you," Damo said.

For that, he got the butt of the sledgehammer punched back into his stomach.

Ellie flinched at Damo's strangled grunt of pain, but she also noted that one of the apprentices took a step towards Chad, his grip tightening around that long knife. The chef laid a restraining hand on the apprentice's shoulder, pulling him back a little.

"Hey, Parker," Chad called out. "The meat locker. Can it be locked? From the outside? Murdoch wants me to put these assholes on ice."

His voice echoed slightly in the large space.

The chef furrowed his brows. Chef Parker, Ellie told herself. His name is Chef Parker.

"What d'you want?" Parker asked, a little confused and clearly annoyed by the intrusion.

"Can I lock 'em in there?" Moffat said, pointing to the walk-in freezer at the back of the kitchen. The door was open, but thick plastic curtains hung over the entrance, keeping the chill inside.

"Fuck no," the older man protested. "Are you crazy? They'll die."

"Chef," Ellie said, looking directly at Parker. "Is there a safety release handle? Say, for when you've pulled two straight shifts, three hundred covers, and you volunteered to lock up 'cause your sous chef is a useless gimp, and you get stuck in that freezer six hours before the breakfast crew clocks on to—"

"Shut up!" Moffat barked. "Nobody asked you."

But Ellie just smiled. She was done.

If the kitchen staff of the Sacajawea Hotel had half a brain between them, they now knew she was one of them. It might mean nothing, of course. They might be all in on Murdoch's fascist wank fantasy. But if this was just a gig for them... maybe there was hope of an alliance.

"There's a safety release, but it's broken," Parker said. "That's why we don't close up at night and why we got the double curtain. Can't get the parts to do repairs."

"So, it's secure?" Ridley asked.

Parker frowned.

"They wouldn't get out if that's what you mean. But if you put them in there for more than an hour or two, they'll die. I just told you that."

Damo, still recovering from the second hit he'd taken today, sucked in some air and grunted from behind Moffat.

"Your boss won't like that, mate. We've got business to do. And I can't do him any favours when I'm dead."

"Shut up," Chad said.

"You're not putting anyone in my damn freezer," Chef Parker said. Obviously, he'd had enough. "And you can get out of my goddamn kitchen."

Ellie could see all the rusty little flywheels in Chad's monkey mind grinding against each other.

"But Jonas said to put them in there," he objected.

"And I said *no*," Parker pushed back. His two apprentices had stopped work entirely. One had been adding duck legs to a giant pot of simmering goose fat, preparing the confit. The other had stepped away from the butcher's block and the pork belly roll he'd been caving into long strips. A full suite of sharpened steel lay temptingly close.

But Ellie knew it was still too far away. Chad would have more than enough time to put her down if she lunged for the edged metal.

"Tell you what, you old fuck," Moffat sneered at Parker. "You can get outta the kitchen. And take these fags with you."

He jabbed the heavy steelhead of his war hammer at the apprentices.

"You'll ruin the cassoulet, Chad," Ellie said in a sing-song voice.

Chef Parker and both apprentices looked at her. Curiosity piqued.

"That's three days of hard work down the crapper," she went on before addressing Chef Parker directly. "If you're prepping according to the requirements of *La Grande Confrérie du Cassoulet de Castelnaudary*."

He snorted, smiling.

"Well. We ain't got any Toulouse sausage, but we'll make do."

"You'll get the fuck out is what you'll do," Chad snapped.

Ridley stepped forward and placed a hand on Chad's shoulder, mirroring Parker's gesture from a minute earlier.

"Chill out, dude. We want these two locked down, is all."

"No," Chad said. "I want my fucking kid back, is all, and she knows where he is."

He pointed at Ellie.

Damo, almost recovered, straightened up.

"Maxi is safe for now, you dopey fucking bollard," he said. "But he's on a ranch about a hundred miles away, and if I don't cut a deal with your boss, I reckon Murdoch's gonna send your redneck militia mates into that valley to kill everyone. Including Jodes *and* your boy."

"Yeah," Ellie said, picking up Damo's thread. "Maybe you should calm the fuck down, princess, and find somewhere we can sit safely for the next couple of hours while your boss sorts out his shit."

"It's not gonna be in my goddamn freezer, I'll tell you that," Chef Parker said. "You can put them in the wine cellar if you want. There's only one way in and out."

"Perfect!" Damo declared. "Prison with a drinks list. I'll take it."

A titanic heavy metal crash made them jump as Chad Moffat smashed his war hammer onto a stainless-steel bench top. He spoke slowly and clearly into the ringing silence that followed.

"I told you to get out," he said through gritted, blood-stained teeth, pointing the weapon at Parker. "Now."

"Dude, come on," Ridley said. "He said he's got a place to secure them."

"And I told him to get the fuck out."

"And Chef didn't listen to you because this is not your fucking kitchen," Ellie said. "You don't count here. Nobody listens to you, Chad, because you don't count anywhere."

He lunged towards her, and she stepped back.

One step closer to those knives.

Ridley placed both hands on Moffat's shoulders and pulled him back, or at least he tried to. Chad shrugged him off without any real effort. Ellie took another half step away, playing the scared and frail female.

"Settle down, Beefcake McRipplechest," Damo said. "Murdoch told you…"

"Fuck Murdoch and fuck you," Chad snapped back at him. He turned on the kitchen staff. "You can get the fuck out, or you can stay. I don't care, but this bitch owes me."

Ellie backed away another step, trying to make herself look smaller. Weaker. Vulnerable.

The blades were closer.

"Get your gun out and cover me," Chad said.

"What?" Ridley asked.

Chad started to undo his belt.

"I said get your gun out and cover me. I'm gonna be busy."

"What?" Ridley repeated, his voice rising with confusion and some alarm.

"The fuck are you doing?" Chef Parker said. There was no confusion or alarm in his voice, which sounded like an old Harley idling on a cold morning.

"If this asshole speaks again, shoot him," Chad said, jabbing a rigid finger at Parker but giving the order to Ridley. "Shoot the kitchen fags too. And if you say 'what' again, I'll fucking shoot you, Ridley."

"You need to calm down, son," Damo said. His earlier mocking confidence had started to desert him. He sounded worried.

"Dude, no," Ridley pleaded. "This is fucked up. These weren't the orders."

Parker looked like he was about to say something, but Damo shook his head, warning him not to.

Ellie shuffled away. Another half step.

"This bitch was fucking my wife," Chad said. His face was twisted into a sickly grin. He took a step towards Ellie, whose heart was really racing now. This was happening. It'd only been a half-assed notion to grab a knife and stick Chad with it. Probably she wouldn't have even done it, but shit was for real now.

Moffat was undoing his fly. She could see he had an erection.

"She got the pussy I was supposed to get," Chad said, his voice turning thick and guttural. "She took that pussy, so I'm taking some back."

"The fuck you are," Damien Maloney said, making a fist.

"No!" Ellie cried out, but it was too late.

Damo had already swung on Chad, a wild haymaker that came out of nowhere and landed squarely on the side of his massive, box-shaped head. Ellie heard two distinct sounds. The thud of impact and the immediate crack of Damo's knuckles and fingers breaking.

"Fark!" he yelled.

Or at least he started to.

He didn't finish because Ridley drew his sidearm with astonishing speed and fired three shots into Damo's chest.

"*Noooooo!*" Ellie screamed. Much louder this time.

Everything slowed down, letting her see the terrible mistake she had just made in glorious, high definition, full horror slo-mo.

The first bullet struck Damo dead centre. A small, dark hole appeared in his puffer jacket. The next was just an inch or so higher. The third was not as tightly grouped. It blew a hole through his left shoulder, spinning him around as he started to drop towards the floor.

Ellie was still screaming, but whatever she was shouting made no sense.

None of this made any sense.

Ridley staggered backwards. Something wrong with him. With his head.

Probably the meat cleaver embedded five inches into his skull, Ellie thought. Had she thrown that?

No. Parker had.

She had meant to grab one of the long carving knives and stick it into Chad. Stab him fast, three times or more. Then launch herself at Ridley and try to pin him down for Damo and, hopefully, the others. But she hadn't even had a chance.

Damo had thrown a punch neither she nor Chad had seen coming. Now, Damo was full of holes, blood spraying everywhere, and he was falling.

His head struck the edge of the counter with a terrible crack, and for no reason at all, everything sped up. Twice, maybe three times as fast as normal.

So fast she could not for the life of her remember picking up the giant pot full of hot oil and confit duck legs. Could not remember throwing it at Chad Moffat as he tried to get up off the floor.

But she must have done that because she had scalded herself with hot oil, and it hurt. It hurt like a bastard, but not as bad as Chad must be hurting because he was screaming, and the flesh was falling from his face, sloughing away like melted taffy. And Ellie was screaming too, but more in rage than pain. And in frustration, too, because Chef Parker or one of his apprentices was holding her back. And all she wanted to do was close the gap between herself and Moffat so she could kick his ugly, screaming, half-rendered skull right off the top of his fucking spine.

This was his fault. It was all his fault.

Parker stepped past her, and she realised with a distant sort of abstract wonder that the clock inside her head, which synced her with the world, was back in real time. She watched Chef Parker step over the writhing, heaving body, take a knee, and expertly slide the long, narrow blade of a carving knife through Chad Moffat's ribs.

His spastic death throes quickly dropped away to stillness.

"No," Ellie said quietly, but she wasn't sure why. Perhaps she only wanted to turn everything back just a few seconds. To reset the world to the moment before Damo had tried to save her from Chad.

"No," she cried out. Louder this time.

The kid holding onto her let go, and Ellie rushed forward, dropping to the floor next to Damo, who leaned at an awkward, almost impossible angle up against the steelwork bench. He lay gasping in a pool of blood, all his own. Only the rubber latticework of the non-slip mats kept gallons of hot goose fat from reaching him. Ellie tried to undo his parka to check on the wounds.

She knew first aid. They all did. It was a requirement of the job.

"I'm sorry, mate," Damo said softly.

She almost didn't hear him.

His voice was weak and wet as blood bubbled out between his teeth.

"I'm sorry," he said again.

"Damo, no, Damo, it was my fault. Oh God, I'm sorry, I'm sorry…"

"Nah, mate. Nah. You're good," he said.

Ellie clamped her hands on the two closely grouped wounds. She could feel the blood pulsing out between her fingers. If she could press down hard enough, stop the bleeding, and find a bandage. Get help. If only.

But Damien Maloney's eyes fluttered closed, and he said no more.

38

SOME SORTA SPOOK TO ME

Michelle kept the revolver aimed at the man's face while she ground the heel of her boot down on his injured knee. He was a tough motherfucker; she would give him that. The muscles along his jawline bunched tightly as he ground his teeth together to suck up the pain.

"Just tell me what I need to know," she said, her voice calm and reasonable.

She leaned a little further into that kneecap. Tommy 'The Tripod' Podesta hissed and squeezed his eyes shut against the agony.

She knew it would be agonising. Her kick had torn his kneecap away and badly damaged the joint. But this guy wouldn't give it up. It was like he thought he was still in the Mob.

"I really don't think this is appropriate," Mayor Jennings said. Upon request, he'd given Podesta's name – nickname included – to Michelle, but it had been a one-sided introduction. One of Rick's eyebrows had risen sceptically at mention of 'The Tripod.'

"No, it's not appropriate," Michelle agreed. "It's torture. I'm torturing Mister Tripod here because I need information, and I need it quickly. When he gives me the information, I will stop torturing him."

Michelle increased the pressure on the joint.

"Hey man," Rick Boreham said. "Come on. We can do this another way."

Rick sounded very uncomfortable. His panic attack had passed, but he was not enjoying Michelle's enhanced interrogation techniques. Nobody was.

Michelle did not take her eyes off Podesta. She held his Smith & Wesson on him. He might look like a crippled enemy. But they could be the most dangerous. She had learned long ago that you never ever took your eyes off them. You never eased off the trigger. Not unless you wanted to get pulled from the field and deposited behind a desk writing endless fucking memos about Chinese food security.

"Where is Jonas Murdoch?" She said again.

"Miss Michelle," Karl Valentine said quietly.

Again, Michelle did not look away from the man on the office floor.

"Yes, Karl?"

"Do you think I could have a try at talking to him?"

She paused briefly, easing the pressure on Podesta's damaged knee. Keeping the revolver aimed at the bridge of his nose, she carefully stepped back.

"Be my guest, but be aware – the clock is ticking."

Michelle covered their prisoner while Karl came around a desk and pulled up a chair. It was an old, moulded plastic thing that had faded in the sun. It should have been in landfill long ago.

"Hey there, fella, my name is Karl Valentine," he said as he eased himself down.

Podesta let go of a ragged breath and grunted at Karl but said nothing else. Michelle moved around to a spot where she could keep an eye on both of them but stay away from the Three Forks contingent: Mayor Jennings, his engineer McNabb and the Reverend Nikobe.

Of the three of them, she was most concerned about the other woman. Nikobe kept shooting wide-eyed looks at her. She had a serrated, sightly crazed aspect to her expression. If Michelle handed the gun to Dan McNabb, she was sure he would charge out the door and start shooting motherfuckers. Jennings would probably try and talk them all to death. But the Reverend was unpredictable. She might try to snatch the gun away from Michelle and insist they all pray for forgiveness. That would not end well.

"Would you be needing a drink?" Karl asked Podesta. "Some water, or something stronger perhaps? Mister Mayor," he said, turning around, looking for Jennings, and causing Michelle to remind Podesta that she still had the gun, which was pointed at his head.

"Would you have some decent bourbon around, sir?" Karl asked.

Jennings seemed not to understand for a moment. It was such an out-of-context question.

"It's good for what ails you," Karl Valentine smiled gently. "And I fear that our friend here is badly ailed."

"Oh, right," Jennings suddenly realised. "I've got something in my office. If you'd give me a moment to fetch it."

He moved away before pausing and asking, "Would anybody fancy a belt? It's a little early, I know, but it's been a helluva morning."

"I'll take one, for sure," Karl said.

"A double for me," the engineer McNabb said.

"And one for me if it's the good Bulleit," Reverend Nikobe said.

Karl leaned forward in his chair.

"The bartender will be here presently," he said.

Michelle exchanged a look with Rick, who shrugged. She was tempted to pop a cap into Podesta's leg to hurry things along, but he'd been surprisingly resistant to her earlier line of questioning, and she didn't want him bleeding out before he talked. Most of what they knew about him, they had from the mayor.

But Podesta was going to talk, one way or another.

Jennings returned with the bourbon and a handful of Dixie cups. He poured a considerable measure for Podesta and passed it to Karl before serving everybody else.

Rick and Michelle both waved away the offer of a drink. Podesta downed his in one long draw before waving the cup at Jennings for more.

"Easy there, Tommy," Mayor Jennings said. "I haven't even finished serving these other folks yet."

"So, how well do you know this guy, Mayor Jennings?" Michelle asked.

The mayor poured the last drink for himself. He looked upset, but she couldn't be sure whether by Podesta or on his behalf.

"He is not a bad man, Ms Nguyen," Jennings said. "Well, not completely. He got Dan's daughter back from Luke Bolger, and my secretary, Miss Bates, speaks well of him. They've been keeping company the last few weeks."

"What about you, McNabb?" Michelle asked the engineer without looking at him. "You want to give him a character reference?"

Dan McNabb stared at the man lying on the linoleum tiles. His expression was a strange mixture of disgust and reticence.

"He did get my daughter back," he said. "And he did kill Bolger."

Karl took a sip of bourbon.

"What made you do that, Tommy?" He said. "We just got in. We only know the basic details about what happened last night. But it sounds like you did a good thing to rescue that young woman. If you thought that fella was in need of killing for what he done, why not just do it then? Would have saved a lot of trouble this morning, I reckon."

Karl handed him the refill of his bourbon. Michelle got ready to pull the trigger.

Podesta made no sudden moves. He gratefully accepted the drink and knocked half of this one down in a single gulp, sighing with something like relief.

He spoke, to Michelle's surprise.

"Where I come from," he said, struggling with the words and the pain. "People used to think it was no big thing killing a man. But it's a hell of a thing, let me tell ya."

Michelle kept her face neutral but was impressed with Karl's debriefer mojo. She honestly thought this guy would hold tight to some bullshit code of silence. But he took another belt and kept talking.

"It almost never works, you know," Podesta continued. "Everyone thinks whacking some guy solves whatever problem he was causing, but the problem's still there. You didn't solve it. You just whacked a guy. Probably made yourself more problems doing it. That's been my experience."

"I think I get you," Karl Valentine said. "I'm just a truck driver, or I was. But I take your point. So why do that this morning? Why shoot this fella?"

Podesta stared at Michelle for a moment, or rather, he glared at her, specifically at the NSC laminate she had taken out to show the mayor. It still hung from an old lanyard around her neck. Was that his issue with her? That she was a Fed?

Podesta shuddered, and some color drained out of his face. He closed his eyes, threw down the rest of his liquor and held out the paper cup for more.

Karl took the bottle from Jennings and refilled it. He handed the cup back to Podesta while Michelle kept the gun on the wounded man.

"I didn't shoot Bolger because of that girl," he said. "Although, that woulda been reason enough. The sick fuck. I killed him because he was gonna try to take over the operation. For sure. When a guy takes over an operation, if he's smart, he gets rid of the old boss's crew."

Michelle had about half a dozen questions she wanted to ask, but she kept her mouth shut, letting Karl take the lead. Podesta was obviously more comfortable talking to him.

"So, this fella, Mister Bolger, he was like the general of the Legion?" Karl asked.

They could have learned all this from the mayor, and Jennings had given them a quick rundown of the Legion's org chart. But Karl seemed to be making a connection, and Michelle knew that could be more valuable than any amount of pain she could inflict.

Podesta took a long draw off that third bourbon. He closed his eyes, breathed in, breathed out, and nodded.

"The Legion and the Cohort," he said. "But the Cohort is more important. There's not that many of them, not compared to the Legion as a whole, but you're looking at ex-military guys, ex-cops. They're all together, not spread out over four states, and they're like..." His eyes locked on Michelle's for a moment. "... Like special forces or something. They're supposed to protect Murdoch."

"Ex-law enforcement," Karl smiled. "Hoo boy. How'd that sit with you?"

Podesta's gaze shifted back to Karl.

"I didn't have much to do with 'em," he said. "Best not to. Things are different now. But some things don't change. Some-a those assholes, I know they'd-a clipped me on general principles."

"I'll bet," Karl said. "And Bolger, what was he before he ran this business?"

Podesta sneered.

"He was just some mope who worked in a prison."

Karl sipped thoughtfully at his drink.

"Yeah, okay," he said, "it's a bit of a mess, isn't it? Seems to me those fellas are likely to take offence, each against the other. The Legion and the Cohort guys. I don't see this going well."

Podesta threw down the last of his bourbon. His third. All of them doubles. His eyes were watery, but his face had some color back.

"You're telling me, pal," he said. "I was this close to just driving on."

"No reason you couldn't do that," Karl said. "Well, except for your knee. Sorry about that. But you know, a guy walks in with a gun like you did. It creates a bad first impression."

Podesta looked at Michelle over the iron sight of the Smith & Wesson. The fire that blazed behind those eyes had died back a little.

"I got no hard feelings, lady," he said. "If I was you, I woulda shot me soon as I came in. That woulda been the smart play."

"I didn't have a gun," Michelle said.

"You do now," Podesta replied, managing a shadow of a smile. "What are you? Some sort of feeb?"

"National Security Council," Michelle said. "Not law enforcement."

"Never heard of them," Podesta said. "You look like some sorta spook to me. Never met one that I know of. But I heard about them. Some of the outfits back east, they worked with you guys."

"If you like," Michelle said. She lowered the gun a few inches. "Karl is right. We have no quarrel with you. If you want to get into your car and drive away, I wouldn't stop you."

She sensed Jennings and McNabb stirring somewhere to her left.

"I can't speak for the good people of Three Forks, though. Maybe you have something to answer for with them."

Mayor Jennings appeared in her peripheral vision. She didn't take her aim off Podesta.

"All Murdoch's command group need to answer for what they've done in places like Manhattan and Livingston. But as best I know, Mister Podesta is a driver, like Mister Valentine here."

Karl nodded, winked at Podesta, raised his Dixie cup, and took a slug. "Sooner or later, everyone needs a lift," he said.

Mayor Jennings went on.

"Tommy was Jonas Murdoch's driver and bodyguard. And something of a fixer, in my experience. But he was not part of the Legion's military organisation. He didn't even stay to watch them shoot up Manhattan. He drove me home. He didn't partake in any depravity in that club of theirs. And he did get Dan's daughter away from Bolger."

Michelle shifted her position to keep enough open space around herself and a clear line of sight on Podesta.

"Here's the deal then," she said. "It's the only one you're gonna get today, Podesta. We need information. Right now. You give it up; you won't have to answer for Murdoch's crimes. It's up to these good people what, if anything, you answer for in their town."

"I have no issue with this man," Mayor Jennings avowed.

"We're good," Dan McNabb said.

The Reverend Nikobe muttered a quiet prayer.

"So, what's it gonna be, Tripod?" Michelle Nguyen asked. "Another Bulleit? Or a bullet?"

THE SQUAD CAR that Mayor Jennings summoned dropped them at the rear of the hotel. The ride over from City Hall was surreal. Armed thugs everywhere. Technicals roaring up and down the streets. Gunfire from unseen combatants popped and clattered from all directions. So far, it was sporadic and uncoordinated. It reminded Rick of half a dozen really shitty places he'd deployed as a Ranger. Sadr City. The Mog. Manbij in Syria. There was something in the air that had no right polluting a small town in Montana, a sense of things going really bad, fast, in the worst way possible. It left a bitter, almost metallic taste at the back of his throat.

"The Mog, for sure," Rick muttered.

"Say what?" Michelle asked.

"Precious memories," he said quietly.

Sitting next to him in the back of the patrol car, Michelle had spent the short trip pressing the two cops for absolutely everything they knew about the forces occupying Three Forks. Like Rick, she was disguised in a half-assed fashion, sporting a THREE FORKS POLICE DEPARTMENT baseball cap and windcheater. She didn't look much like a cop to Rick Boreham. Increasingly, Michelle Nguyen reminded him of the Agency types he had worked with in the sandbox and Absurdistan. Fly-in/fly-out deniable assets. She was very good at her job, whatever the hell it was. Or had been, once upon a time.

By the time they pulled into the small lot behind The Sacajawea Hotel, Michelle had mapped out the Legion's order of battle and the Cohort's current duty roster, at least within the limits of Three Forks. Stuff the cops didn't even know that they knew.

The last thing the city provided was weapons. Two Glock semi-autos and three spare clips for each. No suppressors, unfortunately. They were hardly standard issue for a small-town police department.

Rick dropped the magazine and racked the slide, catching the ejected round with his left hand. He glanced at the magazine and then into the pistol's empty chamber. He thumbed in the loose round and reinserted the fully loaded mag with a click. With his other thumb, Rick pressed the slide release with a snap. The weapon was ready, a full seventeen shots.

The panic spiral he'd felt dragging him under back at Mayor Jennings's office had dissipated. The crippling anxiety and deep psychic dysmorphia had not just eased but altogether vanished. It was not necessarily a good thing. He was back in the funnel, falling towards absolute darkness. But at least it was a functional darkness. One he could use. He was changing. Turning back into something he'd tried hard to escape.

"Thank you, officers," Michelle said. "If you would be so kind as to word up your colleagues over there?"

A second Three Forks PD squad car and a Legion technical secured the rear entrance.

Michelle rechecked her weapon, exited the patrol car, and waited for Rick to join her.

The hotel loomed over them. More gunfire crackled a few streets away.

Podesta had told them that Damo and Ellie were being held somewhere inside. Probably locked in cold storage.

Jonas Murdoch was hiding out in the hotel, too. And all of his top henchmen.

Usually, they wouldn't get within spitting distance of the place, but the Cohort squads that were supposed to secure the hotel had dispersed. Podesta thought some had probably bugged out. Others were openly moving against their former comrades and overlord.

Rick heard one of the cops in their car call up his buddies on the radio.

"Ten eighty-six. Officers on duty."

He pulled the brim of his police cap down low, and Michelle walked ahead of him. She waved to the cops in the second squad car as they drew level but ignored the three men on the back of the weaponised Toyota.

There wasn't much love between local law and the outsiders.

They did their jobs and tried their best to ignore each other.

Rick wondered if the Legion goons would ignore the two pretend cops heading into their bosses' Führerbunker. He didn't fancy trying to bullshit his way past if not, and there was no quiet way of neutralising them otherwise.

As it turned out, that wasn't an issue.

They were halfway there when Ellie Jabbarah appeared. She was running and covered in blood.

THIS WAS A RISK WORTH TAKING, Michelle judged. Everything was in free fall. The Legion had cracked apart before they had even arrived to give it a tap. Podesta had not done that, or not on his own, anyway. The fault lines had run deep long before he put a bullet into Luke Bolger. You saw it time and again in autocracies, large and small. That's what Maloney had been talking about on the drive over from the valley. When violence was the organising principle, true consent could never be given, and the natural differences of opinion, the interplay of competing interests, none of it could resolve peacefully. The pressure just built up until something gave.

That was why this was such a risk but one worth taking. Murdoch and his crew were off balance right-the-fuck *now*, and a man without balance lost most of his strength until he got his feet planted again.

She'd just seen that with Rick back at the mayor's office. He'd had a bad turn. A full-blown PTSD meltdown. But, as soon as he faced a tangible threat, he got his footing back. He'd been weakened and vulnerable for a short time, but that had passed.

Murdoch was still vulnerable, which made this the moment to put him down and ensure he never got back up.

Michelle lowered her head and marched towards the hotel loading dock.

"Picking up a couple of prisoners," she called out to the three-man gun team in the rear cargo bed of the pick-up.

One of them called back.

"Huh? Nobody told us."

"That's because they're Cohort," she said.

Wonderful things can happen when you sow distrust in a garden of assholes.

This asshole hopped down and started toward Michelle.

She might have talked her way past him. That was her first choice, but before she could even get into character, Ellie Jabbarah appeared, racing alongside another man who was wearing a chef's hat and apron for reasons that were not immediately obvious.

They were both a mess, covered in blood. But Ellie was much worse, and she looked deeply distressed.

"Hey!"

The Legion fighter who had jumped down to question Michelle shouted at Ellie instead and started to reach for his gun.

Michelle Nguyen took two steps towards him, drawing the fighting knife from the plastic sheath in her pocket. She kicked out his knee and slashed his neck open as he fell. He forgot about his sidearm and spent the last moments of his existence trying to squeeze together the gross, lipless wound through which his lifeblood was gushing.

The two remaining gun crew, still up on the back of the Toyota, scrambled to turn their primary weapon on Michelle. It was a poor choice, and they died because of it, tripping over each other, fumbling with the mechanism of the mounted M60 instead of just shooting her down with their personal weapons.

It gave her half a second to draw the Glock 17 nestled in the small of her back. She snapped off four shots, dropping both men but blowing any chance they had of maintaining cover or stealth. A siren howled behind her.

Rick swore loudly and ran towards Ellie.

CHEF PARKER HAD to drag Ellie away from Damo. She would have sat there, crying and holding him close, until more of Murdoch's men turned up. Bob Parker was having none of it. He yelled at his apprentices to get the hell out, to go home and get their guns if they had any.

Then he gently but firmly pulled Ellie away from her old boss, mentor, and friend.

It was amazing to her that she allowed him to, but she was numb and incapable of resisting. She had lost her tether to the world, and the world broke up and floated around her in jagged, disconnected shards of shattered continuity. Damo was alive. Damo was gone. Damo was laughing on the deck of his yacht. Damo yelled at her to get down as they tried to escape the pirates on the lake. But it wasn't Damo; it was Parker. Yelling at her to get down. And they weren't on the boat. They ran out of the hotel kitchen and down through the loading dock. And there was Michelle Nguyen, except it wasn't Michelle. It was a cop who looked just like her. And there was more yelling and shouting, and more blood, and more shooting.

Ellie could make sense of none of it, which was fine because Damo was gone, and that made the least sense of all. Even less so than Rick Boreham suddenly appearing, pretending to be a cop, and charging her like a football player. Like the rugby player Damien Maloney had been a long time ago, in a country far, far away. Rick pounded across the car park asphalt, his arms wide to gather her up.

Parker tried to pull her away, but Rick just changed course, blew past him, and scooped Ellie into his arms. Parker yelled something, and she yelled something, and maybe it was her yelling at him that it was okay. She knew this guy. Even though he wasn't really a police officer.

There were real police officers in the car park. They had uniforms and everything. Rick threw her across his shoulder and ran at full tilt toward one of the police cars, where a frightened-looking younger cop stood holding open the back door.

Was she being arrested?

RICK TOSSED Ellie into the back of the squad car. She was in shock. He had seen it before, been through it before. The blood, the trauma, the wide eyes dulled with pain and horror.

"Get her out of here," he shouted at the cops. "Now."

"Wait!" Michelle shouted. "Where's Maloney?"

The man who had emerged from the hotel at a run with Ellie came jogging up behind her. He was out of breath, struggling to talk.

"The guy she... was... with," the man in the chef hat panted and gulped. "He's dead. They... shot him."

Michelle mouthed a single obscenity.

Rick kicked the side panel of the squad car.

"Hey, that's enough," one of the cops shouted. An older guy. A sergeant. "You better get in. This thing is going sideways. Radio says these assholes are turning on each other all over town."

Rick took a moment to reset. He needed a couple of deep breaths to do that. Needed to force his runaway mind to settle back on track. As he breathed in and breathed out, he could hear that the cop was right. The volume of gunfire was much greater.

"You sure about that?" Michelle said. She was talking to the cook. He had to be a cook from the hotel, the way he was dressed.

"I was there," he insisted. "They murdered him. He was trying to save her. Moffat was gonna..." He had to force it out. "Moffat was gonna rape her."

He pointed at Ellie, who had curled up into a ball on the squad car's back seat.

"Jesus," Michelle said.

Automatic weapons fire cycled up from somewhere nearby.

"That's the gun wagons out the front of the hotel!" one of the other cops shouted from the second car. "We gotta get out of here now."

"Go," Michelle ordered. "All of you. But I'm going in there, and I'm getting Murdoch. We get him; we finish this."

Nobody argued with her. The hotel cook looked at her like she was mad as he climbed into the back of the squad car next to Ellie. The other cops ran back to their vehicle.

"Hey," the sergeant called out. "Take this." He tossed a pump-action shotgun and a bandolier heavy with shells to Rick.

"Thanks," Rick said, but the cop was already getting back into his car.

They were all gone less than ten seconds later.

"This is a very poor idea," Rick Boreham said as he slipped the ammo load over his shoulder.

"Got a better one?" Michelle asked.

"No."

They checked their weapons and headed for the rear of *The Saca-jawea Hotel.*

39

NOT EVEN RHETORICAL

This was not like Silverton. This was much worse. Jonas wasn't sure how that'd happened. He had a whole army around him here. His own personal Legion. There were no barbarians at the gates. No outlaw biker horde threatening to storm the defences.

But there was no Sheriff Muller to lay a steady hand on things. Jonas had killed Muller himself. There was no Dale Juntii quietly taking names and efficiently kicking ass. Bolger had killed Dale, and Jonas had done nothing about it.

He wasn't even sure where Brad Rausch had got to.

All Jonas had now was the questionable loyalty of those assholes in the gun wagons out front and the unquestioned hostility of Luke Bolger's surviving lieutenants.

He desperately wanted to peek out of the curtains and see how it was going downstairs, but he was worried that somebody would snipe him if he showed his face at the window.

He heard gunfire everywhere, even inside the hotel. It sounded like someone was firing a cannon downstairs.

It had started about two minutes after those Cohort jerks got on the radio to muster the rest of their company back to the hotel for a loyalty check.

It had seemed like a good idea at the time, even though it wasn't his. That had been the Tripod.

And where the hell was he now? Jonas paced the room some more. The bed was unmade and damp with the residue of all the sport fucking he'd done that morning. A thousand years ago.

Where. Was. Podesta?!

Dude was supposed to be coming back with Jennings and local reinforcements. There weren't many cops in Three Forks. Less than two dozen of them, and they weren't tooled up for urban combat like some places used to be. Not since he'd disarmed the town. But they still woulda been useful to have in his pocket.

He stalked another circuit of the suite. The girls were gone, and fuck knows when they had cut out. Probably when they heard the first shots. Fuck them, anyway.

He was not in the mood for pussy.

He was...

Well, to be truthful, he wasn't much good for anything.

His internal alarms were screeching so loud he could barely think. Every instinct for self-preservation pushed him to get the hell out and start over again. The way he had after Silverton.

A machine gun clattered nearby, and he jumped.

He jumped even higher when somebody hammered on his door.

"Jonas? You in there? It's Leo."

Jonas swore to himself and shivered involuntarily. It was just the adrenaline backwash, that's all. Nothing to be ashamed of. He'd come through Seattle. He'd come through Silverton. He'd dealt with the threat from Muller, and he had survived even greater, deadlier threats in the weeks and months after.

He would deal with this, too.

"Get in here, Leo," he shouted at the door.

Leo Vaulk let himself in.

He was even more of a caricature than usual if that was possible. Vaulk had so many guns hanging off him that he rattled and clanked like a soup spoon caught in a waste disposal unit.

"Chad's gone, man," Leo said, his eyes haunted and shifty.

"What?" Jonas said.

His first thought was that Moffat and the girls might have fucked off together. But that was crazy. Chad was downstairs with the dyke and that stupid Australian.

"He's gone, man," Leo said. "They fucking killed him. Down in the kitchen."

Jonas squeezed his eyes shut.

"What? I don't understand. Who killed him? The lesbian?"

Leo threw his hands up, setting off a metallic clatter as all the items of his considerable armoury banged into each other. One long gun slipped from the strap around his shoulder and dropped to the hardwood. It went off with a loud bang, and a cloud of plaster dust fell from the ceiling.

"Jesus Christ, Leo!" Jonas yelled. "Watch out, man."

"Sorry, boss," Vaulk said. "I'm just a little freaked out, is all."

"Just a little? What the fuck is going on out there?"

Leo Vaulk took a deep breath, like the dumbest kid in class having to finally stand up and do his book report for which, of course, he had not prepared.

"Runeberg says the Cohort's in revolt," Leo said. "And maybe a third of the Legion has gone over to them. What are we gonna do?"

Jonas made his decision quickly. There was a hotel courtesy car downstairs. Some bullshit hybrid or something, but it was always full of gas, and the battery charged off the solar cells on the roof. They could get over to Bozeman, rally the garrison there, and get this thing under control.

"We're gonna get the fuck out, that's what," Jonas said. "You coming?"

"Is that even a question?" Leo said.

"Not even rhetorical."

Jonas had a go-bag stashed in the cupboard. He told Leo to wait in the hallway and look for trouble. One thing he would say for Leo Vaulk, the guy knew how to do as he was told. Leo stationed himself outside the suite while Jonas went for the bag. He had learned after

Silverton that no matter how secure you might feel, you were always one lousy card away from disaster.

He was no raging prepper. His go-bag was just a Nike carry-all with some food-for-the-road and basic medical supplies, spare clothes, a gun and a box of ammo. Enough to get gone in a hurry – and he was in a goddamned hurry this morning. The gun battle outside was getting really fucking gnarly. He reefed open the door, looking to grab the bag and...

It wasn't there.

Fuck!

He didn't even bother wondering what had happened.

The bitches had taken it, for sure. Kimmy and whatever the fuck the other one's name was. If he still had a wallet, they'd have swiped that from the bedside table, too, the treacherous whores.

Okay. Cool. Everything was cool.

They still had the getaway car.

He turned and headed for the door where Leo was waiting for him.

"Hey, who the hell are you?" Leo called out, suddenly fumbling for his weapon.

The problem was he had so many weapons hanging off of him that he got tangled up in all the options.

Jonas flinched at the sound of three shots, very loud, very close.

Leo Vaulk crashed to the floor. But he wasn't dead, not yet.

His mouth worked like a fish just hauled into the boat, and his eyes stared at Jonas, full of questions he couldn't answer.

Jonas Murdoch didn't hesitate.

He ran for the window.

THEY FOUND Maloney in the kitchen. There was no question of whether the other two were alive. Not with what'd happened to them. But Damo looked like he was resting, and Michelle kneeled to check for a pulse. Nothing. He was gone.

Rick swapped out his Glock for the shotgun and kept her covered while she stripped the weapons from the other two bodies. It was quite a haul, even if she didn't bother taking the oversized demolition hammer from the deep-fried gym Nazi.

"Sorry, mate," she said quietly to Damien Maloney. "But we have to go now."

They moved in sync, sweeping through the kitchen and into an empty dining room. The remains of a buffet breakfast still lay on a side table. Pastries, fruit, containers of cereal, and plates full of cold congealed bacon, sausages, hash browns and scrambled eggs. At any other time, she might have stopped to take a picture of the spread, collecting data for later analysis. Not this morning. They swept past, their weapons trained on the main entrance at the other end of the dining room.

Rick used hand signals to communicate that he would breach the door. It made sense. He was packing more firepower than her and had more urban combat experience, even if it had been a few years back. Rick moved with the machined precision you only got from long practice under the most unforgiving conditions. Michelle kept up with him, but her training in close-quarter work was much more elementary. She had transitioned from fieldwork to analysis, from the Agency to the Council, well before Rick had returned from his final tour.

She could still read hand signals, though; she knew not to sweep her partner as he moved in front of her. Michelle held her weapon in a two-handed grip, angled down as Rick Boreham pushed through the mirrored French doors. The Glock came up as she followed him through.

They passed into a large open lounge area. Lots of polished wood and deep leather armchairs. It was all a bit woodsy for her taste, vaguely recalling that weird lodge from Twin Peaks, a bizarre, almost fantastical memory to come floating up out of nowhere. Michelle forced her mind clear of everything but the instant now. She opened all of her senses to let the world in.

The world sounded like Beirut.

It smelled like old socks, cleaning wax and coffee.

And this all felt like one of the dumbest things she had ever done.

Something moved in her peripheral vision, and Rick moved quickly, turning and firing. The shotgun boom was huge inside the relatively confined space of the lounge. Michelle did not ask him why he was shooting. She was already shooting in the same direction herself.

There were three men, all of them armed and dressed in army surplus Apocalypse Chic, an eccentric mix of jeans and cargo pants, desert camo and tactical costume jewellery. They had been standing around a coffee urn, which seemed a hell of a thing to be doing in the middle of a violent insurgency, attempted *coup d'état* or whatever the fuck this was. Michelle had not seen them at first because of a thick wooden pillar blocking her line of sight.

Rick Boreham, however, did see them. What he didn't do was call on them to throw down their weapons. He just opened fire, and, trusting his judgement, Michelle added seven or eight rounds from her clip to the four blasts from the police department shotgun. All three men went down without raising a hand in their defence. Not a fair fight then, but in Michelle's experience, fairness and survival were strangers to each other.

"Where to?" she asked.

"Upstairs," Rick said in a low voice, still scanning for targets. Waiting for follow-on forces. "He'll have the biggest room in the place. If he's hiding, it'll be there or somewhere down in the root cellar. That's if he's even here."

"Worth finding out," Michelle said.

They mounted the staircase to the second floor, side-by-side. Rick swept the area ahead and above them at the turnaround. Michelle checked their six. She flinched a little at the sound of heavy machine gun fire outside the hotel but relaxed marginally when it was obvious the fire was headed out, not in.

The second floor was deserted, as best she could tell. The staircase narrowed and topped out at an attic-level third floor.

Rick signalled he intended to clear the top floor and work his way down.

Michelle nodded her assent.

Halfway up the flight, they stopped. She could hear voices. She didn't recognise them. There was no reason she would, but she did hear the name 'Jonas'.

"Jonas? You in there? It's Leo."

'Leo' was almost certainly Leo Vaulk, the former director of a small security company based in Washington state. He ran logistics for the Legion and, on the best intelligence that Michelle had gathered, he had been phase-locked on some *Cobra Kai*-level rivalry with Mathias Runeberg's operations division.

And he was calling out to Jonas Murdoch. The douchebro in chief. She and Rick nodded to each other. They understood what they were about to do. He loaded four replacement shells into the shotgun. She ensured she could access a spare clip for speed-loading the Glock if needed. It was a proven weapon. The guns she had scavenged from the dead men in the kitchen were not.

They listened to the shouted exchange between Murdoch and his henchman long enough to be sure it was them. They heard a single gunshot, and Michelle thought that one of the men must have murdered the other, but Murdoch's voice, muffled and indignant, reached them almost immediately after the blast.

"Jesus Christ, Leo! Watch out, man."

"Hey," Rick said, almost below the level of hearing. He nodded to her and held up a fist. She bumped her own much smaller fist against it.

"For Damo," she said quietly.

Rick nodded.

They mounted the stairs two at a time, swung around at the top of the landing and found the corridor blocked by a large, barrel-shaped man absolutely festooned with weapons, like a terrorist's Christmas tree.

"Hey, who the hell are you?" he shouted.

Michelle put three shots into him before Rick could even pull a trigger.

KARL FOUND the Expedition parked a block and a half away from the Sacajawea Hotel. Ellie had the main set of keys with her, but he had a spare. Karl always kept extras. Before he keyed the engine into life, he used a pocketknife to lever off the door panel. Rick had hidden weapons and ammunition in there before they set out. It wasn't much. Just a couple of handguns, but it was a hell of a lot more personal protection than he'd enjoyed while sneaking across town from the mayor's office. Nothing enjoyable about that at all. The weather was foul, and the hospitality worse.

There were some hairy moments, too, while he extracted the weapons cache. These Legion fellas had turned on each other like feuding cousins at the reading of a rich uncle's will. A stray bullet cracked the windscreen while he was working on the door panel, and he nearly filled his pants because of it. But it was only a stray bullet; he was pretty sure of that. If anybody had meant to finish him off, they could have done so quickly with him just sitting there in the middle of all the brouhaha.

Karl retrieved the two guns, placed them on the passenger side seat, and started the engine. He was about to back away when he saw the most surprising thing. A man carefully climbing out of a window on the very top floor of the hotel and gingerly tiptoeing across the sloped veranda roof before lowering himself over the edge and shimmying down a pole. He looked like a fella might have been caught out playing cute with another fella's wife, and he must've been quite desperate to get away, given how exposed he was to gunfire the whole time and how slippery those shingles musta been from all the sleet and drizzle. If you could trim the scene of all the idiots trying to kill each other, it was almost amusing in its whimsy. The rascal escaping from another bedroom escapade. Karl was inclined to wish him luck and slowly reverse away from the hotel towards the rendezvous point he had agreed to with Rick Boreham. But he saw an even more surprising thing: little Miss Nguyen climbing out of the same damn window as though to chase after that first fella. A long arm reached out from inside and grabbed her back just before a whole heap of bullets chewed into the woodwork, throwing off splinters and shattering the window glass.

Ah. Now he understood.

That fella who had escaped was escaping from Rick and Michelle. He would be some sort of baddy, for sure. And he was now signalling to his accomplices on those gun trucks, waving frantically, pointing at the window. Karl could not hear him over the general racket and clamour of all the fighting, of course, but it did not matter. It was pretty obvious what he wanted. At least half of the gun wagons turned their weapons on the hotel and opened fire. The roar of the big guns was enormous and terrible, squashing all the little bits and pieces of battle noise beneath their fury. Karl Valentine was not in the least bit surprised to see how quickly they demolished the once charming face of the building. He had seen plenty of what heavy, crew-served weaponry could do during his taxpayer-funded jaunts through the livelier byways of Iraq.

If the effect on the hotel was salutary, the effect on Karl was even more immediate. It was as though his entire blood supply had been replaced by cold spring water. He did not care to imagine what was happening on the receiving end of such concentrated fire. He could only hope that Rick and Miss Michelle were able to crawl away.

Another gun truck joined the demolition effort. This one mounted a couple of 50 calibre Brownings in the cargo tray, and there was no imagining that anyone might escape the consequences of that much heavy weapon's fire.

Karl did not hesitate.

There was nothing he could do to help from this far away. And lightly armed, Karl couldn't do much if he got close enough for a few shots with the two popguns he'd retrieved. He'd have to park right next to the damn things as though for a tailgate party. Instead, he floored the accelerator and drove straight at the pickups.

Karl Valentine had been a driver of one sort or another his whole working life. If you laid all the miles he had driven end to end, you would undoubtedly find that he had circled the globe several times. And it was not so far, this last run. A little more than a single block in a very small town. But he had never been more determined to make his delivery.

He did not stomp the accelerator, but he did keep feeding boot leather to it until there was no more play in the pedal. It was fully depressed, and the seven and a half thousand pounds of American steel was fairly rocketing downtown, accelerating towards its top speed. He started to attract fire as he got closer. Windows shattered. Multiple rounds punched into the doors, the grill work, and the engine block. About twenty yards away, the gun crew finally realised what was happening. They swung those two big gun barrels of 'Ma Deuce' around, spraying twin rivers of hot yellow tracer in a wide arc. Three of the massive BMG rounds punched through the windscreen, Karl's rib cage, the driver's seat, the passenger seat behind it, and the rear door of the SUV. It made no difference. Speed, mass, and the unstoppable momentum of one man's decision to do what he could to try and save two friends all combined to ensure Karl Valentine's final delivery arrived at its intended destination. The big Ford slammed into the other truck with force enough to flip it onto the smaller Toyota on the other side. Some of the crewmen were thrown far away. Others died, crushed between tons of crunching steel.

But Karl was not one of them.

He was already dead.

———

RICK MISSED his first grab at Michelle but not his second. She made it out the open window, chasing Murdoch, and maybe she'd have caught up with him, but she would have done so under the guns of his men.

There were hundreds of them out there. There were more still at war with them.

Diving out the window into that shit storm was just about the worst of her many bad ideas that morning. Rick launched himself out after her, grabbed hold of the police department jacket she wore and yanked her back in through the window just before hundreds of rounds smashed into the antique wooden boards of the hotel's street frontage.

They tumbled to the floor as even heavier fire poured in.

"We gotta get out of here," Rick yelled.

She yelled something back at him, but he couldn't hear it over the uproar.

Maybe it was thanks. That would have been appropriate.

They belly-crawled out of the room, their heads down and eyes slitted against the storm of splinters, bullets and broken glass.

Even snaking their way past the body of the fat Rambo enthusiast and out into the hallway, they still weren't safe.

Rick recognised the terrifying death metal hammer of a fifty-cal Browning. It filled the corridor with flak and debris, dismantling the graceful old building around them. They double-timed their crawl across the carpet and down the stairs.

On the landing at the first level, they stopped.

A squad of Legion fighters had taken cover in the entry hall downstairs.

Or maybe they were anti-Legion Cohort.

Like there was a fucking difference to him.

They started shooting at Rick and Michelle, too.

He heard the tiny pop-pop-pop of her Glock as she returned fire. He added the percussive bass of shotgun blasts, but he was firing blind, not willing to risk putting his head up to take better aim.

They were trapped.

It was only a matter of time before the bullet storm caught up with them.

"WE'VE GOT to go back! We've got to go back for my friends," Ellie shouted, but the cops weren't listening.

Parker was, but the hotel chef was no more interested in turning around than the cops were.

She had no idea what part of town they were in or where they were going.

The police radio crackled and squawked. Cops and dispatchers yelled at each other through the static.

The officer driving slammed on the brakes, and they came to a screeching, sliding halt. Gunfire hit the car like a dozen hammer blows. The windscreen exploded inwards, and the car crashed into something hard. Ellie's door sprung open, and she clicked off her seat belt, rolled out, hit the ground, crawled, staggered to her feet, and ran. She was vaguely aware of Parker bolting away in the other direction. The police officers were both dead.

The tiny western town was a hellscape of warring militia fighters, overwhelmed cops, and townspeople popping up here and there in windows and doorways or from behind solid cover to add their volleys to the crossfire.

So much for suspending the Second Amendment.

Ellie scuttled under a vehicle. Some sort of soccer mom tank.

She banged her head painfully against the axle and scrunched up as tightly as possible in the claustrophobically confined space.

Finally, safely settled, or as safely as she was ever going to be, she found that her hiding place afforded her a view of the pitched battle in front of the hotel. She didn't understand any of it.

People seemed to have turned on each other.

Her mouth hung open. Tears stung her eyes as she shook her head in horror and denial.

What the fuck was up with everybody? Weren't they all still Americans?

This had nothing to do with the Chinese or the Russians fucking everything up, she thought. *We did this to ourselves.*

She saw Karl nearly a block away and wanted to scream in relief. She also wanted him to come get her. He'd found the Expedition where she'd left it and looked to be backing away from all the chaos and madness.

A bullet struck the grill of the SUV under which she was hiding, and she flinched, banging her head hard enough to raise a small galaxy of stars. They cleared from her vision just before Ellie witnessed Karl's charge into the line of gun wagons.

"No," she said, her voice small and cracking. "No."

But he couldn't hear her, of course, and it would have made no difference if he could.

The hurtling Ford slammed into the first vehicle in the gun line with a titanic crash she felt as a hammer blow, transferring its destructive energy through the earth's crust and into her skin a couple of hundred yards away. She saw bodies flying and a pick-up explode into flames. The gunfire abated for a few seconds before returning with even greater power.

Hundreds of men and women charged into the space Karl had carved out of the Legion's defences.

They raced forward, yelling their stupid war cries and firing into the air, into the building, at unseen enemies and at the last few defenders sheltering around the only remaining gun wagon.

It was insanity, brute violence, murderous and primal, and Ellie could not understand any of it. These people had been neighbours once and friends. Or, at the very least, they had lived and let live. How had it come to this?

She realised with dread and creeping terror that Rick and Michelle were probably trapped in the hotel. They were going to die in there like Damo.

Like Karl.

There was nothing she could do about it. She hadn't been able to save Damo. She'd probably doomed him by enraging Moffat the way she had. She didn't know for sure what had happened to Karl, and maybe, just maybe, there was a slight chance he had survived that crash. The Expedition was a big, heavy cage of a thing, and he was a stickler for seatbelts and safety.

But she could not stop this.

None of it.

The earth itself seemed to rumble with portents of doom and the end of days.

Ellie crawled forward, careful not to bang her head against the undercarriage as a deep but rising thunder overwhelmed the sound of battle. The horde of fighters, dozens, maybe hundreds of them, once moving in concert, suddenly lost momentum and sputtered to a halt. Confused and unfocused, but only for a second. They started back into motion, but their flight was not directed this time. It was atomised as they suddenly fled in all directions.

Ellie blinked, her eyes burning with tears and grit as she tried to render what she saw into a coherent narrative. The madness resisted all efforts at reason until she finally recognised what she was witnessing.

A cavalry charge.

Two dozen riders, some with reins between teeth and both hands filled with guns, others more conventionally mounted and armed with a single weapon. And one guy all but standing in his stirrups, loosing arrows into the disintegrating mob. Fucking arrows!

"Shit!" she said and started to crawl out from under cover.

A single bullet glanced off the tarmac and slammed into her like the fist of an angry god.

She cried out, but no one heard.

40

OUTCOME HARBINGER

James O'Donnell recognised the voice but not the phrase.

"Outcome harbinger," Pablo Bruh said, his words distorted by the radio. The others looked to James for the meaning of the transmission.

They had laid up north of the three-river junction in a thin patch of forest on a small hill overlooking the Jefferson River. The I-90 swept past, not two hundred yards away, but it was empty of traffic. The terrain was a morass of worn-down mountains, sandy riverbanks, boggy fens, and open fields. It was inaccessible by vehicle but easily navigable on horseback, at least for a practised rider who took care with their path. It had been years since James had saddled up regularly, but the long ride over from Livingston had knocked the rust off his muscle memory.

His actual memory was fine.

"What's that mean? Outcome harbinger?" Collins asked.

James reviewed the checklist that Michelle had forced him to commit to memory. He grimaced.

"Nothing good," he told the small group of riders gathered around the radio set.

The weather was turning bleak. They'd enjoyed mostly clear skies until yesterday. While the mercury never climbed far above freezing, it had not been a hardship to be out under the stars – not until they got deep enough into Legion territory that they could no longer set campfires to keep warm or heat their food.

The group around James had no formal leadership. They were not a military outfit or a commercial operation, but between them, they constituted the voices to which most of the posse would attend when it came time to make a call. His cousin Simon. Doc Matheson. His old high school friends Stephen Collins and Darren Tuer. And standing next to Tuer, drinking cold coffee and chewing on a strip of pepper beef jerky, Laura-Marie Lawson, also late of Park High.

Even now, James still grew nervous around Laura-Marie.

It had been many years since the senior prom, but they said you never really grew out of who you were in high school. And at seventeen, James O'Donnell had made quite the fool of himself over Laura-Marie.

She had let him know, too. She had let everyone in the town and all of the valley know, which was fair enough, but it had also been part of why he ended up on the East Coast working as a financial consultant instead of staying at home to take over the ranch.

"Outcome Harbinger means the situation in Three Forks has reached a point of critical instability," James said, feeling awkward with Michelle's phrasing and the intensity of Laura's gaze, "and the... er, away team, I guess, are moving to exploit."

He blushed at stumbling over the 'away team' thing. Michelle and Rick had both referred to the convoy as the 'force away', but that had sounded weird to James, and he'd defaulted to 'away team'. *Star Trek.*

His favourite show when he was seventeen years old.

He'd stayed in his room and watched a helluva lot of *Star Trek* after that prom debacle.

"So, what next?" Dave Matheson asked.

"Ass-kicking boss battle, Doc," Steve Collins grinned, holding his hunting bow like a trophy.

"James?" Laura-Marie said. Her tone was grave, and the chuckling died away.

James tried not to be so obvious about how he couldn't look directly at her. His discomfort was amplified by a fresh and livid scar across her face. She had been in Livingston when the Legion attacked, unwilling to abandon the animals in her care at the veterinary clinic. James tried not to stare at the scar line.

"It means we're supposed to move up as close to the edge of town as we can. Get on the horses and wait."

"Wait for what?" Laura-Marie asked.

"A call for help."

She frowned, and he quickly looked away.

"What if they can't make a call, but they still need help?" Laura-Marie asked. "My brother is in there. And your friends."

James nodded.

"I know. Michelle said we can't plan for specific situations. We can only prepare for what's likely. She thinks it's likely that things are going sideways fast. We need to move."

He thought Laura-Marie might push back on the need, perhaps because it was Michelle's plan, but she surprised him.

"We best haul ass then, city boy," she said.

Simon packed up the radio unit, and the others spread the word. They were breaking camp and readying to move into town to support the convoy's mission. They might have to move fast, and that support could mean violence.

THE FIRST GUNSHOTS reached them a few minutes after they had followed a winding course along the sandy banks of the river to a ridge line a mile north of Three Forks. Most of the riders stayed hidden in the gully, but James, Simon and Laura-Marie walked their horses to the crest, where they could observe the town through binoculars.

"That's gunfire," Simon Higgins said.

"Sounds like," Laura-Marie said.

James swept the town with his glasses, east to west and back again.

He spied cement works and a light industrial development at the north-western corner of town. Suburban lots tracked southwest for maybe a mile on one side of the cement factory, while the greensward of a golf course gone to seed ran wild on the other.

"I can't see much of anything beyond the edge of town," James lamented.

The distant fireworks pop and crackle died away for a minute.

He resisted the urge to ask if they had heard anything on the radio. It was a dumb question.

But it was hell not knowing what was going on over there.

His breath plumed out in front of him. All three horses were also blowing steam as the air temperature fell away.

"Maybe we could send one man in to check things out," Simon suggested.

"We already have more than one person in town, Simon," Laura-Marie pointed out. "Got three carloads of them. If they have something to say, they'll tell us."

"If they can," James said.

"If they can," she agreed.

She lowered her binoculars and caught him looking at her. He quickly looked away.

"Something I can help you with, James?" Laura-Marie asked.

He blushed.

Why the hell was he doing this to himself?

"It was a long time ago," she said. "We were both assholes. Build a bridge. Get over it."

The gunfire cycled up again before he could say anything in reply.

All three of them went back to trying to spy something, anything, that might tell them what was going on.

They stood on the bluff for another five minutes, and in that time, the situation in town deteriorated badly. There was no way of knowing exactly how or why, but there was also no denying the increasing density of weapons fire.

"I think we should go in," Laura-Marie pronounced at last.

"I think we should at least send a scout," Simon suggested.

They both looked to him to cast a vote. It was an impossible situation. Michelle was in there. Rick and all of the others. Laura-Marie's brother, Mark. If it were up to him, James would be galloping in already. But Michelle had been adamant that precipitate action was worse than none.

He shivered and cursed under his breath.

He really needed to take a piss.

And fate, deciding to mock him for that realisation, chose that moment to reach out.

The radio squawked behind them.

They all turned around.

Collins was working the tiny Alinco ham radio set. A dozen riders had dismounted and gathered around him.

"Say again?" he said.

The unit crackled, and a male voice replied, but James couldn't quite work out what he was saying. He didn't need to. He could see from Stephen's face that something had gone wrong.

Stephen Collins looked up the slope to Laura-Marie.

"It's your brother," he said. "The Legion has started fighting each other."

"That's good," somebody remarked.

Doc Matheson shook his head, "Not if you're caught between them."

"What about Rick and Michelle?" James asked.

Collins held up a hand. More distorted transmission. He leaned into the ham radio box.

"Say again?"

James caught more words this time. Something about a siege at the hotel.

"Got it," Collins said, "We'll be there."

He replaced the handset and stood up, looking like a mountain giant assembling itself from boulders and grim intent.

"That was Mark Lawson," he announced to the group. "He and most of the envoys are safe. They're staying with Katherine Bates' sister. But she says some of their party have been taken prisoner at the main hotel in town. The fighting is heaviest there. The mayor has turned out the local militia, but they're not doing so well."

James had come all the way back down the slope by this point.

"Who's at the hotel?" he asked. His heart felt like it was trying to speed punch its way out of his ribcage.

Stephen Collins looked almost guilty when he answered.

"Your friends," he said.

James didn't wait.

He spun around, mounted his horse and spurred it forward.

"Let's fucking ride," Collins yelled out.

"For Livingston!" Simon Higgins yelled.

The rest of the riders took up the call.

"FOR LIVINGSTON!"

IT HAPPENED SO QUICKLY that James could not recall any moment of decision or stasis between spurring his horse forward, intending nothing more than to get to his friends and Michelle, and finding himself at full gallop across the open fields just outside of town.

James was halfway across when he realised he had no idea where the hell he was going, but by then, it didn't matter. The entire troop had formed around him, and they were all charging. Simon and Stephen had raced to the front of the pack. His cousin had drawn a pistol, and Collins was somehow nocking an arrow into his bow while steering his goddamned horse with his knees. They seemed to have zero doubts about where they were going. They plunged on at breakneck speed, and the solid mass of riders spurred their mounts on behind them.

The cold wind of their passage burned at the exposed skin of James's face. Tears streamed down his cheeks, and all the muscles that had ached so much after the first day of the ride now screamed in protest as he tried to brace against the violent buffeting of a mad, headlong cavalry charge. All around him, men and women had drawn their weapons. Firearms, for the most part, handguns, some rifles, and that damned hunting bow of Stephen's. James had his rifle with him. He dared not try to remove it from the case, which was jumping around down by his right leg. Instead, he concentrated on urging his horse forward and not crashing into ditches or obstacles. Falling now would mean bringing down most of the charging pack with him.

As they drew closer to the edge of town, everything seemed to accelerate. They did not increase their speed; they could not. They were already riding at full tilt. The distance between them and the settlement collapsed, and the rate of that collapse accelerated with impossible swiftness.

Suddenly, they were inside the city limits, steel-shod horses' hooves throwing up scatters of sparks as two dozen horses and their riders powered down a wide, tree-lined boulevard.

It was beyond surreal.

He could hear the gunfire all around them until their answering volleys drowned out everything except the endless thunder of the charge. He shook his head in astonishment to see Laura-Marie Lawson dual-wielding handguns, steering her mottled brown stallion with her knees. On his other side, Stephen Collins was sending one shaft after another downrange, peeling off four, five, and six arrows while James struggled and fumbled with the straps of the pouch where he had stored his Ruger.

He could see their objective.

A line of pickup trucks converted into gun wagons. James nearly lost control of his bursting bladder as one of the gun crews opened fire on the hotel with the sort of machine gun they used to put on tanks. The industrial jackhammering din was a sonic Armageddon. His heart tried to lurch to a stop as he saw part of the three-storey hotel coming apart under the assault. Michelle was in there.

On they charged.

He realised that dozens, maybe hundreds of local people had emerged from their homes and businesses, from all of their various hiding places to race on in the wake of the flying wedge of irregular cavalry. Many of them were armed. Some with baseball bats and gardening tools. But they all added mass to the stampede.

Closer and closer, they charged. James didn't believe they would get there in time. Nor was he sure what they would do if they did manage to overrun the position. At any moment, one of those gun crews would realise they were about to be flanked, and they would rake down riders and runners alike with a couple of bursts of machine gun fire.

It was only when he saw and recognised the dark blue Ford Expedition accelerating towards the gun trucks from the opposite direction that he thought they might have a chance. He also knew that one of his friends was probably driving that vehicle.

In his mind, he screamed when he saw the snaking lines of tracer fire suddenly whip away from the hotel to hose down the onrushing Ford. He screamed out loud, too, but no words – merely a howl of rage, frustration and fear as the Expedition crashed into the line of vehicles, ploughing through steel and flesh like a giant battering ram.

A few seconds later, James crashed into the madness and disarray of the broken fighting force. He still had no weapon to hand, but a man on a charging horse is a weapon as old as human civilisation.

He put his head down and spurred on for the hotel.

THE KINETIC MAELSTROM stopped dead as though a guillotine had dropped. It severed them from the insanity of the last, endless minute. Michelle did not flinch at what had to be done. She knew she was already dead; she might as well make something of her final moments.

"Cover me," she hissed at Boreham, pushing the second shotgun at him – the cut-down monstrosity she had scavenged from the body of that hairless, half-melted ape who'd killed Maloney.

Covered in plaster dust, spitting blood and shaking off the debris of shattered masonry and raw splinters, Rick Boreham started racking rounds and firing down range. He emptied the combat shotgun he'd borrowed from the cops before switching to the weird, customised model Michelle had just gifted him.

She was already gone, vaulting the handrail on the staircase, dropping through clear air into the narrow space behind the reception desk.

The small unit of Legion fighters, or Cohort rebels or whoever the fuck they were, had scrambled for whatever cover they could find when the heavy machine guns started chewing through the architecture. She had one whole second, and maybe even a lazy two or three, before they recovered their mojo and decided whether it was worth taking the fight back to her and Rick.

Michelle Nguyen, former threat analyst, former DIA field agent, and former Delta Track operator, had zero intention of giving them the luxury of choice.

The dense, explosive cadence of shotgun blasts kept them pinned down while Michelle slammed a fresh clip into her Glock. Dual wielding the 17 and the Kimber Custom semi-auto she had stripped from the second dead Nazi in the kitchen, she advanced on the clump of cubicle farm militia gimps, unloading round after round of 9mm wrath. She ploughed her way through them, a ballistic threshing machine, until the hammers clicked on empty chambers, and she dropped the useless weapons at her feet.

One enemy combatant remained.

JONAS MURDOCH DIDN'T CRASH through the window. He wasn't a fucking idiot. A man could slice open a damn artery or something doing that. But as soon as Leo got clipped, he turned and ran.

He almost didn't make it out.

The window latch was some old-timey frontier bullshit that wanted to kill him or at least delay him long enough for whoever was coming up the stairs. He finally got it loose, and the sash slid up just before they trampled over poor Leo's cooling corpse and into Jonas's suite. He distinctly heard two voices, male and female, as he climbed out of the window and onto a balcony roof. The authentic wooden shingles were a bitch to walk on, and he was nowhere near getting clear when some crazy little Asian bitch launched herself out after him.

For one demented second, he imagined that all of the rumours of a Chinese invasion had come true and that Beijing had sent some wet-work specialist Suzy Wong, deep into Montana just to lay hands on him. But the scene in front of the Sacajawea Hotel deep-sixed any such notion. The feral blood swarm exploding all over downtown Three Forks was exclusively American carnage. It was Murdoch's apocalypse.

Those were his war wagons arrayed in a rough half-circle, their guns turned outward on the Cohort traitors.

They were his loyal fighters battling his treacherous usurpers for control of his conquered lands.

This was all his doing.

And he was not yet done.

Scrambling down the challenging incline of cedar roofing shingles, he yelled for somebody, anybody, to shoot that bitch coming after him. He almost lost footing, waving at the assholes sheltering around the war wagons to get their attention. Finally, one of them did. A single rifleman turned around, noticed Jonas, and guessed what he wanted.

A bullet cracked past his head. Jonas felt like every organ in his body had come free and dropped toward the ground.

Perhaps he should have waited before calling fire on his pursuer.

More rounds zipped past as he hesitated at the jump, but there was nothing for it. He had to get off this fucking roof.

Jonas crouched at the edge, nervously grabbed at the gutter, and swung himself over the edge, wishing he had been better at keeping up with his CrossFit training. Six months ago, he'd have performed a one-armed cartwheel off the goddamn roof and landed on both feet with his cock out, demanding a blowjob as a reward.

Now, he was just pathetically grateful to have lucked out on a well-placed column that he could scramble down like a frightened fucking marmoset.

He hit the ground and rolled, more from a reflexive, unthinking need to make himself as small as fucking possible in the middle of a raging bullet storm than from any super-commando style fast-twitch muscle programming.

His bladder let go as he shrank even further into himself to escape the sudden torrent of hellfire pouring into the upper storeys of the hotel from the heavy weapons mounted on the war wagons. The rain of hot cedar fragments and shards of shattered window glass drove him back to his feet, which carried him, with zero conscious thought, to the nearest shelter he could find.

Jonas ran up the steps of The Sacajawea Hotel. He shoulder-charged the front doors, stumbling into the relative calm of the lobby, intending to keep running right through the building and out the back, down the street, out of town and all the way to North Dakota if that was what it took to get away from this murderous fucking chaos and absurdity.

"Get down," someone shouted. Jonas recognised the accent before his panic-addled brain could process the image of Mathias Runeberg, hidden inside two ballistic vests and wearing a bright yellow safety helmet with FIRE WARDEN stencilled on the front.

Jonas got down, diving for cover behind a nest of leather lounge chairs already spewing their internal stuffing from multiple gunshot wounds. He banged his elbow as he fell, jolting his arm with shooting pains that felt like he had grabbed hold of an exposed electrical wire. He tried to crawl away, but the ferocity and volume of gunfire robbed him of all will, and he cowered on the floor like a chicken-fucked bitch.

It was only when the thunder of battle faded to the singular rhythm of one discrete shot after another that he realised he had to move. It was all over, save for the executions.

MICHELLE NGUYEN MARCHED through the slaughter she had wrought and the debris of collapse. One of the men she thought she had killed was still alive. Some dweebish middle-aged math-Nazi character eccentrically clad in two sets of body armour, neither of which saved him when Michelle stomped her Docs down on the back of his neck as he tried to crawl away from her. His legs didn't work anymore, and she did not hurry to catch up with him.

His vertebrae cracked after the second hammer kick to the base of his skull, and he fell still.

The man she really sought stood with his mouth agape, staring at her.

Jonas Murdoch.

Michelle had no idea what malign sorcery had delivered him back to her after losing him out of that window, but she did not intend to let him escape a second time.

He shuffled backwards as she advanced on him.

The fighting knife she had kept from the border guards was already in her right hand.

"Michelle, don't..." somebody called out.

Rick?

Rick was still with her?

But she ignored him.

Michelle Nguyen knew what had to be done. Hard and thankless duty. Dark enough without wavering in the performance of it. It was not as though she was innocent of wrongdoing and would dishonour herself in the commission of one more misdeed. She had failed in her sworn oath to defend the republic and all those souls who dwelled within. Millions had died. Countless millions. And she had schemed in the death of even more beyond these shores.

What was one more killing measured against all that?

———

JONAS TRIED to make his legs work, but they felt like they had fallen asleep. They weren't his anymore. He tripped and stumbled backwards as the crazy bitch advanced on him with a blade in her hand and murder in her eyes.

She was dressed in cop merch, but she was no cop. He could see that.

She was a killer.

"Hey, come on now," he said, his voice cracking.

He smiled.

Or tried to.

Nobody's gonna cut a dude with a smile.

Right?

———

MICHELLE NGUYEN HACKED HIM DOWN.

41

REQUIEM

He was going to be a while getting over this. James staggered out of the hotel lobby and collapsed in a heap on the top step. He had not even done that much. Not really. He'd ridden his horse for a couple of days. Ridden hard and fast for the last few minutes of that journey. But he hadn't had to fight, not really. Why was he so tired?

He sat on the top step and tried to forget what he had just seen. He tried to see only what was in front of him, but that was horrific. Bodies everywhere. Burning vehicles. Cruelty and sorrow. He felt so unutterably sad. James O'Donnell had never felt so sad.

He tried to blink away the picture of Michelle carving on that guy. He'd called out to her to stop, but she had not. He had seen her gun down three other men as he charged into the lobby. He had seen her stomp one to death. As awful as that was, it was nothing compared to what she had done at the end.

He blinked and blinked again.

The weather was clearing. Or, clearing as much as it ever did in Montana at this time of year. The sleet had stopped falling, and the wind had dropped away. There was a break in the clouds, with a few shafts of sunlight piercing the gloom.

Try as he might, he could not unsee what he had witnessed. He tried to concentrate on the world as it was, not on the memories burned into the back of his eyeballs. The fighting had stopped. At least there was that. The Legion's gunmen had thrown down their weapons and now sat, kneeled or even lay on the cold ground with their hands up. The townspeople of Three Forks were moving to clear away the debris and attend to the wounded.

James O'Donnell squeezed his eyes shut, blocking it all out.

"James?"

He flinched.

It was Michelle.

"Hey man," another voice said. "You okay?"

Rick.

They sat down, one on either side of him.

James O'Donnell said nothing.

They all sat in silence.

Ross Jennings held his feelings tight. He squeezed them so tight, swallowed them so hard that he knew they may well explode later. For now, though, he had a job to do, a town to save.

It had all happened so quickly. He still wasn't sure he had done the right thing by agreeing to help the outsiders who had come into his office. Had they decided to help him? He wasn't sure now. He wasn't sure of anything beyond what a damn mess he had made of all this.

He strode through the wreckage and ruin, sometimes shouting orders, sometimes speaking softly. People turned to him, needing to be told what to do. If he was being honest with himself and with them, he didn't have a clue. Not about the big questions. But for now, he could at least make himself useful by giving people small things to focus on.

He detailed the police department to ensure all outsiders were disarmed, including their notional allies from Livingston and the Valley. There had been more than enough gunplay in Three Forks for

the next little while. He told Dan McNabb to round up every municipal employee for the clean-up and asked Reverend Nikobe if she
could liaise with the town's doctors to establish aid stations at the
high school and the volunteer fire department.

He could hear an engine approaching from that direction and a
siren blaring. It was an oddly soothing sound, given the violent chaos
and anarchy of the last few hours. It promised a return to something
like normalcy.

He hurried out of the way as the fire engine raced up, turning its
hoses on the burning pickups and SUVs in front of the hotel. The
upper floors were smoking and threatening to catch aflame, but there
was ammunition in the back of Murdoch's improvised gun trucks
threatening to cook off.

"Get everyone back," he shouted at McNabb as the first rounds
popped and crackled.

A cry went up, and hundreds of people suddenly flowed away
from the scene. A couple of police officers came running up to help
with crowd control.

Jennings found himself retreating to the hotel's front steps,
where he recognised Boreham and that young woman from the
National Security Council. They were sitting on either side of
another young man he did not recognise, but they all seemed to
know each other.

Ross Jennings did not much feel like talking to them, but he
forced himself to walk over. The government woman, who was
covered in blood—drenched in it, now that he was close enough to
see—was trying to get their unknown companion to engage with her.
Boreham looked like he'd been dragged through a demolition site,
ass-backwards, recognised Jennings and got to his feet. It almost
looked like he was coming to attention.

"Mister Mayor," Boreham said, adding to the air of unreality.

Miss Nguyen gave up on her one-way conversation with the quiet
fellow and came to her feet, too.

"The town is yours, Mister Mayor," she said. It seemed a strangely
formal gesture, given the circumstances.

"Yeah," Jennings answered. "And... Murdoch, do we know what...?"

"Terminated," Nguyen said abruptly before seeming to catch herself out. "I'm sorry, I mean... I killed him. He's gone. His cronies, too."

"I see," Jennings replied. "I would... thank you, I suppose."

He looked around.

They all did.

There did not seem much for which to be thankful.

"KARL'S DEAD," James O'Donnell said at last.

They were the first words he had spoken since telling Simon and Laura-Marie, 'We need to move' and galloping away. Michelle was not there to hear James's report. She had gone to look for Ellie. Rick Boreham was still sitting there, refusing to leave until James moved or spoke up or did something to show that he was emerging from his fugue state.

"Over there." James pointed out the wreckage of the Expedition, which Karl had salvaged from the lot back in Livingston.

"Oh," Rick said, flicking a glance at the still-burning heap of scrap metal and dead bodies. "I'm real sorry to hear that. He was a good guy. They both were."

"Both?" James asked, turning to him. His eyes were red-rimmed and watery.

Rick nodded. "Maloney. They killed him," he said, looking at James with a quizzical expression. "Murdered him, it looked like."

James sighed. A ragged sound. Sadness seemed to fold over on itself, completely covering him like a weighted blanket. "I didn't know that."

"Yeah, you did," Rick said, still looking concerned.

James looked at him. Confused. "What?"

"Michelle told you. Just before. But that's okay, James. All this..." Rick waved a hand at the devastation around them. "It can take a while to sort out something like this. Memories. Feelings. It's a hell of a thing."

James shook his head, a slight movement, a gesture of refusal.

"She didn't just kill him, Rick. I've... never seen her... She..."

There was no form of words to recall what he had seen Michelle doing to Jonas Murdoch without reliving it, and that was not something James O'Donnell wished to do ever again. Rock Boreham laid a hand on his shoulder.

"Brother, what she did needed doing. Trust me. The same way you did what needed doing back at the Cavalry Memorial. And this morning. The way Mel made her choice all the way back in West Virginia, with that fella who had designs on Tammy and Roxarne's little ones. We've all been doing what's hard and what's necessary ever since this thing started. That's what you saw, James. It's all you saw. There's nothing else to it. It was just something Michelle did, not who she is."

Rick let his hand fall away, but he wasn't finished talking.

"Who she is," he went on, "is the woman who loves you. Trust me on that, too."

James was listening, but he wasn't looking at Rick anymore. He stood up, peering through the smoke and the chaos.

"Is that..." he started to say.

But Rick Boreham was already off and running.

RICK TOOK the stairs in front of the hotel three at a time and launched into a sprint when he hit the gravel. He covered the ground to Michelle Nguyen in less than a minute.

She was carrying a body.

No.

She was carrying Ellie Jabbarah, and Ellie was still alive.

"Medic!" Rick called out. "Medic!"

Michelle had Ellie draped over her shoulders in a rudimentary fireman's carry, and she was struggling to go on.

"Been shot," she said, panting for breath, as Rick reached her. "Shoulder wound. A lot of blood gone."

Michelle started to lay the other woman down, but her strength gave out, and she collapsed. Rick stepped in quickly and took the load as James came running up.

He had Katherine Bates with him. The ER nurse from Livingston who had come along as part of Peter Tapsell's crew. She was already covered with blood.

"Put her down over there," Katherine said, pointing at a patch of soft grass.

Rick laid her down gently. Ellie felt as light as a child.

"James, run back to the triage point and get me some bandages," said Katherine. "Rick, I need something to clean the wound. Alcohol, something like that."

"Vodka?"

"Sure. But quick."

He took off toward the hotel at a run.

———

BY SIX THAT EVENING, all the wounded who were likely to pull through, including Ellie, were under medical care. Her wounds were severe, but in time, she would make a full recovery. James thought Jodi Sarjanen would be upset, but at least Ellie was alive and safe, and they would be able to mourn together.

The perfectly composed photograph that Jodi took at that feast on their first night in the valley would eventually take pride of place in their family home for many, many years to come. They would make that home in the valley, not far from the O'Donnells. Nobody ever made it to Damien Maloney's salmon farm. Over the years, Jodi would often find herself standing in front of the mantelpiece, holding a simple picture frame and contemplating the smiling faces of long-lost friends. But, one day, every year, she and Ellie would both sit down with that fading image and a handful of others captured on the road with a cheap cardboard camera, and they would remember when their odd little family was reduced by unutterable loss. There were at least fifty smiling faces in the framed shot of the welcome banquet at the O'Donnell Ranch, but two stood out among the long tables, the glowing fire pits and the candlelit warmth of the frontier homestead. A simple truck driver and a loud-mouthed Australian, the finest men either woman would ever know.

In Three Forks, a small and more immediate celebration was planned, a memorial and a thank-you to distant neighbours. James O'Donnell was not sure he would show up for that. The mission from Livingston remained in town for the moment, either billeted out to local folk or bunked down in the undamaged sections around the back of the *Sacajawea*. He had a small cottage with Michelle, a luxury villa on the hotel grounds, and Rick and Nomi were right next door. Ellie would soon rejoin them, but for now, she was resting after surgery at a medical clinic on the other side of town. Her shoulder was a mess, but the doctors said the bullet that struck her had lost a lot of its force and did not interfere with any vital organs or blood channels.

James sat on a bench overlooking the small garden where the hotel had once hosted wedding receptions. Dog paw tracks criss-crossed the light dusting of snow on the cold ground. Pete Tapsell had reunited Nomi with Rick, and they had spent an hour out here, Rick throwing a ball for Nomi, who had barked up such a storm of canine joy that it had brought James outside to watch them and finally to share a drink with his friend. Rick and Nomi were gone now, off searching for dinner, and it was peaceful in the garden. Quiet and beautiful under the delicate frosting of snow still falling and threatening to get much heavier. James was rugged up in a lambswool jacket, gloves and a scarf.

He nursed a glass of bourbon poured from a bottle he'd liberated from the hotel restaurant.

"Hey."

He turned around toward the voice.

It was Michelle.

"Hey," he said.

"Mind if I sit with you?"

"No. Of course not."

He made room. Michelle sat but a good foot or so away.

"Spare a drink, cowboy?"

He passed her the glass, but she leaned over and took the bottle instead. She had showered and changed. Her hair smelled of apple-scented shampoo.

James closed his eyes and kissed the top of her head. All of the dye and color was gone. She was jet black now.

Michelle put the bottle down, took his face in her hands and returned his kiss on the lips, deeply and urgently.

When they finally came apart, James was a little breathless and somehow ashamed, but not by the kiss.

"I'm sorry," he said. "I just..."

Michelle put a warm finger on his lips.

"It's okay. I should have told you."

"Told me what?" James asked.

"Everything." She took a solid hit off the bottle.

"So, you're not really a threat analyst?" James said.

She smiled. Took another swig. Passed the bottle back.

"I am. Or I was. I was good, too."

Her voice was flat.

"That's why I worked for Panozzo and Holloway," she said. "But I didn't always work for them, James. I came to NSC from DIA. The Defence Intelligence Agency. And to DIA from the CIA. I didn't work office hours for the Agency."

"You did other things," James said. His voice wasn't flat and devoid of feeling the way it had been when he was processing his shock and horror earlier that day. But he still sounded wary.

"I did other things," Michelle confirmed. "I've never told you about them because... I swore an oath, and, to be honest, some of them were not things I'd be proud to talk about. What I'm doing now, telling you the truth? I'm breaking that oath."

"You..." James started but trailed off when he couldn't find the words he wanted.

He took a swig of bourbon. It burned going down, and he gritted his teeth against it.

"You don't need to tell me what you did before," he said at last. "I just want to know what you're going to do now."

Their eyes met. Neither of them looked away for a long time.

"I'm going to be with you if that's okay," Michelle said.

IT WAS.

The End.

John Birmingham

PO Box 437

Bulimba, Queensland 4171

Australia

❀ Created with Vellum

ALSO BY JOHN BIRMINGHAM

The *End of Days* series.
Zero Day Code.
Fail State.
American Kill Switch.

The Axis of Time.
Weapons of Choice
Designated Targets
Final Impact
Stalin's Hammer
World War 3.1
(World War 3.2 & 3.3 coming in 2024)

A Girl Time in Time.
A Girl in Time.
The Golden Minute.
The Clockwork Heart (coming in 2024)

The Cruel Stars series.
The Cruel Stars

The Shattered Skies
The Forever Dead (2024)

Dave vs the Monsters series
Emergence.
Resistance.
Ascendance.
A Soul Full of Guns.
A Protocol for Monsters.

CHEESEBURGERGOTHIC

Hi. It's me, JB. If you liked this book and you'd like more of the same, sometimes for free, please join me over at my blog/book club/dive bar on the internet.

At the moment, it's hosted on Substack, but it kind of moves around, and wherever it ends up, it's *always* called CheeseburgerGothic.

Just throw that into el Goog or whatever AI chatbot runs the world now, and I'm sure they'll hook you up. I give away free stories there at least once a month. And my faves—everyone who signs up at the Burger is my favourite—get steep discounts on new releases.

Everyone else? Well, my friends, don't be like them.

I look forward to seeing you there.

Milton Keynes UK
Ingram Content Group UK Ltd.
UKHW011955281223
435113UK00001B/86